FULL MOON RISING

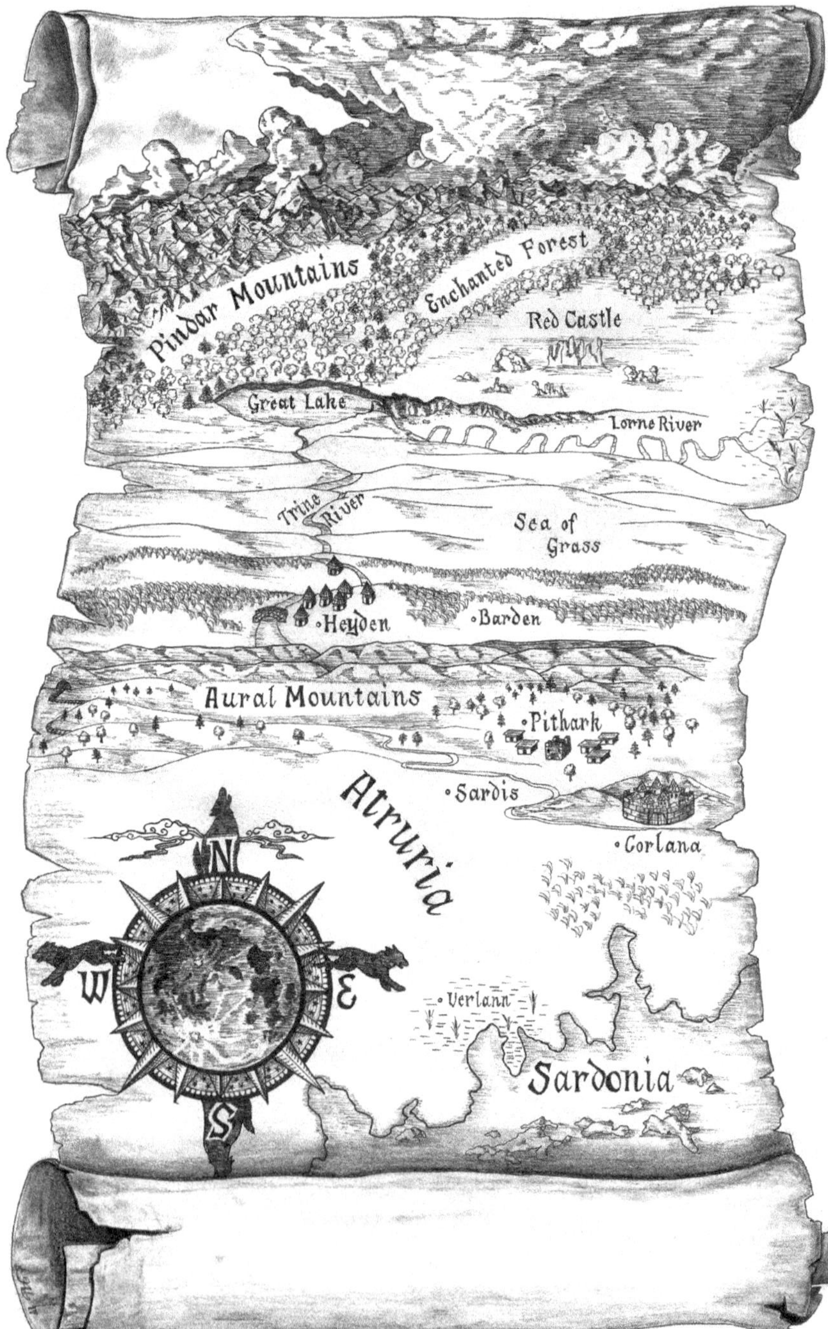

Pindar Mountains
Enchanted Forest
Red Castle
Great Lake
Lorne River
Trine River
Sea of Grass
Heyden
Barden
Aural Mountains
Pithark
Atruria
Sardis
Corlana
N
W
E
S
Verlann
Sardonia

FULL MOON RISING

T. M. BECKER

PROSPECTIVE PRESS

TEEN

P ROSPECTIVE P RESS LLC

1959 Peace Haven Rd, #246, Winston-Salem, NC 27106 U.S.A.
www.prospectivepress.com

Published in the United States of America by P ROSPECTIVE P RESS LLC

TRADEMARK

FULL MOON RISING

ISBN 978-1-943419-63-0

First P ROSPECTIVE P RESS trade paperback edition

Printed in the United States of America
First printing, January, 2018

1 3 5 7 9 10 8 6 4 2

The text of this book was typeset in Minion Pro
Accent text was typeset in Cinzel and PetitFleur

PUBLISHER'S NOTE

A huge thank you to my colleagues and friends in the Central PA Writers' Workshop, without whom this book would never have been published. Thank you for all your great critiques and encouragement over the years.

A special thanks to Jen Henry, my fabulous friend and artiste extraordinaire, for capturing my vision of Atruria on paper.

To my daughter Sarah, my first and biggest fan.

"Hard right, Harry."

PROLOGUE

 hush descended over the courtroom as the three judges rose, their stiff black robes rustling. I willed myself to stand steady, clenching clammy hands in my rough skirt to hide their trembling. My chains rattled, and the pockmarked guard glared at me. The chief judge unrolled the scroll, pushed his spectacles up his nose, and without so much as a glance in my direction, read in his harsh, guttural voice, "Arabella of Maitlan, daughter of Vigo of Maitlan, of Heyden-on-Trine, of Atruria." Somebody in the gallery coughed, and the judge paused, clearing his throat. "This tribunal, convened by the order of King Sarduk, king of Sardonia, Atruria, all the southern flood lands extending to the sea, laying claim to the Great Lake, and all the wasteland and northern foothills as far as the Pindar mountain range..." Someone coughed again, and the judge stared reproachfully. A guard pushed through the crowd to remove the offending person. After the disturbance subsided, the judge resumed. "This tribunal does hereby find you guilty of: learning and using a forbidden language; reading banned material; consorting with unfavorable persons, including the known devious enchantress and enemy of the king, one Elissa; unlawfully performing magic; disseminating poisonous and dangerous materials to unsuspecting law-abiding citizens... and treason against our noble king." A jeer erupted from the gallery, and the other judges pounded their gavels to restore order. I stood motionless as the blood drained from my face. "For said crimes..." The chief judge looked up from the scroll and peered solemnly at me over his spectacles. "Young lady, notwithstanding your tender age, this tribunal does hereby sentence you to death."

A roar swept through the gallery, the room swam, and although I clutched at the rail, my knees buckled as the room turned black.

I

ith a hiss and a pop, the candle stub sputtered and burned out, plunging the tiny closet into darkness. I exhaled in frustration and scrabbled at the crumbling plaster, trying to enlarge the hole I had gouged in the wall.

The fleshy part of my forearm hit the candleholder, and I yowled as the hot metal seared my skin. "Oh...that...hurts..." Amid moans between gritted teeth, I listened for sounds in the adjoining classroom. Fabius had left hours earlier, and though I had no reason to think he would return, I did not want him or one of the few remaining servants to discover me.

Not now...not when I was so close.

I peeled wax from my throbbing arm and leaned against the wall. The movement stirred the thick grime, and a layer of dust sifted down on my head and shoulders. I sneezed once, then twice more.

I sighed and sneezed again. This was the reward for my impatience. Though I had removed a hundred years of Maitlan family castoffs from the storeroom, I had neglected to scrub away the accumulated filth. My nose itched and my eyes watered as I crawled across the floor and fumbled for the latch. I would have to clean the closet thoroughly before it was fit for use.

As I retreated to my room, the eyes of long-forgotten forebears watched disapprovingly from faded paintings lining the corridors. The peeling gilt frames and moth-eaten tapestries were reminders of earlier times, before the Maitlan manor had sunk into poverty and decay... before the Sardonians invaded Atruria.

My nurse, Nanni, was waiting in my room with my nightgown and a washbasin. "Arabella, you look like you been rollin' in the dustbin." She attacked my face with a washcloth. "What've you been up to at this hour? Dustin' shelves in the classroom again?"

My breath caught. Had she guessed...?

"I've no idea how a destitute lord of the lowest rank like yer father can afford a tutor the likes of Fabius. Of course he's ancient now, but did you know he taught at the university in the capital, Pithark? Jus' think—our Fabius might've rubbed shoulders with royalty," Nanni continued, enamored, though her expression turned suddenly wary. "Still, I did overhear that he was suspected of providin' ferbidden books to students. He was even accused of teachin' a *woman*!"

I exhaled in a whoosh. Nanni had a good heart, but I was aware of her penchant for sensational gossip. "Well, not all women need be illiterate."

She cuffed my cheek. "None of that mouth, girl. I can read...an' write, too. There jus' ain't much use fer fancy book learnin' fer women. No good can come of it as long as Sardonians rule Atruria."

I winced as she yanked a nightgown sleeve over my tender arm. "Father gave permission. Fabius said there was no harm in polishing my arithmetic skills and writing."

She snorted. "I doubt Vigo would've fussed if Fabius had suggested you take up *blacksmithin'*. It's a wonder he even remembers you live here."

"He certainly never forgets Pyrrin." I couldn't keep the bitterness from creeping into my voice. My father, a widowed lord with four grown daughters, had wanted a son and heir. When I was born a girl, he stormed off to finish an interrupted game of Kings without ever laying eyes on me. And when my brother was born two years later, my father seemed to forget that I even existed.

Nanni's lips tightened. "The way yer father spoils that child. Iffen yer Mamma weren't dead..."

I tossed the unruly corkscrew locks that passed for my curls.

"She's *not* dead! A wicked sorcerer is holding her captive in a tower. She will return after she escapes."

Nanni looked pained. Three years had passed since my mother's disappearance, yet I still clung to the belief that she would come back to me. I *had* to. I could not allow myself to think otherwise, or I would sink into despair.

My father's neglect only served to heighten my desolation. My kind, beautiful, beloved Mamma had been my world...my life...my everything.

Nanni sighed. "Child, yer gettin' to be as good a storyteller as yer mother. Last week it was a wicked ogre."

I shook my head. "An ogre is too easy. Only a sorcerer's magic is strong enough..."

She gave an exclamation of horror. "Hold yer tongue, child! Such talk will bring soldiers poundin' down the doors!" Nanni's eyebrows knitted, and she wagged a finger at me. "I can still remember when the mere whisper of magic doin's was enough to drown a woman."

She brandished a brush and set to work on my hair. "I can't imagine where you get such tangles. If only you had inherited yer mother's wavy tresses an' light red color, instead of hair the color of—"

"Carrots." I cringed every time Nanni compared me to Mamma.

"Now, child. I don't know if I'd be that harsh." Nanni tilted my face and studied my features. "Of course, if you would wear a hat when you ride, you might not have so many freckles. We ought to bleach 'em with lemon juice."

"Don't bother," I muttered, pulling away.

She shrugged and gave me a peck on the forehead before tucking me into bed. She could be brusque and crabby, but I loved her like a grandmother...most of the time.

~ † ~

Two surly soldiers conversed quietly as they leaned against the side of a building.

"Stupid lass. Wouldn't've had to end this way if she'd jus' told us," said one.

The other shrugged. "No skin off my nose. What's it to me if there be one less Atrurian wench?" Their laughter was chilling.

The first one kicked a bundle wrapped in sacking at his feet. "Still, there'll be questions, and we ain't supposed to make a stir. I say we should've gone straight to the source."

The second soldier shook his dark head. "You heard the order. Not a peep."

"Right," the first interrupted. "This is to be an accident, jus' like the last time. Hopefully, it'll be jus' as convincing." He spat into the weeds next to him, then bent and hoisted one end of the bundle. "Well, let's get on with it."

The other soldier helped him half carry, half drag the sack over the dew-covered grass. One of the men stumbled, and a piece of sacking unrolled. A thin, white arm flopped out and dragged on the ground. Tall rushes growing at the edge of the water hid them from view, but after some grunted curses and a splash, they returned to the shore with the empty sacking, their breeches wet to the knees.

I sat up with a start, entangled in the bedcovers I'd been grappling with. Burying my head in my arms, I stifled a shuddering cry. Though I'd endured nightmares for years, this one was worse than usual.

I waited until my shivering ceased and my racing heart returned to normal, then tossed away the covers and slid out of bed. The sky was graying to the east, so I lit a lamp and pulled out my dream diary. Though I loathed the chore, Mamma had made me promise to continue the task she had begun when I was small.

After writing the newest entry, I caressed the leather bound cover and opened the diary to the beginning. Tears blurred my mother's fine, spidery writing. My early dreams had been delightful, even heroic—a prince with a scarred cheek wedding a gorgeous princess with diamonds in her hair, a dashing enchanter shooting fireworks to the heavens, a unicorn in distress...rescued from a vicious wolf by a lovely maiden with a bow.

I slammed the diary shut and indulged in a fit of sobbing. These wakeful hours of the early morning were the moments I missed Mamma the most. I would even have welcomed the bitter drink she used to urge on me after I tearfully recounted a nightmare. The drink made me groggy, leaving only faded memories of the dream.

Drawing a long breath, I composed myself and tucked the diary away. As it was too early for breakfast, I dressed and took a walk through my mother's garden. Though *I* tended the plants now, I still thought of it as her garden. My memories of Mamma were strongest when I walked through the beds she had cultivated with such care.

She had been renowned as an herbalist, and villagers had sought balms for injuries and cures for toothaches, as well as remedies for hair loss and fatigue. As soon as I could toddle, I followed her as she ministered in the village, and as I grew older, I helped with whatever infusion, tea, or poultice she thought might help. She never turned anyone away, and she never accepted money as payment. Yet after every visit to the village, we would return laden with vegetables, eggs, chickens, and other items the grateful villagers heaped upon us. I once overheard Nanni boast that though my father owed notes on the land and the house was falling down around our ears, the manor never lacked for household goods after his marriage to my mother.

I wandered through the garden, stopping to pull weeds or snip dead flowers. I knew every plant by name—more than a hundred—liverwort, bloodroot, fireweed, stinging nettle, widow's bonnet, lavender, and statice. I stopped in front of a plant with gray, waxy leaves. I still remembered the day she had planted it.

"What is that, Mamma," I asked as she knelt and tamped earth around the roots.

She swiped her glove at some wisps of hair that had escaped her elegant twist, leaving a smudge of dirt on her cheek. "Mararoot, but you must never touch or eat it."

That was not surprising; Mamma forbade me to touch several herbs.

"What does it do?" I dipped my dress hem in the waiting water bucket and wiped the dirt from her cheek.

Her lovely face clouded. "It has no curative powers."

All the plants in the garden were useful for alleviating some ailment; even rosehips made a relaxing tea. "Then why did you plant it?"

Mamma gazed at me for a long moment. "Mararoot has...other uses," she said as she dampened the soil around the base of the plant.

She never explained its purpose further, and I had yet to discover one. The plant smelled like rotten fruit and grew like a noxious weed, poisoning other herbs and leaving nasty blisters if I brushed against it. I could not imagine why she wanted the foul plant.

~ † ~

"The foreign kings of Sardonia have ruled our tiny kingdom for two hundred years. Little of Atruria's history before the Sardonian invasion is remembered now, except for legends and songs traveling minstrels and bards recite around smoky fires."

"Why must we learn Atrurian history?" Pyrrin interrupted my recitation. "Sardonians rule Atruria now."

"The history of Atruria is the story of your heritage," Fabius said. We had just begun, and already the lesson wasn't going well.

"I don't care about my *heritage*," Pyrrin replied, crossing his arms over his chest.

Fabius sighed. "What *do* you care about?"

My brother leaned forward. "I like watching cock fights and dice games at the fortress. The soldiers pass around a jug and tell stories... and sometimes they let me fetch their knives off the target after they throw 'em."

"I see," Fabius said, running his gnarled hands through his snowy hair. "Is your father aware of how much time you spend at the fortress?"

Pyrrin shrugged. "As long as I come to lessons, he don't care what I do after."

Fabius looked troubled, and I gazed at him in sympathy. Though my father doted on Pyrrin...giving him presents, clothes, and a horse he couldn't afford, he cared nothing for manners or education. He wouldn't have bothered with a tutor, except Sardonian law demanded one for the heir of a lord...even one reduced to poverty like my father.

"Perhaps you think an education is a waste of time," Fabius said. "Yet, if you intend to be lord of this manor someday, you will need to keep ledgers and accounts. If you cannot read and do sums, how will you know if your steward is cheating you?"

Pyrrin wrinkled his nose. "Fine, but history ain't much use."

"Sardonian law dictates instruction in reading, writing, mathematics, Sardonian history, and a cursory knowledge of the ancient language of Lattrian..."

Pyrrin scowled.

"...so you can attend a university and receive the education required for the son of an Atrurian noble. Our libraries and universities still boast numerous Lattrian texts. Unless you wish to remain wholly ignorant of literature or the sciences, you *must* achieve fluency."

"There's only one good thing about Lattrian," Pyrrin said with a sneer. "*She* ain't allowed to attend."

"True," Fabius said, his gaze lingering on me. "King Sarduk's predecessors saw fit to bar women from such studies."

I looked away, praying my expression would not betray me.

"Still, she *is* permitted to learn geography." With his walking stick, he rapped the map pinned to the wall and looked at Pyrrin. "Please pay attention. Our hamlet of Heyden-on-Trine is the only settlement north of the Aurals. These mountains run east to west and serve as a formidable barrier, isolating the village from southern Atruria except for a single pass—the northern gateway of Atruria. A Sardonian fortress stands guard on a hill overlooking the Trine River. Unlike the rest of the rivers in Atruria..." Fabius turned to Pyrrin.

"The Trine runs north into the Great Lake," Pyrrin recited.

"Correct." Fabius indicated the huge lake to the north. "Arabella, what can you tell me about the lake?"

"The Great Lake is a huge freshwater sea, fed by the Trine."

"Yes. East of the lake lies grassland, wasteland, and...the Enchanted Forest."

"*Enchanted Forest*?" Pyrrin asked. "The map says Black Forest."

"Once known as the Enchanted Forest, fantastic creatures and magical beasts may still dwell among its ancient trees."

"Ha!" Pyrrin scoffed. "Sardonian armies eradicated magic from Atruria years ago. There probably aren't even any magic toadstools left in that forest."

"Perhaps not," Fabius said, pausing for a long moment before turning back to the map. "North of the forest lie the tallest mountains in the world, the Pindar Mountains. And north of them..."

"There ain't *nothing* north of the Pindar Mountains," Pyrrin said.

"Isn't *anything*, Pyrrin," Fabius corrected, turning back to his desk. "Please mind your grammar."

Pyrrin rolled his eyes.

~ † ~

It was late morning before Fabius closed the mathematics book on his desk and gave me a nod.

"Time for you to leave, Arabella."

"Thank you, sir," I said, bobbing a curtsy.

I could feel his eyes on my back as I exited, so I made myself count to three hundred before sneaking into the closet. The musty smell of mildew assaulted my senses, and the crumbling plaster and a fine layer of dust belied my scrubbing over the weekend. I laid a ragged quilt on the floor, propped a slate and pencil on a pillow, and peeped through the hole I had made in the plaster. A thrill surged up my spine as I listened to Fabius and Pyrrin recite grammar. At last, I was going to unlock the secrets of Lattrian!

2

egin again," Fabius told Pyrrin. "You still haven't memorized the form."

Pyrrin groaned and started over, stumbling yet again on the last two endings.

I peeked through my spy hole and mouthed the words, ticking the cases off on my fingers. I knew this form by heart—just like the last seven Fabius had covered.

"Once more..." Fabius began, but a knock on the schoolroom door interrupted him. "Enter," he called.

"Iffen you please, sir..." The maid gave a clumsy curtsy. "The master sent me to fetch you."

Fabius gathered up a sheaf of papers. "Of course. That shall be all for today, Pyrrin."

My hands grew clammy. I had left the closet door ajar to let in light and air—the musty smell had never gone away.

My heart raced, but it was too late. Pyrrin sprinted past my door, shouting like a hellion, and Fabius followed. I held my breath and willed him to keep going, but his shuffling footsteps paused outside the closet. "Go on ahead, my dear," he said to the maid. "Tell the master I shall be there shortly."

As her footsteps pattered down the hall, I crouched in the back of the closet. The door creaked open and Fabius peered in, eyeing my spyhole and the slate. Dread settled in the pit of my stomach. Though I had always found him kind and generous, he was certainly within his rights to thrash me. Worse, he might tell my father. I could not bear the thought; tears welled in my eyes and try as I might, I started to cry.

"How long have you been watching the lesson?"

I sniffled and whispered in a tear-choked voice, "Three months."

He shook his head, gazing at me for a long moment. "Your father has called for me, but I expect to see you this evening in the classroom. Understand?"

I nodded. After he left, I sat for a while in the gloom, struggling to breathe as my heart raced in panic. Finally, I ran to the stable to seek solace among the horses.

After Mamma's disappearance, my father had sold everything of value in our shabby manor. My walnut four-poster bed and matching wardrobe were the first items to go, followed by my pure white pony, Moonbeam, which my mother had given me on my fourth birthday. Now I had an old swaybacked mare who liked to kick and nip. She was such a disappointment after my beautiful pony, I had not even named her and always referred to her as the nag.

She disliked going faster than a walk, but today I kicked her into a run. I rode until her sides heaved and foam flecked her neck, then dismounted and flopped in the grass. Usually I was gentle and patient with her, and she stood with trembling flanks and flaring nostrils, eyeing me as if I had suddenly gone mad. I rolled on my side and stared into the distance.

Tears collected again, but I swiped them away. It was my own fault Fabius had caught me. I held several conversations with him in my head, in which I begged him to whip me instead of barring me from the classroom, and I promised never to look at a Lattrian form again. Yet the Fabius I conjured remained implacable despite all my pleading, and somehow my promise sounded hollow.

I lay wallowing in the grass until the wintry cold seeped through my cloak. Then I dragged myself to my feet and led the nag back to the stable. She seemed to have forgiven me and allowed me to water, wash, and curry her before sinking her nose into her feed.

I had plenty of time to think about my impending appointment with Fabius while I finished my chores. My stomach churned, but a bath fortified my nerves. Then I chose a dress from my trunk...another gift from my mother.

She had given me the silver-bound trunk right before my seventh birthday, along with an ornately carved jewelry box overflowing with winking diamonds, rubies, and emeralds in settings that rivaled the best Atruria's silversmiths had to offer. When she showed me the beautiful gowns, she told me there were two for every birthday.

The dresses fit for one year. The day after my birthday, the buttons nearly burst on the old dresses if I tried to put them on...and I *had* tried.

That was not the only mysterious thing about my trunk. Every time I pulled a dress over my head, silk and satin transformed into mundane, everyday fabrics. Hemlines shortened or lengthened; necklines lost lace or added demure collars. Even the jewelry changed from silver and gems to wood and pewter.

If my mother had intended to explain the trunk's secret, she never got the chance; she disappeared only two weeks after giving me the silver key that opened the lock.

There was only one explanation. My mother's trunk was...

But I could not say it. I didn't even dare *think* it. Magic was forbidden—no—magic had been erased in Atruria. As they stormed across the kingdom, the advancing Sardonian troops had confiscated and burned everything remotely magical. After two hundred years of Sardonian rule, there was nothing left. No books on casting spells or brewing potions, no strange creatures, no mysterious, unexplained occurrences, and *definitely* no magic trunks...spilling over with gorgeous gowns...that transformed into everyday dresses.

Right.

And that was why I had never told anyone about the trunk—not even Nanni.

My current selections were of delicate gray silk with white crocheted collar and cuffs and deep-brown crushed velvet with a matching sash and ivory buttons running down the front. I slipped the silk over my head and checked my reflection in a tiny handheld mirror. After Mamma's disappearance, my father had sold every large mirror in the house to help cover his debts, but I did not need one to tell me how I looked in the dress. My hair was carrot-colored and curly—crinkly really, high cheekbones jutted over hollow cheeks, my sharp nose was too long for my face, and my crooked front teeth peeked through thin, pale lips. I even detected a couple pimples hiding among the freckles speckling my ashen skin.

The lovely silk had changed into simple gray wool with white cuffs and a lacy collar. Though quite pretty, it could not hide my gangly legs or ungainly hands and feet. I placed a tortoiseshell comb in my unruly hair and started towards the classroom.

Fabius took no notice as I entered the darkened room, and I felt like a drab, gray duckling going to slaughter. I stood motionless until he looked up, his eyes thoughtful and somber.

"What happened to your mother, Arabella?"

I tried to hide my surprise as I scuffed my toe into the floor. I had not expected him to ask about Mamma. "One evening she left for the village to tend a sick woman. She never came back. A search party combed the fields and hills..." I paused and drew a deep breath before continuing; I did not like to talk about her disappearance. "They didn't find any sign of her, so the next day my father called on the Sardonians to search farther afield. That evening a contingent of soldiers returned carrying my mother's silver filigree necklace. They'd found it among some daisies on a hillside near the Trine River. Soldiers and villagers hunted for another week, but they found no other trace of her."

"Nobody has any idea what happened to her?"

"My father decided she drowned in the river. Other people suggested she returned to her home..."

He raised an eyebrow. "And where was that?"

"Nobody knows, sir. One spring morning my mother...Mirella... wandered into the village. The old gossips say she was barefoot and dressed in tatters, with nothing to her name but a ragged satchel. She claimed she was the daughter of a trapper living on the shores of the Great Lake." I knew I was merely postponing my inevitable punishment, but an edge of excitement still crept into my voice.

"Hmmph!" he snorted. "A student once told me a similar story, and I no more believe it now than I did then."

"Where else might she have come from, sir?"

He waved his hand dismissively. "An infant could invent a better tale."

"My father did not seem to care. Nanni says he fell in love with her beauty and genteel grace and offered to marry her. They wed in midsummer, and I was born ten months later."

Fabius drummed his fingertips on his desk. He seemed to be lost in some inner debate. At last, he said slowly, "I suspect your mother was a Northlander."

"A Northlander?"

He pulled a string behind him, unrolling a huge map of Atruria. It was different from the other maps on the wall, labeled with cities I had never seen before and roads I was certain did not exist. Oddest of all, the top of the map continued beyond the Pindar Mountains, showing a vast plain labeled Northland. The plain also had a few sparse roads, towns, and cities.

"I have never heard of the Northland."

"I'm not surprised," Fabius said, sending the map back into the roller with a snap. "Sarduk's predecessors went to a lot of trouble to eradicate all mention of it from the literature and cartography of Atruria."

"Why?"

Fabius leaned against his desk, riveting my attention with his gaze. "The one law most sacred to the king is the prohibition against teaching Lattrian to women. In generations past, the Sardonians hunted, branded, and imprisoned women suspected of reading the language or possessing Lattrian books." He stood up and paced behind his desk. "It's foolish of me to even consider teaching you..." Once again, he seemed to wrestle some inner question. "I can only guess at your mother's intentions..." Looking up at me, he said, "If I am to instruct you, Arabella, I must have your solemn vow that you will tell no one. The Sardonians no longer search for grannies with hidden caches of books, but a single misspoken word might still be disastrous."

I couldn't believe it. I had hoped for a stern lecture...expected a whipping. At the very least, I had been sure he would board up the closet and throw me out of class. Yet here he was...offering to teach me Lattrian.

"I...won't breathe a word, sir, even if they box my ears...or...or send me to the mines." Sometimes criminals were condemned to Sarduk's gold and silver mines in the south; it was the worst punishment I could imagine.

A tiny smile lifted a corner of his mouth. "The mines would be a death sentence, so let's hope it never comes to that." He held out his hand, which I clasped solemnly. "Your lessons will commence tomorrow evening. Then I can see if you've learned anything despite your brother's incessant mewling."

I grinned, and he waved me toward the door. "Go on. We don't want your nurse to come looking for you."

3

y days fell into a predictable pattern. I rose early, attended arithmetic and Atrurian grammar lessons with Pyrrin, then exercised my nag. During the afternoon, I worked in the stables mucking stalls for the horses my father boarded. Afterwards, I tended my garden or delivered medicine to the village, for many villagers now looked to me for simple remedies. After supper, Nanni brushed my hair while she scolded about the straw and twigs tangled in it.

After she left me for the night, I stole to the classroom and spent an hour learning Lattrian, history, and science. When I returned to my room, I usually spent thirty minutes yawning over my books before tumbling into bed.

My tenth birthday fell two months to the day after my clandestine lessons with Fabius began. Despite my protests and Pyrrin's tantrum, Fabius gave me the day off, so I spent the glorious May morning reading on a windswept foothill overlooking the village.

I had already read every tattered book in my father's meager library. His books were moth-eaten, water-stained, and decayed, like all the other vestiges of the former glory of the Maitlan family. Still, I treasured them, for they were reminders of sweeter times in Atruria.

With the whole morning to myself, I decided to reread my father's *Geography of Atruria,* hoping the book might shed some light on Fabius's mysterious Northland. I pored over the keys and descriptions, but by noon, I had to admit defeat. Although there were maps detailing every geographical feature south of the Aurals, none showed anything north of the range.

I set the book aside and unpacked the hamper Nanni had sent along, smiling when I discovered the sweet roll she had added in honor of my birthday. I lay down in the grass and savored the solitude. The wind swept through the grasses, swirling them in little eddies and whorls, and sparrows sang from a lone tree. The warm sun and my full stomach made me sleepy...

The mare's snort woke me, and I rolled on my back and lazily watched the fleecy clouds soaring overhead. A nap was a luxury, and I sought to enjoy it as long as possible.

"Well, lookee here. What's this sleepin' in the grass?"

I sat up, startled. A burly lad stood less than five feet from me, staring with dark eyes. He was Dirk, the youngest of the village black-smith's strapping sons. Behind him, Pyrrin was climbing the rise. He idolized the older boy; wherever Dirk went, Pyrrin followed.

He stopped beside Dirk and appraised me. "It's a hideous beast, if you ask me."

Dirk chortled and slapped Pyrrin on the back. "Good 'un, Pyrrin. A frizzy, orange beast. I like that."

"If you two *gentlemen* will excuse me..." I dropped a mock curtsy, and then I searched through the grass for my book.

"Lookin' fer somethin'?" Dirk asked, lifting the geography over his head.

"Give that to me."

He danced back a few steps, holding the book out of reach. "Or what?"

I snatched at it, but he gave me a push that sent me stumbling backwards and opened the book. "What is this? No pictures?"

"Some people actually *read* them."

His face turned purple, and he yanked out a page.

"Stop!" I screamed, leaping up and grabbing his arm.

He shoved me again, and I sprawled on the ground.

Pyrrin stood watching, hands thrust deep in the pockets of his breeches. "I think she's mad, Dirk."

Dirk ignored him and started pulling out pages.

I ripped off my shoe and hurled it at him. The heel hit him square in the face, and a thin line of blood trickled from a gash on his upper lip. Stunned, he dropped the geography, and I scooped up the book and damaged pages before he could recover. Tearing off my other shoe, I sprinted down the hill.

Dirk shouted hoarsely, and I glanced over my shoulder. He was chasing me, his face contorted with fury. Without missing a stride, I tucked the book under an arm and raced toward the village. Though tall and awkward, I was fleet, and few boys could catch me. Dirk was two years my senior, but he was stocky and heavier. I might outstrip him in a sprint, but I wasn't sure I would fare as well in an endurance race. I needed a place to hide, and the mill was the only building on this side of the Trine River.

I settled into a lope at the base of the hill. Still, by the time I reached the millrace, a stitch had formed in my side. On the bank of the millpond, I veered toward a diminutive figure waving at me. It was the miller's daughter, and she gestured toward a dingy shed by the dock.

"Come on," she called. "They is a ways back."

"Thank you," I said, gasping, and collapsed behind a pile of old paddles and ropes.

She covered me with a musty oilcloth and closed the door, plunging the shed into darkness. After a few minutes, I heard running feet, and the shed quivered as someone collapsed against the side.

"Where'd she go?" Dirk asked in irritation.

"I had no idea she could run so fast," Pyrrin said, wheezing. He sounded muffled, as if he had sprawled on the dock.

Both boys sucked air, and then Dirk called, "Hey, you. Miller's runt. Did you see that book totin', orange-haired beast run by here a few minutes back?"

"Yeah...where'd she go?" Pyrrin asked in echo.

I winced at Dirk's description of the girl. She was small, with mousy hair and huge brown eyes.

"Hey, miller's idiot! Can't you hear me?" Dirk shouted.

"I heard you," she said, sounding distant.

"Well? Did you see her?"

"Yes, but I imagine she be long gone by now. You should check the village. Or she might be home by now. Who knows how far she ran."

Dirk snorted. "Come on, Pyrrin. Let's go find somethin' else to do. I'll look fer her later."

Pyrrin gave a muffled groan, then howled, probably because Dirk kicked him. "I said *come on*, you lazy oaf!"

"I'm comin'," Pyrrin said, whining. They tramped away toward the village.

I pushed the dank oilcloth aside and sat up. The door squeaked and the girl peered in. "They be gone now."

"Thank you..."

"Melora," she said.

"Melora...I don't think I could've run another step." She seemed amiable, and I smiled shyly and emerged from my hiding place, cradling the ruined book in my arms.

"Did you give him the cut on his lip?"

I nodded.

"Well, it's a start, anyway. Someone needs to poun' that Dirk down to size." Her seriousness and candor was delightful, and I burst into laughter. A slow smile blossomed on her face.

"I am afraid he has wrecked this book," I said, sobering.

"Lemme see." She inspected the damaged pages. "Is this yourns?"

"My father's, though I doubt he'll miss it. Yet I am sorely disappointed that Dirk ruined it."

"I don't think so. These leaves were pulled out in pairs." She opened a page and showed me one large piece of parchment. "They be folded in half like so," she demonstrated, "an' then sewn into the bindin' with needle an' thread."

When Dirk yanked on the pages, the ancient stitching disintegrated, leaving the parchment intact.

"This book needs to be reboun', but it can be fixed fer certain."

"I don't have the skill to repair this, nor money to pay another," I said and sighed.

Her small shoulders straightened as she said proudly, "I can do it."

"Where did you learn to bind a book?"

"Me Da makes small leather books fer keeping track of his share of the grain the villagers bring. He taught me how to sew 'em. This book is larger an' uses parchment, but it be mostly the same. I will gladly be doin' this fer you."

"But I cannot pay you."

She looked crestfallen. "I was hopin' we might be friends, an' friends do such things fer each other..."

I caught her hands in mine. "I'd like nothing more than to have you for a friend, but it would be selfish of me to ask! This will take hours and hours, and I've nothing to offer you in return."

"Can you read?"

"Of course," I said, puzzled.

She gazed at me. "Would you be willin' to teach me?"

It hadn't occurred to me that she could not read. "Didn't you attend the village school?"

"Not a day. Da decided it was a waste of time, an' when Ma died he needed me here to keep house."

My breath caught, and a lump grew in my throat. I remembered hearing somewhere that the miller's wife had succumbed to fever. We were two motherless girls. I wrapped my arms around her and squeezed. "I would be happy to teach you to read," I whispered.

She beamed at me, joy shining in her eyes.

~ † ~

After rescuing my picnic hamper and shoes and stabling my mare, which had meandered home on her own, I stole to the classroom. Fabius was at his desk checking sums by the light of a single candle.

"I thought we agreed there would be no lessons this evening," he said, leaning back in his chair and kneading his knees. Fatigue lined his face.

Before tonight I hadn't considered how old he was or how tirelessly he worked. "Are you all right?" I asked, my mission forgotten in a sudden rush of worry.

He smiled, his blue eyes crinkling at the corners. "Nothing a good night's sleep won't fix. I am afraid your brother was more taxing than usual today."

"I can come back tomorrow," I said, retreating to the doorway.

"Nonsense." Fabius gestured toward a seat. "What's on your mind?"

"I want to teach someone to read, and I don't know how to begin."

"At the beginning, of course," he said with a chuckle. "Who is the lucky student?"

"I met a girl in the village today—the miller's daughter, Melora. She wants to learn how to read."

"Has she been to the village school?"

"She is too busy doing chores. Her mother died..." I looked away, unable to finish.

Fabius removed a slim volume from a shelf behind him. "This primer will teach her the sounds of the letters. Assuming she has a modicum of intelligence, with your help and this book she should soon be able to read simple words."

"I'm sure she is quite smart. Thank you, sir. I will take perfect care of it."

He waved off my thanks. "When she finishes the primer, I have a first reader as well. Make sure you obtain a slate and pencil for her so she can copy letters and words." He paused. "Arabella, I know how much young girls like to chatter..."

"I will not say anything about our lessons," I assured him.

4

n my excitement over meeting Melora, a week passed before I remembered my trunk. The next day after lessons, I locked myself in my room, anxious to admire my new dresses. The first was of brown wool, elegantly cut with a flared skirt and beaded cuffs and bodice. The next dress—of emerald velveteen with a pale green silk underskirt—was the loveliest gown I had ever seen. I stretched out on the floor, surrounded by my colorful finery.

After a while, the ornate carvings on the open trunk caught my attention. An intricate pattern of leaves and vines trailed across the front, encircling a prancing unicorn whose long spiral horn pointed to the lock. A burst of afternoon sunlight caught the unicorn's ruby eye, making it wink at me as if the trunk knew a secret I had yet to discover. Laughing at my foolishness, I pressed the jeweled eye.

I gasped as a panel beneath the jewel tilted forward on silent hinges, revealing a hidden compartment. Breathless, I edged forward and peeked into the revealed space. I slid my hand inside and pulled out a heavy bundle wrapped in a red velvet bag. Slowly I peeled back the velvet to reveal two large, gilded books with Lattrian titles on the spine.

I opened the first to the flyleaf and traced the elegant inscription... Elissa—not Mirella, as I had half expected. Questions whirled through my head. Had Mamma meant for me to find these books? Had she even known about the secret compartment? And who was Elissa?

I flipped the page and painstakingly translated the title: *Tudyre Salutori Erbaym*...The Study of Medicinal Herbs and Plants. Was this a recipe book for medicines and potions? Columns of ingredients lined the top of the page, followed by drawings of plants—some of which I recognized—and numbered lines of text that probably gave instructions for blending and preparing the mixtures.

As I turned the fragile pages, a folded piece of parchment slid out of the binding. I smoothed the creases and attempted to decipher the cramped letters. Written in green ink, the spidery writing wandered across the page. *Acerbysradyx* sprawled across the top, followed by several indecipherable lines and then *Admonityem* in capital letters. The writer had boldly underlined and dotted the word with three exclamation points. The next dozen lines may have offered an explanation, but the Lattrian was well beyond me. Baffled, I tucked the page back in the binding and turned to the other book.

This one was titled *Legereya Atruriym yt Latrettym*...Legends of Atruria and Latretta.

Elissa graced this flyleaf as well. Gorgeous hand-painted plates teeming with princesses, knights, and battles illustrated the stories. I pored over the pictures, wishing I could read the accompanying text.

The dimming light and lengthening shadows reminded me of the late hour. I returned the books to their compartment before hurrying to the stable for my round of chores.

Nanni was waiting impatiently when I finally made it back for supper. "Where have you been?"

"Currying the horses," I answered, sitting down to lukewarm stew and brown bread.

"I wish you would spend as much time with yer needle an' thread as you do with them horses," she snorted, yanking at my hair fastenings. "Ye ain't never goin' to have a dower ready when the time comes."

I ducked my head, letting the freed hair fall over my face as she brushed it. Marriage was the last thing I wanted to think about. Who would want to marry me? I was ugly and poor and...ugly. I still had some years of girlish fancy left, and I found it much more pleasant to dwell on my lessons, the garden, the horses, and my budding friendship with Melora.

Though she only managed to get away from her housework and the mill two or three afternoons a week, Melora made excellent progress. Within weeks, she had learned the sounds of all the letters and could read simple phrases.

Writing proved more difficult, but after lots of practice, Melora was able to form passable words and sentences on her tablet. By midsummer, I proclaimed her literate.

I wished I could say the same for my Lattrian skills. I savored my newfound treasures in secret for several months because of an irrational fear that Fabius would take them from me. At last common sense won; if I was to decipher the books, I needed his help. On the pretext of requesting the next reader for Melora, I wrapped the velvet bag in a piece of burlap and carried the bundle to his room.

His gnarled hands caressed the leather covers as I laid the books on his desk. "Arabella, where did you get these?"

"I found them hidden in my mother's trunk."

He raised an eyebrow as he opened *Legereya Atruriym yt Latret-tym.* "Do you know what these are?"

"I think this one contains recipes for potions and herbal reme-dies," I said, pointing to *Tudyre Salutori Erbaym.* "That one is a book of legends," I added, nodding to the book he held.

He set the books on his desk and pushed them aside. "These works are quite old and valuable. This one," he said, tapping the book of leg-ends, "is also very much banned in Atruria. Are you sure they will be safe in your trunk?"

I nodded as I ran my hand over the gilded spines. "Will you teach me to read them?" I asked.

He smothered a smile. "Of course. I just want you to understand what they are."

"But I *don't*! I can only read one word in fifty, and the recipes are gibberish. The other is supposed to tell legends of Atruria *and* Latretta, but I have no idea where Latretta is!"

Fabius rose and slowly pulled down the map I had seen months earlier.

I noted once again the plain above the Pindar mountain range.

"You remember I thought your mother was a Northlander?" he said, pointing to the label Northland. "The people north of the Pindar Moun-tains call their country Latretta. I believe your mother was born there."

"But our maps don't show anything beyond the Pindars."

"Just like the previous Sardonian kings, Sarduk denies its existence, but the land is real." Noting my bewildered expression, he crossed to the hall and checked the corridor before returning to his desk.

"Legends tell of a mighty and magical realm to the north. They built magnificent cities, created a stable government, and tamed the magical beasts of the wild. For a thousand years, their kings governed wisely, and both our lands enjoyed peace and prosperity.

"Then a powerful sorcerer named Toryn rose within the ruling family. He built Ravensdell in the east, a stronghold fortified with towers and protected with dark magical spells. It is said that evil seeped from his fortress and poisoned the Eastern Fen."

For the first time I noticed a vast swath of coastal marshland along the eastern shore north of the Aural Mountains. "I thought the Pindars stretched all the way to the coast."

"Rubbish straight from the fertile imaginations of Sardonian map-makers. *This* map is a copy of an ancient one; the geographical features are quite accurate," he added.

"Toryn delved deeply into dark magic, and legend says it destroyed his humanity. He gathered horrible beasts and evil men to his castle. When his army was strong, he launched an attack on Latretta. There were epic battles, many of which are described in this book," Fabius said, laying his hand on *Legereya Atruriym yt Latrettym.* "Toryn waged war until he had destroyed, killed, or enslaved most of the country. Yet in Latretta's darkest hour, a remarkable young enchanter named Mortekai rallied the last remnant of free men and creatures. In a final battle on the banks of the Lorne that devastated both armies, Mortekai sacrificed his life to slay Toryn, and Latretta was free once again."

Fabius sat down at his desk.

"Are those castles?" I pointed to three crude emblems on the map.

"The remnants of Toryn's army fled to Ravensdell in the marsh, led by his apprentice, Rowena. Secure in the magical fortress, she was free to nurse her hatred. To protect against future attacks from Rowena or her successors, the Latrettans built a line of castles and fortifications across the land for defense."

"Only three?"

Fabius smiled. "Legend says they erected nine, but the other six locations have been lost to time. Although," he added as an afterthought, "I've heard rumors that they built a fourth in the center of the Great Lake." He shrugged. "Regardless, Ivory Tower, an architectural marvel of white marble, was the crowning jewel of their capital city. The Lorne River drains the Great Lake into the Eastern Fen," he said, indicating a blue line meandering between the two. "They constructed Red Castle on its northern shore and built a third fortress here in Heyden."

Heyden was not labeled, but I recognized the sweeping bend in the Trine River where our mill sat. An emblem overlooked the river.

"Surely that's wrong. There is no castle here."

He chuckled. "It is better known as the fortress. The limestone fort fell into ruin, and the Sardonians salvaged the stone to build their outpost."

I glanced at the book of legends. "How does Atruria fit into Latretta's legends?"

"Atruria had long been Latretta's ally, exchanging goods, knowledge, and culture along established trade routes. When Mortekai sent out his desperate battle cry, Atruria's best soldiers marched northward to their aid. They reached the battlefield in time to turn the tide in Mortekai's favor. Scores of valiant Atrurians fell along the shores of the Lorne River that day. In gratitude, the Latrettans helped build the fortress in Heyden."

He paused, looking weary and sad. There was no trace of emotion in his voice when he continued. "The long war exacted its toll; Latrettan civilization lay in ruins. Gradually they abandoned their settlements south of the Pindar Mountains. As vegetation and wild beasts took over, the trade routes connecting us became dangerous. After a time, travel ceased altogether, and our two nations were cut off from one another." A smile blossomed suddenly on his tired face. "Yet even after all the years, a few remnants of Latrettan influence still remain. A trace of Northland blood runs through our veins, and every now and then we get a beautiful anomaly like you."

I blushed and ducked my head. "My *mother* was beautiful."

"So I have heard. You shall grow up to be just as lovely, I am sure."

I wasn't the least bit certain of this, and I mumbled something disparaging under my breath.

Fabius laughed. "Red hair is a sure sign of Northlander heritage, and most Atrurian nobles can locate a redhead somewhere in their lineage. You can probably trace your ancestry to Latretta through your father *and* your mother."

"Do you really think my mother was a Northlander?"

He nodded. "These books offer even more proof than her hair."

"But a different name is written in the front."

He turned to the flyleaf on each and examined the signature. Furrows creased his forehead. "Did your mother ever mention this person to you?"

"Never."

Somewhere in the house, a clock chimed. "It's very late," he said, handing me the books.

I wrapped them securely again.

"I don't suppose I need to tell you to keep those hidden."

"No, sir."

After I curled up in bed, I pondered everything Fabius had told me. Had my mother *really* come from Latretta?

~ † ~

I met Melora the next day, and she read her lesson flawlessly. She sat smiling as I heaped praise on her.

While I leafed through the next lesson, she unwrapped her lunch. "I've got somethin' fer you," she said.

My breath caught as she presented the geography. It bore no resemblance to the ragged book I had given her months earlier. An embossed flower design surrounded the title on the new leather cover. Melora had dyed the intricate diamond pattern on the spine a brilliant scarlet and sewn the pages into the new binding with the smallest stitches imaginable. My eyes misted with tears.

"This is gorgeous!"

She smiled. "I foun' a strange map," she said, reaching over my shoulder and flipping to the back of the book.

The map looked hand drawn; it lacked a key, and the geographical features were crudely inked in black. Two mountain ranges ran across the top and bottom of the parchment. A plain gray rectangle sat beside a river, and a squat yellow crown was inked in the center of a large body of water. Well to the right of the water was a tall rust-colored crown, and directly below in the smaller mountain range was a skinny green crown.

"What do you think those are su'posed to be?" Melora asked. "No other map shows any colored thingies."

"I have no idea," I said.

We glanced through several pages, but the rest of the maps had traditional labels. Finally, I closed the book and hugged it to my chest. "I don't know how to thank you, Melora."

"You already have."

I grinned. "You're an amazing student and a wonderful friend."

She scuffed the dirt floor with her toe, and her ears turned pink. "I must go help Da."

I sat in the dim shed after she ducked out the door. I had not realized how lonely I had been before I met her. We were two motherless girls, and we depended on each other for comfort and friendship.

5

 was thrilled when Fabius began introducing advanced Lattrian grammar, but it required intensive studying. One evening during our lesson, my chin slid off the palm I had propped under it. As I jerked awake, Fabius laid down his book.

"I've been pushing you too hard."

I shook my head. "I can keep up."

"Not if you can't stay awake." He plopped down in his chair. "You have a lot on your plate. You're an excellent student, a teacher, an herbalist...and you work as hard as any servant."

I knew he was complimenting me, but I still felt tears brimming. "I don't want to give up Lattrian."

"Who said anything about giving it up? I'm merely suggesting we switch our lessons to every other night. To be honest," he continued, "I could use the respite as well. These old bones are not as spry as they used to be."

"Okay," I agreed reluctantly.

"Now," Fabius said. "You are welcome to go if you wish, but perhaps you might like to hear about the Sardonians...?"

I leaned forward, my fatigue forgotten. "How did they conquer Atruria?"

He leaned back and propped up his feet. "The Sardonians are first mentioned in our history shortly after the defeat of Toryn. They were a warlike, seafaring people living across a warm shallow sea to the south on an archipelago of some three dozen islands. They were a disorganized group of tribes, bickering and fighting amongst themselves, until Sarduk's forebear Galen united them. He dominated trade...and piracy...in the Southern Sea. We signed a few trade agreements and non-aggression pacts, yet from his vantage in Corlana, the old fortified capital of Atruria, King Hadrian didn't view them as a threat.

"That was a grave mistake. As the Sardonian population overran their islands, they coveted our land, our treasures, and our resources: small gold and silver mines to the southeast, scattered diamond and precious stone sites in the Aurals, and a rich timber belt south of the mountains."

He massaged his temples. "The Sardonian ships docking in our ports carried a disease. They were immune, but the plague devastated our people and killed nearly one third of our population in thirty years. Subsequent internal unrest left us weak and vulnerable; Galen's son Hartuk, who was educated at one of our own military academies, seized the opportunity and led a brilliantly executed military campaign against us."

He sat up suddenly. "They are not a tolerant people. What they do not understand, they fear, and what they fear, they persecute and destroy."

"Magic," I murmured.

"Yes," he sighed, settling back in his seat. "Though we were never capable of the legendary magic of the enchanters of the Northland, some Atrurians...primarily women...learned healing arts and other small spells.

"The Sardonian kings viewed the trifling skills we had mastered as a threat to their domination. They stamped out our culture, obliterated our history, and persecuted any woman suspected of practicing magic. In a final assault, they championed cock fighting and bear baiting, and enforced illiteracy and ignorance on the majority of the population."

"You must find us quite ignorant after teaching at a university."

"Not at all, my dear. Atrurians in the south have embraced Sardonian culture...or lack thereof, and they consider magic a quaint fantasy of yesteryear. But here, north of the Aurals, magic has not been completely forgotten. People here may have less education than their southern counterparts, but they still possess a healthy self-identity and an ingrained hatred of Sardonians."

"I thought all Atrurians hate the Sardonians."

"Oh, they hate them, but businessmen in the south will fraternize with them for the sake of money." He gazed at me. "If we are ever to be a free people again, it may be because of innate Sardonian clannishness. The best way to subdue a conquered people is to intermingle and intermarry, but the Sardonians cannot tolerate the idea of intermarriage; even after two hundred years, we are still two distinct peoples.

Hatred, discontent, and unrest simmer just beneath the surface. Contrary to outward appearances, this is not a peaceful kingdom."

Fabius pulled down the map. "And Sarduk has no idea what lies out there," he said, gesturing to the wasteland stretching between the Aurals and the Pindars. After contemplating the map for a long moment, he allowed it to snap back into place. "I think that's enough for now. I shall see you in two nights."

I stood at the door as he set his desk in order. The sputtering candle illuminated the bags under his eyes, and his face creased into deep wrinkles when he flashed me a tired smile. "Enjoy your evening off," he said.

~ † ~

I was prepared to hate our new arrangement, but barely two weeks went by before I had to admit it was beneficial. With every other evening free, there was more time for study, sleep, gardening, or extra moments with Melora.

I could even pay more attention to the horses. They rarely boarded more than six months in our stable, yet I enjoyed every moment with them. Granted, most of the stable work was pure drudgery: mucking stalls, laying clean straw, giving them hay, feed, and water—gallons and gallons of water, which *someone* had to tote from the well in the courtyard. The work was backbreaking, and there were never enough stable hands. One afternoon I discovered Dirk, the blacksmith's son, forking straw from the loft into a stall.

"What are *you* doing here?"

"Yer father hired me to help with the horses," he said, appraising me with his dark eyes.

I hadn't seen him since the incident on the hillside, but I detected a faint white scar on his upper lip. I turned away, hiding a small smile of satisfaction. I kept my distance; Dirk was not likely to forget who had given him that scar.

Seeing Dirk every afternoon was unavoidable, but he only had time for a couple mocking comments or catcalls and long insolent stares. Still, with another person cleaning stalls and carrying water, I had extra time to work with the horses, which I preferred.

By my twelfth birthday, I had learned the grammar and vocabulary necessary to translate *Tudyre Salutori Erbaym,* and I spent many free hours poring over the indices. One detailed common ailments, another indicated possible remedies, and a third gave an extensive list of plants in alphabetical order. Besides some unfamiliar herbs, the book had a listing for every plant from my mother's garden...except mararoot.

I kept searching the book, examining the line drawings, tweaking the translation...looking for the nonexistent entry. One rainy afternoon I even made a drawing of the hateful plant on a piece of parchment and added my own description. *Mararoot: Causes painful blisters to bare skin, flourishes like a weed, poisons soil. Keep away from other herbs, unless you wish to kill them.*

As I scribbled the entry, I couldn't fathom why my mother had planted it. I had been sure the book would give me an explanation, but I still didn't have an inkling.

Though I had mastered the recipe book, *Legereya Atruriym yt Latrettym* was a different story. Even Fabius admitted the complex grammar and extensive vocabulary were difficult. He used the book on a regular basis for translation exercises; together we translated two legends in their entirety.

I loved stories. My mother had been a masterful storyteller. When I was young, I sat for hours by her knee, watching her spinning wheel turn as she wove tales of fearsome dragons, majestic unicorns, lovely princesses, and powerful enchanters who battled the forces of evil over the fate of the earth. We were still in the midst of translating when I realized the two legends were uncannily similar to my mother's stories.

The discovery that her tales may have come from the book made me impatient to find my favorite. Whenever I awoke from a nightmare feeling gloomy or tired, I would beg my mother to tell me about the beautiful maiden who fled her homeland to escape an evil marriage. She wandered homeless through a wilderness until a noble lord rescued and married her. The story never failed to cheer me up, although Mamma would always gaze into the fire after she finished, her spindle idle in her hand.

Fabius cautioned against haste, but I pored over the book until the words ran together in a frightful jumble. Humbled, I set it aside for those lessons when we painstakingly translated two or three sentences—or even a whole paragraph. I wrote the translations on loose pieces of parchment and placed them in whatever book Melora and I were reading.

The two of us treasured our time together. We would recline on a piece of sacking as we ate lunch in the ramshackle shed. She would read to me for a while, and then we talked—or not, as the mood suited us. The shed leaked like a sieve on rainy days, and in frigid weather, our numb fingers made it difficult to turn the pages. Sometimes we sought refuge in the mill, but the grinding millstone often made it too noisy for conversation.

One day in midsummer, huge storm clouds were gathering as I left the manor to meet Melora. I neared the tavern, hurrying by two soldiers and an officer lounging outside. Lately, they always seemed to hang around at lunchtime, and I marveled that they had so much spare time. A bolt of lightning seared the sky, followed by a crash of thunder; wind whipped my clothes and tore at my books. As I turned a corner, I collided with a running housewife, and my books and her basket went flying. She scolded in a shrill voice as I apologized and helped collect her goods. Gathering my books, I rushed toward the mill and ducked inside the shed just as another huge flash of lightning jagged across the sky. Rain fell in torrents, and water dripped through the many holes in the roof.

"Is your father milling, Melora?" I asked, scrambling to protect my books.

She laughed as a raindrop splashed off my nose. "Not today. Let's run fer it."

We collected our lunch pails, hitched up our skirts, and dashed through the driving rain to the mill. Breathless and soaked, we fell laughing in a heap beside the huge, silent millstone.

Tom the Miller emerged from an adjoining storeroom. "Iffen it be too wet fer you lassies to have yer leetle tea party, you may as well help with these sacks."

We grinned and shrugged, and in no time we were employed sewing closed the bottoms of new flour sacks. I was less than skillful with the huge needle. Several times the miller growled and made me take out a messy seam, claiming it would never hold flour. Despite his gruffness, he loved Melora dearly. He tolerated me because I was her friend, though he complained I was 'puttin' uppity idears in her head 'bout that book learnin' nonsense.' Illiterate himself, he saw little value in reading, but he'd been quick enough to put Melora in charge of record-keeping for the mill.

The rain slowed to a sprinkle after an hour, and I waved goodbye to Melora and the miller. After cleaning a few stalls, I returned to my room to study. I took out the slightly soggy *Flora and Fauna of Atru-*

ria I had borrowed from my father's collection and leafed through the pages.

The translations were gone! My breath caught in my throat as I frantically fanned through the book looking for the loose parchment. After ransacking everything I had taken to the mill, I slumped to the floor, hot tears pricking my eyes. How could I have been so stupid? Not only did the four pages represent many weeks of tedious labor, but I had assured Fabius I would keep them safe.

I told myself to be sensible. They had probably slipped out during the collision with the goodwife in the village. If so, the pages were water-soaked and ruined, but I still dreaded informing Fabius of my mishap.

I dragged my feet to lessons the next night, but we worked on grammar and vocabulary instead of translation, and I could not bring myself to tell him.

Two days later, I visited Melora again. My pace quickened to a trot when I saw her waiting outside the shed, waving something that looked like parchment.

"I thought you might need these," she called.

"Where did you find them?" I asked, breathless.

"In the mill. I figgered you dropped 'em during the storm."

"You found them in the mill?" There were no water stains, although I detected a dirt smudge on one page and some flour on the edges. "When did you find them?"

"This mornin'." She grinned. "Atop the millstone. You are most fortunate they didn't get groun' into the flour."

Lucky indeed. As water frothed around the mill wheel, I tucked the loose sheets securely into a book.

I was glad I hadn't needlessly worried Fabius about the misplaced parchments. That evening we translated two whole paragraphs.

6

 here was a swirling mass of wolves, slinking behind rocks, seeking protection from a hail of arrows raining from an outcropping of limestone ahead, where an overhanging boulder provided a shallow cave. Numerous wolves lay dead or dying, pierced by arrows, their blood staining the rocks black. Still the living ones stayed, pressed against stones or cowering in crevices, intent on their prey, which remained out of sight. A massive wolf sat on a huge boulder to the left of the pack, his glassy red eyes staring toward the rocky outcropping while arrows fell harmlessly around him. Suddenly, with a bellow, a powerfully built man bounded out of the cave brandishing a long sword. He charged over the rocks toward the huge wolf. Its concentration broken, it crouched down and barked sharply to the rest of the pack. The man's momentum carried him halfway to the wolf before the pack responded, but then they attacked, snarling and biting ferociously. He beat them back with his sword and massive bulk. With a furious yell, he leaped on the wolf, hacking with his sword. The remaining wolves piled on him until nothing was visible but a writhing mass of gray fur and snapping jaws. A wail erupted from the outcropping, and a furious volley of arrows hissed forth, scattering the wolves in all directions. The man lay in a pool of spreading blood, sprawled atop the crumpled form of the great wolf he had killed.*

I woke, choking back a cry and drenched in sweat. I threw off the bedclothes and hugged my knees to my chest, rocking back and forth. Why wouldn't these nighttime apparitions stop? I longed to feel my mother's arms around me as she held me and wiped away my tears, whispering into my hair that it was only a dream.

By the light of the full moon streaming in the window, I penned the dream into my diary with a trembling hand. I lay down for a while, but visions of red-eyed wolves haunted me. Somewhere in the manor, a clock chimed four times. I kicked off the covers, threw on a dress, and headed for the stable. Tending the horses always helped put my mind at ease.

After grooming my father's horses and a visiting mare—the blacksmith often borrowed space in return for shoeing—I worked on mucking stalls in preparation for the fall festival in two weeks.

Every autumn, a huge festival on Heyden's green drew craftsmen, horse traders, and artisans from southern Atruria. Every stable and stall in the village filled with horses as festival goers piled into town. The tavern, hostel, and any house with a spare room overflowed with people. My father supplemented his meager income by turning the manor into a boardinghouse and renting our stable.

I was ankle-deep in muck when Dirk sauntered into the stable. He leaned against the stall door and watched me fork dirty straw into a wheelbarrow.

"You better hope the gener'l don't come searchin' fer a horse while yer lookin' like that," he said and snickered.

I paused to brush some straggling hair off my sweaty forehead. "Heyden doesn't have a general."

"Does now. One came with the extry contingent of soldiers sent to keep order durin' the festival. Pop says he's here to stay."

I rolled my eyes. What did the blacksmith know about rank? The soldier was probably a lieutenant or a captain. Heyden was hardly large enough or important enough to warrant a general. "That's just grand," I murmured under my breath, throwing down the pitchfork. "Finish these stalls and exercise the horses...all except the gelding in the corner. He has an injured foot."

"Yes, ma'am," Dirk drawled, bringing his knuckles to his cap in a gesture of mock obeisance.

Irritated, I tossed my head and was rewarded with a face full of hair as my hastily pinned bun chose that moment to come undone.

Dirk reached out as if to touch my hair, and I ducked away, glaring.

He held up his hands in a gesture of surrender. "I ain't never seen yer hair down afore."

"Well, don't count on ever seeing it again."

He remained planted in the doorway, staring at me.

"Are you going to move? I need to get to class."

Dirk retreated with a half smile, and I picked up my skirts and ran back to the manor to change.

~ † ~

"North of the Bearded Hills..." Murmuring, I scratched the translation onto my parchment. I leaned over *Legereya Atruriym yt Latrettym*, studying the phrase. "Bearded Hills?" I asked, raising my eyes to Fabius. "Can that be right?"

"It's an old-fashioned term for the Aurals, though it's only used in Atruria. Odd that it would appear in a book from the Northland..." He broke off, and we both froze as the muttering sound of voices echoed down the corridor.

"The map!" I whispered.

Alarm played across Fabius's features as he sent the map into the roller. He only had time to shuffle some items on his desk before my father swung the door open.

"Here is the tutor I spoke of...and my daughter." My father's eyebrows rose when he saw me.

My father was taller than most men, but he towered over the soldier who trailed him into the room. Gold braiding, scarlet thread, and half a dozen medals adorned the man's coat. The blacksmith had been right after all.

"Ah, and she iss hard at vork," the general said, a thick Sardonian accent garbling his speech. He extended a hand as he stepped toward me, his gleaming boots ringing smartly on the floor. A cobweb—no doubt collected during his tour of the manor—sullied impeccably creased breeches.

"General Attark, may I present Arabella, my daughter," my father mumbled, red-faced. He obviously hadn't expected to find me in the classroom at this hour of the evening.

I clenched my skirt with both hands to hide their trembling and bobbed a quick curtsy to the general. "Pleased to make your acquaintance, sir."

"And vaat might you be writing?" the general asked, picking up the piece of parchment on my desk.

"A poem." At least I hoped it would pass for a poem.

He cleared his throat and read, "North of the Bearded Hills, the streams flow in rills, horses dot the hills, and pies sit on vindowsills."

"What do you think?" I asked. My voice resonated shrill and tremulous in my ears.

"Lovely, young lady. Absssolutely lovely," he said, dropping the parchment back on my desk.

"Thank you, sir." I gave what I hoped was a demure smile and lowered my head.

General Attark wheeled toward Fabius. "And vaat are you teaching this young lady? Hisstory? Science and mathematics?"

I sucked in my breath. Sardonians considered all of those subjects unsuitable for females.

"Arabella has a great love of literature," Fabius said. "She works hard on refining her penmanship, and as you can see, her poetry is spirited and full of life."

I had to clamp my lips together to keep a nervous giggle from escaping.

"Indeed," the general said. He turned toward me and clicked his heels together as he gave a stiff bow. "Vell, I vill not keep you from your vork any longer."

My father and the general said their good evenings and left us. We listened as their voices faded down the corridor. A cricket cheeped from a corner, and I exhaled in a sudden whoosh. I hadn't realized I'd been holding my breath.

"That was too close..." Fabius shook his head. "Where on earth did you put the book?"

I rose and swept my skirts aside, revealing the book on my chair.

"You sat on it?"

"I couldn't think of anywhere else to put it. It was quite uncomfortable," I added, wrinkling my nose.

A slow smile spread across his tired face, and he chuckled. Then we were both snorting and chortling in an effort to hold our laughter in.

"Pies on vindowsills...you...my dear...are no poet!" Fabius gasped at last.

"I should think not. I scribbled those lines in about thirty seconds," I said between giggles.

Sobering, Fabius wiped his eyes with a handkerchief. "We must be cautious, Arabella," he said, his voice barely above a whisper.

And we were. From then on, I always had a piece of parchment prepared...examples of my penmanship, a half-written story, a sketch, or some other innocuous busy work I could present if the need arose. Yet General Attark never set foot in our manor again. In fact, on the few occasions when I passed him on the streets, he seemed to have forgotten me entirely.

~ † ~

It dawned calm, clear, and frigid for late October. I broke a thick rime with an ax and pumped water into the ice-encrusted troughs. As the buckets filled, I stamped my feet and slapped my mittened hands to warm them; the blood still ran sluggish in my veins. I welcomed the warmth of the stable as I toiled over the horses, feeding and grooming them.

I had started to organize and polish the tack when Dirk finally burst in. "Fine morning to be late," I grumbled as he grabbed a pitchfork.

He paused with his foot on the first rung of the ladder to the loft. "Some lass went missin' in the village las' night. Got herself lost an' we was up most of the night lookin' fer her."

A bridle fell from my hand and my voice quavered, "Did they find her?"

He shook his head. "Not when I lef', they hadn't."

"Who is she?" I whispered, barely audible.

He shrugged, avoiding my eyes. "Some lass."

I flung the brush away and ran for the door, tripping over a bucket as I entered the courtyard. My knees hit the cobblestones, but I picked myself up and ran toward the village.

I raced over the deserted streets, scattering a few stray pigs and chickens the villagers had not butchered against the approaching winter. A part of my brain noted the empty tavern porch ...unusual for even the coldest morning. My lungs burned from gulps of freezing air as I crossed the bridge over the Trine at a dead run. Knots of people huddled around the millpond. Women turned as I approached, some wringing their hands, others weeping. They parted in a wave, and I saw the miller lying prostrate over a limp bedraggled form.

A wailing scream erupted, full of unspeakable loss and agony. A figure reached out and tripped me, yet I struggled forward on hands and knees. I clawed and scrabbled at the icy ground, desperate to reach the still figure, but strong hands pinioned me from behind.

Still the wailing went on and on. My vision contracted and focused on a limp, pale hand reaching toward me from beneath the covering blanket, beckoning to me. Then everything spun, and the world turned dark.

~ † ~

As I returned to consciousness, my first sensation was pain. My head ached, my knees and hands throbbed; my entire body felt pummeled and beaten. I lay with my eyes closed as pain washed over me. I heard Nanni's distraught voice in the hall. The words didn't register, but Fabius's response echoed her concern.

Why were they so worried? I struggled to remember, but my thoughts were fragmented and disjointed.

Bitter cold.

Dirk was late.

Frozen troughs.

I tried to connect those thoughts, but the pain radiating through my limbs pushed them away.

I opened my eyes. It was dark outside. The fire burned low, sending shadows flickering across my bedroom ceiling. Some of them resembled hands, and I shivered.

Images flitted through my mind, leaving me bewildered.

Knots of huddled people...weeping women...a thin, pale arm reaching out...

Disturbed and exhausted, I closed my eyes and succumbed to sleep.

Daylight peeked around the drawn curtains when I woke again. I moved under the covers, and pain stabbed my knees. Gasping, I groped at the bedcovers, and my palms throbbed. Nanni appeared at my side.

"Are you feelin' better?"

"What happened?" I held up my swathed hands.

She peeled off layers of bandages, clucking like a mother hen.

I examined my palms and winced. The skin was raw, my nails broken and bleeding. "What happened?" I murmured again.

"Don't you remember, dearie?" she asked, anxious. After dressing my hands, she pulled back the covers and removed similar bloody bandages from my scraped knees.

"Melora is dead." My throat constricted as I spoke.

Nanni's eyes glistened, and I turned my face to the wall. No tears would come, but I felt hollow inside, and my chest ached as I struggled to breathe.

Nanni rubbed my back and fussed over me. At last she brought a tray, but I couldn't eat. My fault...my fault...my fault, echoed in my head.

I dozed fitfully, haunted by dreams of soldiers and burlap sacking. Then I dreamed of Melora. We were playing a game of chase around the mill. I caught snatches of her laughter up ahead, just around the next corner, but she always remained elusively out of sight. Finally, I rounded the shed and caught a glimpse of her beckoning to me from the reeds at the edge of the millpond. She had vanished when I reached the place, and I waded into the water, calling to her. Suddenly I parted the reeds and discovered Melora's lifeless body staring up at me.

I woke, screaming, and Nanni appeared at my bedside. She pressed a cup into my hands and helped me drink. I gagged and nearly vomited; it had been years since I had tasted the bitter liquid.

Sleep came again.

I spent three days in my darkened room, but when Nanni arrived on the fourth morning with a tray, I was up and dressed. I picked at breakfast while she pinned my hair, keeping up a steady stream of prattle about the new babe in the village and an engagement announcement. Her chatter grated on my tattered nerves, and I escaped to the stable.

A week passed before I realized people were avoiding me. Pyrrin was uncharacteristically immersed in his books whenever I glanced in his direction; Dirk headed the opposite way when he saw me coming; servants and stable hands gave me a wide berth. Two soldiers looking for a horse tripped over each other in their haste to leave when I rounded a corner. I even caught my father ducking into the kitchen when I passed. With Melora dead, I had no reason to go into the village. Yet no one had come asking for remedies, which was unusual since winter was prime season for rheumatism, coughs, and fevers.

"Why is everyone avoiding me?" I asked Fabius one evening as I stared listlessly at my Lattrian book.

"Because they are all a bunch of irrational, superstitious simpletons!" he roared after a long pause.

I looked up, shocked. Fabius never raised his voice, not even to Pyrrin.

He sank into his chair with a sigh. "If only I could shield you from ignorance and malice."

I shook my head, bewildered

He continued in a gentler voice. "When you ran to the mill...you were frantic. The tanner tried to stop you before you reached the millpond, but you broke free and fell, clawing the ground as you tried to crawl towards Melora. Blood covered your hands and knees as you screamed over and over, *mie celpe...mie celpe.*"

My fault. The phrase kept echoing in my head. I closed my eyes as tears squeezed through the lids.

In his creaky, arthritic fashion, Fabius knelt and cradled my face in his hands. "Melora's death was not your fault, my dear."

My breath rasped in ragged hiccups. "How...did she...drown?"

He rose slowly to his feet. "The miller thinks she must have slipped on the icy bank and slid under the water. They found her close to shore."

"Do you think...it was an accident?" I asked, my voice wavering.

Fabius knit his brows together. "I would like to think so..." He shrugged his shoulders helplessly. "I can't imagine why anyone would want the poor, unfortunate child dead, but it wouldn't be the first time an Atrurian suffered an untimely 'accident' at the hands of the Sardonians."

I gave a long, shuddering sigh. "How can I go on without her, Fabius? We were like sisters."

Fabius laid his hand on my shoulder. "Treasure the wonderful times you had together. You shared a beautiful friendship."

We lapsed into silence. Finally, I asked, "And *why* is everyone avoiding me?"

"When you spoke in Lattrian, an old biddy claimed you were uttering curses. She carried on about her grandson's death..."

"That must have been Girty, the cooper's son." I shook my head. "I was young...maybe five or six. I overheard Mamma and Nanni talk about him, but I don't know any details."

Fabius looked grim. "I gather the old woman is convinced his death wasn't an accident...and now the drowning has started the rumors all over again."

"I loved Melora," I whispered, tears spilling again. "How could anyone think I was uttering curses?"

"People who are sad and angry can forget reason and lash out...even when their target is hurting as much as they are." He patted my shoulder. "Be patient. I think this will blow over soon enough."

I stared blindly at my desk.

Fabius closed his book. "I think that will be all for this evening."

Swiping at my tears, I asked, "Will there be lessons tomorrow?"

"Of course. Pyrrin isn't going to get off that easy."

As I lay in bed, I thought about the villagers. Why couldn't they see I was the same girl now as before Melora died? Older, wiser, and sadder perhaps, but still the same.

Sleep found me at last. I had a vivid dream about a large gray wolf sitting on a rock. He spoke to me, but when I woke, I did not remember what he had said.

7

hen Nanni came to wake me the next morning, I was already dressed.

"G' mornin', love," she said, drawing back the curtains. A blood red dawn streaked the eastern sky.

She brought my breakfast tray and then bustled around the room, making sure everything was spotless. I ate slowly, gathering my nerve.

"Nanni, what was in the cup you brought after Melora died?"

"To be sure I don't know what you mean." She gazed intently at the pitcher she was polishing.

I opened my dream diary to a page I had marked and read aloud: *"A boy fled across a foothill with three soldiers in pursuit. He kept looking back in terror, until he stumbled and fell headlong. Two soldiers seized him, pinning him to the ground, while the third paced back and forth, holding a crossbow. He asked the boy a question over and over, but the boy only shook his head, weeping. At last, the soldier lifted the bow and shot the boy in the chest. His head lolled to the side and blood trickled from the corner of his mouth. The soldiers laid the crossbow next to the boy and marched away without a backward glance."*

"That was my very first nightmare, Nanni. The next time I woke screaming in the night, Mamma dosed me with the same bitter drink."

Nanni wilted into a chair and fanned herself with her polishing rag. "Yer mother would be furious."

"What did you give me?"

"She tol' me it was dangerous. 'Nanni,' she says to me. 'Never dose her unless she really be in need.'" Nanni waved her hands helplessly. "I never woulda given it to you, but you were beside yerself…" She trailed off. "It's a mararoot tincture."

I blinked. Of course. Mamma had planted mararoot soon after that first nightmare. "What does the tincture do?"

"I don't know, 'zactly." Nanni was pleading now. "She never tol' me. Jest said it would dim yer memory of the dreams."

"Did she teach you how to make it?"

"Goodness, no! She jest gave me a little packet of powder an' said to administer it sparin'ly. Though I did see her prepare some," she admitted. "She groun' the dried root into a powder an' infused the merest smidgen in liquor."

"Do you think mararoot might prevent my nightmares?"

She gasped, and I gave her an imploring look.

"Yer mother...seemed to think so," she said at last.

"Thank you, Nanni. Please bring me what you have."

"Ye mustn't take too much! It's no doubt like poison."

"I'll be careful," I promised, though I had no idea how much was too much.

She brought me the powder, and I tucked the tiny packet into my trunk. According to Nanni's mixing instructions, it would last for a while, though there was plenty of mararoot growing in the garden.

I couldn't remember a time when I wasn't cursed with nightmares. Though few were as terrible as those with red-eyed wolves or soldiers slaying children, most of them left me horrified and exhausted. I had never considered the possibility of ending my nightmares for good.

I had not noted the pattern of my dreams until I noticed a lunar chart on the wall of the classroom. Using Fabius's old charts, I plotted the frequency of my dreams and discovered they occurred in a seven-day span around the full moon. Bad ones came in the three days prior, horrible nightmares fell on the full moon, the occasional nice dream two or three nights later.

This knowledge had proved useless...until now. I was anxious to see if I could prevent the nightmares.

While the next moon waxed large in the sky, I experimented with the mararoot powder. Even the tiniest amount was horrible, so bitter I could barely choke it down. I considered adding honey, but that sometimes destroyed an herb's efficacy, and my mother hadn't sweetened the drink.

The first month I stirred the tincture into tea and drank for four nights until the full moon. I had no dreams, but I couldn't concentrate during lessons, I forgot basic Lattrian vocabulary and grammar I had known for years, and I struggled to remember the horses' names as I cleaned their stalls.

When I recovered from my mararoot-induced stupor a week later, I realized I had overdone it. Since the effects lasted for multiple days, I decided to take one dose four nights prior to the full moon. I hoped that would be enough to prevent any dreams until after the moon waned.

After doing so effectively for several months, I woke on the night of the full moon, screaming in terror. I had no memory of the nightmare, but a feeling of intense horror lingered for hours.

I fiddled with the mixture the following month and settled on two small doses, one four days before and one the night of the full moon. The adjusted dosage prevented any dreams, good or bad, and as time went on, I learned to tolerate the side effects.

Nanni fussed over me whenever she recognized the effects of the mararoot. She vacillated between criticizing me for drinking the potion and crying because I deemed it necessary.

As Fabius had predicted, in time many of my former customers returned, though I made myself scarce during the full moon. Once, I gave a woman a balm for sore muscles instead of a salve for an itchy rash. She came back when the treatment did not work, and I realized I couldn't trust myself to dispense properly.

Dirk and Pyrrin noted the difference the most. One afternoon I overheard them talking in the stable.

"Something's got her brains addled," Pyrrin said. "If Fabius were healthy, he'd notice all the wool between her ears."

"Mebbe it's her time of the month," Dirk said.

"Ain't that supposed to make women cranky? This is Arabella we're talking about. She's been thick as a brick all week."

"I say we ask her."

My heart raced. I retreated into the back corner of the stall I was cleaning, clutching a pitchfork.

"Don't touch me!" I said, leveling the tines at them as they entered side by side.

"Nobody's gonna mess with you in a smelly ol' stall," Dirk said and snorted, pointing to the manure caked on my boots. "We's jus' wonderin' why yer actin' so addlepated..."

"None of your business." I shifted the pitchfork to get a better grip.

Dirk stared at me for a long moment before backing away. "Come on, Pyrrin. Best let her be."

As they left the stall, he muttered, "We got to do a better job hidin' those pitchforks."

I sagged against the wall, shaky from the confrontation. Dirk was growing more unpredictable; sometimes he heckled me mercilessly, at other times he sank into sullen silence punctuated with long raking stares. In many ways, I feared his looks more than his blistering tongue.

I flexed my hands around the smooth pitchfork handle as I rose—now I knew why I had to hunt for implements every day. At times like this, I wondered if the mararoot was worth the side effects...but then I would reread my dream journal. For the first time in my life, I could fall asleep at night knowing I wouldn't wake up biting back a scream or strangling the blankets. Nor did I have to relive each terrible moment when I recorded the dream in my diary. For that, the mararoot was worth it.

8

I f Melora's death had marked the end of my childhood, Fabi-us's passing marked my entrance into adulthood.

It was a harsh, frigid winter, and he suffered terribly. Nanni and I tended a racking cough and fretted as he lost weight. My herbs scarcely alleviated his discomfort, and he had little appetite for the hot soup and tea we pressed on him.

Throughout the winter, Nanni predicted that Fabius would not live to see April. But when spring bloomed in all its glory, she changed her tune, claiming she'd known he would pull through. I also thought the arrival of spring would prompt his recovery, so his death came as a shock.

Pyrrin and I entered the classroom one morning and for the first time in six years, Fabius wasn't waiting for us. A servant found him lying in his chambers; he had slipped away in his sleep.

Though relieved his suffering was over, I mourned the loss of my dearest friend and teacher. I sat in the empty classroom with tears streaking my face as a flurry of funeral preparations began.

Nanni found me midmorning and asked me to choose something for Fabius to be buried in. Her task kept me busy until lunch. Afterwards I sought solace with the horses.

We laid him to rest in a corner of the manor graveyard. I threw the first clod on the wooden coffin, but I wept into Nanni's shoulder as the pall bearers filled in the grave. My father erected a simply carved head-stone: *Fabius—Friend and Teacher*. He didn't bother to say any words over the grave, yet I was grateful for the small kindness he showed in burying Fabius properly. At least the inscription was appropriate.

~ † ~

My fifteenth birthday fell the following week, and I spent the morn-ing inspecting my new dresses. On the first, a lacy purple underskirt peeked out beneath exquisite lavender-colored linen; delicate ruching complemented a bodice finished off with intricate beadwork and lacy cuffs. I found amethyst eardrops and a matching necklace in the jewelry box. Were I pretty, I would have looked like a princess in the shimmery creation.

Cinnamon-brown crushed velvet came next, more plain in design but luxurious to the touch. I rubbed the dress against my cheek and detected the faint hint of violets—my mother's favorite scent. I laid out an exotic silver filigree necklace—a dragon with a shiny emerald for an eye—and equally intricate silver eardrops. The artistry was beyond the skill of Heyden's silversmiths. I wondered how my mother acquired such treasures—and where. According to Nanni, she had arrived in Heyden dressed in tatters.

I pulled out my collection of books. Besides *Legereya Atruriym yt Latrettym* and *Tudyre Salutori Erbaym*, Fabius had bequeathed me several books, and I'd added *The Geography of Atruria*. My father would never miss it, and the book was a sweet reminder of Melora.

First, I paged through the legends. I had read them many times, and I recognized every tale from my childhood—except one. My favorite story was missing. I often thought of Mamma's fleeting sadness after she finished telling of the maiden fleeing her homeland.

Setting the legends aside, I removed the notes tucked into *Tudyre Salutori Erbaym* and fanned the pages. I had read the book many times cover to cover, but today as I browsed, a piece of folded, yellowed parchment wafted out of the binding and landed on my lap. I opened it. Written across the top in green ink was *Acerbysradyx*—mararoot—several lines of instruction, followed by *Admonityem*—warning. My memory flashed back to the day I first discovered the books. I had seen this page then, but I'd forgotten about it.

My heart pounded. This had to be a recipe for mararoot. I laid the paper on my desk and searched for pen and parchment to write a translation. A noise outside my room startled me, and I jumped when someone rapped on the door.

"Who is it?" I hastily gathered my scattered books and deposited them in my trunk.

"Pyrrin."

I shut the trunk with a bang as the door opened. My brother strode in. He was not quite thirteen; dark red hair and eyebrows accented an aquiline nose and haughty gray eyes.

"I didn't invite you in," I said icily.

He was dressed in a green riding coat and snowy white tunic with brown breeches tucked into polished black leather boots. A black cap perched on his head, and he sported a whip and a riding crop. He gave the impression of a wealthy lord's son. Where had he come up with money for such clothes?

"Father wants to see you." His eyes traveled over my homespun dress, bare feet, and unpinned hair. "Perhaps you ought to tidy yourself up a bit first."

My cheeks flamed, and I whipped around toward the window.

"Why does he want me?" I asked, trying to compose my voice. In all my fifteen years, he had never sent anyone to fetch me.

When Pyrrin didn't answer, I stole a glance at him. My heart nearly stopped. He was paging through my sheaf of notes from *Tudyre Salutori Erbaym.* I had left them on the floor in my haste to put the books away.

"Give those to me."

"What is this?" he demanded, shaking the parchment.

I took a deep breath. "Notes for herbal remedies," I said, trying to sound calm. "Recipes for headache cures and wart removers. Nothing important." I gave an affected titter and flopped on the bed. "They're recipes. Terribly boring."

After he leafed through every page with agonizing slowness, he said, "If they're not important, you won't mind if I borrow them, will you?"

I clenched my fists in my skirt. "Of course not," I said. "But when villagers come looking for cures, I'll have to send them to you."

His eyes narrowed. "Perhaps you're right," he said at last. "Wouldn't want the poor idiots suffering from chilblains, would we?" He dropped the notes on my writing table. "Father is expecting you, and you'd best make yourself presentable."

As soon as the door shut behind him, I leaped up and stuffed the notes into my desk. "You'd best make yourself presentable!" I mimicked, seething. It was just like Pyrrin to be insolent and presumptuous. How dare he waltz into my room uninvited and rummage through my things?

Taking a deep breath, I tried to steady my frayed nerves. I dreaded seeing my father, but I didn't dare keep him waiting.

I tossed my shabby dress on a chair and pulled out the new cinnamon gown. I fastened the jewelry and surveyed the result. The velvet was now brown wool decorated with ruffles at the wrists and a handmade lace collar. The jewelry had become a carved wooden pendant on a simple metal chain, and my fingers confirmed the earrings matched. It was clothing and jewelry my father might expect me to own. I slipped on worn leather shoes and headed toward his study, my trepidation mounting with every step.

I knocked tentatively on the door, and his gruff voice bade me to enter. I tried to appear demure: back straight, hands clasped in front, eyes properly downcast. My father had once been striking, but age, debt, ill nature, and too much wine had turned him into a haggard old man. Deep wrinkles and hair heavily laced with gray betrayed his age; shaggy, unkempt brows jutted over a nose crooked from a drunken fight. Poorly tailored clothes hung on his bony frame.

He looked me over, a calculating light in his sunken, watery brown eyes.

"How are you, Arabella?"

"Fine. Thank you, sir." I dropped a stiff curtsy.

He gestured to a worn horsehair chair. "Have a seat."

I settled gracefully on the chair. Nanni would have been proud.

He poured himself a glass of wine. "Would you care for some?" he asked, holding up the decanter.

I shook my head, and he eyed me over the rim of his glass. "I imagine you are wondering why I called you."

I managed a thin smile. "I am...quite curious."

He gave a mirthless laugh. "The long and the short of it, Arabella...I am broke."

"I don't know how I can help you, sir."

He pursed his lips. "I owe a sizable sum to the blacksmith for services rendered over the years. The time has come to settle my debt."

"Umm..." A knot was forming in the pit of my stomach. "How are you going to do that?"

"You will settle it for me."

"How?" I asked in a flat voice.

"Have you a dower prepared?"

I blinked. "It...um...should be satisfactory."

"Good. Although I doubt Dirk would object even if you didn't."

A hand seemed to squeeze my lungs. "You wish me to marry Dirk?"

He nodded.

My blood stirred. "Why would I want to do that?"

"Because the blacksmith will forgive all my past and future debts." A menacing tone crept into his voice.

My head whirled. "Are you sure I'm good enough or pretty enough for him?" I managed to say.

He frowned. "I *had* hoped to marry you to someone of better position, but with no dowry I cannot afford to be choosy. As to your looks…" He appraised me. "I think you are fair enough for the black-smith's son."

I stared. "If I refuse?"

His face turned red, and his eyes darkened. "I wouldn't recommend it."

"You can't make me." Technically this wasn't true. According to Sardonian law, a woman was the property of her husband or father and had no rights. Still, longstanding Atrurian tradition held a maiden could refuse a potential husband if she chose. I hoped my father would be reluctant to force me to marry against my will.

The veins stood out on his neck and forehead, but he choked back whatever retort rose to his lips. He rose and paced behind his desk. "Arabella, far be it from me to thrust you into a marriage you do not desire. All I ask is that you think about it. After serious consideration…I am certain you will find this is best for you." His tone slipped from coaxing to intimidating. Catching himself, he gave a strained smile. "Just give the lad a chance."

I turned away, unable to answer. He seemed to take my silence as compliance, because he said triumphantly, "Good. I will discuss plans with you in several weeks. I'm sure Dirk will make you a fine husband." He gestured toward the door. "That's all."

Back in my room, I ripped off my gown and yanked on a house-dress before reeling to the stables. I had always known my father would seek advantage in my marriage; my four half-sisters had been bartered for his debts. Still, they had all married nobles of some sort; his willing-ness to sacrifice status was a telling indication of his desperate financial straits.

As I hauled water from the pump, I splashed my skirts and wet my shoes. Frustration mounting with every step, I berated my clumsiness as water sloshed on a pile of horse blankets. Unbelievable.

I kicked the soggy pile of ragged quilts. Maybe I could add *them* to my dower. Calling it satisfactory was a stretch. I hated sewing, and I had just a few of the desired linens and only four poorly pieced quilts.

I'd convinced myself I had plenty of time, despite Nanni's wrathful warnings.

Besides the handsome princes populating my childhood fantasies, I sometimes indulged in a daydream about a faceless young noble—with a stable full of beautiful horses. Now reality slapped me in the face, and I recoiled in horror. Dirk was a boorish, cruel oaf, but I also couldn't bear the idea of living in the shadow of my childhood home, the object of scorn and ridicule for my fall from the manor to a filthy smithy.

I climbed to the loft, seeking refuge from the thoughts churning through my head. After a good cry, I fell asleep in the fragrant hay.

The afternoon sun was peeking in the end of the haymow when I woke. Dust motes danced in the sunbeams, and a spider snared a hapless fly in a web strung from a crossbeam. I heard a swishing sound and lifted my head. At the other end of the loft, Dirk was tossing hay down into a stall. He grinned when I sat up.

"Me lovely maid has awoken," he said, removing an imaginary cap and making a sweeping bow.

"I am *not* your lovely maid." I struggled to my feet in the soft hay.

"Well, me hid'ous beast, then."

"I'm not that, either."

"Ah, but you will be soon enough."

Someone must have informed him of my father's plans. I glared. "Are you sure I'm pretty enough for you?"

His eyes traveled up my form, lingering too long on my bosom. "Oh, I think yer jus' fine," he said with a leer.

My face burned. "I haven't said yes."

"Hah! An' what choice do you have?"

Furious, but knowing he was right, I shouldered past him toward the ladder.

"Hey! What's the rush?" He jumped in front of me.

"Let me by."

He grabbed my arm.

"Let go!" I jerked away from him.

"Come on. How 'bout a little kiss?" He puckered his lips and leaned toward me.

"Get away from me!" I flailed at him, and one of my hands whacked him across the lip. He dabbed with his sleeve at a small cut welling with blood.

"You cold, uppity wench!" He leapt at me.

I dove for the ladder, but he grabbed my hem. My dress made a great ripping sound as he yanked me backwards and flung me into the loft. My bun came loose, and I landed on my back in the hay, tangled in my skirts. I gasped in panic and terror.

He lunged at me, a look of pure hatred twisting his face. As I scrambled away, my knee caught in my torn hem, and he grabbed a fistful of my hair. As I screeched in pain, he slapped me across the face, shoved me down, and straddled my body.

"Shut up," he whispered harshly.

My cheek stung, and my eyes watered from the blow. At seventeen, Dirk was a strong, barrel-chested young man who outweighed me by forty pounds. He pinned me with his knees and grinned as I struggled.

Twisting and squirming, I screamed and pounded his chest with my fists.

He slapped me harder, and I tasted blood. Then he pressed his forearm against my neck. I clawed at him, choking. He grabbed my wrist and twisted sharply.

"Shut up!" A wild light filled his eyes. "No one can hear, but iffen you don't shut up, I'll choke you till you pass out. Understan'?"

I tried to nod, and he released the pressure on my neck. I lay in the hay, gasping and panting. Dirk reeked of sweat, horse manure, soot, and garlic, and my stomach rebelled. I clawed the hay as I fought the urge to vomit. My right hand closed over the smooth handle of the forgotten pitchfork. Dirk leaned forward and pawed at my hair. I winced, and my fist knotted around the handle just above the tines.

"Relax. You might like it."

As he lifted his arms to yank his grimy tunic over his head, I swung the pitchfork and hit him across the chest. He yelled and fell backwards in the hay, tangled in his shirt. Dizzy from his choking, my rubbery legs gave way as I jumped up, and I sank to my knees.

Freeing himself from his tunic, Dirk leaped at me with a howl. I dealt him a savage blow with the handle, and blood spurted from his nose. Feeling stronger, I clambered to my feet. When he came at me, his face streaming blood, I whacked him again. There was a satisfying crunch as I hit his mouth. He staggered back and spat teeth.

Fleeing past him, I shinnied down the ladder and dashed toward the manor.

Dirk howled from the loft, lisping through missing teeth, "You'll be sorry, you wretched wench!" He hurled obscenities as I ran.

Safe in my room, I stripped off my ruined clothing and called tearfully for Nanni.

"Yer hair...yer *dress!*" she wailed. "Who did this to you?"

"I'm not hurt, Nanni. I just need a bath."

"That animal...that wretched Dirk...I'll wring his bloody neck, I will...an' yer father...How could he let this happen...?"

After she filled my tub in the antechamber and poured in some precious lavender oil, I scrubbed until my skin was tender—as if removing Dirk's stench could wipe away the memory of his pawing hands. I washed again and again before collapsing against the side of the tub and sobbing.

I would never marry Dirk, despite my father's threats. He could lock me in my room or beat me if he liked, but I would run away before marrying the blacksmith's son.

Somehow, these thoughts calmed me, and I relaxed in the luxuriously scented bath until the cooling water drove me from my refuge.

My back stiffened as I entered my room. My desk had been ransacked. A quick search proved the notes from *Tudyre Salutori Erbaym* and the mararoot parchment were gone. I had left them under the stack of writing paper now strewn across the floor. Pyrrin must have returned and taken them.

I spent the rest of the afternoon huddled on my bed, wondering what Pyrrin would do next. He and Dirk were best chums...and Dirk wanted...me...?

Towards evening, I drifted to sleep and dreamt about my mother. I was a young child, sitting at her knee, listening to a story. As we discussed the moral, she gazed at me with her beautiful gray eyes. "Arabella," she said, and she seemed to speak to me across the years that separated us. "'Tis truthfulness and strength of character I value most. Never forget that."

I awoke refreshed and fearless, drained of all emotion. It was odd to contemplate the future without a hint of feeling. I wandered through the manor and then the village, searching for Pyrrin. I found him outside the tavern, speaking in hushed tones with two soldiers.

"Pyrrin, I wish to speak with you."

He scowled as I approached.

"You took some papers from my room."

He opened his mouth as if to protest, but I held up my hand. "You can do as you like, but I will never marry Dirk."

His expression changed from wary apprehension to anger. "You're a fool. If you would just marry him, I would forget about this."

"You already know I won't or you wouldn't have come here." I gestured at the soldiers. "Are they going to arrest me?"

They stared at the ground. One of them scuffed his boot against the stair.

"I thought not. I'll be in my room." I maintained as regal a posture as I could muster as I walked away.

I sat on my bed for several hours, halfheartedly paging through the *Geography of Atruria*, wondering how long it would take the soldiers to arrive. When I heard the stamp of horse's feet in the courtyard, I put the book away, repinned my hair, and straightened my dress. I sat with my hands in my lap, listening to the drama unfolding below.

A soldier rapped on the door and asked for my father. He spoke in an indistinguishable monotone, then came my father's roar of denial and cries and shouts from servants. The tumult continued into the hall; footsteps hurried down the corridor toward my room. From the huffing and puffing, I knew it was Nanni. She burst through the door.

"They want to arrest you!" she cried, red-faced and breathless.

I rose and offered her my seat. "I know." I handed her a glass of water.

"Why?"

"You must be strong, Nanni," I said, kissing her cheek.

Soldiers' boots tramped up the wide, rundown staircase. "Go," I said, taking her by the hand. I led her to the door, kissed her again, and pushed her into the hall. I watched her retreat down the dark corridor before returning to my chair.

The door flew open, slamming the door handle against the wall. Plaster chunks fell with a thud; fine plaster dust sifted onto the floor. Four soldiers filed into my room, followed by a sergeant clutching a scroll.

"Arabella of Maitlan, I arrest you upon the order of General Attark."

"The general must have thought I would be a lot of trouble if he sent five soldiers to the do the job of one."

The sergeant flushed and snapped open the parchment. He stumbled as he read, butchering words so badly I had to listen closely to understand. "You are hereby charged with: treason against our king, the most noble Sarduk; unlawfully learning a forbidden language; possessing, reading, and disseminating banned and treasonous material; corrupting innocent civilians; consorting with unfavorable persons; performing magic with the intention of doing harm; assaulting servants of the king; and possessing and disseminating dangerous and poisonous substances to law abiding citizens with the intention of doing them bodily harm." The man was out of breath by the time he finished.

I raised an eyebrow. "What does that mean?"

"It means you'll go straight to the mines when yer convicted," a soldier said. "If they don't burn you first."

I blanched and rose; the ice in my veins was thawing. A soldier clamped a pair of shackles around my wrists, and the sergeant led me downstairs. Two soldiers flanked me with the other two following closely. They kept their spears leveled at my back, and I worried they might stumble and spit me by accident. Both Pyrrin and my father were conspicuously absent as I descended the rickety staircase.

Except for Nanni, the servants had assembled at the bottom of the stairs. Though teary-eyed, not one of them offered a word of comfort. I held my head high and set my shoulders as the soldiers paraded me down the hall and into the night.

9

he last shreds of fearlessness melted as the cell door shut with a clang. The finality of the door closing, combined with the chains fastening me to the cold stone walls served to jar me back to reality. Honesty and character seemed irrelevant now. The dank walls of my jail reeked of fear and hopelessness. Overwhelmed, I huddled on the filthy pallet and succumbed to tears.

After my initial shock and grief subsided, I sat up against the wall, resting my cheek against the worn stones. A smoky rush light in a holder by the door provided dim illumination for the small room. A tiny barred window set high on the wall revealed a patch of night sky. If I leaned to the right as far as my chains allowed, a tiny sliver of moon was visible.

I rolled over, attempting to find a more comfortable position. The rush light sputtered and burned out, leaving me in darkness with my disjointed thoughts. Today was my fifteenth birthday...or was it yester-day? Had I really admired my new dresses just this morning?

~ † ~

A boot jabbing my ribs woke me the next morning. I sat up slowly, massaging my side.

The soldier shoved a bowl of disgusting-looking gruel into my hands. "Eat," he said with a growl.

The gruel was runny and looked thoroughly revolting. I wondered about the brown things floating in it and set the bowl aside. I wasn't hungry enough to eat...not yet, at least.

A few hours later, the soldier returned. Without a word, he un-hooked my chain from the wall and led me down a poorly lit corridor through a nail-studded door. He unshackled me and pushed me to-wards a hard wooden chair. I stumbled into the seat, grateful to have my wrists free. A moment later, General Attark strode in, his spit-shined boots ringing on the flagstones. At a nod from the general, the soldier bowed low and exited.

The general settled into a plush upholstered chair, which looked out of place in a room fitted with rings for chains and shackles. Faded tapestries depicting a gruesome battle hid the wall on the left. A barred window on the right allowed ample light, and two ornate oil lamps sat on a battered desk, wicks trimmed and ready for lighting.

General Attark stuffed a carved pipe full of tobacco and lit it. He puffed methodically, studying my disheveled hair and grimy face.

"How iss your cell? Are you in need of anything?"

"A warm bath, a comfortable mattress, palatable food, and hot tea."

"Perhaps something can be arranged. Vee are cifilized people, of course."

"Of course," I said with a tinge of sarcasm.

He leaned back in his chair. "So, tell me what happened in this business vith Dirk."

"He attacked me in the hayloft—"

"You broke hiss nose and knocked out a couple teeth," the general said.

"Dirk behaved like a pig...worse than a pig!"

"Come now...surely it vass just a misunderstanding—a luffa's quarrel."

"A lover's quarrel?" I leaned forward, punctuating my words with a fist on the desk. "He sat on my chest...slapped me when I screamed... choked me till I couldn't breathe!"

General Attark flushed at my account of events. He lowered his gaze and shuffled through a pile of parchment on his desk. "You have been a wery busy girl? And not just writing poetry. You recognize these, no?" he asked, shoving the notes from *Tudyre Salutori Erbaym* under my nose.

"My brother stole those from my room."

He waved his hand dismissively. "Vere did the notes come from?"

"A book."

"*Vaat* book?"

"From a book of recipes for medicinal potions and balms. I make cures for villagers who seek my services."

He ground his teeth, took a deep breath, and enunciated each word clearly. "Vaat iss the name of the book?"

"The Study of Medicinal Plants." If he thought I was going to spout the Lattrian name, he was mistaken. Fabius had seen an Atrurian translation in the university library.

"That iss not the name!" He pounded his fist on the desk and purple veins bulged in his neck.

A tentative knock sounded on the door.

"Enter," the general said in a strangled voice.

A thin, sallow-faced man in spectacles pushed the door open. "You asked for me, sir?" he said, peering over an armful of books.

The general gestured at the papers and withdrew to a corner. He leaned against the wall, sucking his pipe and fouling the air with smoke. The man eyed the plush chair. With a vicious kick, General Attark sent a wooden chair banging into the man's legs. He winced and settled on the chair with a sigh.

"You are Atrurian," I said.

The man cleared his throat. "How did you know?"

"Your accent and features. Yet you work for *him*."

"No." He banged his books on the desk and plopped a copy of *Tu-dyre Salutori Erbaym* in front of me. "These notes came from this book, correct?" He tapped his long fingers on the parchment.

I ducked my head to hide my astonishment. I lifted the cover and blew out my breath in relief. There was no inscription on the flyleaf. My stash of books was safe.

"Who are you?" I asked, pushing the book away.

"A Lattrian professor from Sardis."

Sardis was in central Atruria, not far from the capital, Pithark.

The general growled from his corner, and the man thumbed through the book until he found a marked page. "This is the recipe, correct?" He jabbed the parchment with a long index finger.

Careful to ignore the book, I studied the notes. "Sage tea is for nursing mothers who produce too much milk. The tea decreases their supply and makes them more comfortable, but too much can make them dry up."

The general made snorting noises.

"But the recipe came from this book," the man said again.

"What is your name?" He raised an eyebrow, and I asked, "Isn't it the custom of *civilized* people to introduce themselves?" I aimed a pointed look at the general.

"Curmyck," the man said grudgingly.

"Well, sir...Curmyck, the recipe came from a book called *The Study of Medicinal Plants*. It proved most useful for the poor mother who told me she would explode if I didn't help."

He grimaced.

The interrogation lasted another two hours. Curmyck fumbled through my notes, matched each recipe to a page in the book, and insisted they came from *Tudyre Salutori Erbaym*.

Each time I offered a similar reply. I administered lady's mantle to stanch bleeding in a peasant who nearly severed his foot while chopping wood; birthwort and smut rye induced reluctant labor; wormwood, henbane, and poppy petals alleviated pain; belladonna relieved menstrual cramps.

The last piece of parchment was a recipe for raspberry leaf tea sweetened with honey. "What is this?" Curmyck asked. He sounded exhausted.

"It's a healthful, relaxing tea for pregnant women and aids in preparing their bodies for delivery." I gave an angelic smile. "You ought to try some. You might find it soothing."

The general choked on his pipe, and Curmyck turned pale. "I think we're done here," he said, slamming the book shut.

After the general recovered from his coughing fit, he roared for a guard to haul me back to my cell. The soldier had the decency to remove my shackles before he closed the door.

"What's your name?" I asked when he brought dinner.

He gazed at me as if I was the first prisoner who had ever spoken civilly to him. "Taren."

Unfortunately, the meal was hardly an improvement over the gruel: a hunk of dry bread; slimy cheese; a small piece of tooth-defying jerky of uncertain origin; a revolting dish of boiled turnips, and a jug of stale water.

I came to dread the dish of gummy turnips. Taren was adamant I eat them to prevent scurvy and remained unmoved when I expressed how much I detested them with gagging and retching sounds. Though he lacked a sense of humor, he wasn't cruel or mean.

~ † ~

Curmyck was waiting when Taren deposited me in the interrogation room the next morning.

"Isn't the general joining us?"

"He's busy. You're my responsibility today."

He tented his hands and gazed at me. "You think you are quite clever, don't you?"

My eyes widened, and he waggled his fingers at me. "Ahh, yes. You know that recipes similar to yours have survived in Atruria through oral tradition...passed down from one dabbler to another." He frowned. "Unless we find your books, you can argue that you gleaned those notes from other sources."

He leaned forward. "But what about these?" he said, laying a sheaf of parchment on the desk.

As I sifted through the parchment, the blood drained from my face. They were copies of the notes from *Legereya Atruriym yt Latret-tym* I had misplaced so long ago. Sick to my stomach, I buried my face in my trembling hands.

"Do you know what they are?" he asked again.

I lifted my head, tears coursing down my cheeks. "They murdered Melora because of these." My voice rose to a wail as I fought for breath. "And it was such a stupid, stupid waste. She had no idea what they were!"

Curmyck looked astonished. He leaned out the door and called into the hall. A sergeant appeared, and they held a whispered conversation in the doorway. Visibly shaken, Curmyck returned to his seat. "How—how did you...how did you know about the girl?"

My racking sobs subsided, but my chest ached. I rubbed my temples; a headache was brewing. "They don't tell you much, do they? Ask the general why they killed her. Ask *him* why they dumped her in the pond!"

In a shaky voice, Curmyck called for the guard.

Back in my cell, I wept bitter tears. Melora's death *was* my fault. Soldiers must have found my notes, copied them, then placed the originals on the millstone. Girty's crazy old grandmother had been right. Yet I had no idea why the soldiers killed Melora.

After I cried out all my tears, I felt hollow and empty inside, and I couldn't eat lunch or dinner.

Taren came to check on me late in the evening. I heard him unlock the door, but I lay on the filthy pallet with my face turned to the wall, feigning sleep.

His boot tapped a nervous cadence on the floor. "I...heard about... what happened today. I remember when the girl died."

I rolled over to demand that he leave, but his expression stopped me.

"I have a little daughter to an Atrurian wife."

I gazed at him with new interest. Fabius had said intermarriage was rare.

"What happened to that poor girl was horrible," Taren added through tight lips.

"Do you know why they killed her?"

He shook his head. "Foot soldiers are commanded to do this and do that; there's never an explanation. If a soldier is asked to do something unsavory, a commanding officer gets him a couple of extra tavern passes and a new pair of boots to keep his mouth shut. Sometimes generals use squads of handpicked men who have stomachs for such things." He leaned back against the door, a sickened look on his face. "I know things—more than most. That unfortunate girl wasn't the first to die, and she won't be the last, either. They are deathly afraid of people like you and your mother."

"Who is afraid of me...and my mother? Why?"

"The soldiers, the general, the king..." he shrugged. "Take your pick. You are different, your mother was different, and what Sardonians don't understand they fear."

His words echoed those of Fabius. "Why are you telling me this?"

"You don't deserve this. You're just a motherless girl with a wretched excuse for a father. If you lose your courage, you'll die in this wretched cell, and I don't want that on my conscience." He scuffed his toe into the floor. "You won't get a fair trial, and you deserve one."

"Thank you for your...candor...and your kindness," I said as he shouldered the door open and left.

I didn't expect a fair trial.

Villagers accused of petty crimes were brought before my father, who presided as magistrate once a month. He had the authority to fine the accused, put them in stocks, have them whipped, or, if the offense was serious enough, to remand them to a Sardonian court in Pithark. I had once heard my father scoff that Sardonian justice was no justice at all; he had never sent anyone before a Sardonian judge.

I had all the next day and the following to think it over. When I entered the interrogation room on the third morning, both Curmyck and General Attark were waiting.

The general began, "Now vaat makes you think *I* had something to do vith the miller girl drowning?"

"Do you deny it?" I asked, gazing at him.

He straightened in his chair. "Sardonians are cifilized people. Vee don't murder our citizens."

"You spoke before of how *civilized* you are."

"I had nothing to do vith that girl's death," he said.

I gathered the subject was closed.

"These are translated from a Lattrian book, no?" he said, shoving some parchment across the table.

I shrugged. "What does the professor say?"

Curmyck's eyes narrowed. He opened *Legereya Atruriym yt Latrettym* to a marked page and read aloud, mispronouncing some of the words. Jabbing his finger at the parchment, he asked, "Vyy do you bother denying it? These notes match the passage, and this book is the only possible source. Unlike your potion book, there's no Atrurian translation of *Legereya Atruriym yt Latrettym*."

I paused for a long moment. "I made one," I said at last.

"Treason!" the general shouted. "That iss treason!"

"Treason? These are just fanciful stories."

"This book iss banned! It's treasonous to our sofereign king to own it...translate it...read it..." The general turned red in the face. "Or for a VOMAN to learn Lattrian!"

"It's not treasonous to be educated—"

"Where did you get the book?" Curmyck asked, interrupting me.

"I found it."

The general snorted, and Curmyck raised an eyebrow. "Who taught you Lattrian?"

"Fabius."

"Aha!" the general crowed. "From the moment I saw that man I knew he vass a seditious traitor."

"Fabius was a great man! He was kind, intelligent, and intensely patriotic...only not to your king. He believed the law forbidding women a proper education was wrong."

"Vell, what he *beliefed* iss going to get you condemned for treason," General Attark said and sneered. "And him too, vere he still alife."

"If reading books is treasonous, then I'm guilty. I read them both, cover to cover." I leaned forward. "Yet I have a clear conscience. Can you say the same?" I asked Curmyck.

The general sputtered, and Curmyck turned pale. He dismissed me back to my cell.

~ † ~

Curmyck's butchered Lattrian pronunciation started me thinking. When Taren brought supper, I asked, "Is Curmyck really a Lattrian professor from Sardis?"

"Hardly," Taren snorted. "He's Sarduk's chief advisor concerning magic and such, but I don't think he had any formal Lattrian training. His father wasn't a lord that I'm aware of, yet somehow he wormed his way onto the court." Taren shook his head. "I can't imagine why General Attark thought you warranted questioning by him."

"Such irony," I said and sighed. "If I did know magic, I could wave my hand and bust out of this jail."

Taren looked grim.

IO

urmyck interrogated me every day for two more weeks. He pressed me about my mother, classes with Pyrrin, Fabius's clandestine Lattrian lessons, teaching Melora to read, Dirk, and my 'magical' remedies—as he called them.

One interesting line of questioning concerned the mararoot parchment. He laid it on the desk one morning. "Do you recognize this?" He settled back in the plush chair—which he chose when the general was absent—and peered at me over his spectacles.

I reached out, recognizing the green ink, but he jerked the page away.

"What is this tincture for?" he demanded.

"I don't know, sir."

"Of course you do," he scoffed. "This recipe was among your other treasonous papers."

I tilted my head, straining to see the writing.

He slapped a book over the parchment. "The warnings suggest it is dangerous. How many people have you poisoned with this recipe?"

"None, sir."

He raised an eyebrow. "Where does the mararoot grow?"

"My mother planted some in her garden, but I don't know why. It's a scourge, growing like a weed and poisoning other plants."

Eyes narrowed, he tapped the bottom of the page. "Do you know this woman...Elissa?"

I shook my head. "Perhaps she was the previous owner of the recipe."

Curmyck's gaze probed me. After questioning me further about the mysterious Elissa, he sat back, drumming his long fingers on the desk.

"General Attark's men ransacked your bedroom. They dismantled every stick of furniture...your writing desk, your dressing table and wardrobe...they even left your bed in splinters and shredded your mattress. Where are your books?"

My desk, dressing table, wardrobe, and bed...but not my magical trunk. "Safe from dirty hands and prying eyes," I said.

Curmyck slammed his fist on the table. The general may have been satisfied to charge me with lesser crimes, but not Curmyck. He wouldn't be mollified until I was convicted of high crimes against the king.

While most of the soldiers shared Curmyck's sentiments, Taren seemed genuinely concerned about my wellbeing and comfort. He brought a pillow and two well-worn blankets. I used one to cover the stinking pallet, for without a bath or even a change of clothes, I had developed head lice, and the cot seethed with bed bugs and disgusting creepy-crawlies. He even smuggled in fresh fruits and vegetables when he could. Though usually just a carrot or an apple, I was so grateful for the variation in my diet that they tasted better than pie or cake. If only he could smuggle in a washtub. I itched...and scratched...everywhere.

Four weeks after the soldiers hauled me to jail, Taren announced that my interrogation was over.

"What happens now?"

"You'll be transported to Pithark for trial."

"Trial? Why do they bother?" I scootched myself into the tiny square of pale sunlight traveling across the floor. June blossomed outside, sending the sweet perfume of flowers and the sound of buzzing bees wafting through my window, but my cell was damp, clammy, and chilly.

"There is *always* a trial." He spat. "Curmyck and General Attark may have already decided your guilt, but a judge must make it official."

"Why Pithark?"

Taren fidgeted. "Treason is a capital offense; all capital cases are tried in Pithark, the seat of King Sarduk."

"What will my sentence be? Drowning? Burning at the stake? Or shall I be drawn and quartered?"

"Hanging is preferred...but since you're a girl, I think they'll send you to prison instead of the gallows..."

"Lovely."

"...or the mines."

"Even better." I gazed up at him. "Do you still believe I'm innocent?"

Taren studied his hands. "I used to think I served a great king and country—that Atrurians were backwards, ignorant people, and better off with Sarduk ruling them." He lifted his eyes, looking troubled. "But then…I…fell into disgrace. After my transfer…" He shrugged. "Living in Heyden made me rethink old assumptions." He scuffed his boot on the dirty flagstones, seemingly intent on scraping off some piece of filth. "Something is rotten in Pithark when a nice girl is labeled a traitor, while a greedy, lecherous, spiteful man like General Attark is considered a hero."

I leaned back against the wall, basking both in the warmth of the sun and Taren's words. After a long moment, I cleared my throat. "Taren, what would happen to you if I…escaped?"

His face remained emotionless, but an edge crept into his voice. "If you escaped during my watch, my family would be made to serve your sentence."

"That's what I thought," I said softly.

He snapped to attention. "Get some rest. We leave in a week, and the journey won't be pleasant."

"Taren," I called after him. "Will you be my jailer in Pithark?"

"I wouldn't trust you to anyone else," he said, pausing on his way out the door.

Nanni visited three days later. Taren led me to a tiny room. I thrust my arms through the iron bars separating us and clung to Nanni's hands as if I were drowning.

"Oh, baby," Nanni moaned, taking in my filthy attire and disheveled appearance. "They be starvin' you, an' they don't let you bathe, do they?"

"Sardonians are hardly ones to waste water on a bath." Nanni always disparaged the soldiers' notoriously smelly condition.

"And I miss good cooking, but don't despair; they feed me turnips every day." I had never relished them, and I stuck out my tongue.

Nanni laughed in spite of her tears and hugged me through the bars. "That's me gal. Keep up yer spirits."

"Careful," I whispered, also tearful. "You might get lice."

She snorted and clutched harder. "I should like to see one try an' roost on me head. Iffen they jump in me hair, I'll attack 'em with turpentine an' camphor." To Nanni, turpentine and camphor cured everything from ringworm to warts. If the lice knew what was best, they would stay away from her.

"They're sending me to Pithark for trial."

She pulled back in alarm. "Pithark! Why would they be sendin' you there?" She shook her head and frowned. "Mind yerself, gal. It's a wicked place, is Pithark."

"Don't worry, Nanni. I'm sure I won't be wandering the streets at night." I paused. "Do you have any news of Pyrrin?"

Her face turned dark and stormy. "I'll not speak his name, an' he's fallen from yer father's graces, too. I've seen precious little of him since you were arrested, an' a good thing too, fer I'd box his ears till they bled. He spends all his time at the fortress."

"Here? I haven't seen him."

"Of course not! He wants to dis'ssociate himself with you, so he does. He's made a lot of noise about you bein' guilty of treason, but he'd better keep his mouth shut if he knows what's best fer him. More'n one person wants to knock him silly for turnin' against you like that, love."

Nanni cheered suddenly. "You did a number on Dirk. Broke his nose, knocked out his teeth, and cracked a rib from what I heered. Brought him down a peg or two. Beastly lad. He acted all broken up when you were arrested, but I think he were only upset because he won't get the chance to use yer face as a punchin' bag." Nanni muttered under her breath, and I grinned.

"Knowing I don't have to marry him almost makes my cell bearable."

Nanni's face fell. "They...they won't...hang you or anythin', will they?"

"I heard they don't hang carrot tops."

Nanni's breath caught, and she squeezed my hands tightly through the bars. "I want you to take this," she said, pressing something into my palm.

It was Nanni's prized possession—a small gold brooch my mother gave her shortly after I was born. Intricate filigree lacework encircled a tiger's eye stone polished to a mirror finish.

"I can't, Nanni. This is your special treasure."

She shook her head and closed my hand firmly around the brooch. "It's not me treasure anymore. Bury it in the corner of yer cell if you like, but that was yer mother's, an' now it belongs to you." Tears threatened to spill down her cheeks. "She always meant fer you to have it..."

"Thank you, Nanni."

"Take care of yerself," she choked.

I squeezed back tears and secreted the brooch in my clothing. I could not bear the thought of some soldier taking it home to his mistress.

II

 t's a grueling thirty-five league journey to the capital," Taren said, gesturing to a crumbling limestone marker alongside the road. The obelisks displayed the distance to Pithark, the center of Sarduk's empire.

Taren and five soldiers flanked my cell on wheels. Another soldier guided the two horses. Besides the low ceiling, the short chain attaching my shackles to a ring on the floor forced me to sit facing a large barred door in the rear. The June sun beat mercilessly on the roof, making the vehicle an oven. We managed only three leagues on the bumpy, rutted road. By the end of the day, everyone was coated with a layer of dust from the constantly churning hooves.

We camped on the outskirts of a village at dusk, and a soldier rode into the square to commandeer supplies.

"Tell me about Pithark," I said when Taren brought dinner.

"The city is built to Sardonian design...everything laid out in squares." He cast a sidelong glance at the rest of the soldiers, who were regaling each other with bawdy stories as they reclined around the fire. One soldier raised his mug of cheap wine and erupted into a vulgar song. Heaving a sigh, Taren sank down against the cart. "Pithark is filled with courtiers and soldiers eager to claw their way up the social ladder. It's not a place for a lady like you."

Nightfall brought relief from the burning sun, and I drifted off to sleep, lulled by a symphony of crickets and a chorus of raucous snores from the intoxicated soldiers. They slept in their uniforms, lying haphazardly around the smoldering fire. Taren had to kick them awake in the morning.

We traveled for ten days in this manner. Only a two-day journey remained when the storm began. A stiff wind sent brooding clouds scudding over the sun. Wind-driven rain pelted from every direction.

The roof leaked, and water puddled on the floor, soaking my skirts. The cart reeked in the dampness, as if it had last carried a combination of rotting corpses, pig manure, rancid meat, and moldy cabbage. The smell infiltrated my hair and sodden clothing, until none of the soldiers except Taren would suffer to be downwind of me. But since the swirling wind made every direction downwind, everyone was nauseated by the time we stopped.

We sought refuge at several taverns, but the nicer ones wouldn't allow a filthy, stinking convict through the door. We ended up in a cockroach-infested rat hole with food on par with prison fare. After spending the night on a lumpy pallet that stank of vomit, I awoke with bedbug bites.

"I'd rather sleep in the cart than endure another night like this," I said, scratching viciously at my stomach.

Taren said nothing, but I caught him itching his arm.

That night we slept in a grungy, rundown stable behind a seedy tavern. I enjoyed the relative peace of sharing my quarters with chickens, two pigs, a cow, and some horses. At least the animals didn't snore.

The torrential rain washed out the road in low areas, and the cart mired in muck. The wheels made slurping sounds as the suction of the mud pulled them down; the men shouted as the wagon halted with a sickening lurch and listed to one side. Soldiers yelled and cursed at each other as they fought to free the wheels. It took four miserable days to slog the last five leagues.

As the mud-spattered cart rolled through the gates of Pithark, the rain slowed to a sprinkle and sunbeams peeped through chinks in the clouds. By the time the jolting cart reached the uneven cobblestones of the central boulevard, the sun was blazing and wisps of mist curled above the steaming roofs.

People bustled into the streets as the weather cleared. Men, women, and children sprouted like mushrooms, overflowing into the lanes just like the gutters spilling over with rainwater and filth from the city. Women carried baskets on their shoulders for their shopping, sellers chanted or sang their ditties, and buyers and sellers haggled. Children ran underfoot, pickpockets sized up their targets, beggars installed themselves on familiar corners, and dogs, pigs, and stray poultry darted around adding their voices to the noise and confusion. Rich merchants strode by carrying heavy purses, wealthy men and women rode horses or reclined in litters, and on every corner, in every street, everywhere—were soldiers.

They looked nothing like the muddy contingent that led my wagon. They carried gleaming swords, pikes, and halberds, and wore crisply ironed breeches, snowy white tunics, polished boots, and sparkling breastplates and helmets.

The cart slowed, and Taren appeared at the door. His gaze followed mine, and he snorted at the smartly dressed soldiers. "Those milksops are the highborn sons of wealthy Sardonians and Atrurians. They vie for Sarduk's favor like vultures over a carcass, hoping to win the wealth and prestige of a bodyguard contingent. They're the cream of the soldiery, but if anyone ever laid siege to these walls, they'd abandon the city and run like the cowards they are."

Guards barked orders in harsh guttural speech; my entourage halted, and Taren presented papers. After a long delay and many shouted orders, a huge gate creaked open, and the wagon entered a courtyard.

Taren let me out, and I blinked in the bright sunshine. Green flagstones surrounded an immense black fortress. The low, squat building reminded me of a huge frog crouching on a giant lily pad. A crenellated gateway, with massive iron-studded doors topped with two barred windows and arrow slits, hunched between short flanking towers. With no spires to draw the eyes heavenward, the effect was ugly and grim. I shivered despite the brilliant sunshine.

Two guards, devoid of armor, escorted us through a maze of corridors and stairways. "Here vee are," one said, gesturing to an empty cell.

Taren removed my shackles. "Keep up your spirits," he said before closing the door behind himself.

A noise from the courtyard drew me to one of the barred windows, and I discovered I was in the right-hand tower. I could see a portion of the green courtyard and the massive gated wall separating the fortress from the rest of the city. The other window allowed a view of the barracks and three soldiers patrolling a catwalk behind battlements, armed with halberds and crossbows.

The modest furnishings in my cell were luxurious compared to those in Heyden: a chamber pot; a washbasin in a dilapidated wooden stand; a wooden chair with a well-worn cushion; an iron bed frame topped with a pallet, clean sheets, and a neatly folded woolen blanket. It was dry, bright, and immaculate, and I stood in the center of the room, loath to place my dirty, smelly body on the clean sheets.

The door flew open, and a short, morbidly fat Sardonian woman with several chins and copious quantities of greasy gray hair burst into my cell, arms flailing. "Don't tetch anythin'!" she bellowed. She continued in a torrent of Sardonian, but I only caught one word in twenty of her fast, adulterated speech. Her furious tirade caused her warty chins to wobble, and a huge hairy mole on the side of her nose was both disgusting and mesmerizing. Her shapeless smock may at one time have been blue or green, but it was hard to tell with all the filth embedded in the weave of the fabric. Ragged, yellowed stockings bagged at her ankles, revealing vivid purple veins. A few black teeth wobbled in her gums, and the stench of garlic and rot emanating with every breath could have repulsed an entire regiment.

Saliva dribbled down the corner of her mouth, and I stepped back to avoid flying spittle. She screamed louder, and by her gestures indicated that I was to follow her. Still ranting, she led me down a long corridor to a laundry where a huge tub of water steamed. She unceremoniously stripped off my clothes and pushed me into the tub, then scrubbed me from head to toe. The water was delightful, although a little too hot at first. I would have enjoyed my first bath in more than a month if she hadn't been so intent on rubbing my skin off with a stiff bristle brush. The caustic soap burned, and she doused my head with turpentine to kill the lice. After an intense scrubbing, I emerged five shades lighter. My tender skin felt raw, and my scalp burned from her treatment, but I was clean. It was delightful.

Still grumbling, she handed me a gray smock. After I dressed, she directed me to a chair and picked the remaining nits out of my hair with a fine-toothed comb, yanking until tears streamed down my cheeks. An alarming amount of hair lay strewn in snarls on the floor when she grunted to indicate she was finished. She gave me a pile of pins and a wooden comb, and I pinned up my hair. Then she handed me a pair of coarse woolen slippers and led me back to the cell.

I crawled on the pallet, tugged the blanket over my shoulders, and fell into a dreamless slumber.

~ † ~

I finally woke around dusk. I sat up, stretched, and padded over to the southern window. The sun had dropped below the wall, plunging the courtyard into murky shadow. I stood at the window until nightfall and listened to crickets chirping, then ambled to the other window and leaned against the sill as stars appeared in the sky. Raucous laughter echoed from the barracks, and a sickly sweet smell wafted up from a refuse pile below.

Booted feet tramped down the hall, followed by a knock on the door. Taren entered, bearing a torch.

"Taren!" I grinned.

He stuck his torch in a holder on the wall. "You didn't touch your dinner," he said, pointing to a tray by a food slot in the corner.

"Actually, I didn't notice it. I slept for awhile, and now I'm just enjoying being clean."

"I understand. Make sure you eat. I think you'll find the food better than the swill in Heyden."

"Who was the woman who scrubbed me down?"

"Kefra, the matron of the women's ward. Completely disagreeable, but she keeps the place tidy."

"Perhaps she would benefit from a bath herself."

Taren laughed. "She thinks water is only for criminals and prisons. They say her house is as filthy as she is. She's a mean old bat, but she's fair. She treats everybody the same. Just don't get her sheets dirty."

I could abide by that.

Taren sobered. "I'm not your only jailer now. Another soldier named Prell will share the duty. I don't much like him. He's superstitious and narrow-minded. Try not to run afoul of him."

~ † ~

Kefra was not a 'mean old bat,' as Taren described her; she was a fiend. Twice a week she blew into my cell like a whirlwind, armed with clean linens, a broom, a mop, and a pail of water. After thrusting the broom into my hands and commanding me to sweep, she changed the linen and scrubbed and mopped, ranting the entire time in garbled Sardonian and spraying spittle liberally. I kept my cell neat and I was always polite and respectful, but she glowered at me with unmitigated hatred.

If Taren didn't 'much like' Prell, I abhorred him. The first day he arrived for guard duty, I heard him whining to Taren outside my door.

"She won't put some spell on me, will she? She won't turn me inta a toad, or something?"

"Not a toad. Maybe a skunk or a rat," Taren said as he unlocked the cell door.

A hulking brute of a man, pockmarked and piggish, peered around the doorjamb, assessing me with nearsighted eyes.

"Come on," Taren sighed. "She's perfectly harmless."

After Prell got over his initial fear, he tormented me endlessly, swearing and cursing in broken Atrurian. I hated his long, ogling stares, and the crass comments he repeated under my window to other guards made me acutely uncomfortable. I dreaded the nights he had guard duty.

Taren did his best to keep Prell in check and my growing anxiety at bay. Whenever he received a letter from his wife, he kept me abreast of the news from home. He furnished me with books and brought tidbits of food or drink. I had a comfortable cell, edible food, a selection of Sardonian literature—if it could be called that—and I was clean; Kefra scrubbed me down once a week without mercy. Yet the long days turned to weeks and then months—and still no trial.

<h1 style="text-align:center">12</h1>

hate this game," I said, glaring fiercely at the board.

Kings was one of the few aspects of Atrurian culture the Sardonians had embraced with gusto. They loved playing, and Taren excelled at the game. He took especial pleasure in defeating me with a different strategy every time we played.

"Are you ready to concede?" Taren asked, leaning back in his chair and grinning.

I chewed my fingernails as I studied the board. I had lost my queen early in an ill-conceived gambit attempt, and now his dragon held my last cavalry *and* turret immobilized. Though I might stall my demise a few turns with some savvy moves by my foot soldiers, his assassin was breathing down the neck of my king, and I couldn't do anything about it.

"I *hate* this game!" I said again, jumping to my feet.

My skirt caught a corner of the inlaid board, somersaulting it into the air. It hit the floor and splintered along the grain; carved ivory and ebony game pieces ricocheted off the walls.

I stared at the wreckage and burst into tears.

"Hey," Taren said. "It's all right."

"I ruined your beautiful board." I sank onto my pallet.

"Please don't cry, Arabella." Taren brushed my shoulder with his hand. "I never much liked that board anyway."

I shook my head. "It's not just the game...it's...everything. All day long, the sun bakes that...that dung heap outside and the flies drive me *mad* with their ceaseless droning. At night, the behemoth stones of this granite prison radiate heat into my cell. For one blissful hour after sunset, a breeze wafts through the windows. But King Sarduk's father, in his *infinite* wisdom, decided to build Pithark on a marsh. Every evening without fail, mosquitoes come to dine, and *I'm* their favorite meal. I wake up splotchy and itchy from their wretched bites. Yet if I close the shutters, this room becomes a furnace and I can't breathe."

"Why didn't you tell me the insects were so bad?" Taren asked. "I'll bring some muslin to tack over your windows."

I held up my hand. Misery and tension had been building in me for weeks, and I wasn't half finished with my tirade.

"You remember the storm that made our journey here so miserable?"

Taren nodded. "Of course."

"Well, it has rained exactly *zero* times since we've arrived, and the warden has instituted water rationing. Once a week, Kefra resorts to dousing me like a drowned rat, and the boiled drinking water is about as refreshing as hot tea in August. I'd give my left arm for a draught of cold water from a well."

Taren looked pained. "Arabella..."

"And another thing...all the smoke and haze makes my throat burn and my eyes smart."

"Trade winds sear acres of grassland to the south," Taren explained. "Lightning sets the brittle grass ablaze, and the smoke blows over the city. The fires should die out once we get a drenching rain..."

I sagged against the rickety headboard. "I didn't mean to whine."

"You have every reason," he said.

"Sorry about the game. I truly like playing Kings...I'm just bone tired of waiting for trial. I'm sick of reading and pacing my cell...sick of thinking. Instead of sleeping, I mop sweat and swat mosquitoes." I picked at the mattress ticking.

"Why don't you write a letter to your nurse and I'll post it for you."

I shook my head. "You can't keep doing that. Nanni sent a few bits in her last letter...but I have nothing to tell her." I put my hands to my temples. "If something doesn't happen soon I'm going to lose my mind!"

Taren started cleaning up the scattered pieces.

With a sigh, I rose and gathered up shards of the board.

"I can fix it," he assured me.

"No, you can't. But thank you for saying so."

~ † ~

The sky opened up in mid-October, quenching the fires and the heat—but it did nothing to quell the simmering unease pervading the barracks. The signs were subtle: grudging salutes; lazy parade attention; soldiers slow to respond to orders, and a general resentment of the officers in their fancy uniforms. Did Sarduk know all was not well in his stronghold?

The following week I was called before a judge at last. After shackling me, Taren loaded me into a wagon for transport across the compound to a huge courthouse resembling the massive fortress. Sardonians seemed incapable of producing beautiful architecture.

The judge wore an austere expression, but his long flowing black robe and curly powdered wig bordered on the ridiculous. He did not bother to glance up as he perused a lengthy scroll. "Charges are treason and so forth...disseminating banned materials and so on and...performing magic?" The judge's voice rose sharply. "Magic?" He peered at me for the first time. "These are serious charges. Where is counsel for the defense?"

A tall, rail-thin Atrurian with a pinched face, harried expression, and wig askew rushed up to the lawyer's stand next to me, clutching an overflowing satchel to his chest. "Counsel for the defense, my lord," he wheezed, vainly trying to straighten his rumpled robes.

"Ahem, Devolin," the judge said. "What says the defendant?"

I tried to speak around the lump in my throat. "Ummmm..."

"Guilty or not guilty!" the judge asked.

My father had ignored my repeated requests for a lawyer, so the court had appointed one. But Taren had told me my best strategy for defense.

"I would prefer to represent myself."

"Represent yourself?"

"Yes, sir."

The judge shuffled parchment in a befuddled manner. "This is highly unusual. Highly unusual!"

An imposing man in impeccably tailored robes stepped forward and cleared his throat. "Glessim, the king's prosecutor, my lord. Might I make a suggestion...?"

The judge waved for him to continue.

"The girl is of such a tender age and the charges are of such a serious nature that I would contend she is foolhardy to proceed on her own without..." He glanced at Devolin with obvious disdain. "Without such distinguished counsel to aid her. Perhaps Devolin might act as her co-counsel."

The judge looked relieved. "Excellent idea! Devolin, I hereby appoint you as co-counsel for Miss Arabella of Maitlan." He turned to me again. "Now, how do you plead?"

"Not guilty, my lord."

"Hmmm. Devolin, help the girl prepare a suitable defense. This case involves capital offenses, and General Attark has requested that this matter be bound over for trial before a special tribunal convened by King Sarduk. Trial date to be set at their behest."

The judge banged his gavel and bellowed, "Next case."

13

n early January, after spending weeks worrying about my preparation and wearing paths in the flagstones as I paced my cell in restless anxiety, the tribunal called me to trial.

The immense courtroom was shaped like an amphitheater. Three judges sat behind podiums at the bottom. Rows of stairs marched upward to a massive gallery. My box was stationed midway up the stairs in the center with Devolin's box to the right and the prosecutor's to the left. Curmyck occupied a seat behind the prosecutor. He never spoke to the court, but occasionally I saw Glessim confer with him. Taren and Prell stood at attention behind me after chaining my shackles to an iron ring on the floor.

Trial convened three days a week. Over the first two weeks, Glessim gave an eloquent elegy of my life, including a catalogue of wrongs I had committed against General Attark and King Sarduk.

When it was my turn to give a rebuttal, I could only explain the prosecutor's mistakes and assert my innocence.

The prosecution then presented a list of witnesses, including Dirk, Pyrrin, my father, Nanni, and villagers. In keeping with the travesty they called justice, no one who might have said something on my behalf was actually present. Sardonian law allowed the prosecution to take sworn statements from witnesses and read them before the court. It worked wonderfully well—except the statements were falsified and witnesses couldn't be cross-examined.

According to Nanni, I was a difficult child: ornery; contrary; petulant, and obstinate. Not only did I ask her to aid me in producing poisonous concoctions to give the villagers, I threatened to put a pox on her if she didn't hide incriminating documents for me. She, being an honest, honorable citizen, refused to do so, and the prosecutor declared she had heroically reported me to Pyrrin despite the risk to her life.

No less than five absent villagers accused me of poisoning and cursing them. I had done everything from causing their milk to curdle, preventing their butter from churning, making their ewes and lambs die, giving foot rot to their horses, and turning the village well bitter.

The miller, in absentia, accused me of encouraging his daughter to engage in seditious behavior, including learning Lattrian and reading banned books. Our relationship culminated with me strangling my best friend and throwing her in the millpond. However, since the general had not charged me with murdering Melora, the judges threw that statement out.

I could do little to refute absent witnesses, though I did present a letter Nanni wrote and pointed out that the statement did not match her handwriting.

The trial may have been a farce, but it was a lengthy, entertaining farce. Every day cityfolk piled into the courtroom, seeking relief from January's bitter temperatures. The press of humanity overflowed the gallery, but as long as they maintained relative quiet, the judges allowed them to remain. Even after the icy cold lifted, crowds kept coming to watch the proceedings. Every morning before the judges filed in, a chant of, "Hang her high, hang her high," began somewhere in the back of the gallery and traveled around until the guards bellowed for silence. Most spectators added their voices to the raucous chorus, though I did notice a few abstainers—most notably a knot of fresh-faced students hunched in a back corner, pencils poised over their slates—but they were probably university students taking notes on trial procedure.

I had no illusions about the outcome of the trial. Each morning Devolin served the court with a petition begging them to bestow mercy on me. Each time the judges ordered him back to his box where I would glare and berate him with acerbic whispers. Worse than useless to my defense, Devolin never questioned the legitimacy of the proceedings or the prosecution's evidence.

Dirk was the first witness to appear in person. Glessim began with questions about the assault in the hayloft. To my surprise, Dirk couldn't meet anyone's gaze.

I passionately hated the prosecutor, so I reveled in his growing discomfort at Dirk's subdued answers. He kept glancing at Curmyck, until he threw up his hands and said, "Your witness."

I was not permitted to approach the witness box, so I gazed down at Dirk. "Why did you attack me in the loft?"

Glessim made several loud hems and haws.

"I guess..."

Glessim coughed loudly, and I looked over at him, wondering what he was up to. He grew red in the face and made wild gestures.

"I was angry 'cause you wouldn't kiss me." His eyes lifted, but his gaze flitted over the gallery. "I's sorry, Ar'bella, I..."

I was astonished to see tears well in his eyes.

He brushed his sleeve over his face. "I never meant fer this to happen!"

"Objection!" the prosecutor roared.

A judge banged his gavel. "You will keep your comments pertinent to the proceedings, young man, or we'll throw you out."

"When I broke your nose and knocked out your teeth, was I defending myself?" I asked quickly.

Dirk's eyes reverted to the cap clutched in his hands. "I reckon any lass woulda been in her rights to do the same."

Glessim looked ready to eat his parchment, and a judge dismissed Dirk.

The next time we convened, Glessim called Pyrrin as a witness. He questioned him about his discovery of my notes, Fabius's Lattrian lessons, Melora, the horses, and a hundred other things. Pyrrin had nothing good to say and twisted things I had said or done to make them sound conniving. He outright lied several times. I was seething when the prosecutor turned him over for cross-examination.

"Pyrrin..."

He turned to the judges and said smugly, "I refuse to be examined by a woman."

"What?" I said, taken aback.

One of the judges nodded. "It's his right to decline questions from a woman."

"His right! How on earth can I cross-examine him if I can't question him?"

"Your co-counsel will do it," another judge said.

"My co-counsel?" I stabbed a finger at Devolin. "This whiny...idiotic... sniveling..." I grasped for the appropriate word. "This...this...imbecile doesn't know the hind end of a horse from the front! How can he possibly question my brother about all the lies and half-truths he just fed the court?"

"Young lady," a judge said sharply. "That's no way to speak of an officer of the court, nor of a sworn witness."

"Officer of the court? Sworn witness? Devolin's only interest is to ingratiate himself to this court, and Pyrrin is calculating which lies will put the most nails in my coffin!"

A burst of noise erupted in the gallery and crescendoed rapidly through the room. All three judges rapped their gavels and shouted, "Order! Order!"

"Hold your tongue, young lady," a judge said, "or we'll remove you from this trial."

"This trial is no better than a festival sideshow!" I cried. "And the three of you are more qualified to run a circus than a courtroom!"

The gallery erupted again, and one of the red-faced judges grimaced. "Get her out of here!"

~ † ~

Back in my cell, I fumed. After Glessim's wild antics while Dirk was in the box, I should have known he had something up his sleeve. Devolin had conveniently neglected to inform me that witnesses could refuse questions from a woman. Not that it would have made a difference.

I paced in fury until, overcome with fatigue, I curled up on the cot and drifted off to sleep. I woke well after midnight, pondering Dirk's statements in a new light. Like Pyrrin, the prosecutor obviously expected him to refuse my questions. Still, he told the truth about events in the hayloft, even saying I was justified in whacking him with the pitchfork.

I shook my head to clear the cobwebs. A day ago, I would have called Dirk unrepentant and irreclaimable. Yet he had apologized for his behavior and defended me, while my own brother had betrayed me. And Pyrrin seemed perfectly content to watch me suffer at the hands of Sardonian injustice.

The following day the judges allowed me to return to the courtroom, but Pyrrin was gone. I didn't know if Devolin had questioned him after my exit from the courtroom, and I didn't care. The whole charade was exhausting; I was relieved the trial was nearly over.

General Attark refused my examination when he came to the stand. My interest in the proceedings waned as Devolin sniveled and groveled with every inane question. As the general expounded on his illustrious military exploits, I let my gaze travel over the gallery.

By now, I recognized many faces: the red-cheeked matron in the corner rocking a baby while a runny-nosed boy tugged her skirts; the tall, hook-nosed man by the door carrying a sketchpad and charcoal pencils who never drew anything; a rotating gaggle of bored boys darting through the gallery covertly passing an inflated pig's bladder back and forth—which a guard had confiscated only once; four whispering sisters, kerchiefs covering their wavy brown hair, who batted their lashes and tittered every time a boy dashed by; the skinny, earnest-faced student in the corner holding whispered conversations with his friends; in the rear, the poor tailor flexing his stiff fingers as he worked a cuff or collar, and the lazy clerk lolling against the back wall as he dozed off.

I often found the entertainment in the gallery more fascinating than the trial, and one of the judges seemed to as well. Sometimes his eyes flitted to the audience, and he even cracked a smile when one of the boys made a daring catch, the clerk caught himself as he tumbled over, or a noble woman's peacock feather tickled someone's nose and made them sneeze.

Today, however, I noticed a newcomer. Striking in appearance, she stood taller than most Atrurians. Snowy hair streamed down her shoulders, and a pale green sash girdled her sparkling white dress. She had an aquiline nose, high cheekbones, and the most piercing eyes I had ever seen, though I could not tell their color. Her skin appeared smooth and unwrinkled, though I was sure a closer inspection would reveal crow's feet and laugh lines. Despite her serious expression, she looked as if she might burst into laughter at any moment.

She leaned against the wall at the top of the gallery to my left, and when a judge rapped his gavel to announce the end of the day's proceedings, people filed past her. Yet not one of them looked at her twice.

The woman glanced away from the judges, and our eyes met. She inclined her head and smiled as Taren led me away.

The next day I searched for her in vain. Then, right before the afternoon recess, a man in the upper gallery rose to leave, and I spotted an ancient crone in a shapeless brown smock hunched against the back wall, holding a walking stick in gnarled, arthritic hands. Her wrinkled skin was brown with age spots and dotted with moles. A gray cloak hid her face, but then the hood slipped back, revealing snowy hair and piercing eyes. Our eyes met again, and a curious look stole over her face as she noted my surprised expression.

~ † ~

It snowed briefly the night before I took the stand in my own defense, and I awoke to a basin full of solid ice. The shutters on the windows offered little protection from the cold, and my fingers went numb as I ate my rapidly cooling breakfast. My thin slippers did nothing to hinder the icy cold seeping through the flagstones. Clouds of frozen breath wreathed my head, and I snuggled into the woolen horse blanket Taren offered when he loaded me into the wagon for the short trip to the courthouse.

An officer of the court bade me swear to tell the truth and then directed me to the witness box. My shackles were removed for the first time in two months, and I flexed my hands, enjoying the freedom. Taren and Prell stood at attention on either side.

Glessim rose and strode down the steps. He paused to straighten his impeccably coiffed wig and brush imaginary dust from his crisply ironed robes before drawling, "Your name, please."

"Arabella of Maitlan."

He strode away a few steps. "Where is Elissa?"

"Elissa?"

"Yes!" He turned abruptly and paced the courtroom. "That cursed recipe for brewing misery and death, found among your treasonous materials, belonged to the most villainous of traitors ever to walk this earth. That recipe was no doubt penned by the hand of the most wicked and devious enchantress to ever draw breath, this...Elissa." He spat her name out as if the very mention tainted his mouth. "I implore you, if you wish to save yourself, tell me where Elissa is and when and how have you consorted with her."

I stared in disbelief. "I don't even know who she is."

"Impossible!" Glessim roared. "Her paper was among your things!"

"I don't know who wrote that parchment or where it came from."

He lifted his fist, as if he would have liked to wring the desired answers from me with his bare hands, but a judge cleared his throat, and Glessim let his hand fall to his side. He paced the room in agitation, asking more questions, but he didn't seem interested in my responses. As the crowd wearied of his badgering, they booed and catcalled. The judges banged their gavels for silence, but after several minutes, the din began again. This cycle of noise and enforced silence continued until someone yelled, "Jus' burn the gal already!"

A judge slammed his gavel and yelled, "Clear the gallery!" Once the guards expelled the grumbling crowd, the prosecutor continued his questions. Without spectators, however, his enthusiasm waned, and Prell shackled me for the return trip to my cell before the bell rang for noon recess.

In a way, I was sorry to leave, for the courtroom was warm compared to my cell. As I lay shivering under my inadequate blankets, teeth chattering uncontrollably, I couldn't decide which was worse: the misery of the torrid summer or the bone-chilling cold.

When Taren brought dinner, he said, "The judges will announce their verdict next week."

14

ope.

It sat on my shoulder and twittered relentlessly.

Yet false hope was a mockery, its promises reduced to ashes in my mouth. Every morning, I woke with hope bubbling inside me like water in a spring—telling me truth must prevail. No matter how much I railed, hope blossomed unbidden and unwanted in my breast.

Snow-laden clouds hung low and ominous over the courthouse as Taren and Prell helped me out of the wagon. Taren led me to my box and shackled me to the rings. I stood unsteadily, waiting, as the judges filed into the room and took their seats. A clerk announced the verdict was ready.

A hush descended over the courtroom as the three judges rose, their stiff black robes rustling. I willed myself to stand steady, clenching clammy hands in my rough skirt to hide their trembling. My chains rattled, and Prell glared at me. The chief judge unrolled the scroll, pushed his spectacles up his nose and without so much as a glance in my direction, read in his harsh guttural voice, "Arabella of Maitlan, daughter of Vigo of Maitlan, of Heyden-on-Trine, of Atruria." Somebody in the gallery coughed, and the judge paused, clearing his throat. "This tribunal, convened by the order of King Sarduk, king of Sardonia, Atruria, all the southern flood lands extending to the sea, laying claim to the Great Lake, and all the wasteland and northern foothills as far as the Pindar mountain range..." Someone coughed again, and the judge stared reproachfully. A guard pushed through the crowd to remove the offending person. After the disturbance subsided, the judge resumed. "This tribunal does hereby find you guilty of: learning and using a forbidden language; reading banned material; consorting with unfavorable persons, including the known devious enchantress and enemy of the king, one Elissa; unlawfully performing magic; disseminating poisonous and dangerous materials to unsuspecting law-abiding citizens...and treason against our noble king." A jeer erupted in the gallery, and the other judges pounded their gavels to restore order. I stood motionless as the blood drained from my face. "For said crimes..." The chief judge looked up from the scroll and peered solemnly at me over his spectacles. "Young lady, notwithstanding your tender age, this tribunal does hereby sentence you to death."

A roar swept through the gallery, the room swam, and although I clutched at the rail, my knees buckled as the room turned black.

~ † ~

The wagon creaked and swayed in tune with my misery when I woke in the back. Fainting in the courtroom was *not* the way I had hoped to show fortitude and courage. My conviction came as no surprise, but a death sentence...

Taren had said female offenders were sent to the mines. They slaved away their existence feeding the miserable souls condemned to a life of toil in the darkness. Devolin had confided that the Sardonians had not executed a female prisoner in over fifty years, and even the gallery had seemed shocked at the verdict.

My strength and will sapped, I lay weakly beneath the horse blanket, half listening to snatches of a conversation between Taren and Prell. Then their voices rose, and I heard them clearly.

"Come on," Prell whined. "She'll stink to high heaven once we start back. Don't tell me you haven't thought 'bout it all these months. You know what they say 'bout redheads..."

Taren's voice held a steely edge. "If you even *touch* her..."

"Fine," Prell retorted. "But with looks like that..."

Taren removed the blanket and shook me gently when we arrived at the jail. I feigned sleep. He passed smelling salts under my nose, which made me gasp and cough.

"Are you all right?"

I nodded as he helped me out of the wagon. "When is the execution?"

He did not answer, and when I glanced at him, he seemed choked with emotion. He kept his face averted from Prell, who slapped me on the shoulder. "It's not jus' an execution, me gal. It's a spectacle as well."

"A spectacle?"

Taren brushed his sleeve over his face. "You'll be transported back to Heyden and executed there."

Prell cackled. "Yer leavin' out the best part, Taren." He jostled my shoulder, and I stumbled.

Taren steadied me. "You'll be pilloried in villages along the way." He looked weary and defeated.

"Why?" I murmured.

"You're to be an example for the whole country. A spectacle." He spat out the word.

So hanging wasn't enough...I must also endure the pillory?

I swayed and nearly fainted again. Taren grabbed an arm before my wobbly knees gave out, but he had to support me the rest of the way to my cell. Prell followed closely, snickering.

By evening, my spirits were lower than they had been in months. Indifference settled over me like a suffocating shroud, and I huddled on the pallet and stared at the wall.

The slot rattled. I chewed the tasteless food and drained the cup, then waited numbly for sleep to come.

I awoke after dark with a strange taste in my mouth and an odd clutching in my throat. A wave of nausea assailed me as I sat up. I stumbled toward the chamber pot, thinking I might vomit, but the nausea passed, and I sank to the floor. There was a sound outside the door. I tried to call for help, but only a croak came out.

The door swung open, and Prell entered. He placed a torch into the bracket beside the door. "Are you sick?" He glanced into the chamber pot. "It's an unfortunate side effect of the drug I gave you."

His words took time to register. I dimly remembered a strange aftertaste. I opened my mouth to scream, but only a squeak emerged.

He laughed. "Renders you incapable of speech fer a while, so it does." He squatted and reached out a grubby hand toward me. I jerked away from him, overbalanced, and sprawled against the wall, paralyzed by drug-induced weakness.

I grimaced and turned my head aside as he pawed at my hair. He loosed its restraints, and it fell cascading around my face, blinding me. His breath reeked of onions and tooth decay, and I gagged. A sudden memory of the dark hayloft galvanized my muscles into action. Giving the best rasping call I could muster, I struck Prell in the chest with both feet. He fell back, cursing. I scrambled toward the door, but a wave of nausea drove me to my knees. Bile rose in my throat, my stomach churned, and I vomited all over Kefra's clean floor. I struggled toward the hall, dragging myself through the mess.

Prell had left the door unlocked, but as I scrabbled at the latch with my fingertips, he grabbed me by the hair and tossed me on the pallet like a sack of grain. My head hit a post and a million tiny stars danced in my vision.

"Look at you," he grumbled. "You made a mess of yerself."

Vomit caked my hair and stained my dress, and I sprawled over the mattress, dizzy and weak.

With agonizing slowness, Prell reached out to stroke my face.

I croaked again and tensed every muscle, ready to claw him. A sudden movement flashed behind him, and his gloating look turned to one of surprise. His head lolled sideways as he crumpled to the floor.

There stood Kefra, brandishing a broom.

"Ignorant pig! Slovenly monsssster...!" A string of Sardonian epithets erupted from her, and she stomped her foot and kicked him. I had never been so happy to see anyone in my life.

Kefra's bellow brought several guards running. Prell was coming around, and two soldiers grabbed him under the arms and dragged him out the door. He started to struggle and curse halfway down the corridor, but a guard must have struck him for he went suddenly quiet.

Kefra stripped off my soiled clothing, put me in bed, and scrubbed the floor, grumbling all the while. For the first time I felt something akin to affection for her. My apathy had evaporated, and I soon slipped into an exhausted slumber.

~ † ~

A battle was raging—a fight to the death between two men. One was tall, his filthy tunic torn and soaked with blood from a fresh wound. He was weaponless and clutching his ribs. The second man, dressed in black, stood over him, his face twisting as he gloated in triumph. He pointed a long sword at the first man's throat and lunged. The victim stumbled, and the sword grazed his cheek, leaving a gash that welled with blood. My vision narrowed until I could only see the man in black. He stared straight at me, his pointed, yellowed teeth bared in exultation. As he raised the sword over his head, the tip of a dagger sprouted from under his left shoulder blade. Blood spurted from the wound, his mouth opened soundlessly, and the sword fell to the ground as his hands faltered.

As I sat up, wrestling with the blankets, a dark figure started up from the chair and came toward me. Thinking it was Prell, I tried to scream. The drug had not worn off; all I managed was a short burst of sound before my voice cracked.

"Easy now, rest easy!"

I slumped back when I realized it was Taren. He lit a torch and moved his chair next to my bed. I shuddered from the memory of the dream. Taren, no doubt mistaking my trembling for fear, took my hand in his.

"Prell invented an excuse to keep me away. Thank goodness I asked Kefra to watch you."

"Thank you for that," I croaked. "And for staying with me. I had a nightmare."

"I shouldn't wonder," he said, dismay evident on his face.

"What will happen to Prell?"

"Not enough," he muttered. "If I had my way, he would be drawn and quartered. But he'll not have charge of you again. I'll kill him first."

"Thank you," I whispered.

He sat until I grew sleepy, before tucking the blanket around me and tiptoeing to the door.

"What is it they say about redheads?" My voice rasped.

Even in the dim light from the guttering torch, I saw a deep flush spread across his cheeks. When he regained his composure, he said, "Nothing I can repeat in the company of a lady." Then he fled out the door.

I lay on my back and watched shadows play across the ceiling. Why did I have the misfortune to attract miserable men like Dirk and Prell? Were they the only type of men who could stand to look at me? I rolled into a ball and huddled under the covers as hot tears seeped out beneath my closed lids. I felt ugly, afraid, and terribly alone.

15

n a wintry March morning, Taren loaded me into the same stinking cart that had transported me from Heyden. Dirty brown snow lay heaped in piles at the edges of the streets, and the previous day's snowmelt had pooled in puddles and frozen overnight. The air was raw, and when the creaking wheels ran over a frozen puddle, the ice groaned and cracked, splashing freezing water into the cart. I huddled under the horse blanket Taren had wrapped around me.

By afternoon, we reached a sizable town, and my dread grew as the wagon stopped in the town square. Taren stayed with the cart while the rest of the soldiers dispersed through the village. A bell tolled, and soon the soldiers reappeared, herding bunches of refuse-laden townsfolk toward the green. The air was ominously quiet as two guards dragged me from the cart and positioned me in the stocks. One of them clambered on top of the wagon and read a long list of my crimes, both in Sardonian and Atrurian. Then they took up positions on the fringes of the crowd.

A sigh traveled through the bystanders, as if they had all exhaled at once. The crowd seemed hesitant. For a moment, I thought I detected expressions of pity on those closest, but their faces hardened when a soldier shouted and brandished a flaming torch.

I twisted in the pillory, trying to see. What was he threatening to do...? My thoughts fled as a rotten potato hurtled through the air and exploded on impact, spraying my face with foul-smelling slime.

Their reluctance forgotten, for the next twenty minutes the crowd jeered, hissed, and booed, hurling insults and taunts at me. They threw every piece of rank garbage imaginable; chicken heads, rotten eggs, spoiled apples, stinking cabbage, and slimy rotten turnips with hard cores that hurt as much as rocks. Someone even dumped a manure bucket over my head. The stench was horrible; when a rotten egg burst on the pillory, I vomited until there was nothing left in my stomach.

Some boys began chucking stones, and one grazed the crown of my head. Taren sprinted out of a nearby shop and collared the surprised boys. He retreated after boxing their ears, but the crowd lost its fervor and dispersed.

After several minutes, a soldier released me from the stocks. Swearing liberally about the garbage plastered all over, he doused me with a bucket of freezing water and threw me in the cart. My temples throbbed, and I gingerly touched a growing knot on my head where the rock had struck. Blood caked my hair around a gash on my scalp. I huddled miserably under the blanket, shivering violently as my extremities turned numb. Icy water dripped from my damp clothes and hair and froze on the floor. I reeked like a cesspool, and I heaved again in a corner of the cart.

We bedded down in a stable for the night, and Taren applied a poultice to my bruises. His mouth drew into a grim line as he cleaned the gash with spirits.

The fiery burning made me gasp, and I tried not to wince as he stitched the wound. I found the pain reassuring in a way; at least I could still feel *something*.

Somewhere along the jolting wagon ride on the never-ending journey back to Heyden, we developed an entourage—a sober-faced knot of young men plodding behind the cart. At each village, they clustered on the fringes of the crowd, always silent, always watchful. At first, I wondered who they were and why they followed us, but my curiosity dulled as my bruises turned brilliant shades of violet, green, and yellow under the layers of filth. I endured the stocks once or twice daily, ate what my stomach did not reject, and snatched sleep in whatever wretched hole Taren found for me. Even though a gallows waited, all I could think about was an end to the journey.

~ † ~

Despite the rutted road, I managed to fall asleep, the first warm breeze of spring a balm to my face. When the eternal jolting of the wagon ceased, I sat up, waiting indifferently for a soldier to lead me to the stocks. Instead, Taren appeared at the back of the wagon.

"This way," he said, helping me out.

My heart thrilled. There, across the Trine, were the pastures and fields surrounding my father's manor. I was home.

"It's been a long time," I said.

Taren led the way, but I could have walked the familiar passage-ways of the brooding fortress blindfolded—past the well-traveled cor-ridor to the interrogation room, down the hall and around the corner to my cell. Tiptoeing into the small room was like returning to an old friend after a long journey. Tears pricked my eyes as I glimpsed a patch of blue through the bars of the tiny window. The pallet was lumpier and smellier than I remembered, but it seemed like a feather mattress after the hard jolting wagon.

In the evening, Taren brought a dinner consisting of the same wee-vily fare and slimy turnips I remembered. He leaned against the wall as I picked at the food. For once, he did not urge me to eat.

"You don't deserve to die," he said, sounding bitter and angry. "And I'm not the only one who feels this execution is wrong. I tried to use what little influence I have left to have your sentence reduced, but the king would have none of it."

I raised an eyebrow. Was it possible Taren had the ear of the king?

"I could help you escape."

I considered his offer for the eternity of one exhalation. "You can't do that. After executing you, they would kill your wife out of spite, and then what would happen to your daughter and little son?" A baby boy had been born to him while we were in Pithark. Taren had not even seen him yet.

Taren turned away, agitated. "You didn't do anything wrong! How can I live with myself if I stand by and do nothing? I can't let them hang you."

"I won't let you sacrifice yourself and your family for me." I watched his unyielding back and tears welled in my eyes. I had not expected to find such a friend in a Sardonian uniform.

"I'm not afraid to die." Somehow, speaking the words made them true. "Besides, where would I go? Into the wilds of the north?"

"I can't watch them slip a noose around your neck," he said in a choked voice.

I understood, though I would miss his comforting presence.

"Go kiss your children for me."

He turned abruptly, his face twisted with emotion. He thrust a bat-tered satchel into my hands. "Here. Prisoners aren't supposed to have personal possessions, but they won't care now."

"This isn't mine," I said, shaking my head.

He shrugged. "The soldiers took it from your room. Besides, it has your name on it."

And so it did. 'Arabella' was stitched in flowing letters on the faded brocade.

"I hope it gives you some comfort." His voice sounded hollow.

"Thank you."

He nodded curtly, then closed and locked the door.

Where had the satchel come from? I traced the neatly stitched letters. Had Nanni done this...hoping I would get it? I opened the satchel and examined the contents. It held an unfamiliar shabby dress and a paper-wrapped parcel. I undid the fastening cord and emptied Nanni's tiger's eye brooch and the silver chain and key to my trunk into my hand. Taren had kept them safe for me during all the months in Pithark.

After fastening the key around my neck, I clasped the brooch in my hand and sank to the floor, gazing at the dust motes dancing in the sunlight. I would never marry, never watch my children run through the flowers in a garden, never grow old. I thought all the emotion had been wrung out of me during the endless journey back to Heyden, yet I mourned for the life I would never have. I curled up on the pallet and sobbed.

16

y cell was freezing when I woke. An unfamiliar soldier brought watery gruel for breakfast, which I declined to eat because of the black and brown flotsam riddling it. Weevil skeletons, I knew from long experience. I spent the morning huddled in a corner, watching thin wispy clouds scud across my tiny patch of sky.

At noon, a guard brought lunch, and I attempted to engage him in conversation. "What is happening in Heyden?"

His face impassive, he answered with a thick Sardonian accent, "They beeld the gallows. Hear?" He put a hand to his ear and cocked his head.

All morning, I had heard saws and banging hammers, but I had not realized what the racket imported. My appetite gone, I set the bowl aside.

The temperature rose throughout the day, and by afternoon water dripped steadily from the eaves. Nightfall brought a warm southerly wind and sounds of water trickling outside.

Light snow was falling when I woke the next day, but it changed to a steady drizzle midmorning. The hammering on the gallows ceased with the rain, but a new sound prevailed during the afternoon—river ice creaking and booming as it broke up.

Despite my pending execution, excitement coursed through me. The breaking of the ice signaled the beginning of spring—green pastures, nesting birds, fluffy lambs, and new foals were sure to follow. I longed for a glimpse of the outside world. I felt new life quickening all around.

The guard woke me the next morning with an insistent nudge from his booted toe. "Got a vissitor," he said harshly. Holding his nose, he scowled and backed away. The stench of the pillory still clung to my clothes and hair.

When I glimpsed Nanni's beloved face, I rushed into her arms despite my shackled wrists.

"Oh, me baby! I been tryin' to visit since you arrived, but they wouldn't let me in till this mornin'!" she cried, pulling me close in a tender hug. "The soldiers searched me, the nerve! Down to me very petticoats, they did—as if I might be smugglin' somethin'." She sniffed in outrage, squeezing me fiercely. I nestled my head against her, wishing my hands were free so I could cling to her. After several moments, she pulled back, wrinkling her nose.

I grinned. "Lovely, isn't it?"

"Goodness, gal! You smell as if you were burrowin' in a dung heap. An' I think yer hair might be alive."

"Probably."

"Jus' look at you! Yer freckles are gone, and you growed a couple of inches. An' yer hair..." She reached out to touch it.

I pulled away, eager to change the subject. "I missed you desperately in Pithark."

Her face turned stormy. "That gen'ral. He tol' me I couldn't go to Pithark lest I paid me own way. Oooooh, they could pay fer Pyrrin an' Dirk, but not fer good ol' Nanni," she fumed. "An' yer father! I asked him fer money, but he said I couldn't be spared from the manor. Such nonsense!"

"How *is* my father?"

Nanni snorted. "Oh, he screamed at Pyrrin till he was blue in the face, but I guess he saw which way the wind was blowin'. He fell over hisself in his rush to help Gen'ral Attark smear you. Made nary a fuss when they searched yer room an' everythin'." Her brows knitted in anger. "An' when they found you guilty..." I thought she might fall apart, but she collected herself. "When they declared you was to be hung, he disowned you! Claimed you was always an ungrateful miscreant. Yer own father declared you come from bad blood...!" Her lips quivered, and I placed a soothing hand on her arm.

"How is Dirk faring?"

She shook her head. "That boy! I don't know what to think of him no more."

"What do you mean?"

"After yer trial, he came to the manor, all mopey faced and hang dog like. He weren't nothin' but a bag of bones, ablowin' in the wind, yet he had some nerve," she sniffed.

I raised an eyebrow.

"He asked me to write a letter fer him apologizin' fer the way he treated you!" She sounded outraged. "I tol' him iffen he had somethin' to say to you, he could say it hisself."

An apology? From Dirk? I found it hard to believe. Still... "He did seem different at the trial."

"Hmmph. A snake may shed its skin, but it's still a snake. One thing is fer sure—Dirk an' yer brother have parted ways."

"Really?"

"Aye. When he found out Pyrrin turned over yer papers to the soldiers... He showed up one day, near 'bout to bust a vein, lookin' fer Pyrrin. Iffen yer brother had been home, I think the boy would've killed him. Dirk lit out of Heyden after that, an' we ain't seen him since."

I turned this information over in my head. "What about Pyrrin?"

"Pyrrin! That horrid boy! He's now a fav'rite of the gen'ral, an' a mister Curmyck took him under his wing." She spat.

"*Curmyck?*"

"That's the one. He decided to continue Pyrrin's education hisself. Even took him to Pithark to meet the high society." She rolled her eyes and clenched her fists. "When I think 'bout what that boy did, I could jus' wring his neck..."

I had not intended to start Nanni on a tirade. "Tell me all the news."

I perched on the corner of the table as she began a breathless whirlwind monologue about every possible piece of news in Heyden. Nanni thrived on gossip, and she brimmed with juicy tidbits about the villagers and everyday life in Heyden. When she told me about the carter's adorable new baby and how she worried when he caught the croup, I couldn't bear her chatter any longer. She was detailing the wonderful ordinariness of village life—a life that was gone forever.

My chest heaved, my throat constricted, and I moved to the window. Nanni's gaze followed mine, and her voice trailed off as we both stared at the grim view. The structure was finished. A man tied a noose around the neck of a straw dummy. He pulled a lever, a trapdoor opened, and the dummy fell, jerking with such ferocity that the head snapped off and rolled across the platform. Held by the noose, the body swayed gently for a moment before slumping in a crumpled heap on the ground.

"I hope my head stays put," I murmured in a flat voice, and Nanni gasped and began to sob. I turned away from the grisly sight and pressed on my eyes with my shackled hands. "When do I hang?"

She blinked and swiped at her tears, swallowing hard several times before she croaked, "Day after tomorrow, if the weather be fine."

I wouldn't live long enough to see my sixteenth birthday. I sank into the chair. Perhaps it would have been better not to know.

Nanni sniffled and blew her nose into a large handkerchief she produced from her bodice.

The door opened and a guard said harshly, "Time's up." He stood at attention, waiting.

Nanni clung to me and wept. The guard had to forcibly remove her hands. "I love you, Arabella!" she wailed as he led her away.

I sat dry-eyed in my cell all afternoon, unable to think coherently. My mouth was dry, and my chest hurt. Once again, I could not force myself to eat the revolting fare the guard brought in the evening. I lay on my pallet, emotionally spent, watching the tiny patch of sunlight traverse the room until it faded away with the sunset. The chill of evening settled over the cell, and numbness sank into my soul. I had less than two days to live.

~ † ~

I started up and pressed my back against the cell wall, listening for the sound that had woken me. The moon had yet to rise, and my window was barely visible in the starlight. From the depths of the fortress, I heard a muffled noise—a groan perhaps, shuffling feet and whispery sounds—then some thumps, possibly a scuffle, a dull thud that might have been a guard slumping to the floor, and finally the unmistakable clank of a weapon falling on flagstones. Soon the glow of a torch lit the corridor; after several long moments, it stopped outside my cell.

"Ah, here we are," said a pleasant female voice. "The keys, Talmage."

"Wait! Let me." This voice was male.

There was a brief pause followed by an orange flash, then the door creaked open, the bolts of the lock neatly severed.

"My spell worked!" the male said.

"So it did," the female answered. "But a gentler approach would have been equally effective, such as using the *keys*."

The woman stepped into the cell carrying a torch. She wore a pure white gown and a pale green sash. Snowy hair crowned clear blue eyes; she was none other than the striking woman from the gallery at Pithark.

A tall young man entered behind her. He had impeccably groomed black hair, dark eyes, a sharp nose, and high cheekbones. Though handsome, thin, pale lips and a weak chin detracted from his striking looks. He smirked as he studied me, his expression triumphant.

A second young man hovered behind them, clasping huge work-worn hands in front of him as he ducked powerful shoulders beneath the doorframe. He looked older than the first man but less sure of himself. He sported an unruly thatch of strawberry blond hair, gray eyes, a rounded nose, and a smattering of freckles.

I wanted to ask who they were, how they had opened the door... anything, but I was frozen in place, unable to blink, move, or speak.

"I hardly think she required a stunning spell, Mortimor," the woman scolded as she studied me.

Mortimor shrugged. "We've no time to explain ourselves now. Besides, I've always wanted to use one. Look at her—she can't move." He waved his hand back and forth in front of my face.

The woman frowned. "She *can* hear you. Stunning spells aren't to be used lightly."

He shrugged again and then made a gagging noise. "Uggh! Something in here reeks!" He pinched his nose between two delicate fingers.

"She does...from the pillory. Such a barbaric practice. Though after traveling a hundred leagues in those clothes, you don't smell so sweet yourself." She handed the torch to the red-haired man and knelt in front of me. "Poor lass. You needn't be afraid, dear." She gave a warm smile full of compassion. "What you need is sleep." She laid a smooth, cool hand on my forehead and murmured something unintelligible. My eyes closed, my body relaxed, and I was asleep.

<h1 style="text-align:center">17</h1>

aking was like climbing out of a deep dark pit. First, I heard an orchestra of birds, lapping water, and a crackling fire. Next, I inhaled wood smoke and grass—the fresh scents of spring. Morning dew misted my cheeks, and I opened my eyes. Two spitted birds sizzled over a fire, and the aroma brought saliva rushing into my mouth. I sat up, ferociously hungry after days of meager food. A wave of weakness assailed me, and I crumpled to the ground with a faint moan.

"Careful." The man with strawberry blond hair stepped around the fire and knelt beside me. "Sit up slowly."

"Who are you?" I croaked through dry, cracked lips.

His lips twitched in a shy smile. "You can call me Tal." He helped me to a sitting position. "Are you all right? Any dizziness or nausea?"

"I'm fine," I murmured, though I still felt faint.

"Are you hungry?"

"Ravenous," I said, eyeing the roasting meat.

He removed the birds from the spit, cut off several succulent slices, and laid them on a flat rock. After skewering the slices on a sharpened stick, he handed them to me. "I'm sorry we don't have better implements. We had to pack light."

The meat tasted of smoke and was juicy and moist. He prepared another skewer as I devoured the first.

"This is...delicious," I mumbled around a mouthful of bird. "I haven't had meat in...months." He handed me a cup of steaming tea, which I sipped while I scanned our surroundings. We were on the bank of the Trine, nestled in a protective growth of willow trees. Bushes, low scrub, and last year's rushes overhung the river. Swelling buds on the willows showed a hint of green at the tips, and in several places the curl of a new leaf peeked through the undergrowth. The river was clear of ice and swollen with melted snow, moving swiftly in its rush to the Great Lake.

Spring had come. Tears spilled down my cheeks as I gazed at the river for the first time in nearly a year. For many weeks, I had wondered if I would ever splash my feet in its chilly waters or trail my fingers across the rippling surface again.

Tal rose to tend the fire, and I studied him from beneath my damp eyelashes. His hair stood up as if he had rubbed it vigorously with a towel while it was still wet. He wore soiled tan breeches tied at the waist with a rawhide thong, a well-worn and patched brown tunic, and scuffed leather boots.

He caught my glance, and I turned away. He cleared his throat, but an uncomfortable silence stretched between us.

"Your friends...?"

"They're out reconnoitering. Morty fancies himself an expert out-doorsman, so Balissa took him along to fetch the boat."

I raised an eyebrow. "Balissa wore a white dress...and Morty opened the door?"

He looked confused. "I don't know about any white dress, but Morty did blast the door—showing off, of course. Morty does that... wanted Balissa to see his stunning skills. He's hoping word of his superior spellcasting will get back to Oryn." He scowled and scuffed the toe of his boot in the sandy ground. "Not that anything impresses *him*."

My head spun. "Spellcasting? Stunning skills? Who are you?"

"Enchanters...well...only Balissa is a real enchantress."

"Who is Oryn?"

"Our master. We...Morty and I...are his apprentices, which is what you'll be when we get back. If Oryn likes you. Balissa is his friend from Latretta."

"Talmage! Douse the fire!"

I jumped at the rich, melodic voice of the woman, Balissa. She had the same regal, ageless appearance, but she wore the simple homespun frock and gray hooded cloak I had seen the second time in the gallery.

"Egad!" Tal cried. "I forgot!" He stamped on the fire, scattering the burning embers.

The tall, black-haired young man leaned against a tree behind Balissa. "Just like you to forget, Tal. You'll bring a horde of soldiers down upon us." He sounded hopeful at the prospect.

"Mortimor!" Balissa said, a sharp edge to her voice. "We should never seek violence against others, no matter who they are."

His jaw clenched, and he toed a stone with his boot.

"Help him," Balissa added, nudging him with her walking stick. "Smother the fire. We don't want any smoke."

Turning to me, she smiled. "Hello, Arabella. I'm glad to see you awake. Have you eaten?"

I nodded.

"Good. We must be on our way. Soldiers are probably already in pursuit." She studied the makeshift camp. "Tal...Morty...clear up this mess and follow as soon as possible." She turned to me. "Come."

I stood carefully, thankful my knees did not buckle, and followed her to the riverbank. She steadied a small rowboat nestled among the rushes at the shoreline, and I climbed in. There was one seat in the pointed prow and a board across the blunt stern, but she gestured to a low bench in the center.

She sat beside me and produced a gray woolen cloak from beneath the bench. "This ought to keep you warm. Later, I'll find you some new clothes and help you get clean. We'll sit here and let the boys do the work."

While we waited for the 'boys,' I glanced around the boat. A burlap-wrapped bundle and two oars rested on the floor; a third oar lashed to the gunwale served as a makeshift tiller. A battered satchel was stowed under the stern seat beside several bedrolls and three packs, and a warped panel hid a compartment beneath the front seat.

"Don't worry. I procured your belongings for you," Balissa said, indicating the satchel.

I nodded my thanks.

Morty and Tal arrived at the water's edge. Tal offered me my neatly folded blanket as a cushion before he took his place in the stern. Morty plopped down in the bow, untied the boat from an overhanging bough, and aimed us downstream.

~ † ~

We drifted for a while before I found my voice. "Thank you for rescuing me."

Balissa smiled. "You don't seem too sure about that."

I ducked my head. "I...don't know who you are or why you rescued me...though I did see you at the trial."

Balissa's brow furrowed. "I noticed. I was surprised when you picked me out of the crowd."

"Your dress and stature made you...conspicuous."

"Really?"

"A tall woman wearing a white gown sticks out in a crowd of short, drab Sardonians. Your disguise the next day was much better."

Balissa raised an eyebrow.

Morty snorted. "What white gown? We haven't changed clothes since we left Red Castle. She just aged her face and hunched over during the trial."

That explained the age spots, moles, and wrinkles I had seen in the gallery, but my unreliable eyes had played tricks on me again.

"We attended the trial almost from the start, dear," Balissa said.

"You mean the circus."

She sighed. "It did resemble a side show more than a trial; unfortunately, I have come to expect that from Sardonian justice."

"Why were you at the trial?"

"Reports about you reached Oryn...quite a while ago, actually. He didn't pay much attention at first, but when you were imprisoned..." She laid a gentle hand on my arm. "He deemed it prudent to determine if there was any merit to the rumors. He sent the three of us to spirit you away to Red Castle."

"What rumors?"

"Hmm..." Balissa paused. "For one, he heard you are accomplished in Lattrian."

"Oh...why does he care if I know Lattrian?"

"Because Lattrian is the language of magic."

I exhaled in a huff. "I can't do any magic! Why does everyone think I can?"

She smiled. "Perhaps not, but you will still be helpful to Oryn if you can read Lattrian texts." She hesitated and pursed her lips before asking, "How fluent are you?"

I considered for a moment. "Fabius declared I was quite good."

Morty laughed. "What would an ignorant *Atrurian* schoolteacher know about fluency? We'll be lucky if she can read nursery rhymes."

Heat flooded my face, and I clenched my fists. "Fabius was *not* ignorant. He was a Lattrian master and a professor at a university!"

Balissa's voice took on a steely edge. "Mortimor often speaks thoughtlessly without regard for others' feelings. His scornful banter and cutting remarks bolster his ego. Be patient with him. I believe in time he will learn humility and kindness."

I shot him a look. Morty's ears were bright red.

We drifted for several minutes, and I leaned to the side and peeked over the edge, watching the greenish, foam-flecked water rush the boat downstream. "How did you get past the guards?"

Balissa laughed. "A combination of stealth and disguise, a couple of sleeping spells, a pilfered set of keys, and we were in."

"There was one guard who was kind to me..." I lifted my eyes to hers. "If they think he helped me escape, the general may execute him and his family."

She put a hand to her mouth. "Oh, I do hope he wasn't the soldier Morty knocked over the head." She leaned to the side in an attempt to catch Morty's eye. "Which was uncalled for, by the way."

I shook my head. "Taren wasn't on duty."

"Well, then don't fret. Given the...excessive nature of Morty's spell, I doubt very much your Taren—or any other Sardonian—will be implicated in your escape."

"You mentioned sleeping spells...is that what you used on me?"

She gave an impish grin. "They are effective...and quiet. Blasting your door added unnecessary flair, but Mortimor was aching to use that new spell he learned. A blunt instrument, but it did the trick."

"How else was I to practice?" Morty said in complaint. "My spellcasting was getting rusty." He flexed his fingers, and a burst of light whizzed into the river, making me nearly jump out of the boat.

"Mortimor! Now is not the time to show off," Balissa said, her voice stern.

Morty scowled, and I offered him an appeasing smile. "You and Tal are Oryn's apprentices?"

"I am the most talented apprentice Oryn will ever have," Morty said.

"And the most arrogant..." Tal muttered.

"'Tisn't arrogance if it's true." Morty's expression was smug.

"That is quite enough," Balissa said. To me she added, "Despite their squabbling, they do manage to help Oryn with Red Castle."

"Red Castle...is that on the Lorne River?"

"Yes," Balissa said. "'Tis one of nine fortresses built generations ago to defend Latretta and Atruria."

"Fabius said many of the castles are lost, but...how can someone lose a castle?"

"He taught you well. Powerful enchantments protect the castles, making them invisible and inaccessible to those not privy to their secrets and locations. Unfortunately, over the years many of those secrets were forgotten. Sometimes the enchanters and apprentices guarding the strongholds were killed in battle, taking their locations with them."

I frowned. "If the strongholds were invisible, how were the stones of Fort Grey scavenged to build a Sardonian fortress?"

"Ahh. Fort Grey wasn't protected by magical spells. While your fort fell into ruins, Red Castle has survived for generations. 'Tis always tenanted by a powerful enchanter...a bastion against the forces of evil, if you will."

"Oryn is the 'powerful enchanter?'"

"One of the best," Balissa said.

A hundred questions flooded my mind. What if he didn't like me, or I proved worthless to him? Would he regret sending Balissa and his apprentices to rescue me? Might he even send me back to Heyden? I shuddered as a vision of a straw dummy slumping to the ground passed before my eyes.

Balissa wrapped a reassuring arm around my shoulders. "You have nothing to fear, my dear. Oryn is a kitten disguised as a lion. He bloviates and bellows, but he's loyal to a fault. He will defend those in his care with his life."

For the first time in months, a thrill surged through me. I was free! No gallows, no chains, no bars, and no revolting prison fare overshadowed my future.

At the thought of food, my stomach rumbled and gurgled.

"I'm starving," I murmured.

Balissa turned from gazing upriver and smiled. "Perhaps we can do something about that. Talmage, have we anything for Arabella to eat?"

I glanced back at him, and he nodded. His calloused hand never left the tiller as he effortlessly yanked a pack out from beneath the board. He rummaged through the contents and pulled out a small packet wrapped in a napkin. He turned pink and nearly dropped the bundle when I reached for it.

"Thank you," I said softly. He blushed even harder and ducked his head. He must have had little contact with females if I made him react this way. I faced forward again, smiling slightly; there was something endearing about his painful shyness.

I unwrapped the napkin to reveal a slab of shortbread flavored with nuts, honey, and dried fruit. It had a sweet delicate flavor.

"Don't eat too much," Balissa warned. "The cake is filling."

I obeyed, eating only a small piece. She was right. I felt full, then pleasantly sleepy.

Balissa must have noticed my drooping eyelids. "Why don't you curl up on the bottom of the boat and rest?"

I snuggled into my cloak, using a bedroll as a pillow. The gentle rocking of the boat, warm sunshine, and water lapping against the hull lulled me to sleep.

18

hey're here, Balissa!"

Tal's urgent whisper woke me. I glanced toward our wake and gasped. A sleek craft was coming into view around a bend in the river. A sergeant sat at the helm, and a double row of uniformed soldiers stood at attention behind him. Lances bristled over their shoulders, glinting in the sunlight. Built for the speedy transport of a dozen soldiers up and down the river, the Sardonian skiff flew over the water with each dip and pull of the six oarsmen.

A cry rose to my lips, but Balissa hushed me with a shake of her head. She nodded at Tal, and he steered our boat skillfully toward the calmer water near the shore. Balissa murmured several unintelligible words, and a look of intense concentration came over her face. The hair on the back of my neck prickled and stood on end, as if lightning charged the air. I heard—or rather felt—a faint tingling, and as I peeped over the gunwale at the oncoming craft, wisps of silvery mist drifted across the edges of my vision.

My heart thumped, and I held my breath as the skiff bore down on us. They had to have spotted us by now; at any moment, they would give a shout of triumph. Incredibly, the oarsmen maintained their steady rhythm. They were scarcely twenty feet away as they drew abreast, yet the helmsman continued his ceaseless scanning of the river as the boat swept out of sight around a bend in the Trine.

"They never saw us!" I cried breathlessly. "How could they just row by...?" I trailed off as Morty snorted.

Balissa's tense face relaxed, and my goose pimples subsided. She cast a warning glance in Morty's direction. "You did well, Arabella. Thank you."

"But...why didn't they spot us?"

Balissa laughed. "All in good time, dear. We should stop for lunch."

While Balissa and I lugged water from the river to fill a large kettle, Morty and Tal searched for sticks and built a fire. Balissa sent Tal off to replenish our firewood supply and suggested that Morty try his hand at hunting. He wandered off, a quiver of arrows and a huge bow slung over his shoulder...no doubt the contents of the bundle in the boat.

After we ate shortbread, Balissa leaned back against a rock and curled her hands around a steaming cup of tea. "Now for those questions of yours."

I leaned forward, squeezing my cup tightly. "Why didn't the soldiers see us?"

"I was hiding the stern all morning, but when Tal saw the Sardonians, I placed a masking spell around the entire boat."

I blinked. "How does a masking spell work?"

"It fools the eye."

"So...when they spied our boat..." I frowned. "They saw...something else?"

"Exactly! Instead of a boat with four passengers, we were a log floating low in the water. Hence they steered clear."

"What if they *had* run into us?"

Balissa grimaced. "They would have destroyed our boat and discovered us."

"And if they had...?"

She gave a wry smile. "I prefer to avoid drastic measures."

Fabius had assured me magic was real. Still, I was enthralled and amazed by what I had witnessed...and felt. "The static...the tingling feeling...was that from your spell?"

Balissa raised an eyebrow. "You felt something?"

"Umm." I wished I had not been so eager to expose my ignorance. "It was a notion I had."

"And correct, at that." She gazed at me, cocking her head. "Few people can detect a masking spell. If you did sense it, 'twould be a rare gift indeed." She rose to stir the water in the kettle, checking its temperature with a few drops on her wrist. "I think this is warm enough for a bath."

"Here? Now?"

She set up a rickety screen with some sticks and a blanket. "Don't worry. I'll make sure we are discreet." She gestured towards the wildness, and I felt the familiar tingling again.

"You put a spell around us," I said, laughing.

She grinned, flashing perfect white teeth. "Now the wildlife won't spy on us."

"What about the boys?" I said, halting in my undressing.

"They will be busy for a good long while."

"What if they return?"

Balissa laughed. "I made us look like a bathhouse with a 'Do Not Enter upon Penalty of Transformation' sign. They'll stay away." She scanned my anxious face and said, "I'm sure this is new and unsettling for you. Let's have a quick bath, and then I'll comb your hair for nits."

After secreting my brooch in the folds of my cloak, I took off my filthy, ragged dress, which she promptly burned. I was still self-conscious, but I sat on a smooth rock, and she helped me sponge-bathe. It took a long time to remove the caked filth from the pillory. When I was reasonably clean, I wrapped a towel around myself, and she scrubbed my hair and scalp with a sweet smelling soap. I curled my toes and stretched, delighted to be clean and shiny for the first time in weeks. After I dressed in a simple smock and fastened my cloak around me, I sat on a rock while she deloused my scalp and hair with a fine-toothed comb.

A question burned on the tip of my tongue, but Morty had mocked me earlier, and I did not want to appear foolish. "Ummm," I began.

"Yes, dear?" she said sweetly.

I hunched in my cloak and fingered the hem. "In the gallery at the trial...you never wore a white dress, did you?"

A smile creased her face. "I did not. But set aside your misgivings. I think you will be a charming surprise to Oryn. You may have been raised in a world devoid of magic, but you belong with us."

I wanted to believe her.

After she disbanded the bathhouse and dumped the water, Tal returned with a mammoth bundle of firewood strapped to his back. Such a burden would have crippled another man, but he bore it as if it were no heavier than one of the packs stowed in the boat. He glanced my way as he tossed the wood down, and then looked again, his eyes widening.

I reddened and murmured tartly, "Didn't you know my hair was carrot-colored under all the dirt?"

"I didn't mean to stare. You look different, that's all. Cleaner...and... beautiful," he stammered, flushing crimson.

"Beautiful? I imagine you don't encounter lasses often if you call *me* beautiful."

"'Twas meant as a compliment."

"Keep your compliments for someone who cares for them!" I fled toward Balissa. Why would he say such a thing to me? I shook my head to clear it as I tidied up the campsite.

Balissa and I had packed the boat and helped Tal extinguish the fire before Morty finally returned, a small hare dangling from his hand.

"There you are!" Balissa said. "When I sent you out, I didn't expect you to play in the woods all afternoon. Arabella, stow the hare in a sack. We should continue downriver."

I reached out to take the hare, but Morty stood frozen, gawking at me just as Tal had. I snatched the hare from his hand.

"Don't say anything," Tal warned. "She about bit my head off..."

I already regretted my hasty reaction. Tal seemed kind and honest... nothing like Dirk or Prell. Perhaps he had been sincere—even if he *was* a woeful judge of beauty. I gave Tal what I hoped was an apologetic smile. "Don't mind me. I've been in a cell for months and months. It may take me awhile to readjust to civilization."

"I'm sorry if I said something..." he mumbled.

Balissa brushed his sleeve, and he fell silent.

We took our places in the boat, and Morty pushed off. After drifting for a moment, the swift current caught the skiff and sent us hurtling downstream. Tal steered expertly, guiding the boat past snags and choosing the smoothest route. Balissa seemed much more relaxed; she reclined against a pack and dozed off.

Morty was still eyeing me. After awhile he said, "I cannot believe Sarduk was going to hang you. I should think he would rather have added you to his harem."

Balissa's eyes shot open. "Mortimor! Besides the fact that Sarduk doesn't possess a harem, that is the most tactless, ignorant, and offensive remark I have ever heard you utter!"

Morty hitched sideways in his seat so he did not have to look at her, but his neck turned crimson.

"If you can't curb your tongue... 'Tisn't appropriate to speak every word that comes to mind." Balissa's expression was troubled.

Not even Morty could dampen my enthusiasm. I leaned over the side of the boat, gazing into the rushing water as intense happiness bubbled inside me. I was alive! I was free! The future stretched before me rich with promise. I grinned and trailed my hand over the side of the boat. The icy meltwater left me breathless; my hand burned like fire, as if a hundred needles pricked it. I withdrew my hand and watched in delight as droplets sheared off my fingertips.

I spent some time repeating this performance—dangling my hand until I could not take the cold, and then watching droplets splash on the frothy surface as feeling slowly returned. Then plunging my hand and arm back into the river.

"'Tis fine here, but I wouldn't do that once we reach the Great Lake," Tal said.

"Why not?"

"Your fingers might look like bait."

"The whole boat may look like bait," Morty retorted from the bow.

"Ancient creatures live in the Great Lake," Balissa said, removing a sleeve from her face and sitting up.

"But if the lake is so dangerous..."

"Why are we going there!" Morty finished in disgust. "We've left Atruria behind, so we don't have to hide our magic anymore. I don't know why we can't just open a portal."

"Who would close it behind us?" Tal asked. "You know the rules, Morty. No portals in uncharted or hostile areas."

"They ought not to apply in this situation," Morty said, glaring at Tal. "The *rules* will only serve to blister our feet, dirty our clothes, and turn us into dragon fodder or monster chum. All this dangerous travel, when we could simply step through..."

"Very well," Balissa interrupted, leaning forward. "Go ahead."

Morty's eyes widened.

"And you can stay behind to close it," she added.

He scowled.

Turning to me, she said, "As long as we stay at the edge of the lake, we shouldn't be in danger. Besides," she paused, winking, "we are not venturing out on the lake unprotected. We have Morty the Great Apprentice to stun things for us."

He folded his arms across his chest and turned red.

"A little humility goes a long way," she said to him. "You have skill, but lack control. And your blatant disregard for the tenets of magic..."

He snorted and turned his back. Balissa sighed and fell silent.

We halted when the deepening dusk made it difficult for Tal to navigate safely. Balissa deemed us far enough from civilization to risk a fire, so after mooring the boat, Tal went in search of firewood again. I thought fleetingly of the huge stack he had collected earlier.

Morty dressed the hare while Balissa devised a makeshift spit. Sooner than I could have hoped, we had a merry fire crackling, and the enticing aroma of sizzling rabbit and roasting potatoes reminded me that I was famished. Balissa stewed some turnips, which I gracefully declined.

I filled myself to bursting with the savory hare and hot, delicious potatoes. Then I curled into a ball, covered myself with a blanket, and drifted to sleep, lulled by a full stomach and Balissa and Tal's muffled conversation.

19

he Great Lake was still and calm in the deepening dusk. Half the full moon had risen over the eastern rim of the lake.

"We must turn back, sir! The open lake is not safe!" A nervous lieutenant gripped the side of the boat so tightly his knuckles turned white with the strain.

"The moon is full," the commanding officer said, gesturing. "We can continue our search. They cannot be far ahead."

"But we don't know where they went. We may have missed them on the river, and the lake..."

"What about the lake?" The officer's words were clipped and short.

"It's not safe!" The lieutenant's eyes flitted over the surface, straining to see any faint ripple that might bode their doom. "The monster and the maelstrom..."

"Ha!" the officer snorted. "Enough of your superstitious babble. It's just a big lake. A really big..."

A commotion broke out among the oarsmen. "Look!" one of them shouted, pointing. To starboard, swirling bubbles were breaking on the surface. With them came an odor of death and decay. Tiny whirlpools were forming; bubbles collected around the boat, and an eerie phosphorescent glow lit up the water. As the bubbles burst, bringing a sulfurous stench, the lieutenant shrieked in panic. Ripping off his sword, buckler, and coat, he dove headfirst into the lake, surfacing fifteen feet from the boat. He swam madly toward the dark, distant shore.

The boat erupted in pandemonium. The officer screamed for order, but oarsmen and soldiers scrambled over each other. The boat rocked back and forth violently, and then capsized, throwing men and weapons into the lake. The men, yelling and shouting, tried to clamber aboard the slippery hull. They grappled and fought with one another. Some of the soldiers, including the commanding officer, could not swim; their sodden *clothing and heavy weapons dragged them below the surface. One man, thrown farther than the rest, was caught in a whirlpool. The eddy carried him around and around, shrieking, until he slipped underwater with a last gurgling wail. Two men struck out after the lieutenant for the nearest shore, several clung to the hull, and a couple more treaded water around the capsized boat.*

The surface roiled, a geyser spewed muck, then something flailed and splashed around the boat. The remaining men screamed; the hull flew twenty feet through the air, splintering into fragments as it struck the lake. Water frothed around the men, and they disappeared beneath the surface.

By the time the lower edge of the moon rose above the rim, not a single ripple disturbed its reflection on the mirrored surface of the lake.

Sweaty and shaken, I sat up, hugging my knees. I shook my head to clear the image of drowning soldiers and waited until a full moon rose over the rocky plateau to the east. Too early in the year for night creatures and insects, the rushing gurgle of the Trine River hurrying north to the Great Lake reverberated in my head. I shivered and threw a handful of sticks on the smoldering embers before lying down again.

~ † ~

The first predawn twittering of a bird roused me. Stars faded in the east as the purple sky turned brilliant shades of pink, orange, and magenta. I stretched, savoring the warmth of my bedroll. The others were still sleeping, so I rose and wrapped my cloak around me, scanning the cliffs to the east.

The Trine River had worn a sizable canyon through the plateau, and steep bluffs rose on either side of the river. Detecting what appeared to be an animal path leading out of the gorge, I trotted off, hoping to catch a view of the sunrise from the top. After a hard, rocky climb of seventy feet or more to the summit, I was blowing hard. I scrambled to the top of the highest boulder in time to watch the leading edge of the brilliant disk push above the eastern horizon.

The view was worth the climb. Twenty feet below my perch the plateau stretched east and west, covered in dry brown grass. Winter storms had flattened huge patches of the chest-high stalks, but green sward peeped through the bracken. I had heard men talk of the Sea of Grass, but I had not known how to imagine it until now. In summer, this would be an ocean of green, dotted with brilliant patches of wild-flowers. The grass would billow like swells in the quickening breezes, scarred only by a rim of rock jutting into the sky, marking the gorge snaking along its back.

The land sloped away sharply to the northeast. Beyond a dense dark smudge to the north, the land lay flat and gray.

The sun rose higher, and the flat gray land turned pink, then yellow. The smudge partially hid the edge, but there was no mistaking the lake's massive silvery surface stretching to the horizon. Images from the nightmare flooded my head, and I shivered.

"Scared of the lake, are you?"

I whipped around. Morty was perched on a boulder watching me intently, head cocked to one side.

"What are you doing here?" I demanded. I hadn't heard him, and the image of a cat stalking a helpless mouse came unbidden to my mind's eye.

"Sorry to startle you." He leapt from his rock and landed beside me, reinforcing the image of the cat and mouse.

I drew my cloak around me in a protective gesture and gazed at the lake. The sunrise glinted off the surface. It looked quiet and peaceful.

"Are you frightened?" he asked.

"Should I be?"

"Oh, yes." Morty plopped down on the rock at my feet and lazily stretched his long, lean frame.

I took the opportunity to study his face. He was impossibly handsome, but a shroud of dark unshaven whiskers coupled with his bored, petulant pout and ill humor spoiled his looks.

"Any person of good sense stays off the lake." He broke a dead stalk from a stray weed growing in a crevice and dissected its layers.

I cleared my throat. "What do you think happened to the boatload of soldiers?"

"Well, they were either stupid enough to be sucked into the maelstrom, or they were eaten by the monster of the lake." He crushed the remaining stalk in his hands and flung it away. The tangled mess landed only a few yards away, and with a snarl he picked up a rock and hurled it after the stalk. "Or, they stayed off the lake and are waiting to ambush us when we get down there."

For once, I knew he was serious.

He leapt to his feet. "Come on. Balissa sent me to fetch you." He set off along the rim of the gorge, away from the steep track I had climbed.

"Isn't the path that way?" I asked, pointing to the right.

Morty shrugged. "Go ahead...if you want to slip and fall on your backside. But there's an easier way down in this direction."

Heat rose to my cheeks as I followed him.

The descent—which *was* decidedly easier than my climb—brought us to a switchback overlooking a sweeping curve in the river upstream. A glint of sunlight drew my attention to the riverbank. I stared, trying to decipher what I was seeing. "Is that a boat?"

"Where?" Morty demanded.

"There, moored at the river's edge beneath the overhanging branches," I said, pointing.

Morty's eyes narrowed as he sighted along my finger.

Another reflection flashed between the trees, and Morty's breath hissed. "Soldiers," he said. "They must have dispatched a second boat." His brow puckered and he glanced down the path for a moment, then back again.

"Should we get Balissa?" I couldn't keep my voice from trembling.

Morty's jaw set. "No." His hand closed over a knife belted at his waist. "I'll take care of them."

"What are you going to do?"

"Lead them straight to you, of course," he said, his voice laced with sarcasm.

My eyes widened, and he snorted. "I'm going to put a big hole in their boat." He gestured down the path. "Go back to camp. I'll be there soon."

"Are you certain...?"

He thrust out his chest. "I am the grandson of the most powerful spellcaster in all of Latretta. I can take care of a few measly soldiers." His eyes darkened as he leaned close. "And there's no need to worry Balissa."

"Morty..."

"Go!" he yelled. With a grunt, he plunged off the switchback, scrabbling and sliding down the steep bank of the gorge, using brush and stunted trees to arrest his descent.

My heart pounding, I scurried down the path.

Tal was stirring the fire when I reached the campsite. "Hey! There you are." He glanced behind me. "Where's Morty? Didn't he find you?"

"Umm..." I kneaded my fingers into the rough wool of my cloak. "He...went down a different way." It was technically the truth, but my stomach still churned.

Balissa shook her head. "He was supposed to fetch you, not go exploring." She smiled at me. "Did you find a good view?"

"Yes, ma'am. Spectacular."

She shouldered a bedroll, and I did the same, shadowing her to the boat.

"I'm sorry to have disturbed your sightseeing, but we need to get an early start. 'Tis a full day's journey from here to the lake."

"Do we *have* to go out on the lake?"

"Are you still worried, dear?" She took the bedroll from me and stowed it securely, then reached out and brushed my forehead. "You are, aren't you? Tal! Go find Mortimor. We need to get moving."

Tal set out upstream, splashing through the shallows where overhanging bushes crowded the shore.

Balissa and I took our places in the boat and waited in silence. In only a few minutes, Tal and Morty strode into view around the bend.

"Where have you been?" Balissa called as they neared the boat. "We should have pushed off already."

His eyes locked on mine for a moment. Then he shrugged. "I had to take care of business."

Balissa sighed. "A little warning would have been nice."

As the boys climbed aboard, Balissa asked, "Are you hungry?" I nodded, and she broke off a small piece of shortbread. "We'll stop mid-morning for a proper meal, but this will have to do for now." She parceled out small amounts and brushed the crumbs from her faded skirt.

"Look, Arabella. I'll show you." Balissa produced a cylinder of parchment from a pocket and unrolled it to reveal a hand-drawn map.

The small parchment was only eighteen inches long by six wide. At the bottom was Heyden on Trine; the Great Lake filled the top left corner. Between the two ran a detailed drawing of the Trine River with all its twists and turns.

Balissa pointed to a spot midway down the river. "This is where we are now. Soon the plateau will end, and we'll exit this gorge onto a sandy, barren plain filled with rocks and bushes. Then we reach the Dead Forest." She indicated a ring of glyphs around the border of the lake. "We only have to circle the edge of the lake to the eastern rim. The Dead Forest is flooded and impassable, and the plain is dusty. 'Twould add days to our trip to avoid the lake. Besides, we won't go past the shadow of the trees, and real danger lies in deep water. After skirting the lake, we'll make our way on foot down the face of the rim to the Lorne River."

Only a small portion of the Lorne River emerged from the Great Lake on the top right corner of the map. It was little more than a scrawled squiggle ending at a red crown.

"After that we must cross the Lorne Valley, which will be the longest and most difficult part of the journey." Balissa studied the river in front of us.

"Where did you get this map?"

"Oryn made it for me. 'Tis a strip map, and though the Trine section is almost perfect, the Lorne is not to scale." She pointed to the squiggle. "We'll spend a great deal more time trekking through the wasteland than drifting on the Trine."

"Is that our destination?" I asked, pointing to the crown.

Balissa nodded.

The symbol tugged at my memory. "Why is a crown used to represent Red Castle?"

"Each of the nine fortresses was represented by a colored crown, except Fort Grey."

I laughed. "Why? Wasn't it good enough to warrant a crown?"

"I suppose you could say that. 'Twas the only one called a fort, and 'twas garrisoned with troops instead of enchanters. Fort Grey was never intended to host the king of Latretta." Balissa sighed. "Latrettans of old were snobby that way. Unfortunately, many of them still are. They view those who are unaccomplished in magic as inferior. Such ideas brought suffering for both nations and contributed to the collapse of the alliance between Latretta and Atruria." Balissa stared into the distance. Then she rolled up the strip map and returned it to her pocket.

I considered what she had said. In Atruria, people were superstitious because of ignorance, and cruel because of superstition. In Latretta, people were proud of knowledge, understanding, and magic. But to hold Atrurians in contempt for their ignorance...? I did not know which was worse—cruelty based on ignorance, or contempt based on knowledge. Yet sometimes the poorest, most ignorant people were the noblest, and sometimes the richest and most fortunate were the most contemptible.

By late afternoon, we reached the end of the gorge. One moment, canyon walls soared fifty feet above our heads, the next, only a narrow strip of cattails and scrub separated the river from the dry, rocky wilderness beyond. We had reached the wasteland.

"Let's find a place to camp," Balissa said.

The evening sun cast long shadows over the water. We moored the boat and made camp close to the river.

~ † ~

The small fire Tal had built had grown cold when my eyes fluttered open. I sat up in my bedroll and gazed into the darkness, wondering what had woken me. Gauzy clouds shrouded the sky, reducing the moonlight to a pale, ghostly glow. A shadow melted away from the scrub and knelt at the water's edge, accompanied by the rattle of last year's cattails. A quick glance told me Morty's bedroll was empty.

I rolled out of my blankets and padded across the damp grass towards the riverbank.

"Morty?" I called softly. "Is that you?"

"Gah!" The shadow jumped and something splashed into the water. Morty swore softly under his breath. He retrieved an object from the river and wiped it on his breeches. "Creep up on me again and you're liable to get a blade in your gut."

"Sorry. I didn't mean to scare you."

The watery moonlight glinted off his knife as he stowed it at his waist.

I eyed him. "What were you doing with the knife?"

"Trimming my fingernails," he said tartly. "Go back to sleep. We'll have to shove off soon enough."

As I curled up in my bedroll, I wondered what he had *really* been doing with his knife.

20

I awoke bleary-eyed when Balissa shook me in the predawn. "Hurry. We need to be off the lake before nightfall."

We tumbled into the boat. After eating a quick breakfast of bread and drinking from the river, Balissa and I rested. I jumped when Tal nudged me with his toe.

"Look," he whispered.

Morning fog obscured our surroundings, but just ahead, a wall of massive conifers hundreds of feet tall emerged from the mist. They began abruptly, as if a giant finger had drawn a line in the earth and forbidden the trees to cross. We drifted into the misty gloom of the massive forest, overhanging branches creating arches above our heads. Huge buttress roots spread out at ground level, some ten feet across at the base. The earth was clothed in moss and ferns, and the rocks glistened with damp.

"We've reached the lake," Balissa said, rousing. "Time to row, boys."

The river slowed as it widened and fanned out into the forest, lapping at the buttress roots. Balissa and I took Tal's place at the tiller, and he and Morty took turns rowing. Tal was stronger and more skillful, sending our light craft leaping over the water with each stroke.

"This forest is amazing," I said, gazing at the trees towering above us.

"According to legend, this was once the grandest forest in the world. Ages ago, this lake was a huge volcano spewing lava and ash. When the volcano died, this forest grew in the rich soil. Over time, the mountain sank into itself, leaving a huge bowl covered in trees. As the bowl formed, the Trine flooded the forest, and the Great Lake was born." Balissa gestured at the trees. "This is all that remains of the Dead Forest."

"It doesn't look dead to me," I said.

"Only a few trees around the rim of the lake survive."

Water spread in all directions. As we went farther, more tree roots were underwater, and skeletons and snags thinned the dense trunks. Sunlight increased as denuded branches took the place of the leafy canopy, and then we broke through the last row of dead trunks and entered the lake.

The sun had burned through the mist while we were in the forest, and the water sparkled in the sunlight. The lake was exactly as I imagined the ocean would appear—never-ending water and a disappearing shoreline. In the distance, on the western shore, the horizon swallowed a dark, hazy stripe of trees. To the east, the tree line faded, and endless water met endless sky. A smudge directly ahead on the horizon resembled an island, a cloud...or perhaps nothing.

"Stay clear of the trees, boys, but don't go out too far," Balissa said, her voice taut. "Keep your eyes peeled. Pick up the pace, but don't wear yourselves out. We need to reach the landing area before dark."

The edge in her tone made me nervous. The danger had to be greater than she had indicated earlier.

I scanned the surface of the lake but saw no evidence of the Sardonian boat. Occasionally, a fish jumped and cascading ripples fanned out until the surface absorbed them. Besides the swish of the oars, the surface of the lake stretched quiet and peaceful.

"I'm surprised there isn't any ice on the lake. The Trine broke up only a few days ago," I said.

"The lake never freezes. The edges crust over, but the center is kept open all year by warm springs bubbling to the surface." Balissa dipped her hand in the water and let several droplets fall on my palm. "'Tis not nearly as cold as the Trine."

I peered into the murky depths, but I could see nothing. Tannin released by the trees stained the water black.

"Over there," Balissa said, pointing toward the northeast.

Tal balanced the boat while Morty gingerly stood up, scanning the surface. "That's a big one." He grunted as he sat down again.

Balissa nodded. "All right, we can switch now. Arabella, can you row?"

"Of course." I traded places with Tal and plied the oars. Though gratified I remembered how to row, I grew tired quickly. A year in prison had sapped my stamina.

"What did you see?" I asked when Morty took my place.

"A whirlpool."

"Was it...the maelstrom?"

"Oh no, dear," Balissa laughed. "That's the stuff of legends. The maelstrom is supposed to be near the center of the lake. That was just a whirlpool."

"What *is* the maelstrom?"

"The water in this lake exits through a hole in the eastern rim, rather than over the top," Balissa answered. "Legend says a powerful maelstrom sucks down anything that has the misfortune of getting too close. Trappers and fishermen never go out far from the shore."

"Very wise of them," Morty said. "This lake has other dangers besides a giant whirlpool that sucks you into the abyss."

Balissa ignored him. "'Tis said the maelstrom spawns smaller vortexes and whirlpools that appear out of nowhere on this lake. They are usually in deep water." She gestured toward the center of the lake. "Occasionally a small one shows up in the shallows, but never within the ring of trees. The huge influx of cold water in the spring seems to generate whirlpools like the one we just passed. Of course, the underwater springs and geysers can be dangerous, too." She laughed tightly. "The only certainty is that the surface of the lake is unpredictable."

"Comforting, isn't it?" Morty said, scoffing softly.

"Don't be a worry monger, Morty. As long as we stay in the shallows and are off the lake by sundown, we'll be perfectly safe."

"And if we aren't?" I asked.

"Only the very brave, the very foolish, or the very desperate go out on the lake at night," Morty said.

The four of us rowed steadily. Tal seemed tireless, sending the boat hurtling over the surface with each powerful stroke of his oars. We hugged the tree line, staying within twenty yards of the last row of snags. Here and there, a huge, ancient trunk sprouted in deeper water, though only the upper branches of the tallest and broadest trees still stood after all the centuries. I used them as landmarks to gauge our progress across the lake. In mid afternoon, a flash of color on a snag twenty yards out caught my eye.

"Look!"

Tal rested the oars, and we stared in silence. Wedged in a fork of the sun-bleached tree was a dead man. Morty steered the boat nearer, and I saw from the shredded remains of his uniform that he was a Sardonian soldier. Flies and insects buzzed around welts on his head and bare torso. His eyes were open; a horrible grimace contorted his face. I shuddered, and Tal moved the boat away.

"What happened to him?" I asked.

"Something nasty," Morty said gleefully.

"Mortimor!" Balissa said.

He made a face.

"I suppose we don't need to wonder about the soldiers anymore," she said.

"Maybe some of them survived."

"Maybe," Balissa said, though she sounded doubtful.

~ † ~

I dozed in the warm sunshine until a soft fluttering woke me. Perched on the gunwale was the largest insect I had ever seen. As long as my hand, huge gray wings lay folded across its back. It had long antennae and a pair of curved pincers nearly an inch long. I sat up slowly, eyeing the creature.

"Tal!" I said softly. "Look at this huge bug."

He paused his rowing and leaned over for a closer inspection. "'Tis big."

The bug flexed its wings and took off right towards me. Its huge wings tangled in my hair. I cringed and batted at it.

Balissa sat up, woken by my movement. "Be still, child." I gripped the bench until my knuckles turned white as Balissa extricated the helpless insect. "Hmmm," she mused, studying it as she held it between her thumb and index finger. "A thrimblefly. How strange that it would be out at this time of year." She released it, and the bug fluttered drunkenly away before plummeting into the lake, its wings too damaged to fly.

It struggled on the surface until a silvery fish leapt from the water, ending its misery.

"That's the biggest bug I've ever seen," I said.

"They are rare in their adult form. The larvae, called thrimblites, live for three years underwater until they emerge as an adult. Adult thrimbleflies live only a week before they lay their eggs and die." Balissa frowned. "Usually they don't emerge until midsummer."

"They must have epic battles with those gigantic pincers," Morty said.

"Not every weapon is used for fighting, Morty. In this case, they are solely to impress females."

Morty snorted.

"Although the females *can* bite, and they both emit a horrible stench when attacked." She lifted her fingers to her nose and sniffed gingerly. "Phew!"

I switched positions with Tal, enjoying the exertion of rowing. Dip... pull...lift...rest. And then I watched droplets slice off the blades into the lake. Dip...pull...lift...rest. The rhythmic monotony was relaxing.

As I rowed, a curious cloud in the distance caught my attention. It whirled over the water, expanding and contracting as it approached. "What is that?"

The others turned to look. Balissa watched the writhing cloud, frowning. Suddenly she cried, "Everybody down, into the boat, and cover yourselves!"

Tal was already squatting on the floor, so I squeezed in next to him. I lifted my head to stare at the approaching cloud, and I realized it was a swarm of thrimbleflies. Thousands upon thousands of them massed in a swirling knot inches above the surface of the lake.

They were almost upon us, but I stared, frozen in horror, until Tal grabbed me and pulled his cloak over our heads. The next moment, the angry whine of a million wings rushed over us. I felt some thud into the cloak, and I bit my lip to stifle a whimper. Cold bilge water soaked my skirts as I lay with my cheek pressed against the rough wool of Tal's tunic. Tal's heart pounded, and I concentrated on its terrific thumping as the insects whined overhead and smacked into the sides of the boat. I grabbed a handful of his tunic and burrowed my face deeper into his chest, willing the awful noise to stop.

Finally, the torrent of insects stilled to an aimless fluttering, and we sat up. Hundreds of dead or dying thrimbleflies littered the boat, and the water in the wake of the swarm teemed with struggling insects and feasting fish. They gave off a horrible stench, and I gagged and shuddered as I gingerly picked them off the bench so I could resume rowing.

"I'll do it," Tal said, his voice taut.

"Are you all right?" I asked. His face was as red as his hair, and his gray eyes seemed darker than normal.

"I'm fine. I'll row," he said roughly. He took me by the shoulders and set me aside, then swept away the dead insects and grabbed the oars.

Morty, who had just extricated himself from Balissa's cloak, gave a low hooting whistle. I glared at him, and he winked at me.

"For goodness sake!" I hollered. "You can't make fun of people for being afraid."

He raised an eyebrow, and I stabbed at the dead insects with my toe. "Tal doesn't like bugs. I'm not overly fond of them myself, and you probably aren't either. To mock him for being agitated during a swarm is...is..." I searched for the right word. "*Despicable!*" His behavior reminded me too much of my experiences with Dirk. I was cranky and wet, and Morty's insensitivity was infuriating.

"Behave yourself," Balissa told him.

Morty swiped the bugs off the seat in the prow. "She's a firebrand," he said to Balissa. "Oryn should just *love* her."

A faint smile played around Balissa's lips. I huddled on the floor of the boat, shivering. A cloak draped around my shoulders, and I offered a shy smile of thanks to Tal. His distress seemed to have passed.

As the sun sank steadily toward the horizon, Balissa grew nervous. The bright little ditty she hummed couldn't hide the tension in her voice when she encouraged the boys to row harder, and her eyes roved endlessly from the setting sun to the shoreline and back.

The lake was calm and mirror smooth, reflecting the huge, blood red sun in its shimmery surface as its leading edge slipped beneath the horizon.

"I'll take a turn," Balissa said to Tal. He was the picture of exhaustion. Sweat beaded on his forehead and he had guzzled most of our water, but he was still reluctant to give up the oars.

Balissa plied the oars feverishly, her mouth set in a thin line.

"You'll wear yourself out if you row at that pace," Tal said.

"Oryn advised us to be off the lake by nightfall, and the sun is nearly set," Balissa muttered.

"Advised?" Morty peeled back the cloak he had thrown over his head when he had collapsed in the stern. "More like commanded, ordered, demanded, decreed..."

"Yes, thank you!" Balissa said. "We should be moored already."

"What's making those bubbles?" I asked.

"Where?" Morty and Tal asked in unison.

I leaned over the port gunwale and pointed to a trail of bubbles bursting on the surface.

"Sit down!" Balissa exclaimed, her voice rising to a fevered pitch, but her warning came too late.

A vortex opened beneath us; the boat lurched sideways as the whirling current seized it, and I tumbled over the side.

I inhaled water as the lake closed over my head, and I came up gasping and sputtering. The whirlpool had spit me into calmer water, but it still held the boat, spinning it in a circle as Balissa fought the current.

"Sit down, you fool!" she barked to Tal, who was preparing to dive in after me. "You can't swim!"

"I'm okay," I called. I was treading water, though the cold would soon sap my limited energy reserves.

Something brushed my leg.

I jerked reflexively and peered into the depths of the murky water.

Below me, a series of eerie violet splotches pulsated in the water. The throbbing lights faded, then reappeared, deeper.

"I think something is down there..." I trailed off as the violet pulses shot toward the surface.

"Balissa...!" My cry ended in a choking gurgle as something wrapped around my ankle and sucked me beneath the surface. I kicked violently, but the hold on my leg tightened. Terror surged through me, squeezing the last reserves of oxygen out of my screaming lungs, and I stomped at the creature with my other foot. It relinquished its grip, and I glimpsed one saucer-sized opalescent eye as a triangular head shot past me, trailed by a dozen tentacles flashing deep shades of violet. A luminous cloud of phosphorescent liquid ejected from the creature, enveloping me as I fought my way towards air...and life. My head broke the surface, but I drew only one ragged breath before a tentacle yanked me under again...into the darkness. I flailed and kicked at the creature, but my lungs sucked in water; soon the fight would be over.

Bubbles roiled around me, and I shot out of the water. I somersaulted in the air before landing with a massive splash thirty feet from the boat. My billowing skirt buoyed me, and I lay on the surface, coughing, choking, and vomiting water, until the boat pulled alongside and Balissa and Morty hauled me over the gunwale.

"Are you all right?" Balissa asked, her voice trembling.

My lungs burned with every breath, but I managed to choke out, "What was that...*thing* in the water?"

"I don't know. Nobody knows!" Balissa cried. "The beast isn't supposed to go in shallow water...not before the sun sets."

"'Twas probably only a baby," Morty said. Even he seemed shaken. "My spell never would have freed her from the full grown monster."

I sat up slowly and hitched up my skirt to inspect my ankle. Balissa gasped. A line of welts started just above my waterlogged shoe and wrapped around my leg halfway up my calf. "I don't think I will ever go swimming again," I said.

21

he Great Lake is fed by the Trine and other streams flowing with runoff and ice melt from the Pindar Mountains. The Pindar foothills border the lake to the north and wrap around the western edge in a hook," Balissa said.

I cradled a steaming cup of tea and nestled in my cloak beside a crackling fire. We had moored the boat beside a barren, rocky promontory. Our wet clothes steamed by the fire as Tal and Morty cooked our meal and Balissa daubed my welts with a salve. My stomach full of rabbit stew and potatoes, I savored my tea as I listened to Balissa. Without the diversion, my thoughts would no doubt have taken a darker turn after the attack on the lake.

"The lake is kept in place by a slender spine of granite that stabs the earth and forms the eastern rim. Here the Dead Forest is no more than a few gnarled, stunted living trees, precariously perched on the narrow ledge of rock and thin soil between the lake and the precipice yonder." She nodded toward the east.

"Why doesn't the water spill over the spine?" Tal asked.

"Listen," Balissa said. "You can hear the waterfall."

It was a low-throated rumble.

"The water exits the lake through a hole in the rim before falling several hundred feet to the Lorne River below."

"If there's a hole, why doesn't the lake drain?" I asked.

Balissa gazed into the darkness. "According to legend, long ago the Great Lake had no outlet. As the lake expanded, a powerful enchanter realized the water might break through the rim and cause a catastrophic flood in the Lorne Valley. Thousands of people would be displaced. So he made a hole through the rim to relieve the pressure."

"His name was Mortimor the Great, and he is my namesake," Morty said.

"Do you think the legend is true?" Tal asked.

"For the most part," Balissa said.

"But that's impossible!" I said. "How could he make an opening through solid granite?"

"Magic, my dear," she said.

Of course...magic.

"Now we must sleep," Balissa said. "We've all had an arduous day, and tomorrow we have a difficult climb down the spine followed by a long journey on foot."

I slipped into my bedroll and curled into a ball. A hard lump poked my side. I reached to inspect the bulge, and my hand closed around Nanni's keepsake. I unpinned the brooch and gazed at it. The tiger's eye stone glowed pale amber in the moonlight, and the gold filigree glinted in the light of the dying fire. Intense loneliness and a wave of homesickness churned through me. Tears rose as thoughts of Nanni and the people of Heyden swept through my mind. I fell asleep with the brooch clutched in my hand.

~ † ~

The morning dawned cold and damp. An evil-smelling fogbank shrouded the lake, dulling the senses. The air hung close, cold and clammy, like a dank, musty blanket. The heat from Tal's fire was welcome, but the smoke refused to rise. It burned our throats and eyes until we doused the flames.

"This is poor weather for crossing the rim, but staying here is equally unappealing. I'm glad we didn't encounter this yesterday morning," Balissa said. "Crossing the lake would have been nigh impossible."

Balissa helped me don my pack, which was lighter than I expected, and I looked around suspiciously at the others' shares. Tal was carrying a mountain of a pack that would have felled a smaller man. Morty grumbled as he lifted his pack, though he would probably complain no matter what he carried. Balissa's pack looked to be the same size as mine, and she cinched the straps expertly.

She saw me studying the burdens. "Is something wrong?"

"I just want to be sure I'm carrying my share. I can carry as much as anyone...except Tal, perhaps."

She laughed. "No one can carry as much as Tal. He would carry everything if I let him."

"He can carry mine," Morty offered.

"'Twill do you good to carry your weight," Balissa said. "And if Arabella gets overtired, you can carry hers, as well."

Morty grimaced, and Balissa gave him a tight-lipped smile. "Let's set off, shall we? Keep close. I don't want to lose anybody in this infernal fog."

Balissa led us along the spine toward the northern shore of the lake. To the right, the waterfall thundered far below. I shivered. The rim sloped toward the falls and was slippery in the damp. One misstep might send us tumbling over the edge.

We trudged through the cloud for hours, though we soon left the roar of the falls behind. The fog remained thick throughout the morning, but at noon the sun made a feeble attempt to shine through. Pale, watery light washed the landscape, lending a ghostly appearance to our surroundings. Nothing was visible through the fogbank except the edge of the narrow rock ledge we were traversing.

"I'm told the view of the valley is breathtaking," Balissa said when we stopped for a much needed rest. "On a clear day one can see all the way to Red Castle."

"Are there towns or villages?" I asked.

"Not anymore."

"If Mortimor the Great pierced a hole through tons of granite, there must have been something worth preserving."

Balissa nodded. "The original landscape was partially arid, but fertile. The people grew grapes and olives, as well as vegetables and grains. The Lorne Valley produced enough surplus food to feed half the population of Latretta."

"What happened to them?" I asked.

Balissa sighed.

"The law of unintended consequences. Mortimor the Great created the Lorne River when he made the outlet through the spine. No doubt many people thought this would be a blessing to the inhabitants of the valley; they would never lack for water."

"Sure," Morty snorted. "All the sour, sulfurous water they could possibly want."

"The river is polluted?" I asked.

"All those massive hemlocks rotting in the lake for centuries," Tal remarked. He was busy whittling a piece of wood. "Although no one knows why there is so much sulfur."

Balissa nodded. "Crops withered, soil baked hard in the sun—"

"And washed away," Tal finished. "Rainfall is infrequent but violent in the Lorne Valley. Massive storms blow off the lake and drop torrential rain."

"Rain washed soil into the river, and silt built the delta at the mouth of the Lorne River and created the Eastern Fen. Within a century, the Lorne Valley was a barren wasteland, and the eastern shore—once fertile farmland—became a trackless swamp...or so the legends say. You see," Balissa continued. "Magic gives great power, but requires great responsibility. Actions can have far-reaching consequences."

Morty snorted again. "'Tis probably all hogwash. This area has been a rocky wasteland forever, or as long as anyone can remember."

"As long as anyone can remember is not the same as forever," Balissa said. "Time to move on. We should be nearly across."

We walked for another ten minutes before the landscape began to change. Instead of bare rock, a thin layer of soil covered the ground beneath our feet, and small plants and grasses grew in crevices and cracks.

"We're almost there," Balissa said.

Suddenly, the fog thinned, and hemlocks towered only yards in front of us. "We've reached the northern end of the rim," Balissa said. "Now begins our descent into the valley. Hopefully the fog will dissipate as we go."

She turned right, stepped off the rim, and disappeared. I peered over the edge. A stone staircase was cut into the face of the sheer cliff. I gulped. Was *this* the only way down?

"'Tis all right," Tal said. "I'll stay with you."

"Thank you."

Morty had started down ahead of Balissa, hopping lightly as he went, oblivious to danger from loose rocks or slick stones. Balissa called sharply, "Mortimor! Slow down or you'll break your neck!"

The mist swallowed his taunting answer.

Gingerly, I headed down, clinging to the cliff face as I went. I counted as we descended to steady my nerves, and Tal helped where steps were broken or blocked by debris. As Balissa had predicted, the fog thinned and dispersed as we descended, and the air was clear when I clambered down the last few steps to the valley floor.

I sank down on a handy rock. "Two hundred and twenty-six steps. I hope I never have to do that again."

Balissa's face looked pale and pinched as she offered me some water. "Those steps were harrowing for all of us...or most of us," she said, glaring at Morty, who didn't appear fazed by his lightning-fast descent. "Oryn warned me the steps would be difficult, but I don't think he imagined we would have to descend in fog. What a day to try this for the first time."

I choked on my drink. "The first time! You've never climbed down the cliff or crossed the lake before?"

"I never set eyes on them before," she said, studying my face. "Before our journey from Red Castle to Pithark, none of us had ever been in Atruria before."

I tried to remember how Red Castle and Pithark were situated on Fabius's map. "Pithark is south of Red Castle...but how did you cross the Aurals?"

"There's a pass north of Pithark," Balissa replied.

"I thought the only pass was at Heyden."

"A common misconception...'twas fortunate for us Alara's Pass is so obscure," she said. "'Tisn't much of a pass."

"Alara's Pass?" I echoed. "As in the last queen of Atruria?"

She nodded.

"I wonder if Sarduk knows about it."

"Of course he does!" Morty said. "But he doesn't perceive it as a threat. Only one regiment guards the pass. And the soldiers live in a makeshift barracks and spend more time gambling and chasing skirts than guarding. An army could march through that pass in broad daylight, and Sarduk wouldn't hear about it until they knocked down the gates of Pithark."

"I think *most* of his soldiers spend more time gambling and chasing skirts than guarding," I said.

"And pursuing beautiful, red-haired enchantresses?" Tal asked.

I turned and glared at him. He leaned against a massive boulder, calmly whittling his driftwood. His face was unreadable and shadowed by his thatch of shaggy hair. I wasn't sure which description bothered me more: beautiful or enchantress.

"Sometimes," I said in exasperation. "Sometimes you say the darndest things!"

His lips curled in an almost imperceptible smile, but he did not glance up from his whittling.

Balissa's laugh pealed like chiming bells.

~ † ~

The day remained gray and overcast, though the fog had lifted in the valley. It started to sprinkle when we left the stairs, and by the time we reached the base of the falls two hours later, the spray was indistinguishable from the steady drizzle.

"There it is," Balissa said, resting on a spray-drenched rock. "The mighty Lorne Falls."

A torrent of water shot from a perfectly arched hole a hundred feet below the lake rim. It resembled a geyser turned sideways more than a waterfall. Water plummeted two hundred feet into a massive pool filled with gargantuan boulders, smooth and shiny from an eon of falling water.

"The opening in the rock face is a perfect oval."

"Surprising, isn't it," Balissa said.

"That's magic for you," Tal said.

I picked my way across the rocky ground toward the pool. Steam and spray obscured much of the roiling surface. The water frothed a dirty yellow color and bubbled, as if boiling. A sulfurous odor mixed with the smell of decay assailed my nostrils. I coughed, and my eyes smarted and burned. Nothing could survive in the noxious water flowing from the pool.

"How can the Lorne River be dead, while the Great Lake is full of life?" I asked.

"Some say the lake is the entrance to the mouth of Hell," Morty said.

"That sounds like a bunch of nonsense." I plopped down on a stone.

"Oryn has spent hours poring over old manuscripts trying to find an explanation, but he's only one man. Few others think such things are important enough to devote their attention to," Balissa said.

"Is that all he does? Pore over old manuscripts?"

"Of course not," Morty said. "Oryn pores over musty old books, torn old scrolls, smelly old ledgers, tattered old parchment, *and* illegible old manuscripts."

Terrific. He sounded fascinating. Why would a stodgy enchanter devoted to a pile of moldering books take *me* as an apprentice?

"Come along," Balissa said, "Red Castle awaits."

"How long will it take to get there?"

"Two weeks if we're fortunate."

22

uge sandstone formations, ranging in height from forty to several hundred feet, choked the floor of the Lorne Valley. Snow, wind, and rain had carved the ridges into fantastic shapes. Running north to south, each one formed a wall blocking our journey east. Saw grass and thorn bushes grew abundantly in the shallow, sandy soil between outcroppings. An occasional succulent, sagebrush, or gorse bush clung to the rocks along the faint path. Outside of the fascinating geology, there was little to recommend the valley; it was difficult to imagine the land had once been verdant and fertile.

At times, the path diverged hundreds of yards north or south to skirt a jagged ridge of stone impeding our progress. Sometimes there were no breaks in the ridges, so we had to scramble up their steep faces on narrow ledges only twelve inches wide in places.

After scaling the fourth ridge, we sat on its crest and rested next to a stunted tree struggling bravely to root itself against the elements. "Wouldn't it be easier to follow the river?" I asked, eyeing its meandering course in the distance.

"The river takes a circuitous path across the valley," Balissa said. "'Twould add many leagues to our journey."

"Besides, would *you* want to travel beside that sulfurous stew?" Morty asked.

"How did you get to Pithark? You had to cross the Lorne if you went due south from Red Castle."

"On river ice. 'Twas frozen nice and thick when we crossed. You're lucky 'twas wintertime," Morty added, miming a rope around his neck.

Balissa elbowed him in the ribs. "We'd have found another way, but ice made the crossing easier."

A question had plagued me since she mentioned traveling to Pithark. "Why didn't you snatch me in Pithark, instead of waiting until Heyden...?"

"And save you the humiliation of the pillory?" Balissa finished with a sigh. "Tal begged me to break you out in Pithark, but 'twas too dangerous. I knew we had a better chance of success in Heyden." She paused, fingering the travel-stained hem of her dress. "I *am* sorry. I wish we could have saved you that degradation." Her eyes sparkled with unshed tears. "I thought my heart would break. I couldn't bear to watch you suffer." Her lips curled in a hint of a smile. "Tal was all for blasting our way in and dragging you out by your hair, but I told him that was boorish and foolhardy."

She winked at Tal, who turned away, his ears flushing crimson.

~ † ~

The days crossing the Lorne Valley seemed endless. We would spend a whole morning scrambling over a series of jagged outcroppings, only to find ourselves facing an insurmountable bluff. Then we would squander the afternoon marching north or south around it; sunset would be upon us before we turned east again.

"I think we've traveled far enough to reach Red Castle twice over," grumbled Morty after a particularly exhausting detour.

I remained silent, trying to conserve as much energy as possible. A year of inactivity in jail had reduced my endurance, and the trek was grueling. Our stores were running low as well. Balissa did not think we needed to ration the food, but I had come to enjoy shortbread about as much as turnips. Tal set snares every night, but the barren terrain produced little.

Water was our biggest problem. We had filled every leather flask with the sharp, astringent lake water, and then replenished our supply from a spring at the base of a lone tree. But our flasks were nearly empty.

Balissa consulted her map at regular intervals, staring with knitted brows, though she put the parchment away when I came near.

"We aren't lost, are we?" I asked one evening as we set up camp. We had been in the valley for ten days.

"Goodness, no. Red Castle will loom on the horizon soon enough, though I *am* concerned about finding water. According to Oryn's map, we should reach a rain pool tomorrow, but it may be gone. He assured me there would still be water in April, but today is the twelfth of May."

"The twelfth of May!" I echoed, suddenly distraught. I wandered a short distance across the rock. We were camped on a small bluff. Balissa had hoped to find water collected at the top, but there was none.

I picked my way around the largest crevices toward a stunted pine growing out of a crack. Espaliered against a larger outcropping, it clung tenaciously to the rocky cliff despite eons of wind and drought. I sank down amongst the gnarled roots and surveyed the bleak landscape. Tears splashed my cheeks.

"What's wrong?"

I brushed my eyes. Tal was perched on a rock watching me.

"Nothing," I sniffled. "It's silly."

"What is it, Arabella? Is the journey wearying you?"

"I *am* sick of traveling, but..." I paused, feeling foolish.

He waited for me to continue.

"My sixteenth birthday has come and gone, and I missed it," I said in a rush. Tears welled again, and I swiped them away. "It's foolish, I know. I'm so grateful to you for rescuing me, yet here I sit, blubbering like a baby."

"'Tisn't foolish. A sixteenth birthday is a milestone." After a moment of silence he said, "I made this for you."

I wiped my cheeks and looked up. Nestled in his hand was a beautifully carved bird, every detail perfectly rendered.

"For your birthday. I am sorry 'tis late," he said shyly, "but 'twasn't ready yet."

"It's so beautiful," I whispered, cradling the carving in my hands.

He blushed and ducked his head.

"You couldn't have known it was my birthday," I added softly. "Thank you."

He squirmed and turned even redder.

A sudden gust of wind grabbed my cloak and set it flapping. We heard a commotion at the fire, and a shout from Balissa sent us running. I arrived right behind Tal and gaped at the ruined camp. Bedding and packs were strewn everywhere, and the cooking pot had tumbled off the tripod and lay in the fire.

I gasped. "What happened?"

"Not the wind," Balissa said grimly, holding up a shredded pack. The bottom was sliced open, the contents gutted.

Morty came running, an arrow notched on his bow. "Two wolves," he panted, pointing north. "They ran off carrying something."

"Ayr wolves?" Balissa asked.

He shrugged. "Maybe."

Balissa shook her head. "They haven't ventured out of the marshes in years. I wonder what has brought them now."

We assessed the damage. Wolves had eaten or ruined most of the food. One packet of bread had survived intact, and some of the remaining potatoes were salvageable. But the other stores were either missing or scattered, and razor teeth had shredded two of the four bedrolls.

"Why would they demolish a bedroll?" I asked, holding up the tattered remains.

"Out of spite," Morty said, kicking the cooking pot. "There's nothing left!"

"We're only a couple days from Red Castle. We'll have to ration the remaining food, but we'll be fine," Balissa said.

"What about water?" Tal asked.

As if on cue, a fork of lightning lit the dusky sky, and an answering clap of thunder sent us scrambling to pick up the strewn camp. "Collect what you can and follow me!" Balissa shouted. As we passed the stunted pine, the storm broke; huge drops of rain splattered on the stones, and lightning flashed across the sky. Thunder rolled and rumbled, echoing off the ridges.

"This way!" Balissa called. We followed her down the bluff, picking our way over slick stones. It was pouring by the time we neared the bottom, and the deepening dusk and sheeting rain made visibility so poor I barreled into Morty when he stopped.

"Watch it!" he said, almost tumbling into Balissa.

She put out a steadying hand. "We can't stay in the gulch," she shouted over the wind.

A flash of lightning revealed a torrent of water rushing through the previously bone-dry valley between the ridges.

"Back up!" Balissa shouted. "Tal! Find us a place to camp!"

Tal disappeared into the gloom. Within minutes, he returned and led us northward along the ridge to a shallow cave. Balissa scrambled in next to me, and Tal stacked the packs in front. Still, the rain drenched us to the bone and soaked our bedrolls and blankets.

"I suppose a fire is out of the question," Morty said sullenly.

We spent a sleepless night huddled in misery, and when the first hint of predawn tinted the eastern sky a pale gray, we rose in silent consensus.

The rain had ceased, and the sky was clearing, but the valley was sodden from the storm. We picked our way across the remnants of the stream in the gulch, slipping on wet rocks and bypassing huge puddles.

"At least there's plenty of water," Balissa said with a sigh as we filled our water flasks from a rock pool.

Dawn was pinking the east by the time we reached the top of the next ridge, and Balissa decided to pause for a meager breakfast.

Tal tried to start a fire with some brush, but the damp wood just smoldered.

I wandered away to watch the sunrise.

"Don't stray far," Balissa called. "Wolves may still be lurking."

"I'll scream at the top of my lungs if I spy one," I told her.

The high ridge afforded a good view to the east. I perched on a flat rock to enjoy the sunrise. In the distance, the largest sandstone formation yet speared the sky. As the rising sun struck the formation, it wavered like a vision. When it came into focus again, a red castle with towers and spires glinted in the sunlight. I gazed in breathless wonder, but then the light changed, and it became a pile of rock once more. I sighed, disappointed. The castle had been so beautiful, yet it was only a trick of the morning light.

I joined the others as they approached and took a bundle from Balissa. The wolves had destroyed my pack, so I carried the remaining bedrolls.

She scanned the horizon. "Only a couple more days."

"Any longer and we'd all starve," Morty said.

We descended into the rocky valley. At midday, we ate the last of the bread. Morty strung his bow and searched halfheartedly for game, but the sparse vegetation provided no cover for wildlife. Balissa sighted toward the sandstone outcropping as we set out again.

"Are we headed toward that huge pile of rock?"

"Yes," Balissa said. "I know it doesn't look like much from here, but that *is* Red Castle. We should arrive sometime tomorrow afternoon."

"So it wasn't a mirage," I murmured.

Tal was following me. "Did you see something?"

I nodded. "Early this morning during the sunrise."

"That's impossible!" Morty snorted. "*No* one can see it. Powerful spells mask Red Castle, making it look like a rock formation. You can climb on it, and it *still* looks like rock."

"Does the castle have lots of spires and windows that glint in the sunrise?"

Morty's face turned pale, and his eyes darkened. "Tell her it's impossible!" he said to Balissa.

She looked thoughtful. "'Tis not outside the realm of possibility."

"'Tis impossible!" Morty yelled. "She didn't see Red Castle, and both of you know it! Why do you let her lie like that?" He turned to me. "Do you see it now?"

I shook my head. "I only caught a glimpse before it shifted into rocks again."

Balissa laid a hand on Morty's arm. "I think Arabella is being truthful. She doesn't know what Red Castle looks like, nor does she know what she *ought* to perceive. 'Tis possible she saw the real castle for a moment."

Morty shrugged Balissa's hand away. His fist clenched, then he whirled around and shot out his hand, sending a shower of sandstone rocks ricocheting across the ground.

I jumped...again. Would I ever get used to seeing magic?

Balissa pressed her lips together as he stomped off.

"Thank you," I said to Balissa.

"I have every reason to believe you—more reasons than I gave Morty." She drew me close. "Don't doubt yourself. Mortimor thinks he has nothing left to learn, but the wise enchanter recognizes he will *never* understand all there is to know about magic. We like to think magic abides by certain rules, but it doesn't."

I did not know anything about magic and its rules, nor did I understand how I had 'broken' them. I was just glad what I had seen was real.

When we camped at dusk, Tal made a large fire and roasted the potatoes. We ate slowly; this would be our last meal until we reached Red Castle the following day.

We set out at dawn, tightening our belts. The sun was high overhead as we approached a small sandstone ridge set back from the base of the huge outcropping.

"We're almost there," Balissa said. She led us between two sandstone columns, and I felt a faint tingling sensation.

"We've arrived, haven't we?" I said wearily.

"Indeed," Balissa said.

I blinked in surprise. As we passed through the columns and the protective spell, the ridge before us transformed into a wall built of rough stones joined with red mortar. Two doors bound with iron bands and studded with nails stood just ahead.

Balissa set her shoulder to a door and pushed it open. "Welcome to Red Castle, Arabella."

23

e were standing on a huge green encircled by a high wall. A massive red castle rose before us, looking like something straight from a fairy tale.

Balissa took my arm. "Is it everything you expected?"

"Everything and more. It's magnificent!" I said, breathless, taking in countless arched windows and graceful spires soaring towards the sky.

"Yes, but a tour must wait. First, we eat."

Morty and Tal were already sprinting to the left, and we followed, bypassing twenty-foot tall double doors. "That's the main western entrance, but we stick to the small doors," Balissa said, directing me toward a human-sized door. "This door leads to the kitchen."

She led me down a short hallway and past several passageways into a spacious kitchen. "And here is the food," she said. Tal and Morty were devouring bread, cheese, and salted meat, and we followed their example. After filling their stomachs, they scattered into the castle.

A striped tabby sauntered through an open doorway, arching her back. She rubbed against my leg, and I fed her a piece of salted meat. She purred as I scratched behind her ears.

Balissa studied me over her glass. "Are you ready to meet Oryn?"

"Now?" The cat skittered away, affronted that I had stopped petting her. I glanced down at my dusty clothing. "Shouldn't I change first?" But I had nothing to change into.

"There's no time like the present," Balissa said. "Don't worry, dear. Oryn bellows and roars like a lion, but inside..." She put her hand over her heart. "Inside, he's as gentle as a kitten. Besides, he won't even notice your clothes. The only thing he cares about is your head and your heart. Follow me."

I nervously straightened my skirt and smoothed my hair as she led me down a series of hallways. We stopped in an open doorway.

I peeked around Balissa and studied the room. Floor to ceiling shelves lined three walls—shelves jammed with books, manuscripts, and parchment lying in haphazard piles. Books leaning at crazy angles spilled everywhere; massive tomes lay in messy piles on every flat surface, documents and parchment scraps covered in scribbled writing were strewn on the floor. A long table crammed with bottles holding colored liquids and powders filled the left-hand portion of the room. A massive oak desk strewn with more disheveled parchment and manuscripts faced away from a bank of arched windows on the right.

Six framed oval mirrors sat in a semicircle facing the desk. A tall man stood with his back to us, but two mirrors clearly reflected his face.

He was much younger than I had imagined—barely older than Tal—and devastatingly handsome, despite a livid red scar ravaging his right cheek. His dark brown hair was messy and unkempt; he had a firm jaw, blue eyes, and a strong, muscular build. He stood straight and proud, arms crossed over his chest with his feet firmly planted.

He watched us enter, and I felt him scrutinizing me. I smoothed my dingy skirts self-consciously.

"So this is the famous Arabella of Maitlan."

He turned to face us, and I gasped involuntarily. My experience with mirrors had taught me over and over that they were unreliable, but his smooth, unscarred cheek still startled me.

He raised a quizzical eyebrow. "Does my appearance surprise you?" His voice was deep and commanding. "Were you expecting a cape and a pointy hat?"

"No, sir," I said, dropping a clumsy curtsy.

"I see she isn't gifted in social graces."

"She has other talents," Balissa said, pulling me into the room.

"Yes, sir. I'm an excellent horsewoman..."

He cut me off with a snort. "That will be *extremely* useful, considering we don't have any horses. At least she can cook and clean," he said to Balissa, turning toward his desk. "Sadye seems to have gone on strike, and I'm sick of my own cooking."

"I cannot cook, sir."

"What? Who ever heard of an Atrurian girl who can't cook?"

"I'm a reasonably accomplished herbalist, and I'm fluent in Lattrian, sir." I hoped he would find these skills more impressive.

"Fluent, huh? I'll be the judge of that." He picked up a book from his overflowing desk and held it out to me. "Translate a phrase for me."

Balissa nudged me. "Go ahead. Show him what you can do."

My heart thumped as I opened the book. I moved toward the gothic windows. "You can't be serious."

"She isn't going to be any good to me if she can't read, Balissa," Oryn said, reaching to take the book.

I stepped back, hugging the volume to my chest.

"*Spring rains swelled the rivers till they overflowed their banks. The armies of the great enchanter Mortekai stood on the shore of the mighty Lorne, facing the hideous hordes of the evil enchanter Toryn across the raging waters...*"

"Enough! Obviously you've read this before, but did you translate it or read it in Atrurian?" He tilted his head to one side and stared at me with his deep blue eyes.

"This book was never translated into Atrurian," I said, placing his copy of *Legereya Atruriym yt Latrettym* on his desk. "Doing so earned me a swing at the end of a rope." I lifted my chin and met his gaze.

He held my eyes for several long moments before turning to Balissa. "She's feisty."

I could not tell whether my feistiness pleased him or not. He strode over to one of the bookshelves and pored over the titles.

"Here," Oryn said, selecting a thin volume. "Translate the first two pages and have them ready by tomorrow afternoon." As I took the book, he said with an expression that was almost a smile, "Welcome to Red Castle."

~ † ~

Balissa led me through the hallways. Besides Oryn and the cat, I had not seen a single living soul since we entered the huge castle. "Who lives here?" I asked, peeking through doors at empty rooms, cold hearths, and furniture shrouded with sheets.

"Sadye, Mortimor, Tal, Oryn...and now you."

"And you?" I asked hopefully.

"Just until you're settled, dear. I must return to Sperara. I've been gone far too long, I fear."

"Sperara?"

"'Tis the capital of Latretta and my home," she answered, turning at a low doorway.

I followed her into a vaulted bathroom. A tub of steaming, lavender-scented water waited, flanked by a table piled with fluffy towels, scented soap, scrubbing brushes, robes, and a lacy nightgown. I burst several buttons in my haste to remove my travel-stained clothes. I could not imagine anything more pleasant than a long bath to ease the kinks in my tired muscles.

"As usual, Sadye has taken care of everything," Balissa said with satisfaction. "She knows exactly what a lady needs after a long journey."

After settling into the steaming water, I asked, "Who is Sadye?"

"Oryn's nurse when he was a boy...she followed him here to Red Castle. She holds the title of enigmatic housekeeper, mender-of-all-things-torn, and cook—when she feels like it," Balissa said with a smile.

I relaxed in the tub until I wrinkled like a raisin.

After I dressed in the nightgown and a robe, Balissa took me to my room. We climbed several flights of circular stairs, passing a series of window seats decorated with vases of cut flowers. Some of them were summer bloomers, and I stopped at a bouquet of chrysanthemums to admire their perfect blossoms.

"How can mums bloom in the spring?" I wondered. "Does Oryn have a hothouse?"

Balissa smiled. "Growing things is Oryn's specialty, dear."

He seemed rough and prickly, but if Oryn liked to garden, he couldn't be too terrible.

"Here's your room," Balissa said, stopping at a brass-studded door. "Oryn thought you would be comfortable in the south tower. It has a lovely view of the gardens."

"Thank you," I murmured, suddenly exhausted.

"Don't work on that translation tonight," Balissa said. "After breakfast, we'll find you a pen and parchment."

My hand was on the latch when she added, "Goodness! I almost forgot. Here's your satchel."

"Thank you," I said.

She pressed it into my hands and glided down the stairs.

I opened the door and stepped into the room.

The satchel fell to the floor unheeded as I gaped at the most glorious room I had ever seen. An immense four-poster bed crouched on a plush carpet. Garlands of carved ivy and bunches of grapes wreathed the posts. A burgundy canopy and curtains lavishly decorated with gold and silver thread concealed a matching down comforter piled high with a sumptuous array of pillows and bolsters.

It was a bed for a princess.

Three tall gothic windows looked out to the north, east, and south. Richly colored tapestries hid the curved walls. The room held a wardrobe, an armoire, a writing desk and chair, and a bookshelf well stocked with volumes.

I gazed up at the gilded ceiling, took a step backwards, and promptly fell over an object behind me.

I gasped, "What in the world?" It was my trunk.

Kneeling, I wrapped my arms around it, pressing my cheek against the cool smoothness of the bands. I laughed in disbelief and joy. "But where did you *come* from?" I said again. I had thought the trunk was gone forever, but here it sat in my beautiful new room...

"The satchel!" My trunk transformed into a satchel. How clever. "Thank you, Taren."

I danced around the room, delighted to have a small piece of my old life. I yanked out the key and unlocked the trunk.

I caressed each dress. They were just as I remembered. I had not worn the lavender linen at all, and the cinnamon crushed velvet only once. How much I had grown in the last year? My emotional and spiritual growth had been tenfold, but had I grown taller?

On a whim, I pulled the velvet over my head. The dress fit perfectly! I grinned. Maybe my trunk had decided to allow me some extra use since they had not seen daylight for more than a year. Yet they smelled as sweet as ever, as if I had sprinkled the crushed lavender yesterday.

I dug deeper and found two new dresses. The first was of white damask with a delicate silk overskirt, meticulously sprigged with pink flowers. The long flowing sleeves were of diaphanous silk, embroidered to match the overskirt.

The second dress was a sleeveless, off the shoulder evening gown, fit for a queen, with a figure-flattering bodice, flowing skirt, and vee neck. Sewn of gorgeous emerald green velvet, delicate velvet-covered buttons ran down to the small of my back. I deemed the gown too beautiful to wear.

Next, I pulled out my jewelry box. A perfect pearl necklace with matching eardrops nestled beside an exquisite set of garnet jewelry: necklace; eardrops, and combs for my hair.

I placed the dresses back in the trunk, removed my books and dream diary from the secret compartment, and lined them up on a shelf.

But now I was in a predicament. The trunk prevented me from closing the door. I tried pushing it against the wall, but it would not budge. Confounded, I shoved the trunk as hard as I could. No luck.

I decided to leave the trunk until morning, but the open door made me feel vulnerable once I climbed in bed. I lit the lamp again and circled the trunk, pondering. I had never tried moving the trunk before, yet obviously Balissa and my mother had done so easily. I hefted one end, and the trunk shifted as easily as a sack of feathers! "Amazing," I murmured, closing the door. I crawled back in bed and fell asleep before my head touched the pillow.

~ † ~

True to her word, Balissa woke me the next morning and took me to breakfast. A huge woman towered over the table. A voluminous print apron covered a shocking magenta and yellow dress, and her steel-gray hair stuck out in wiry clumps around a garish paisley kerchief.

"Good morning, ma'am," I said politely.

She grunted and set a steaming bowl of oatmeal topped with honey, dried apples, raisins, and cream in front of me.

"Thank you," I said.

She gave me a searching look before turning back to the dough she was kneading.

I glanced inquiringly at Balissa, who grinned and said, "What Sadye lacks in words she makes up for in perspicacity."

"Hmmph!" Sadye snorted.

After breakfast, I returned to my room to work on the translation. The book was a scientific treatise exploring the wartfly. By the time Balissa came to fetch me for lunch, I had learned more than I had ever hoped to know about the habits of said fly.

After eating, she showed me to the library. Oryn sat with his back to the door, poring over something at the huge table. Balissa motioned for silence. Winking, she stole across the room and delicately brushed her fingers across the back of his tunic.

With a yelp, he jumped, knocking over a beaker of clear liquid at his right elbow. It shattered on the floor, the liquid fizzing and hissing as it spread across the flagstones.

"BALISSA!"

She held both hands over her mouth as she laughed helplessly.

"You take far too much perverse pleasure in scaring me like that!"

"I know, I know," Balissa said, "but I can't help it. You are too funny when you jump." She laughed.

Oryn scowled at the growing puddle on the floor. "And look what you made me do. A whole morning's work ruined."

"I'll clean up the mess," assured Balissa, still chuckling. She motioned to a broom in the corner.

I squeaked in surprise as it danced across the room on its own. The self-propelled broom swept up the mess on the floor, followed by a mop and bucket.

Glancing at my face, Balissa said, "Don't worry, dear. You'll get used to seeing strange things around here."

"You might as well make yourself useful. See those shelves?" Oryn said to me, making a sweeping gesture toward all the books on all the shelves. "Organize them in alphabetical order according to subject. If you can't determine where they belong, put them in a stack, and I'll decide later."

Organize his books. Lovely.

I laid my translation on the table and pulled volumes off one by one, studying their titles and flyleaves to determine their subject matter.

"You should make catalogues, too," Oryn added. "Alphabetize them according to title, author, and subject."

"Of course I should," I murmured under my breath. What did I look like? A librarian? This job would take a year. There was no order or sense to his books; astronomy was next to zoology and botany beside medicine.

By late afternoon, I had organized a third of the books on the first shelf of the first wall. I was tired and dingy, and a surreptitious glance at one of the mirrors revealed dirt streaked across my nose and cheek.

Somewhere deep in the castle, a clock bonged four times. "That's it for the day," Oryn said. "You can head back to the kitchen. Sadye and Balissa will have something for you to do. *Someone* has to teach you to cook."

"Thank you, sir," I said, stealing back to the kitchen.

Instead of putting me to work, Balissa sent me to get a bath. "There will be plenty of time to teach you the basics of cooking, and you look exhausted," Balissa said.

I soaked in the scented water for a long time. By the time I returned to the kitchen, I had missed the others and had to dine alone. After dinner, I retired to my room, organized the wardrobe and dressing table, then climbed into bed and listened to night sounds steal over the castle and grounds.

Although tired, I tossed and turned for more than an hour as sleep eluded me. Finally, I lit the lamp and drew on a robe. As I chose a book to read, a knock sounded on my door. Surprised, I opened it to find Oryn lounging against the doorframe.

"Since you can't sleep either, I was wondering if you'd care to join me for a drink in the library."

"How did you know I wasn't sleeping?"

He shrugged.

I glanced around my room. "You weren't...watching me, were you?"

He raised an eyebrow. "Suspicious, aren't we?" His lip curled slightly. "'Twouldn't do for you to learn all my secrets tonight, would it now?"

I extinguished my lamp and followed him. I found him quite intimidating.

His pace quickened, and I had to jog to keep up. "How did you know I was awake?"

Oryn halted, and I almost crashed into him. He steadied me and proceeded to the library. "'Tis my gift, I suppose."

"Your gift?"

"I know where people are, and I have a general idea of what they are doing," he explained.

"Really? Can you tell me what my father or nurse is doing right now?"

He shook his head. "They would have to be in closer proximity."

"Oh." I paused as he animated the pot to pour tea. "So you know what Tal and Morty and Sadye and Balissa are doing."

"Well...ahh," he said, handing me a steaming cup of tea. "Balissa is able to obscure herself and those around her. As you may have noticed, she thinks it is fun to sneak up on me."

That explained the spilled beaker.

"My mirrors don't work on her, even if she wants them to." He watched the spoon stir his tea, which I still found unnerving.

"Your mirrors?"

"They are for seeing, not for prying."

"You...watch us...?"

He snorted. "What, you don't want me to know what you're up to?"

"No, sir...I mean...yes, sir..." My tongue felt tied in knots.

He grinned into his teacup.

The striped tabby appeared in the doorway. She leapt on the table and nosed my arm, no doubt remembering the salted meat.

"I see you've met Prissy," Oryn said. He poured a smidgen of cream into his saucer, which she lapped up. "She's queen of the castle. She catches a few obligatory mice, and we spoil her shamelessly." He scratched behind her ears, and she purred.

"You did well on the translation," he said suddenly. "And if you keep at it, you'll have my library organized for the first time in..." He frowned, considering. "Well, for the first time ever."

I smiled at his admission, and we sat in silence, drinking our tea. At last he rose and said, "'Twould probably be best if you didn't mention my...umm...ability...to Tal or Morty."

"Of course not." I was surprised he had told me at all; he hardly knew me.

"Tomorrow you can spend the day with Balissa and Sadye. They'll teach you the basics of life in the castle and give you a list of duties. My library can wait for your spare time."

"Thank you, sir."

"Don't call me 'sir,'" he said gruffly. "Just Oryn."

24

fter breakfast, Balissa took me on a grand tour of the castle and grounds. She also taught me a quick way around the castle. On the second story, a hallway ran around the inner perimeter of the castle, lending access to every room on the first and second level. Most utility rooms, including the kitchen, were on the first level, while living quarters were on the second. Oryn's library overlooked the southern green. My chamber was in the southwestern tower, far from the kitchen but close to the library.

The great hall, the ancient keep, sat in the exact center of the castle. Hallways leading in the four cardinal directions connected the hall to four main entrances. Four large courtyards nestled in the right angle formed between the keep and the outer flanking towers. In them were workshops, stables, barns, kennels, and outbuildings. The northwestern courtyard, the one nearest the kitchen, contained a large, deep well, which Balissa said had never run dry.

Tal's workshop was near the well. He nodded shyly when Balissa asked if she might show me around. On one wall hung decorated bows in different lengths. Beside them sat quivers crafted of leather, tooled with intricate patterns and designs. Tal was also a competent blacksmith; tools of that trade lined an entire wall, along with examples of his work wrought in iron and steel.

"Tal! You're a wonderful craftsman!"

He flushed and bobbed his head. The bird he had given me was a lovely example of his skill, but the items in his workshop were breathtaking, combining utility and beauty in a way that defied description.

"His work puts the craftsmen in Heyden to shame!" I said to Balissa as we left.

Balissa smiled proudly. "He has rare talent. I just wish he had more confidence."

Next, Balissa took me on a tour of the outer grounds. Herbs, vegetables, flowers, and an orchard flourished in the sunny southern green. The grass was verdant and lush, cropped close by two resident goats.

"I can't believe how green the grass is."

"That's because it poured last week, but by midsummer the grass will turn brown."

"How do you keep these plants alive in the heat of summer?" I asked, running my hands over the burgeoning foliage. They would still be seeding in Heyden, but here, even further north, everything appeared to have been growing for a month or more.

"Under these greens are huge cisterns. Every drop of rainwater drains into them, and Oryn uses the water to irrigate the gardens. An intricate system of pumps and irrigation ditches connects everything."

"Who mans the pumps? Fifty servants?"

Balissa laughed. "Oryn, dear. Magic enables him to run this castle smoothly. We help as we're able, but the brunt of the work falls on him."

Living here would require a new way of thinking. "Can I take a peek at the herb garden?"

Smiling, Balissa led me through Oryn's herbs. Many of them were familiar, but Balissa pointed out some new ones as well. Clary, chervil, evening primrose, feverfew, hawkweed, and heartsease, along with mugwort and soapwort. We laughed together over some of the names as she told me their basic uses.

"Oryn knows these herbs even better than I do. With his help, you'll become an expert herbalist. He is more than willing to share his wisdom, unlike others."

"What do you mean?"

"Enchanters of old jealously guarded their discoveries and secrets. 'Twas selfish and egotistical, and Latretta has paid dearly for the practice." Balissa sighed. "Oryn is trying to change things; he *wants* to train apprentices and impart his knowledge. Yet his ideas and methods are unpopular with many of the highborn of Latretta. They see the spread of knowledge as a threat to their power. But if knowledge is not shared and passed from generation to generation, important secrets may be lost forever."

"Like the locations of the nine castles."

"Indeed. The loss of such secrets could lead to the demise of our country and culture. If things in Latretta don't change soon...!" She steadied herself and drew a deep breath. "I'm sorry, Arabella. 'Tis not for me to burden you with such matters. Your only concern is to learn everything Oryn has to teach. Who knows, perhaps you'll even rediscover an ancient secret."

That seemed improbable. What might I discover that an intelligent and driven man like Oryn could not?

Balissa wrapped her arm around my shoulder. "Enough exploring. Let's go make bread."

~ † ~

When we finally pulled my finished loaf from the oven, Balissa declared it a success, and Sadye even grunted her approval. We celebrated by feasting on warm hunks slathered with fresh butter and honey.

"This is delicious," I said around a mouthful, "but nothing like the bread in Heyden."

Balissa grinned. "No manchet here. That stuff will stunt your growth and give you rickets. We use *all* the flour. Besides, Sadye's too lazy to sift it so many times," she added, winking.

Sadye nodded sagely, and we laughed together. The bread had a nutty flavor and was filling and satisfying.

That evening we all ate in the kitchen. Afterwards, Oryn dispatched Tal, Morty, and me to help Sadye clean up. Clearly, this was to be our evening routine.

Over the next several weeks, Balissa taught me to milk Lacy the cow and care for the poultry, while Sadye showed me how to churn butter and prepare meals. In my spare time, I organized Oryn's bookshelves or translated documents for him. In the mornings, I often helped him care for the gardens.

As time passed, Oryn no longer seemed so austere and frightening, and Red Castle began to feel like a home.

~ † ~

"You need to learn to shoot a bow," said Oryn as we picked an abundant crop of summer squash. "If Ayr wolves have migrated out of the marshes, they pose a threat if we venture beyond the castle grounds. I want you to practice with Morty an hour each day."

I grimaced, and Oryn said, "I'll make him behave."

An awkward silence followed. "What exactly are Ayr wolves?"

Oryn frowned. "According to one legend, long ago a race of men lived in the Lorne Valley. They could transform themselves into wolves and preyed on human flesh. After the valley was destroyed, they lost the ability to turn back into men. Another legend suggests Ayr wolves are an adulteration of a race of noble wolves that dwell in the foothills of the Pindar Mountains." He shook his head. "I don't know if either is true, but they're bloodthirsty creatures who kill without mercy. A few stray beasts aren't anything to worry about, but a pack..." His eyes darkened with intensity. "A pack is extremely dangerous—a well organized killing machine whose leader can break magical defenses. They are the favored tool of Mortock."

"Mortock?" Images of red-eyed wolves made me shudder involuntarily.

"He is *the* great threat to humanity," Oryn said. He gestured toward the southeastern courtyard, cutting off any further questions. "Morty is waiting for you."

My feet dragged as I walked to the courtyard. I had managed to avoid Morty—except at mealtimes—and I enjoyed the respite from his teasing.

"There you are," he said with obvious irritation. "I don't have all day."

I examined the bows. "Haven't you any crossbows?" The crossbow was the most common bow in Atruria.

"Crossbows are for soldiers and idiots," he sneered. "I prefer a more elegant weapon." He picked up a tall bow and said with an exaggerated flourish, "Meet the longbow, the weapon of choice for distance *and* accuracy. A bolt might pierce armor, but we're trying to hit a bull's-eye at a hundred yards."

He stood the bow next to me. "This one is too tall. I think you can manage something...about this long!" He picked through the assortment of weapons and produced a bow about five and a half feet long. "This is fashioned of yew, the ideal wood for a longbow." He handed me a quiver. "Nock an arrow and take aim at the target." He pointed to the far side of the courtyard, thirty yards distant.

He demonstrated and loosed his arrow, which hit the target within the bull's-eye. "That's how you do it!" he said, grinning smugly.

I nocked an arrow.

"Draw the string back to your right ear," he instructed.

I pulled as hard as I could, but the string wobbled. When I released, the arrow clattered on the cobbles twenty feet away.

"Try again. Hold steady and sight along the arrow's length to the target."

I did, but with only slightly better success.

Morty's contempt grew with every miss. Again and again I tried, and at last an arrow struck the outside edge of the target.

"Finally," Morty said. "I was beginning to think you were too stupid to hit it at all."

"MORTIMOR!"

We whirled around. Oryn was standing behind us, feet planted and arms crossed. "If you *ever* call her stupid again, I'll turn you into a toad!"

"Yes, sir," Morty mumbled, flushing.

"Don't try me." Oryn's eyes bored into Morty, and then he strode into the castle.

Morty watched him go, muttering bitterly under his breath, "He wouldn't have the nerve. 'Tis against the rules to enchant apprentices." He spat on the ground and stalked off in the opposite direction.

~ † ~

Balissa was an excellent shot with the longbow, and despite a full complement of duties, she took charge of my lessons. She helped perfect my mechanics, and when we moved to the green to practice longer distances, I could hit a target at fifty yards once in three tries.

"You're learning quickly," Balissa said. "By the time I leave for Latretta, you should be able to strike at this distance more than half the time."

"Must you leave?" I had come to depend on her companionship and guidance.

"I've been away for many months. Too long, I fear." She grasped my hand. "Besides, I have a feeling I'm hindering your potential. After I leave, Oryn will concentrate his efforts; you'll blossom under his tutelage."

"I hardly think so," I muttered.

~ † ~

Late one muggy July night we had a magnificent thunderstorm. The lightning crackled and snapped, brightening the sky in a show as impressive as a festival fireworks display. Rain poured down in sheets, and wind battered the shutters and set the old castle trembling.

By morning, the storm had spent its fury, and the outdoors glistened with the promise of fresh growth. Before the storm, Oryn had animated the pumps to water the gardens around the clock, nearly emptying the cisterns. Now, with the cisterns overflowing, the crops and flowers were safe from drought.

Balissa and Tal found me after lunch, practicing with my bow. "Come on," she called, holding up several baskets. "We're going mush-rooming."

Copious quantities of fungi had sprouted on the green, and we filled our baskets with a variety of delicacies. Balissa inspected what Tal picked, but she was confident in my ability to choose only edible mush-rooms; both my mother and Nanni had been expert mushroomers.

Balissa left us to pick the last of a patch as she moved off to search for a fresh supply.

"What about these?" Tal asked, showing me some button mush-rooms.

"They look fine. Where did you gather them?"

He pointed out a cluster of mushrooms under a bush.

"Puffballs!" I exclaimed. They were delicious either raw or cooked.

Satisfied with our harvest, Balissa led us to the kitchen. "I'll dry my basket for later use," she decided. "You two prepare your mushrooms for dinner." She grinned with girlish delight. "I'm so glad it rained. No place in Latretta can match Red Castle's green for mushroom varieties. Mushroom soup tonight, Sadye," Balissa said.

"Blech," Sadye rumbled, mopping her sweating brow with her bril-liant orange apron.

Balissa grinned, undaunted. Her enthusiasm was contagious, and we hummed a cheerful tune as we cleaned the mushrooms. Sadye plunked a huge kettle down on the fire, which soon bubbled merrily. The delicious aroma of cooking fungi wafted through the kitchen.

We had baked bread the day before, and Balissa cut generous slices to go with the soup. Grubby from picking, she sent us to wash before dinner. I passed Morty as I ducked into the hall.

I heard Balissa tell him, "I need you to check the soup. I'm going to freshen up before dinner."

After bathing, I hurried to my room to change. I arrived at dinner moments after Oryn, who pulled out a chair for me. "Thank you," I said, embarrassed by his uncharacteristic chivalry.

Sadye exhaled with a snort and stabbed a slice of bread with her fork. I smiled at her, but her face remained impassive as she smeared butter on the bread.

Balissa dished out the hot, savory-smelling soup as she talked to Oryn.

Morty picked up his spoon to begin eating. Steam rose from his soup in little curlicues, wafting and swaying above his bowl.

Suddenly, the steam shifted into the shape of a skull. Gasping, I threw out my hand to stop him as he lifted the spoon to his mouth. He was out of reach, but the spoon flew out of his hand and skittered halfway across the room. I jumped to my feet and covered my mouth in horror.

"What the...!" Morty bellowed. Soup had splattered his face. "What did you do that for?"

"Poison," Sadye said around a mouthful of bread.

"Arabella?" Oryn asked, his brow furrowing.

"I think...I think...there may be a bad mushroom," I stammered.

"Mortimor!" Balissa cried. "Did you check the soup?"

Morty's face turned red.

Balissa gritted her teeth and shook her head. She held out her hand to the pot and commanded, "Venyto!" There was an eruption in the kettle, and a black disk flew into the air and hovered over the pot until she snatched it.

"Look at it!" she cried, opening her palm. I had never seen her so angry. "'Tis as black as a cinder."

The black disk was a silver coin. Nanni always put a silver object into the pot when she cooked mushrooms. She claimed the silver turned black if the pot was poisoned.

Balissa threw the coin down in front of Morty. "'Twas a simple task, Mortimor. You could have killed us all!"

"I'm sorry," Morty began, but Oryn shushed him with a wave of his hand.

"How did you know the soup was poisoned, Arabella?"

Obviously no one else had seen the grinning skull in the steam. I gazed down at my bowl, struggling for an explanation. "I was thinking...about the mushrooms, sir...I may have mistaken a baby Death Cap for a button mushroom..."

Tal turned pale and rose slowly to his feet. "'Twas my fault, sir. I picked a couple I thought were buttons."

Oryn waved for silence. "'Tis not your fault, Tal. Death Caps can be mistaken for puffballs as well. *That* is why we put a coin in the pot." He turned to Morty, rippling veins in his neck belying his calm voice.

"Mortimor, your disregard for Balissa's instruction is inexcusable. You will throw away this poisoned pot and clean the kitchen until it gleams. You are confined to kitchen duty for two weeks. Do not show your face at lessons until the fortnight has passed." Oryn rose to his feet and caught my gaze.

His look suggested he did not believe me. I flushed and dropped my eyes, but he left without further questions. Morty cleaned the table, and Tal silently helped him. Balissa left the kitchen, too upset to speak. Sadye calmly munched another slab of bread. I found her unruffled composure unnerving, and I retired to my room.

Morty accepted his punishment with remarkable grace. He reported to Sadye every day and refrained from most of his sarcastic remarks. He was merciless in one respect, though.

"How did you know the soup wasn't safe?" he asked yet again.

"Why does it matter?"

"You *knew* that soup was poisoned."

I closed my eyes, willing myself to be patient.

"Magic," Sadye said.

Morty shot her a scornful look. "You owe me an answer," he prodded. "I saved your life."

I sighed. "I know. The monster in the lake..."

"That was the second time," he said smugly.

My brow furrowed. "When else...?"

He crossed his arms and puffed out his chest. "I caught two Sardonian soldiers trying to creep into camp the night before we reached the lake."

"What? Where did they come from?"

Morty shrugged. "They must have followed the shoreline after I sank their boat that morning."

"I saw you by the river in the moonlight." My eyes widened. "You had your knife..."

Sadye rumbled deep in her chest.

"I stunned them," Morty said. "And I tied them together. I used my knife to cut the rope."

Sadye hemmed and mumbled under her breath.

"So I think I deserve an answer," Morty said.

I massaged my temples. The truth had to be better than his incessant pestering. "I saw a skull form in the steam above your soup." I raised my chin, daring him to contradict me.

"You saw a skull...?"

"Told you," Sadye said, punctuating her speech with a paring knife.

His dark eyes narrowed. "Fine," he said after a long pause.

That was it? No mocking, no scorn? His reaction was not what I had expected, and I hoped I wouldn't regret telling him.

25

ryn and Balissa agreed on a day for her departure, and we decided the apprentices would throw a sendoff banquet in the great hall. I labored all day in the kitchen; I wanted the meal to be perfect. Though Morty was still on kitchen duty, Oryn allowed him to hunt meat for the dinner. He bagged a sizeable deer, and Tal set snares and caught a brace of hares.

Thrilled with the fresh meat, I entrusted Tal with roasting the hares in the huge kitchen fireplace. Morty would have used magic to keep the spit turning, and when his attention wandered, the meat might have burned. Tal never animated objects and then neglected them.

Instead, Morty peeled and prepared the vegetables while I tackled dessert. It was my first unassisted try at a torte. One of the three layers was a little uneven, but a generous application of frosting helped. I topped the torte with fresh peach slices. I was delighted with the lovely result.

Oryn agreed to transport the food to the huge table in the great hall, where he had spent most of the day animating dust cloths, brooms, and mops to clean every nook and cranny. When everything was ready, I bathed, and then went to my room.

I debated a long time over which of my dresses to wear. At last, I settled on the green velvet; I might never have another excuse to wear it. I slipped on the gown, hooked the long row of buttons, and studied my reflection critically in the small mirror on the wardrobe. The dress was quite elegant, and I practiced my curtsy. When I swept up my hair and added the garnet jewelry and combs, I looked quite grown up.

"Despite what Nanni said," I murmured, "my freckles are still as pronounced as ever and my hair just as orange." I sighed and wrinkled my nose. My mother had once said I would grow into my looks. "I think I'm all grown up," I said to my reflection. I cocked my head and frowned. "Yet no one would call me pretty."

I smoothed my skirts and glided down the spiral stairs, careful not to trip on the long skirt. "That would be perfect. Enter the dining room and sprawl on the floor." I wanted to save myself *that* humiliation.

As usual, I arrived last for dinner. The others had gathered in a knot around the elegantly set table, sparkling with freshly polished silver and crystal wine glasses. As I entered, Morty looked up and gawped in disbelief. The others ceased speaking and gaped as well.

I glanced from one to the other, noting their expressions. As usual, Sadye's face remained impassive, but Tal gazed with open admiration, Morty looked disconcertingly wolfish, and Balissa beamed with approval. Even Oryn's usually inscrutable face revealed something akin to admiration.

"What?" I demanded, acutely self-conscious. "Haven't you ever seen a lady dressed for dinner before?"

A smile spread across Oryn's face. "Indeed. Ladies, gentlemen." He bowed to us in turn. "I think this calls for a change of venue." He lifted his hands, and tapers from the table fluttered around the room, lighting the chandeliers. Lush garlands of greenery sprouted on the walls and festooned the balcony. Richly colored tapestries shimmered into being on the walls, and vases of glorious flowers appeared in the windows. With help from a taper, a fire leapt to life in the massive fireplace, crackling and dancing merrily.

"Perhaps we should dress for the occasion," Balissa suggested. She, Morty, and Oryn each made gestures, and their clothes suddenly transformed into magnificent evening attire. Balissa's pure white gown—the same gown I had seen in the gallery at the trial—sparkled with diamonds, and the jewels glistening in her white hair matched her pale green satin sash. Oryn and Morty's clothing consisted of starched white tunics, pressed black breeches, shiny boots, and perfectly tailored coats. But there were subtle differences; Morty's shirt had ruffles at the ruff and sleeves, his boots came to a long point, and a scarlet carnation graced one of his buttonholes. Just like him, I thought, hiding a smile.

Even Sadye shed her apron, though her astonishing turquoise and yellow gown topped with a matching kerchief reminded me of a jester's attire.

Tal stood bewildered, still wearing a wrinkled tunic and breeches. Balissa waved her hand, and he sported an outfit similar to Oryn's. He blushed, and she patted him on the arm.

I sank into the chair Oryn held ready for me.

The table strained under the weight of the food. "This is a feast fit for kings," Oryn declared. "I think we need dinner music." He waved his hand with a flourish and music wafted across the room. The song began well enough, with violins and horns following a recognizable melody, but it soon deteriorated into a tuneless cacophony of crashing percussion and wailing strings. Oryn sat conducting, seemingly oblivious, but the rest of us clapped our hands over our ears as the din grew louder and louder.

"Mercy," Balissa gasped, laughing helplessly. "Oryn, please stop."

He shrugged, grinning boyishly, and the music ceased.

"I think you should leave the music to me." She lifted a finger, and a beautiful aria floated across the room. The aria swelled and grew, filling every corner of the hall with its lilting melody.

Sadye nodded her approval. "Better," she rasped.

I listened in awe. "Are you creating that, Balissa?"

"Sadly, no. I can only copy what I've heard before. But thankfully my ears are more in tune than his," she added, grimacing playfully at Oryn. She mock whispered, "He's tone deaf."

"I heard that," Oryn said.

Balissa winked, eliciting a shy smile from me. It was good to see Oryn so relaxed and happy.

We ate the delicious meal, talking and laughing as music swirled around us. Tal had turned the hares to perfection, and he rewarded my praises with a blush. Seasoned vegetables complemented the venison.

"Perfect," Sadye declared after tasting my torte.

I basked in the glow of their compliments, and even Morty, who often pretended to gag on my cooking, ate everything with lip-smacking relish.

Oryn ate a prodigious quantity of food. At last, he pushed his plate away with a contented sigh. "That was delicious. Tal, Morty, Arabella... Thank you. Now, who's up for a rousing game of Blind Man's Bluff?"

Sadye huffed, and the rest of us groaned in protest, but Oryn would have none of it. He was as enthusiastic as a schoolboy. Shooing us away, he sent the table and chairs scuttling against a wall, clearing the center of the room for the game.

Balissa produced a blindfold. "Who wants to go first?" Teasingly, she waved it over her head.

"I will!" Tal and Morty chorused.

"How about you, dear?" she suggested, turning to me.

I tied the blindfold. "All right, where is everybody?" A chime of voices—minus Sadye—answered, and I picked out Tal's baritone as nearest. After a breathless chase around the hall, I tagged him. He then touched Balissa, and she in turn tagged Oryn. He grinned as Balissa tied the blindfold over his eyes.

I had raised my voice when Tal and Balissa took their turns. But I found myself tongue-tied when Oryn called, "Where are you?"

Even so, he cocked his head and moved toward me. I fled, but he followed relentlessly.

Sadye stood like a statue in the center of the room, watching him with narrowed eyes. "Cheater," she croaked.

"He *is* cheating, isn't he?" I murmured to Balissa as I sought refuge behind her.

Balissa laughed. "He can't help it, dear."

Finally, he cornered me. I squealed and twisted, but he caught me in his arms. "Gotcha!" he whispered in my ear before releasing me. Oryn handed the blindfold back to Balissa.

Morty scowled and said, "What about my turn?" He had been calling loudly to get Oryn's attention.

After an awkward pause, Balissa said, "How about some dancing? Morty, will you be my partner?" She started a lively waltz, and they sailed around the dance floor.

Tal looked uncomfortable, so I curtsied and offered my hand. He blushed, and we set off. His huge hand dwarfed mine; for once, I felt small and dainty.

"I like your dress. It's...velvety...and you look...beautiful," Tal stammered, his face turning red. He was not a great dancer, but we had managed to make it once around without treading on each other's toes.

I smiled and dropped him a deep curtsy. "Thank you, but only the dress deserves to be called beautiful."

He looked perplexed, but then Morty appeared at my elbow, ready to take his turn. I glanced around, hoping Oryn was available, but he had cajoled Sadye into stomping around once with him. I took Morty's offered hand, and he led me confidently around the floor.

"You are an excellent dancer," I said.

"And you're not."

I flushed and did not speak again until he handed me off to Oryn.

Oryn was also a good dancer, and he led me expertly. Noting my red face, he asked, "What was he teasing you about now?"

I flushed again. "He suggested I'm a lousy dancer."

Oryn glanced in Morty's direction and frowned. "You are better than *I* expected, considering you spent a year in jail instead of practicing such things."

Grateful tears pricked my eyes. Ducking my head to hide them, I said, "You cheat shamefully at Blind Man's Bluff."

He squeezed my waist, drawing my ear to his mouth. "Of course I do."

We had come full circle, and he stepped away, bowing deeply to all of us. "Thank you, ladies, for a lovely evening. Perhaps our guest of honor would like to say a few words before we retire?" He held out his hand, and Balissa curtsied gracefully.

"Thank you. Mortimor, Tal, Arabella." She gazed at each of us in turn. "I leave for Sperara tomorrow morning, but I will treasure the memory of this wonderful evening while I am apart from you. I've already spoken with Oryn and Sadye, and I wish to have a final word with each of you, so Tal, if you will walk with me...?" She held out her arm, and they set off on one final circuit of the great hall. Sadye stacked a great mound of dishes on a teacart and headed in the direction of the kitchen. Oryn busied himself extinguishing candles, though he could have blown them out with one sweep of his hand.

When Balissa and Tal returned, she strolled away with Morty. Soon it was my turn, and Balissa took my arm and led me across the hall.

"I'm going to miss you so much," I said.

She turned to me, tears glistening on her cheeks. "A dark cloud is brewing in Mortimor's future. Oryn has done his best but..." she trailed off and sighed. "Some faults cannot be overcome by discipline and training. Be wary and vigilant." She pulled me close and said in my ear, "I know I needn't ask, but be extra kind to Tal. 'Tis difficult for him here." Her voice fell to a whisper. "You can trust Tal with your life."

"I know."

"Listen to Sadye. She is loyal and faithful. And Arabella, be strong for Oryn. He needs your strength more than he knows."

"But I'm not strong."

"You are," she said, touching her finger to my nose. "Iron runs through your spine. Take care of Oryn." She kissed me on the forehead and whispered, "Good bye, my dear...till I see you again."

26

 rose early, thinking I would tidy the hall before the castle awoke. But the hearth was cold, and the furniture was shrouded in sheets. Since the kitchen sparkled as well, I decided to spend my morning organizing Oryn's shelves. I had made little progress so far, but I was resolved to finish before the end of winter.

Oryn was at his desk. "Up and about already?"

"The great hall and kitchen are clean." I plopped down by a shelf. "I have a few hours till Sadye churns butter, so I thought I would put in some time here." I pulled a book down and opened to the flyleaf. "I hoped to say goodbye to Balissa before she left."

"She left in the wee hours of the morning."

"She's gone? I never saw her pack any food...how long will it take her to get home?"

Prissy had been crouching beneath Oryn's chair, but she suddenly jumped on his lap.

"Ooof!" he complained affectionately, scratching behind her ears. "She's home already," he said, looking up at me.

"But how? Isn't Latretta far to the north?"

"She went by portal."

"By portal? What is that?"

Oryn shooed Prissy off his lap and stood up. "Come stand next to me."

I obeyed.

"Where would you like to go?"

I shook my head, confused.

"Name a place within the castle grounds."

A giggle burbled out, and I berated myself mentally. I did *not* want to sound like a naïve, nervous schoolgirl in front of Oryn. I cleared my throat. "The kitchen!"

"The kitchen it is." He gestured, and a spot six feet in front of us shimmered. The portal expanded to an oval seven feet tall and three feet wide, and slowly Sadye came into focus on the other side. She was mixing something at the kitchen table.

"Amazing!"

"Walk through," he said.

I glanced at him uncertainly, but he gestured and said, "'Tis perfectly safe."

Squaring my shoulders, I stepped through the oval—and I was in the kitchen.

"Dang portals," Sadye muttered under her breath, moving to the other side of the table.

I turned around. Oryn was still standing in the library, watching me. "Can I come back through?" I called.

"I can hear you just fine, and yes, portals work from both directions."

I skipped through, enthralled. "Can a portal take you anywhere you want to go?"

"Almost. Your destination must be somewhere you have already been. For instance, I can open one to the great hall...the courtyards...or the gardens." He gestured three times and three portals opened to the specified locations.

"Fantastic! You can use a portal to get anywhere you want to go, instantly."

He smiled at my enthusiasm. "That's the idea." He gestured again, and the portals closed.

"While we were traveling, Morty said something about opening a portal home, but Balissa said he would be breaking the rules. What did she mean?"

"Ahh," Oryn said and sighed. "Count on Morty to wish to break the rules." He sat down. "Portals work in both directions but can only be closed from the side they were opened. If Morty had opened a portal and all of you came through, the portal would have stayed open... possibly forever."

"Forever?"

"Many enchanters have opened one in desperation, trying to get somewhere or attempting to escape from danger. Sometimes the danger follows them through, or the portal remains open, unable to be closed from the other side."

I raised an eyebrow. "You mean there are open portals out there?"

"Lots of them. People sometimes blunder through and find themselves leagues from where they started. Often they disappear forever, unable to find their way home. That's why strict rules govern the use of portals."

"Wouldn't a gaping hole to another location be obvious?" Another giggle escaped, and I clapped my hand to my mouth. What was wrong with me? Why was I tittering like an idiot? "Surely they could get back again," I said in a more restrained voice.

Oryn shook his head. "Over time, portals fade and become invisible. A person who had no idea such a thing existed would be hopelessly lost and confused."

"Oh. Did you open a portal for Balissa?"

He ran strong hands through his dark hair. "No. Powerful magic protects Red Castle; portals can only be opened to locations within the barrier masking and shielding the castle grounds."

"Then how did she get home?"

"There are other ways to open portals." He looked away. I thought he was finished, but he held out a hand, beckoning me closer. "This is a portal stone," he said, removing a gold ring from his pinky finger.

The ring was simple but elegant; the band was delicate, and an oval tiger's eye stone shone in the setting.

"It's lovely."

"Thank you," he said with a wry look. "But I'm more interested in its function than its beauty."

"How does it work?"

"This stone opens a two-foot-high portal to another stone. 'Tis intended as a communication device, but it can transport goods or people in a pinch." He grinned. "Balissa had to crawl through."

"She has another stone?"

Oryn nodded. "She left it with a trusted friend in Sperara. This ring also belongs to her, but she lent it to me when I first came to Red Castle. It has proved quite useful," he said, shoving the ring back on his finger. "There are huge round portal stones, too," he added as an afterthought, holding his hands in a six-inch circle to demonstrate. "Supposedly there were nine, but only one remains."

I smiled. "I guess one isn't much good, is it?"

He shrugged. "'Tis just a pretty museum piece on display in Sperara without another stone."

He waved me toward the bookshelves. "You'd best get back to work."

"I'm surprised you don't use portals all the time. They seem handy," I said as I went back to sorting volumes.

He grimaced. "They are, but Balissa made me promise I wouldn't use them while she was here. She claims I need the exercise. But now that she's gone..." He grinned. "You can expect to see them pop open anywhere. I hate walking the length of this castle. 'Tis such a waste of time."

I hid a smile. His impatience was in keeping with his personality.

~ † ~

Summer melted into fall; grapes turned purple, pears golden, and apples rosy. We were busy from dawn to dusk preparing for winter. Oryn's herbs were spectacular, and he enlisted everyone's help to pick and dry them. He opened a portal from the garden to a small room at the back of the library where he stored herbs. Tal and Morty picked one type of herb at a time and brought them to the storage room where Oryn and I dried the leaves and stems, chopped and ground the roots, or whatever preparation they required. Sadye packaged the herbs and labeled the packets before stacking them on the shelves.

"Tomorrow we can begin on the vegetables," Oryn said.

Late that night, a clap of thunder woke me from a sound sleep. I listened as the storm broke; lightning brightened every spire, and rain sheeted down the leaded windows. Suddenly, an unfamiliar pounding began on the roof. Alarmed, I rose and went to the window. Hailstones the size of lemons were smashing everything.

Without waiting to throw on a robe, I rushed out the door and sprinted down the staircase, my nightgown whipping around my ankles. I had not descended more than twenty steps before a portal opened in front of me. Unable to check my momentum, I tumbled through in a tangle of limbs and nightgown.

I was in the library. Oryn stood at the windows gazing at the ruined gardens.

He turned as I untangled myself and rubbed a shinned elbow. His sour expression slowly turned to a smile. "That was quite an entrance."

"I can see why Balissa doesn't like portals. You never know when you might fall headlong through one around here," I said tartly.

He gave a short barking laugh and turned back to the window. I stood next to him and watched the garden's destruction with every brilliant flash of lightning.

"Your beautiful garden, Oryn."

Every leaf was shredded, every stalk flattened. Fruit and grapes lay crushed or pitted on the ground.

"The gardens will grow again, but much of our winter food supply has been destroyed. There may be lean times ahead," he said with a sigh of resignation.

The hearth was cold; goose bumps rose on my arms and legs, and I shivered. Oryn gestured, and a blanket high on a bookshelf flew across the room. He moved behind me and draped it around my shoulders. His hands trembled, no doubt from watching the destruction of his beloved garden. Longing to comfort him, I tilted my head back until it rested on his chest. He gave a shuddering sigh, and his heartbeat accelerated. His hands stole to my shoulders. I stood motionless, wishing I could find the right words to say.

"We're strong and resilient. We'll make do...we can tighten our belts."

Oryn swallowed hard. I thought I felt his chin rest ever so lightly on my head.

"Thank you, Arabella," he said hoarsely. We stood watching until the storm's fury abated, and the hail and rain slackened. I moved away from him and huddled in the blanket. I heard him sit down.

"What about the root vegetables? Won't they be all right?" When he remained silent, I turned and looked at him.

He was leaning back in his chair with his hands laced behind his head, gazing at me with an inscrutable expression. I blushed and whirled to face the window; sometimes his behavior bewildered me. Moments ago, he had been devastated, or so I had thought, but now he seemed indifferent to the destruction outside.

"The turnips should be just fine," he said with a crooked grin.

I raised an eyebrow, irritated by his flippant manner. We needed those crops for the winter. "Good. We can eat them every day. Fantastic."

He laughed. "Why do you hate turnips so?"

I lifted my chin. "My jailer in Heyden claimed turnips prevented scurvy. If I never see another boiled turnip, I won't complain." Not eager to discuss my time in jail, I unwrapped the blanket and laid it on a chair. "I'm cold. I think I'll return to my room."

Oryn raised an eyebrow and shrugged.

I stepped through the portal as regally as I could, although the effect was negated when I tripped on a stair before he closed the portal.

~ † ~

The root crops *were* all right, but it took the five of us two weeks to clean up the havoc the hailstorm had wreaked on the grounds and gardens. Oryn set Morty and Tal to work pruning fruit trees and grape vines. The grapes were lost, but Sadye salvaged three bushels of apples and pressed them for cider. I mourned the loss of the fruit; the prospect of no dried apples or preserves over the winter was depressing. Without grapes, there would be no raisins or wine. Morty was bitter about the wine and downright sullen when Tal suggested it would build character to go without.

Oryn had grown a bountiful crop of vegetables, and it made me ill to see the destruction. I found four large winter squash entwined around a railing and protected by an overhang. The cabbages were usable if we ate them quickly, but the peppers, beans, squash, greens, and okra were gone.

We spent a whole day digging root crops: several varieties of onions, potatoes, parsnips, carrots, beets, late radishes, and...I groaned in despair as we turned over row after row of turnips. I knew what we would be eating all winter.

~ † ~

Winter approached steadily; every stray breeze loosed a shower of leaves, ice formed on water buckets during the crisp nights. My weekly tasks included aiding Sadye with meal preparation, butter churning, bread baking, and laundry, among other chores—along with daily target practice with my bow. Oryn also required more help both in the library and in his 'kitchen,' the room he used to prepare concoctions of herbs, philters, and tinctures. The only suitable room was far from herb storage, so he opened a portal between the two. After spending one wintry afternoon grinding gingerroot for an infusion of ginger and heartsease, I returned to the kitchen to help prepare dinner.

Sadye rolled a crust for a mince pie while I chopped damaged cabbage for a creamed dish.

Oryn stalked into the kitchen. He watched me for a moment and then asked, "Where did I put that packet of rosehips you fetched for me this morning?"

"With the sassafras root." He often misplaced things, and I had learned to take note of where he put them.

"Of course. *Exactly* where it belongs."

I grinned and continued chopping.

"Are you tired of cabbage yet?" he asked. We had eaten cabbage in some form at every meal since the hailstorm.

"I am." I sighed, looking at the pile on the table. "Tell me, Oryn. You're an enchanter. Why can't you just make the food?"

Oryn looked serious. "That's not the way magic works. Magic cannot create anything. I can move things..." He gestured, and my knife flew from my hand and furiously chopped cabbage. He flicked a finger, and a taper suddenly dipped, picked up flame from a lit candle, and danced around the room lighting other candles. "I can make things grow faster..." An onion sitting on the counter sprouted a top.

I laughed. "So that's how you grow such beautiful vegetables—and those gorgeous out-of-season bouquets on my stairs!"

He nodded. "I enjoy making things grow. Watch this," he said with an impish grin.

My eyes widened as Sadye's rolling pin handles grew stems and leaves.

"Botheration," she muttered, examining the leafy twigs before setting down the rolling pin.

Oryn smiled and shrugged. "Magic can also make things appear to be something other than they are." The pile of chopped cabbage flew into the air over my head, changed into a rainbow of flower petals, and fell in a colorful shower on my shoulders. Next, the flower petals became butterflies and fluttered around and around the room.

"Incredible," I said, dazzled.

"But this butterfly," he said, reaching up to snatch one, "is no more alive than Sadye's rolling pin." He called it to him with a gesture and broke off the new growth. "This rolling pin is still made of wood, even if it looks like bread." The pin transformed into a loaf of bread, which he handed to me. It was warm, as if just pulled from the oven. "But if you eat it, my 'bread' will offer as much nutrition as if you ate a branch."

Still enthralled, I said, "This is amazing! You're so creative!"

He shook his head. "'Tis all parlor tricks. What Tal can do with steel and an anvil, or a piece of wood and a chisel...He creates things with his bare hands from the wealth of his imagination. *That* is creativity. All I do is fool the eye." The butterflies collected in a huddle on the table and turned back into a pile of cabbage.

"It's still beautiful."

He shook his head. "Some magic is enduring, such as portals and protection and masking spells, but the vast majority..." He shrugged. "'Tis gone like a vapor as soon as we turn our minds to other things."

"What if you changed *food* into a different *kind* of food...?"

He gave a short laugh. "I can fool most palates. What does the damsel desire? Quails' eggs, caviar, truffles...?" He was retreating out the door.

"Just something other than cabbage."

"All right," he replied from the hall. The pile of cabbage turned into a pile of turnips.

"Turnips? Turnips! The best you can do is *turnips?*" Floating laughter echoed along the corridor. "At least *someone* has a sense of humor," I called. The turnips became cabbages again.

Sadye stalked to my side and retrieved her rolling pin. "Crazy," she said, shaking her head.

"What's crazy?" I asked.

"Him."

"He just has a unique sense of humor," I laughed.

"'Bout you."

I paused for a moment, trying to piece together her cryptic meaning. Oryn...crazy...about me? I shook my head. "Don't be silly, Sadye."

27

 *rom a distance the valley seemed empty except for a horde of black ants scurrying aimlessly on opposite banks of a dry creek bed. Then my view zoomed in, revealing two armies poised for battle across the trickling remnants of a once mighty river. Suddenly, a horn sounded, and one of the armies fell into disarray, retreating, the white plumes on their helmets streaming in the wind. Thousands of voices rose in a hideous shriek of victory, and the opposing crimson and black-plumed hordes swarmed across the river. As the first wave of foot soldiers reached the opposite bank, the retreating army wheeled at the blast of a horn, spears at the ready and swords drawn. A drum boomed, and a deadly hail of arrows rained down on the ranks of the advancing army, thinning their ranks. But for every soldier that fell, two more advanced in an endless stream.*

Then a shout passed through the army in the river, turning quickly to screams as a wall of churning water rounded a bend, bearing down on the soldiers. The panicked men clawed their way over one another in their haste to escape the riverbed, but the wave bore down, crushing and drowning everything in its path. The archers of the white-plumed army ran to the riverbank and rained arrows into the remaining ranks on the further shore. Some crimson-plumed archers returned crossbow bolts, but they fell short into the swirling waters. My view shifted to a foot soldier caught in the raging waters. He dragged himself on to a boulder in the middle of the river. He fell exhausted on the slippery rock and removed his battered helmet.

I jerked upright, clutching the bedcovers and scrubbing my eyes with my fists, trying to remove the harrowing image of Dirk's face from my mind.

Dawn streaked the sky with lovely shades of pink and purple as I headed to the library.

Oryn was bent over his desk, scribbling on a piece of parchment. "G'morning," he said.

From the corner of my eye, I saw a shadow flit across the semi-circle of mirrors. I turned quickly, but as usual, the image had vanished.

Irritated, I stalked to the center of the room and glared at my reflection. "What's wrong with your mirrors?" I demanded.

Oryn's head jerked up. "What do you mean?"

"Are they enchanted?"

"Not unless Morty's been messing with them. Why?"

"I've never found mirrors to be dependable, but yours are particularly unreliable."

He rose and studied our reflection in the mirror. "Exactly *how* are they unreliable?"

Now I had done it. From the determined look on Oryn's face, I was already wishing I had not started the conversation. "Sometimes I see flitting gray shapes in them...and the first time I saw your reflection you had a huge scar on your face...but of course...you don't have one..."

His brow furrowed. "Tell me what you see right now."

"You and me."

"Be specific, please," he said dryly.

"Okaaay," I blew out my breath, scrutinizing our reflections. "You look perfectly normal...long nose, dark hair, firm mouth, strong jaw, blue eyes..." My gaze traveled over his clothes. "Very tall, with a muscular build, grimy tan breeches, and torn gray tunic."

He glanced down at his clothes. "No mistake there." I couldn't tell whether he was pleased with my description or not. "Now describe yourself."

I made a face. "Do I have to?"

He folded his arms, and I sighed and scrutinized my smudged brown smock and ragged apron. "What's there to describe...just plain, drab little me."

He frowned at this brief sketch of my appearance. "Humor me."

I sighed again and looked at the mirror critically. "All right. I have crinkly, carroty hair, muddy hazel eyes, a pointy nose with an ugly crop of...pimples, high jutting cheekbones, too large a mouth with thin lips, ashen skin with innumerable freckles..." I was gaining momentum, and I scanned my reflection with a dispassionate eye. "I'm too tall, with bony shoulders. I have angles where I should have curves, my hands and feet are overlarge and clumsy, my dress is dirty...and...my apron is torn."

His eyebrows had risen higher and higher as I continued my description. "Is that the way you always see yourself?"

"Of course that's how I *always* see myself! What other way is there to *see myself?*"

Oryn stared at our reflections until a blush crept up my cheeks. Then he said, "I suppose beauty really *is* in the eye of the beholder. Perhaps you shouldn't always trust what you see in the mirror."

He gestured toward the door, dismissing me, but I left dissatisfied. I shouldn't trust what I saw in the mirror? What did *that* mean?

~ † ~

As frigid weather settled in, the castle grew colder. To conserve fuel we only lit fires in rooms we used daily. Instead of practicing spellcasting in the great room, Tal and Morty moved to the kitchen. Usually, we occupied the room at different times, but one blustery day in late November while Sadye and I were kneading bread, Tal and Morty trooped into the kitchen, declaring it was too cold in the courtyard for swordplay. Morty sent the furniture to the edges of the room, and Tal practiced calling objects. I had guessed his spellcasting was weak, but it was painful to watch him struggle.

After Tal tried unsuccessfully for a fourth time to call a chair from across the room, Morty exclaimed, "That's as easy as it gets, Tal. If you can't call something, you'll *never* be an enchanter."

Tal's shoulders sagged.

Sadye's breath hissed, and she slapped the dough noisily on the table.

My ire rose at Morty's insensitivity. Brushing the flour from my hands, I came to Tal's side. "You must be more assertive when you call something. Like this." Pointing to the chair, I said commandingly, "Venyto!"

To my astonishment, the chair flew across the floor. It stopped in front of me with a screech as if waiting for me to seat myself.

"Well done, Tal!" Oryn stepped into the kitchen, smiling with warm approval.

"I didn't do it, sir. She did," Tal said, his voice filled with awe.

"Really?" Oryn sent the chair scuttling back to the wall. "Show me."

I swallowed hard. To my relief the chair came when I called, though not as spectacularly as the first time.

"Good. You will start spellcasting lessons tomorrow. Boys," Oryn said, nodding to Tal and Morty. "Build a fire in the great hall in the morning. We'll need more space."

~ † ~

As I mastered spells, I learned to use them to help with chores. Any job requiring a tool could be accomplished twice as fast or more if I animated the tool.

Sometimes, however, I came back to the kitchen after drawing water and found Sadye chortling because the overzealous peeler had whittled the carrots down to nubs, or the paring knife had diced the potatoes into shreds. But with practice and concentration—and several snickers from Sadye—I got better.

Magic was *not* suitable for milking the cow or kneading bread. And if I animated the butter churn, I had to watch it like a hawk. Sadye nearly turned blue from a coughing fit after my second batch of spoiled butter, so I went back to churning by hand.

Supplies ran low as winter closed in. We had enough root vegetables, flour, and dry goods, but meat was in short supply. To supplement our stock, Oryn sent Morty out hunting, and Tal set snares beyond the walls surrounding the green. The fresh meat was a welcome change after months of salted pork.

One day, Tal wandered into the kitchen. Sadye was apparently on strike again, and I was preparing lunch on my own.

"What's amiss with your arm, Tal?" I asked after watching him scratch vigorously.

"I think I got into some poisonweed while I was setting snares."

"Let me have a look. Perhaps I can find a salve for you."

He showed me some small blisters on his forearm. They were the tell-tale signs of an encounter with a mararoot plant.

"What a nasty rash. Wait here while I get some ointment." I hurried to the storeroom, scarcely able to contain my excitement. Somewhere beyond the castle walls, mararoot was growing. If I could find the plant...

I forced myself to remain calm. After seizing the salve, I returned to the kitchen and smeared some on Tal's arm. "This ointment will soothe the itching. Apply a generous amount morning and evening. The blisters should subside in a couple of days." I paused. "Could you take me along the next time you check your snares?"

"Why do you want to go?"

"A change of scenery would be nice."

He frowned. "There's not much to see. Just rocks and boulders."

"I'd really like to see how you set snares. Please."

Tal shrugged. "I guess you can come, but bring your bow. Oryn says we're not to go out unarmed."

I grinned. "Thank you."

~ † ~

I packed a bag, ticking off the necessary items—warm cloak, gloves, trowel, knife to cut the root, burlap to wrap it in, longbow, and quiver. I was ready by the time Tal came to fetch me the next day.

"Are you certain you want to go?" he asked.

"Of course. I'm ready."

I felt the air crackle as we exited the northern gate and left the protection of the castle. I followed Tal over the rocky, boulder-strewn landscape, keeping my eyes peeled. As he checked the third empty snare, I spied the plant growing near a stunted gorse bush. Its waxy evergreen leaves had a distinctive dull gray sheen. The plant looked vigorous and healthy.

"Nothing will grow here *but* mararoot," I muttered. "Tal, you go ahead and check the next snare. I'll catch up with you shortly."

He nodded, and I set to work. I donned my gloves and cut off the woody stems with my knife. Then, using the trowel, I painstakingly dug the root from its crevice. I wrapped it in burlap, secured the bundle in my pack, and headed in the direction Tal had gone.

I had just scrambled on to a large boulder when I heard an odd sound—a growl accompanied by a shriek of fear. The growl turned into a snarling bark, and I leapt off the boulder and rounded another large stone. I shouted in surprise. A slinking gray wolf was attacking a small white horse. Two stones trapped the horse's left hindleg, and blood trickled from a gash on its haunch. The horse's eyes rolled in terror, and it foamed at the mouth. Attracted by the blood, the wolf was circling in a crouched position, watching for an opportunity to strike.

When the horse saw me, it gave another frightened whinny . The wolf turned toward me, snarling and growling. Its eyes glinted dull red in the morning light. I whipped off my bow and nocked an arrow, but the wolf slunk behind some rocks before I could get off a shot.

"Easy, there," I murmured, taking a step toward the horse.

It trembled as I approached, then suddenly reared back, bugling.

A blur of movement to the right betrayed the wolf. Unwilling to abandon its prey so easily, the sneaky beast was trying to flank me. I ducked behind a rock for a moment and readied my bow. When I rose up, the wolf had mounted a large boulder above me. As it leapt, I placed a clean shot directly into its heart. The wolf died before hitting the ground, its teeth still bared in a hideous snarl.

Tal came running. "What happened?" he asked, nudging the wolf with his toe.

"That wolf was attacking the horse," I explained, moving slowly toward the terrified creature. "It's okay. You're safe now."

She snorted, her eyes rolling, but as I murmured soothingly, she allowed me to touch her. I patted her neck, talking slowly all the while, and ran my hands gently over her trembling sides and down her legs.

"No broken bones, but this hoof is trapped. I need your help to free her."

Tal was still examining the wolf with an expression of disbelief on his face. "You killed an Ayr wolf...a sneaky, murderous, Ayr wolf!"

"Tal! Forget the wolf. Help me with the horse."

The horse snorted and whinnied in fright. "Calm down, girl. He's trying to help."

Tal was a man of behemoth strength, and after he hefted several large stones, we managed to free her. She sprang away, but stumbled and almost fell on her injured foot. She stood trembling with feet splayed and head bowed.

Ripping a strip from the hem of my petticoat, I tied the makeshift lead around her neck. "Come on, girl."

I took her straight to the stables and fixed up a stall. I doctored her leg with a poultice and bandages before returning to the castle.

The men were gathered in the great hall, deep in animated discussion about the wolf and the horse. Sadye stood listening, her green and yellow kerchief bobbing as she followed the conversation.

"There's no way it was an Ayr wolf," Morty declared as I entered.

Oryn shook his head. "I think Tal is right. Did you notice the color of the wolf's eyes, Arabella?"

"They looked red."

"That confirms it. I don't want anyone going out alone again. Where there is one wolf there may be others. And *you're* not to go out again at all," he said to me.

I frowned. "What's so special about these Ayr wolves?"

Oryn sat heavily in a chair. "Ayr wolves are the minions of evil. Normally they reside in the depths of the Eastern Fen, wild and untamed, but when a dark sorcerer's powers increase so he can control them, they will leave the marshes to do his bidding. A single wolf might be nothing...or it could mean evil is solidifying its power in the marshes. Ayr wolves are often a forerunner of turmoil."

"Who is in the marshes? Who is gathering power?"

Oryn's eyes closed, and his shoulders bowed as if the weight of the world rested on them. "Mortock. He is ruthless, without conscience, and very powerful...and that was ten years ago. Who knows to what depths his depravity has reached."

"You knew him?" I asked faintly.

Oryn sighed. "Yes, and Mortimor as well." He cast a glance in his direction, but Morty stood ramrod straight, chin jutting defiantly in the air.

"Tal tells me you found a horse," Oryn said, changing the subject.

"I named her Aramis. May I keep her?"

Oryn snorted. "I don't know what good a horse will be, but yes, you can keep her."

"Where do you think she came from, sir?" Tal asked.

Oryn shrugged. "I have no idea."

28

ramis soon healed, and I started gentling her. Though not used to a halter or shoes, she learned quickly and was ready for saddle training by the time the mararoot dried enough to grind.

I made a tincture with the ground root, and when the full moon approached, I added a few drops to a cup of tea. The drink left a horrible aftertaste in my mouth.

The following day, a pervading sluggishness afflicted me. Spellcasting lessons were a disaster; I could not perform simple spells I had mastered weeks earlier. With a shake of his head, Oryn sent me to the kitchen to help Sadye, who rumbled disapprovingly deep in her chest as I pared the vegetables by hand.

I fared a little better the next day; objects came when I called them, but animated tools stopped and started fitfully. Oryn watched me with pursed lips and a creased brow, but I persisted valiantly. The next day, more by sheer force of will than anything else, things obeyed me. By then I was due for another dose. As I took the mararoot, I wondered if it was worth the listless fog that accompanied it. Perhaps I should invent an excuse for missing lessons tomorrow.

The next day Oryn set up a large square on the floor of the great hall. "Today you will learn to use the quarterstaff." He sent a long stout stick flying to me. "You must learn to defend yourself in hand-to-hand combat."

He instructed me in basic techniques, and we took several passes around the square. Then a stout blow on my upturned stick splintered it.

"I didn't know I was so strong," Oryn quipped as he examined the broken staff. "Arabella, please fetch another from the storeroom." He opened a portal, and I ducked through.

As I returned to the portal, a glimpse in a mirror brought me up short. I laughed in disbelief. First, none of the usual shadowy gray shapes flitted in the corners. Second...

"You cannot be real," I told my reflection coyly. "The mararoot is messing with your head."

The girl staring at me had perfectly molded features. Her skin was clear with a rosy flush in her cheeks, and not a single freckle dotted her well-formed nose. She had plump red lips and striking green eyes. Her red-gold hair had the perfect amount of curl. She was tall but not gangly, with a lovely rounded figure.

"Unbelievable." I smiled and dropped a curtsy, watching the girl in the mirror mimic me.

"Preening, are we?"

I whipped around. Morty stood just this side of the portal. "Not at all," I snapped, furious and embarrassed that he had seen me.

I swept by him, determined to return to the great hall, but he grabbed my arm. "Do you like what you see?" he asked in a low voice, his dark eyes boring into mine.

"Let go of me." I yanked my arm away. Tightening my grip on the staff, I ducked past him into the portal.

"There you are," Oryn called as he faced off with Tal. "I thought you had gotten lost."

"No, sir." When it was my turn again, I attacked with savage vigor and strength.

"Don't take my head off," Oryn laughed, ducking a poorly aimed blow. He shot me a puzzled look. "Is everything all right?"

"I'm not feeling well. I would prefer to retire to my room."

"By all means," Oryn said. He cast a questioning glance at Tal, who shrugged in bewilderment.

I spent the afternoon resting and wondering about the mysterious reflection. That evening, Sadye coughed and mumbled as I diced another pile of vegetables without the aid of magic.

~ † ~

My abilities returned over the next three days. Oryn did not question me about my temporary loss of skills, and life returned to normal.

I was eager to shoe Aramis so I could ride her. Tal was wary about attempting it because she was so skittish, but after much begging, he agreed.

"She has weird feet," he grunted when I brought her to the smithy.

All four of her elongated hooves came to a pointed ridge in the front.

Tal formed the shoes on the anvil and secured them to her hooves. I held her halter and stroked her nose, speaking gently to calm her.

The task went smoothly until the last shoe. Dissatisfied with the fit, Tal reheated it in the forge so he could alter the shape. When he struck the glowing steel with his hammer, a brilliant shower of sparks burst from the surface.

Frightened, Aramis tossed her head and jerked against the rope holding her. She overbalanced and crashed into me, pinning my right arm against the stall opening. I heard the bone crack, and then I was lying on the floor with Aramis whickering and nibbling on my shoulder.

Tal's white face hovered above me. "Are you all right?" His voice was tight.

"My arm is broken," I said faintly.

Tal swept me into his arms and rushed through the freezing courtyard, calling for help. I must have drifted into unconsciousness because the next thing I saw was Oryn's worried face gazing down at me. Sadye sponged my forehead while Morty and Tal hovered in the doorway.

"It wasn't Aramis' fault," I murmured.

"I know," Oryn said.

Sadye rumbled as she dipped the cloth and wrung it out. She dabbed at my face, but I turned away, trying to see my arm.

"'Tis splinted. Don't try to move." Oryn said, brushing a stray hair off my damp forehead. "'Twas a nasty break, and it will take time to heal."

I shook my head. "You must fix it."

"Arabella," he began.

"You *have* to heal my arm. If you can make plants grow faster, you can mend a bone."

"Normally a bone takes two months to heal."

"Please," I begged. "With a broken arm, I'm useless."

His head bowed. When he lifted his eyes at last, he wore an anguished expression. "I *can* repair it, but I have been told the pain is excruciating. I don't want to make you suffer."

I squeezed his arm until my knuckles turned white. "I can stand the pain."

He gazed at me for a long moment. Heaving a resigned sigh, he rose to his feet. "All right." As he walked to a cupboard, I realized the room was unfamiliar.

"Where am I?"

"In my quarters." He filled a glass with brown liquid and brought it to me. "Drink. 'Twill dull the pain."

I choked and coughed as he poured the fiery liquor down my throat. "I hate whiskey," I croaked.

Oryn set the cup aside and knelt by my bed. He glanced at Sadye. "You will need to hold her down."

My left hand found a rail, which I gripped tightly. Sadye draped her arms over my torso, and Oryn unwrapped the splint.

Excruciating was not the right word to describe the pain. It felt as if someone was stabbing my arm with a thousand red-hot ice picks, driving them into my bones and viciously wiggling them around. I gritted my teeth, and my breath whistled in and out. As I fought to not scream, I focused on the troop of embroidered unicorns parading across Sadye's outlandish purple and yellow dress. Finally, a shriek of agony escaped, and the pain subsided.

"You have to finish!" I gasped.

Sadye released me, and Oryn dabbed sweat from my face with a cloth. "I'm done. The bone is fixed, but I want you to wear the splint for three days. 'Twill ache for a while, but within a week you should be able to use your arm as usual." He ran his hand across my forehead. "You're incredibly brave." His voice was rough. His hand dropped abruptly, and he rose to his feet. "Tal, Morty...help Arabella to her room."

Both of them looked pale and drawn. With Sadye's help, they half carried, half supported me to my room. Sadye closed the window curtains.

"Get some rest," Tal said. "I'll care for Aramis."

I sank into sleep, exhausted by the ordeal.

~ † ~

After the requisite three days, I removed the splint. My arm was stiff and sore, but after I worked out the kinks, it felt almost normal again. At times it twinged if I moved a certain way, but Oryn said that would go away over time.

Tal successfully applied Aramis's last shoe, and soon I was trotting her around the green. She was small, but swift, with a smooth, even gait. I was a little saddle sore after two years without riding, but my form returned quickly. Even Morty admitted I was an excellent horsewoman.

While I recovered from my broken arm, Oryn excused me from kitchen duty. Instead, I worked on his shelves, which were more than half-finished. Sometimes Oryn asked me to read passages aloud while he translated. I think, however, he accomplished more without my help; invariably, we spent more time arguing over nuances of wording than translating.

One evening, as I perused flyleaves, Oryn leaned back in his chair and propped his feet on his desk. "Here," he said, tossing me an apple.

"Oryn, how lovely! I thought all the apples were gone!" I polished the yellow apple on my apron until its blushing pink cheeks shone. "It looks luscious," I said and took a huge bite.

"I've been saving it," Oryn said with a crooked smile.

I chewed my first bite and swallowed, then took a smaller one. Slowly, I set the apple down, unfinished.

"What's the matter? Don't you like it?"

"I'm sorry. Maybe it's the variety. The taste just isn't quite..." I paused, stumbling for the proper word.

Oryn shook his head. "You're unbelievable, Arabella."

"I'm sorry." I picked up the apple, about to take another bite to appease him, but it whipped out of my hand and landed in his.

"I can't fool you, can I?" he said with resignation. The apple changed to a partially eaten turnip. Oryn set it on his desk. "Why can't I fool you?" he asked, gazing at me.

I colored and looked away. "You don't deserve to fool me if you use a turnip. You know how much I hate them."

"I could give most people an apple made from sawdust, and they would eat it down to the core, smacking their lips with delight." He waggled a finger at me. "But you...you can tell the difference." His blue eyes bored into me. "How is that?"

"I have no idea," I said, tossing my head. I hated questions like this. I hated the fluttering feeling in my stomach and the way my heart raced when he gazed at me...I turned away and pretended to study a book.

I heard him munching the rest of the turnip. "I'm glad *you* like it," I said after my pulse returned to normal.

"Unnh," he grunted.

I looked up.

He was preoccupied, studying an unrolled parchment.

I rose and stole to his side, looking over his shoulder. It was a map of the wasteland. The Aural Mountains ran across the bottom, the Great Lake filled the left side of the parchment, and the Pindar Mountains hooked across the center of the page.

"Oryn!" I gasped. Several crown-shaped emblems were smattered across the map.

"What?" he asked.

I was already running toward the door.

"Where are you going?"

"To my room," I called over my shoulder. As I exited the library, he opened a portal in front of me. I sprinted through and pushed open my bedroom door. I found what I was looking for and hurried back in the space of half a minute.

"Portals are amazing," I murmured as I searched through the book I had grabbed.

"I'll teach you to open one sometime," he said. "What's all the excitement about?"

I placed the open book on the desk beside the parchment. "I reread my books while I was recuperating."

"What book is this?" Oryn asked, flipping to the cover.

"It's the *Geography of Atruria*. This particular page has always puzzled me, but the emblems match those on your map!" I pointed out the colored crowns Melora and I had pored over so many years earlier.

"Here is a red crown, designating Red Castle," Oryn said. "And here's a gray rectangle for Fort Gray in Heyden." He tapped the parchment. "My map shows a white crown for Ivory Tower in Sperara..."

"Is that the capital?"

"Yes. Parliament holds session there, and 'tis the home of the king and royal family."

I pointed to a golden crown in the center of the Great Lake on both maps. "My teacher, Fabius, told me there might be another fortress in the middle of the Great Lake. Is that what this is?"

Oryn nodded. "'Twas called Sunset Keep, but no one knows if it still stands. The middle of the Great Lake isn't accessible."

"Look at this emblem in the Aural Mountains." I indicated the skinny crown in my book. "Doesn't that have to be another castle?"

Oryn ran his fingertips over the green crown. "This is an important discovery," he said, an undertone of excitement running through his voice. "I've been searching for definitive proof of a castle in the Aurals for years. 'Twas a single tower built of stone rich in malachite." He turned to me and grinned. "You've found Pine Lookout."

I flushed under his praise and fidgeted, knotting my skirt in my hands. "I didn't know you had lost it."

Oryn gave a snorting laugh. "I have spent hours poring over old texts looking for this very thing. Most documents make roundabout mention of the different castles...what they look like...what stone they were built of." He rubbed his hands across his eyes. "I even found an ancient volume telling about all the tree species growing around Pine Lookout, but until now, I haven't found a single sentence about its location."

"Then this is not going to help you," I said, crestfallen. "The Aurals are long. The tower could be anywhere."

Oryn smiled and pointed to two marks on the map. "These notches show a pass through the Aurals."

"Alara's Pass."

He nodded. "Pine Lookout stands near the pass. Balissa, Tal, and Morty may have walked through the tower's shadow on their way to Pithark. Now the council will have to listen to me," he said abstractedly.

"The council?"

"That's a conversation for another day." Oryn laid his hand on the geography. "May I keep this for a while?"

In answer, I placed the book with the other geographies on his shelves.

I stifled a yawn behind my hand, but Oryn saw me.

"'Tis getting late. You need your beauty sleep."

I grimaced, but he did not seem to notice.

29

here was little snow during January, but a relentless bitter wind chilled us to the bone. Since the weather was not conducive to working outside, Oryn put a table in a storeroom and assigned us the task of copying a faded remedy book. It was an herbalist's field guide, a more concise version of *Tudyre Salutori Erbaym* with no pictures and limited indices.

The old book was tattered beyond repair, so we divided it into sections and passed on each portion as we completed it. Morty and I wrote quickly, and we were in a race to see who would finish their copy first. But Tal found the task slow and laborious, so I made two of some pages to assist him. Sometimes, Sadye joined us, doling out nutmeats from the hazelnuts she was shelling.

One dismal gray afternoon, after blotting several of my letters and ruining the page, I pushed my pen aside and stared out the small window. I had been unable to ride Aramis for a week, and the castle was beginning to feel like a cage. With no warning, a hazelnut shell bounced off my shoulder.

I glanced at the boys, but both were scribbling on their pages.

Sadye coughed into her sleeve. It sounded suspiciously like 'Tal.'

I eyed the pile of shells. With a flick of my finger, I scuttled a hazelnut across the table and hit him on the crown of his head. Tal didn't even flinch, but he furtively reached for a shell. As it flew towards me, I ducked, sending several shells raining down around him. He grabbed a fistful of shells. I squealed and made a wild gesture, sending a barrage of shells across the table toward him. My aim was not precise, however, and the inkbottle in the center of the table teetered and fell over, spilling ink over Morty's completed pages.

Morty slammed his fist down. "Look what you did! You stupid wench..."

Even as he said the words his body shrank, and within moments, he had transformed into a toad.

Tal and I gaped, our mouths hanging open, and then we burst out laughing. "Oryn warned you he would turn you into a toad," I gasped, which sent us into greater convulsions of merriment.

If ever there was an angry toad, it was Morty-the-toad. He swelled to twice his original size, made odd gulping noises, and hopped up and down frantically.

"We shouldn't laugh," I cried. "It's making him angry." At this, Morty-the-toad jumped even higher, like a maniacal jack-in-the-box, making strangled hisses and croaks. His mad antics sent us into further gales of laughter, and we laughed until our sides ached and tears streamed down our faces. Every time we came close to stopping, he made a noise or convulsed and started us off again. At last, he launched himself at us, smacking into our hands or arms.

After fending him off for the third time, Tal gasped between laughs, "You had better behave yourself Morty, or the cat will get you."

As if on cue, Prissy sauntered through the door. Morty-the-toad's mad hopping attracted her attention, and she crouched down like a jungle huntress, frozen except for the tip of her tail twitching back and forth. Morty chose this inopportune moment to launch himself on to the floor, and Prissy stalked him from across the room.

I jumped up, all laughter forgotten. "Catch her, Tal!" I took off after Morty, who was hopping madly across the flagstones. "Come on, Morty," I said as he jumped away from me. "I'm trying to help you."

I reached for him, but he slipped between my fingers just as Tal made a grab for Prissy. He missed, and we collided and fell into a tangled heap on the floor. Prissy leaped over both of us and cornered Morty-the-toad against a heap of storage crates. Tal and I watched, helpless, as she made ready to strike.

As she pounced, Morty-the-toad turned back into Morty-the-apprentice, and Prissy bounced off his leg. He howled and aimed a vicious kick at her, but Prissy was so spooked at seeing her prey transform right under her paws that she was already careening for the door, screeching at the top of her lungs. Morty cursed and kicked the crates savagely, splintering them and strewing their contents all over the floor. His curses turned into howls of agony as his foot found a crate of pig iron. Alternately howling and cursing, he limped out the door.

"Hmmph!" Sadye snorted. She had calmly continued shelling throughout the entire escapade.

"You knew Oryn would never allow Prissy to harm him, didn't you?" I said to Sadye.

Her lips curled slightly as she popped a hazelnut into her mouth.

Tal and I fixed and repacked the ruined crates. I picked up Morty's ink-stained sheets. "I'll fix these for him. It was my fault they were ruined."

"Our fault," Tal said. I acknowledged this with a faint nod.

Morty was not the least bit mollified when I handed him the sheets I had painstakingly reproduced on fresh parchment. He snatched them without a word and limped away.

~ † ~

The next week, Oryn chose to keep us busy—and separated—with individual tasks.

I was close to completing the library shelves when Oryn began teaching me to open portals.

"Picture a room or corridor in your mind's eye," he told me. "Try to include distinctive details that make it unique from other places in the castle."

With practice, I was soon able to open portals to many different locations. Still, I sometimes found myself in the wrong spot.

"You see how easy it is to make a mistake," Oryn said when my portal opened near a different outbuilding than the one I had intended. "Here the portals are all *inside* Red Castle. Imagine how easy it is to get it wrong out there." He gestured to the world outside the protective walls. "That's why it's so important to remember those little details I've been nagging about."

Before I knew it, the moon was nearly full again, and I dosed myself with mararoot in preparation...with the same disastrous effects.

On the day of the full moon, Aramis threw a shoe, and Tal and I spent the afternoon replacing it. I was reminded again of her odd hooves, so after a light supper and a soaking bath, I wandered down the stairs with the idea of asking Oryn about them. I carried my cup of mararoot-spiked tea with me.

"Have you come to chat?" he asked when I entered the library.

"More to question and query."

"Well, query away," he said, pushing a book aside.

I settled in a chair. "While I lived in Heyden, a lot of horses boarded in my father's stable. Draft horses, war horses, ponies...yet not one of them had feet as oddly-shaped as Aramis."

"Aramis has odd-shaped hooves?"

I nodded. "They have a ridge on the front—something like this." I drew a horseshoe on a piece of parchment and sketched a point on the top.

Oryn studied my drawing for a moment before tossing it across his desk. "Interesting," he grunted.

I took a sip of tea, grimacing at the bitter taste.

"I wonder..." Oryn pulled a rolled map from a shelf. "An ancient legend claims that unicorn herds were once tended by elves."

"Elves? Like...fairies?"

Oryn snorted. "Fairies are figments of childish fancy, but elves are real, and they may still reside in the depths of the Enchanted Forest. Strange things are known to happen there, even now."

"Are you saying she's a unicorn? I think we'd have noticed a horn."

"Female unicorns aren't supposed to have horns. Still, 'tis unlikely." Oryn unrolled the map and laid it on his desk. "The legend says elves bred unicorns with horses. Their offspring—called elven horses— roamed the wasteland and Sea of Grass south of the Lorne. Perhaps Aramis is one of their descendants. If so, she's a long way from home."

I took another sip from my cup. Oryn stared at me quizzically as I grimaced again, and his eyes narrowed. "What are you drinking?"

"Tea." I lifted the cup to my lips, but it sailed from my hand. "Please give that back," I said, reaching for it, but he moved away from me.

He lifted the cup to his nose, sniffed suspiciously, and gingerly took a sip. A strange look passed over his face, then he whirled around and hurled the cup against the hearthstones. It splintered, spraying tea and ceramic shards everywhere.

"Why did you...?" I trailed off as he wheeled on me.

"DID MORTIMOR PUT YOU UP TO THIS?"

I gasped, shocked at his violent reaction. "No...no, sir..."

"THEN WHO?"

I was bewildered. "No, sir..."

"WHY ARE YOU DRINKING POISONWEED?"

"It's not poisonweed. It's a mararoot tincture..."

"IT DOESN'T MATTER WHAT YOU CALL IT. WHY ARE YOU...?" He choked mid-sentence and leaned over his desk, hacking.

"I've been taking mararoot for a long time..."

"Let me guess, you can't cast spells after drinking it!"

"That seems to be one of the side effects..."

"Then why do you take it?"

"My mother gave some to me when I was a little girl..."

"ELLY WOULD NEVER GIVE YOU MARAROOT!" He was furious again.

I burst into tears. "But she did...I had terrible nightmares..."

Oryn's brow furrowed. "Mararoot doesn't help with nightmares."

I sobbed. "But it does. It makes them stop."

He paced behind his desk. "Your mother would *never* give you mararoot. Not for nightmares, not for anything. Mararoot suppresses..." He trailed off, staring out the windows. The full moon was just visible over the horizon. Oryn's mouth fell open, and an expression of shock crossed his face. He shook his head and gave an incredulous laugh. "The moon is full," he said softly.

"Yes." I sniffled.

"And you take mararoot because you have nightmares during the full moon."

"Yes!" I wept, relieved that he finally understood. "Bad dreams come...before the full moon...nice dreams after...though they don't happen often," I stammered through shuddering sobs.

He came around the desk and pulled me roughly against his tunic. "I'm so sorry I bellowed at you," he murmured into my hair.

I clung to him, crying. I was as bewildered by his tenderness as I had been by his sudden anger. He dug in a pocket and pulled out a wrinkled handkerchief. I wiped my eyes and blew my nose. The steady beating of his heart and the pressure of his arms around my shoulders calmed me. My crying subsided to dejected hiccups.

"You must stop taking mararoot," he whispered. "Your mother may have given it to you when you were very young to help you cope, but she would never have intended for you to take it permanently..." He sighed and trailed off, releasing my shoulders. "I know this is difficult to hear, but you can't medicate yourself to stop the dreams."

Tears welled in my eyes again. "I know. I hate the way mararoot makes me feel."

"I'm sure..." He paused. "Arabella, in the future, will you tell me your dreams...or write them down?"

I wiped my eyes with the handkerchief. "I've been doing that for years. My mother made me promise...you knew her, didn't you?"

Oryn shook his head, his face unreadable.

"You called her Elly..."

He shrugged, and I knew he wasn't going to say anything more.

I blew my nose and hugged my knees. My head ached. I could not think straight, and I was exhausted from crying.

"You should sleep," Oryn said.

I nodded and retired to my room.

~ † ~

A couple days later, Oryn ambled into the library as I sorted shelves, a picnic hamper slung on his arm.

I raised an eyebrow. "Isn't it a bit cold outside for a picnic lunch?"

He grinned. "That's why we're having an inside picnic."

"We are?" I smiled, delighted.

Oryn swept a pile of manuscripts off the table and laid a crisp linen tablecloth overtop. "We are dining in style today," he said, opening the hamper. He placed a stack of neatly cut triangles on a platter. "Egg salad sandwiches on fresh rye bread, apple chutney..." He removed a napkin from a bowl and set it beside the sandwiches. "Assorted cheeses and spicy pickles..." A platter arrayed with cheese slices emerged next, followed by a cut crystal bowl overflowing with gherkins and pickled peppers. "And..." he finished triumphantly, producing a carafe from the depths of the hamper, "wine—not too sweet and not too dry."

"Did you make this spread yourself?" I asked as I settled in the chair Oryn pulled out for me.

"Of course...except for the chutney and pickles—Balissa preserved those last fall...and Sadye made up the sandwiches...and sliced the cheese for me."

I shot him a wry smile. "In other words, you chose the wine."

He grinned broadly. "And 'tis a fine wine indeed, I assure you." He poured some into a pair of goblets and handed me one with a flourish.

"Thank you." I took a sip. It *was* delicious. "What's the occasion?"

His forehead puckered. "Does a man need an excuse to have a picnic with a lass?"

Heat rushed to my cheeks, and my gaze dropped to my plate. "Yes, sir...I mean...no, sir..." I stammered.

Oryn leaned back in his chair and blew out an exasperated sigh. "Don't tell me we're back to 'Yes, sir,' and 'No, sir.' Come now, surely we've moved past such formality."

My face grew even hotter, and I was sure I was as red as a skinned beet. Why wouldn't my blood stay where it belonged, and why couldn't I speak without blithering like an idiot?

Oryn downed his wine in one gulp and poured some more.

Why was he drinking so quickly? Surely the wine would go to his head.

He stuffed a sandwich with a couple pickles before taking a bite. "You are doing well in your spellcasting lessons," he said around a mouthful.

I grinned. "If Balissa were here, she would say you need a few etiquette lessons."

He tilted his head to the side. "Am I not sophisticated enough for you?"

I grunted. "Don't be silly. People who are afraid to get mud beneath their fingernails are boring."

A crooked grin tugged at his mouth, and my face flamed.

Oryn reached across the table and slid his hand alongside mine, so our pinkies just brushed. "There's something I've been meaning to ask you..."

A knock sounded on the open door, and I jerked my hand away and looked up. Tal's huge frame filled the doorway.

"Tal!" I said, my voice sounding shrill to my ears.

"I was wondering if you were ready," he said slowly. "Unless you are busy..."

I jumped up from the table and smoothed down my skirt. "Of course not. Oryn and I are just having an inside picnic lunch."

A nervous titter escaped, and I pressed the back of my hand to my lips. This whole situation was going from bad to worse. An entire watering can dumped over my head wouldn't be enough to put out the flames in my cheeks.

"You two have plans?" Oryn asked, gazing at Tal through narrowed eyes.

"I'm helping Tal with his spellcasting," I said in a rush. "We're working on calling chairs and animating objects and..." I was babbling again, and I clamped my mouth shut and sank down on my chair. "Why don't you join us for lunch first," I said brightly to Tal. "If you don't mind, that is," I added to Oryn.

"Of course," Oryn said, indicating an empty chair, but something in his tone and the set of his jaw made me wonder if he did indeed mind.

Tal looked from me to Oryn and then at the food spread over the tablecloth. "Umm...okay," he said, plopping into the chair.

Tal was aptly described as a man of few words, but Oryn was always engaging and witty, full of banter and entertaining tales. Yet today, our conversation lagged, sputtered, and finally ceased altogether, despite the wine and delicious food. It seemed to me the tension between Tal and Oryn was so thick I could taste it.

As soon as politeness allowed, I excused myself from the table.

"Thank you for the lovely lunch," I said, dropping a curtsy to Oryn.

He gave a sullen nod as Tal stuffed one last sandwich in his mouth and rose to follow me.

"Tal, I am going to have to bow out of our lesson," I said to him. After our strained and awkward lunch, I needed time to settle and compose myself. I fled before Tal's crestfallen expression could change my mind.

I retreated to my room, curled in bed, and fell asleep, despite the tumultuous thoughts roiling through my head. It was late evening before I awoke.

After lying on my bed with my face buried in a bolster for a while, I rolled on my side and surveyed my bookshelf. *The Geography of Atruria* and *Tudyre Salutori Erbaym* bookended my growing collection of manuscripts and tomes, including two slim volumes I had recently acquired from Oryn's library. My eyes landed on an empty space between two books, and I scrambled to the edge of my bed. That spot usually held my dream diary. Had I forgotten to return it after updating it?

I searched the shelves, the desk, my trunk, under my bed—everywhere I could think of, but I couldn't find my diary anywhere. Where had I left it?

I arrived at the table late and somewhat disheveled after my hurried trot down the stairs. Oryn was savoring a cup of tea, his utensils already stacked neatly on his empty plate.

"Late," Sadye croaked, lifting a cover off my dinner.

"I know. I'm sorry." I slid into my chair. "I was searching for my diary. I can't find it anywhere."

"What does it look like?" Tal asked.

"It's leather bound. About so big," said, holding my hands six inches apart.

"Haven't seen it," Morty said, scrubbing a hunk of bread over his plate to sop up his gravy.

"Neither have I," Tal said. His eyes fell, seeking his plate heaped high with seconds—or perhaps thirds. "I'll help you look for it...if you like."

Morty snorted as he tossed his napkin on the table. "Good luck with that, lover boy."

Tal's ears turned bright red, and I shot a look at Morty's back as he sauntered out of the kitchen. Why did he always have to be so impudent and rude?

I glanced at Oryn, hoping for a chuckle or at least an ironic smile, but his blue eyes were dark and stormy. Was he still upset with me? And why?

"Have *you* seen it?" I asked.

"No." His chair screeched across the flagstones as he rose abruptly. "'Tis probably wherever you left it last."

I bit my lip. He was so very helpful.

"Would you...like my help?" Tal asked again. Now his cheeks above his beard were as red as his ears.

"Thank you for the offer, but I'm sure it will turn up."

For a moment, I thought he looked disappointed, but then he took a great gulp from his mug, and I decided I had to be mistaken. Why would Tal want to spend his evening hunting for my lost diary?

After another two hours of half-hearted and fruitless searching, I returned to my room and readied myself for bed. As I slid beneath the covers, my leg brushed something hard. I reached down and fished out none other than my dream diary. Somehow, it must have worked its way between the sheets.

"Thank goodness," I murmured as I placed my diary back on the shelf. Misplacing it had been too reminiscent of my missing Lattrian papers. And that had been disastrous.

~ † ~

"We've been practicing spells for a while," Oryn said. "But what if someone tries to enchant you? What would you do?"

Citing a need for a change of scenery, Oryn had brought us to the green for spellcasting lessons. He was in his element, but Tal, Morty, and I huddled in our cloaks. My fingers and toes were quickly becoming ice chunks, making it difficult to concentrate.

"You can attempt to avoid the spell or put protection around yourself, but what happens if someone succeeds in enchanting you?" He gazed at us expectantly.

"Break the spell," Morty muttered, stomping his feet.

"Exactly," Oryn said. "I brought you here because cold makes it easier to break free. We'll start with a stunning spell; if you can break this enchantment, you'll be able to break most others." Oryn looked at the three of us. "Who wants to go first?"

"I will," Morty said.

Oryn proceeded to stun Morty and within twenty seconds, he broke free. I was impressed.

"Well done," Oryn said. "I can see you've had practice."

Morty shrugged, but he seemed pleased with Oryn's praise.

During Tal's turn, I moved to stand beside Morty. "How did you break the spell so easily?"

Morty cast me a glance. "My grandfather used to stun me all the time."

"That's horrible!"

"I deserved it! I was a brat and irritated him while he tried to rest. My mother told me I learned to break free when I was only a little tot."

My brow knitted. "Surely stunning toddlers goes against the rules of enchantment. It certainly goes against the rules of common decency."

Morty crossed his arms over his chest. "Rules don't apply to great men like him."

I frowned. "Do you really believe that?"

He shrugged, and I turned away, troubled.

"Your turn, Arabella," Oryn called. Tal had freed himself after ten minutes. I walked to a spot in the snow, and Oryn stunned me. Tal and Morty watched with interest. Oryn came close to me.

"Fight the enchantment," he said in my ear. "Use the cold to your advantage. Eventually, the pain in your feet will force you to move."

It was useless. I could have frozen into an ice sculpture, and I would have remained there until spring.

Oryn freed me after fifteen minutes. "'Tisn't easy, Arabella. Don't be discouraged. Some people only succeed under extreme duress." He hesitated a moment. "For some reason, women find this more difficult than men."

I frowned and kicked the snow with my boot. I hated feeling vulnerable. I desperately wanted to master this skill.

After the lesson, I fell into step beside Oryn as we walked toward the castle. "We're almost out of food."

Oryn sighed. "How much is left?"

"Sadye has two wheels of mediocre cheese and twenty pounds of flour. The potatoes are gone, only the scrapings remain of a barrel of salt pork, and all the preserves are finished. There are a handful of carrots, two dozen onions, and..." I shook my head in dismay. "Lots and lots of turnips. But we can't eat just turnips!"

"I know how much you love them," Oryn said and chuckled. "I guess I'll send Morty hunting." His expression turned serious.

"I was hoping I could go with him."

"No."

"Why not? I'm a good shot, and two hunters are better than one."

"I told you before; I don't want you going outside the protection of the castle."

"I won't be alone."

"No!"

Tal and Morty turned back to look at us.

I frowned and pursed my lips. "Why not?"

He stopped walking and stared at Morty, his brow furrowed. "Because." He lowered his voice. "Because I don't trust Morty. Beyond those walls...I cannot see what's going on."

We continued walking toward the castle. "I could go hunting with Tal."

"NO!" Oryn bellowed.

I halted. Tal and Morty were staring again. "Do not tell me you don't trust Tal!"

"I trust him with my life. But you are *not* going hunting with him!"

Oryn strode toward the castle, and I followed, feeling stubborn and a little miffed. I didn't understand why Oryn was being so unreasonable.

Oryn sent Morty and Tal hunting together, and then shut himself in the library.

In the kitchen, I clanged pots and kettles until Sadye said with a sidelong glance, "Tell Sadye."

With a frustrated sigh, I related Oryn's confusing reaction. "Why was he so upset when I suggested going out with Tal?" I asked. "And it's not the first time, either." I told her about the disastrous picnic. "It was a week before things were normal between us again."

"Jealous."

"Who's jealous?"

Sadye just nodded sagely and coughed.

I frowned. Though Oryn had assured me Sadye's coughing was an expression of her personality, she seemed to be doing a lot of it lately. "Are you all right?" I asked, bringing her a glass of water.

"Hunh!" she snorted once her fit passed.

I sighed. She was no help whatsoever.

30

ven though the full moon was two weeks off, my dream was as vivid and colorful as usual. Despite our argument the previous day, I decided to tell Oryn about it at breakfast.

"I had a dream last night."

"Really?" Oryn looked surprised. Morty and Tal glanced up from their food. Sadye shoveled a piece of burned bacon into her mouth and crunched contentedly.

I took a deep breath. "Tal stood on a huge rock holding a sword. He was an enchanter, and he had just slain a monstrous beast. He knelt and offered his sword to a beautiful red-haired maiden..."

I broke off when Tal turned bright red and choked on his breakfast.

Morty hooted, "Ho, ho! Tal, an enchanter, saving a bee-yoo-ti-ful red-haired maiden!" He poked Tal in the ribs. Tal turned even redder, leapt to his feet, and fled.

I looked toward Oryn, bewildered. His eyes were somber. "In the future," he said, placing a well-aimed kick on Morty's shin, "you ought to tell me your dreams in private."

"I don't understand," I said to Oryn.

"You eavesdropped on Tal's dream," Morty said, snickering. "If he becomes a great enchanter, I'll eat my foot. *Only* in his dreams."

Oryn aimed another kick at Morty.

I clapped my hands over my mouth, mortified. "Oh, tell me that isn't true!"

As Oryn gave an almost imperceptible nod, I flew out of my chair. How could I have humiliated Tal like that? I should have known. I raced to the courtyard. A steady clanging led me right to his workshop. Tal's muscles rippled with effort as he lifted the hammer; with each stroke, it seemed as if he would cleave the bar on the anvil in two.

"Tal."

He ceased hammering and stood with head bowed, his back straight and rigid.

"I'm so sorry. I didn't know it was your dream."

"'Tisn't your fault, Arabella." He stood for a moment. Then he flung the hammer away from him. It dented the wall and fell to the floor with a thud.

I jumped. I had never seen him so upset before. I was heartbroken for him.

"Morty's right, you know. I can't perform the simplest spells. I can't even call my hammer!" He stretched out his hand. The hammer waggled weakly, then flopped back against the wall. He gave a mirthless laugh. "I'm worthless."

"No!" I put my hand on his arm. He stood unmoving, like a statue. Like a man defeated. "No, Tal. Morty may measure the worth of a man by the number of spells he can cast and the power he can harness, but Oryn does not, and I don't either. The measure of a man isn't just in the strength of his arm or the work of his hands, but in his character and heart." I gestured to the beautiful objects in the workshop. "Even if you could not create any of these lovely things, you would always be a better man than Morty because of your loyalty, your courage, your dedication." I covered his hand with mine, willing him to hear to me. "Tal... your worth is in your beautiful heart, wise spirit, and strong character." My eyes were misty.

"From you, that is quite a compliment." He took my hands in his huge ones.

A rustling noise made us turn. Oryn was leaning in the doorway. I pulled away from Tal, suddenly embarrassed. I wondered how much of my eloquent speech Oryn had overheard. He did not move, so I had to duck under his arm to exit the workshop.

~ † ~

Oryn and Tal must have come to an understanding concerning Tal's future because he stopped taking spellcasting lessons and instead devoted himself to his workshop and the smithy. My heart ached for him, but he seemed cheerful and always had a shy smile for me. He even did my chores. Every morning Sadye and I found buckets of freshly drawn water waiting in the kitchen beside a crackling fire. After breakfast, he brought the day's milking and eggs, his eyes downcast.

"I've fed and watered Lacy, and the poultry had their scratch feed."

"Thank you for your help." I smiled cheerfully.

Our food stores were rapidly dwindling. Sadye produced a sack of flour she had secreted in a cupboard, and Tal and Morty doubled their efforts hunting and setting snares. It was late March, but we were still in winter's grip, and game was scarce. Sadye made a lot of custard and served turnips regularly, but every day the pantry shelves were barer.

One evening she served a meager dinner. She was rationing the flour, so we each had one small roll, a portion of a snowshoe hare Tal had snared, a dish of creamed turnips, a wedge of crumbly cheese, and some custard.

"Are we going to run out of food before spring?" I asked no one in particular.

"Hey, you're the one who keeps a diary of your prophetic dreams. You tell us," Morty said.

My head snapped up. "How do you know that? Did you *read* my dream diary...?" My eyes widened as the rest of Morty's words sank in. "What did you say about my dreams?" I gasped.

As Morty opened his mouth to speak again, Oryn stunned him with a furious gesture.

I jumped to my feet, shaking my head from side to side. "No, no, no..." Oryn had a pained expression on his face. "No!" I covered my ears with my hands, as if that would make me unhear what Morty had said.

I ran from the kitchen into the courtyard. My feet carried me to Aramis's stall. "It can't be true," I said, patting her neck. Images from nightmares flashed through my head, and I staggered against the wall. "They *cannot* show the future. They mustn't."

Oryn found me, and I gazed up at him, silently begging him to tell me it wasn't true.

"I'm sorry," he said.

I closed my eyes and tears squeezed beneath my lids. My chest heaved, and I banged my head against the stall. The pain brought order to my thoughts. The dreams...the nightmares...showed the future. Deep in my heart, I had known this for a while—but usually my dreams were so horrible I pushed them from my mind. A hundred images flooded my head, and I babbled as I tried to sort them out.

"When I was little, I dreamed bandits attacked my father. They beat him and took his horses. I told Mamma about it, and the next day..." I swallowed hard, trying to slow the rush of words. "The next day she had a terrific argument with him. He was traveling to the outlying village of Barden with wool and horses to trade. My mother begged him, implored him not to go. When he refused, she insisted he take three servants with him. I can't remember the reason she gave, but she insisted."

I pressed my clenched fists against my face. "A week later, he returned home with this...ugly black eye. Three highwaymen attacked him. They beat him and stole the horses. He told my mother over and over he would have been murdered if he had been alone. He even bought her a silver filigree necklace set with a green stone."

A single image of my mother caressing my disheveled hair after a dream clarified in my mind. The image shifted to one of her bending over my diary as she wrote an entry. "She knew!" I gasped. "She knew from the beginning. That's why she gave me the potion, why she made me promise to write down the dreams." My chest was heaving so much it was hard to breathe.

One last image invaded my head, and I took off toward the castle.

"Arabella!" Oryn called after me, but I did not stop.

I sprinted through the halls and up the stairs until I reached my room. I tore through my shelves, strewing books and parchment everywhere until I found my dream diary.

With trembling hands, I tore apart the corners of the leaves holding the last lines my mother had penned. As I looked over the two pages without reading them, I noted that her handwriting wavered uncharacteristically, and wrinkled splotches smeared the ink.

My eyes welled as I read:

Dawn broke over a rolling hill lush with daisies, buttercups, and cornflowers. At the base meandered a river, and a woman ran swiftly across the hill, her light red hair streaming behind her in the wind. Several gray, flitting shapes shadowed her, leaping and jumping as they bounded after her. Wolves. The woman never glanced back nor missed a step, but they gained on her, bound by bound, until the largest wolf leapt on her back, driving her to the ground. The others jumped on her as well, snarling and snapping in their haste. The woman disappeared beneath struggling gray bodies, and when the great wolf stepped away from the pile, there was blood-flecked foam around his jaws. He gave a short snarl, and the rest of the wolves retreated, their eyes gleaming dull red as the sun crested the horizon. The grass was empty, and the pack milled aimlessly, growling and snapping at one another in confused disarray. The lead wolf gave a final bark and started back over the hill, the rest of the pack falling in line behind. The rising sun revealed lurid red stains on the buttercups and daisies where the woman had lain.

A tear dropped from the end of my nose, mingling with the other splotches on the page, and somewhere deep inside the turmoil in my head it registered that she had been crying as she wrote the entry. The pain in my chest tightened; I could barely breathe around the huge lump in my throat.

The journal slipped from my numb fingers, and I curled into a ball on my bed, tears streaming out beneath my closed lids.

"Arabella?" Oryn called softly from my open doorway. "Are you all right?"

I heard him retrieve the diary. "Your mother," he said after he read the entry.

"She wrote that two weeks before my seventh birthday. A month before she disappeared." My ragged voice echoed in my ears. "What was it like for her to write down those words, knowing what she was describing?" I fought for composure with every breath. I sat up suddenly. "She sealed those pages together so I wouldn't have to read them." Sobs overwhelmed me, and Oryn pulled me into his arms.

"Darling," he murmured into my hair. "I'm so sorry."

"She's dead, isn't she?" I wept into his tunic.

His breath sucked in. "I think so," he whispered.

I pulled away from him. "I'd like to be alone, now," I said, my voice shaky.

"Are you sure?"

I curled up on my bed, and finally he said, "If you need anything…"

I listened to the echo of his boots retreating down the stairs. He had called me darling. Darling.

~ † ~

The memory of Oryn's poignant tenderness stayed with me for days.

"I think I once had a dream about you." Sadye had sent me to deliver a tray to the library when Oryn once again failed to appear for lunch.

He bit into a cold egg sandwich. "When?" he asked around a mouthful of food.

"I was a little girl."

He grinned. "Do I really want to know what you dreamed? Hopefully I didn't end up dead or maimed."

"It was a nice dream. You were the groom in a wedding."

"Really?" he laughed.

"You wore a purple velvet cloak."

His brow furrowed for a moment. "Purple, hunh? How do you know it was me?"

I shrugged. "He looked like you."

Except Oryn had no scar on his cheek.

"How about the bride?" he asked with a grin. "Am I to marry a beautiful woman?"

"She was *very* beautiful. She wore a sparkling white gown and diamonds in her red hair."

A curious expression stole over Oryn's face. "You could be describing yourself."

All memory of his previous tenderness fled. "You're mocking me! She was as similar to me as a stallion is to a donkey!"

A smile played around the corners of Oryn's mouth.

I clenched my fists. "You like making me angry, don't you?"

Oryn's smile turned to a grin. "It makes your green eyes flash."

"Green eyes!" I cried. "You're impossible!"

Oryn was laughing now, a deep belly laugh. I whirled and stomped out.

~ † ~

Oryn made Morty wash the dishes every night in penance—though in my opinion, transforming him into a toadstool would not have been punishment enough for the violation of my privacy. I used my newfound free time to finish organizing Oryn's books. My next task was to produce catalogues. I had written down every title and subject; it was just a matter of alphabetizing the information.

I spent an hour working one night in my room. The hearth was cold when my candle started flickering, so I went to bed. I awoke after midnight in a cold sweat and came to a quick decision. This should not wait.

I slipped into a robe and opened a portal to the corridor leading to Oryn's room. After gathering my courage, I knocked on his door.

He opened it almost immediately. "Come in." Cold moonlight streamed through his windows, making his room seem even starker than I remembered. Oryn lit a lamp beside his bed and sat on the mattress. He yawned and stretched, making his rumpled nightshirt gape at the neck. I blushed and looked away. He tugged the laces to close his shirt and slowly tied them.

"Did you dream, Arabella?" Oryn asked, looking out the window at the nearly full moon.

"I think Balissa may be in trouble."

He called a chair from a corner for me. "Tell me."

"Soldiers wearing scarlet plumes pulled her from her house in the middle of the night. They brought her before a group of six old men dressed in crimson robes."

Oryn slowly rose to his feet. "What did they say?" he asked in a flat voice.

"They accused her of aiding and abetting you. They claimed you are 'Misguided and bent on spreading panic among the populace... your motives are questionable, and despite the support of Beris, they will call you before the council for questioning when you return to Sperara.'" I frowned. "There was a woman with black hair. She was beautiful, but in a sinister kind of way."

"That sounds like Tennala. She's the granddaughter of a high council member. Women are not allowed on the council, but somehow, she has weaseled her way into the council's meetings, and Balissa says she wields considerable influence."

I sighed. "Tennala said you might be banished if enough evidence could be brought against you. They seemed to love the idea."

Oryn stared out the window. "And so things happen just as Balissa feared." He shook his head. "Here I stand, the last bastion between them and destruction, and they wish to banish me." He turned to me, running his hands through his hair. "What else did they say?"

"They implied that they might arrest Balissa, but a woman entered the room. I think she may have been the queen."

"The queen? How did she look?"

"She was dressed in a light blue gown and wore a gold circlet in her silver hair..."

Oryn shook his head. "Did she seem well?"

"Well enough, I suppose. She looked pale and tired, but it was early in the morning. She insisted that Balissa was under the protection of the king. She told them that should still mean something, even to the council. They finally agreed to release her into the queen's custody.

"The women were about to leave when Tennala said to Balissa, 'We know all about your family heirlooms. The council requests that you bring them to us.' Balissa had no choice. They dispatched a soldier with her, and she returned with her necklace. The council took it, and then she left with the queen."

Oryn sat on the cot and lifted his right hand. His tiger's eye ring winked in the light of the lamp. He ran his hand over the stone, and a dark portal opened, two feet high and a foot and a half wide. He peered into the blackness and said, "The stone is still functioning. I hope I can warn Balissa, but she is not scheduled to contact me for another week." He closed the portal with a flick of his finger and folded his hands in his lap. "I was planning to request supplies."

By his tone, I guessed he would rather scratch his eyes out than admit we needed help.

He sighed. "Life could get difficult around here without Balissa's support."

"Who were those men?"

"The high council. Three governing bodies rule Sperara: the king, parliament, and the council. The people choose the king. The king's eldest son usually—but not always—succeeds the father. The populace elects eligible citizens to parliament, which is in charge of domestic affairs. The council is a body of one hundred and fifty men from ancient aristocratic families. They are members for life, and their seats pass to their eldest son. They are the elite of Latretta, important and powerful men. Originally, they were in charge of judicial matters. The high council—the six men you saw in your dream—sit on the highest court of Latretta. But for many generations they have overstepped the bounds of their power. Now they threaten the authority of the king." He rose and paced back and forth. "The last time the people stood up to them was more than thirty years ago, and they were infuriated. Even now, they refuse to believe Mortock poses a threat. They are a bunch of doddering old men who only remember Mortock as a handsome and flattering young man." Oryn sighed. "'Tis a long story, too long to relate now, but they have great influence. They have convinced many people that the king and I are crying wolf. They have nearly silenced the king. As for me..." He gave a snort. "They thought I couldn't make trouble for them here, but the winds of power are shifting. Rumors of roiling unrest in Atruria and elsewhere have reached even ordinary citizens' ears."

"Unrest in Atruria?" I said, but he continued without paying heed to my question.

"I think this is a desperate attempt by Tennala and the council to limit Balissa's influence." He pursed his lips and stared ahead, deep in thought.

I was hesitant to break in again.

At last he said, "Thank you. Try to get some sleep." He attempted a smile. "Don't worry about Balissa. She's a wise woman. She'll be fine."

I nodded and returned to my room. It seemed as if Oryn had the weight of the world on his broad shoulders. Balissa said he needed my strength, but Oryn was the strong one. He did not need anything from me.

31

hy do the names of so many Latrettan men start with m-o-r-t?" I was bored. A late blizzard had obliterated the landmarks outside, so Oryn and I had spent the morning in the library. After completing the catalogues, I had amused myself shuttling books back and forth with a flick of my finger until Oryn cleared his throat in irritation. Then I retreated to a comfortable chair and watched the snow swirl outside while I flipped through a Latrettan history.

"There's Mortekai, Morticus, Mortifor, Mortolla..." I laughed. "Who names their son Mortolla?"

"The same kind of person who names their son Mortoryn."

"Mortoryn?" I raised an eyebrow. "Is that your name?"

Oryn nodded. "'Tis tradition. For generations my family has given the eldest son a name beginning with m-o-r-t. Mortolla's mother was probably desperate for a name."

"There's Mortred, Mortonious, Mortimor..." I paused. "Are you related to Morty?"

"We're cousins."

"Oh." I wondered why no one had mentioned this before. Suddenly my eyes widened. "And Mortock...? Surely you're not related to him as well!"

Oryn sat back and sighed. "He is my grandfather's older brother."

Horrified, I gasped, "Do you think he would...?" I stopped, unable to continue.

"Family means nothing to him. He would kill me if he had the chance."

Late that night, I lay thinking of Mortock. I did not know what he had done, but I understood betrayal. A man who could kill his nephew...or betray his own sister. I huddled under the covers and shivered, and not just from the cold.

~ † ~

I sat up, startled. The blizzard had ended sometime after midnight, and a slim fingernail of moon gleamed through the window. Stillness reigned throughout the castle. Then the sound echoed again and again—Sadye's deep, hacking cough. A chill traveled up my spine. It was too similar to Fabius's final illness.

I found Oryn after lunch. He was clearing paths to the outbuildings.

"Sadye is sick," I said, coming up behind him. "She's been hiding a cough for months."

He gestured, and a huge spray of snow flew across the courtyard. "I know. She's been swiping ginger from my shelves, as well as honey and whiskey for a tonic."

"I don't think she's getting better." His faced sobered as I told him about her late night coughing fit.

"Perhaps I ought to send her home to Sperara," he said.

"I don't think she'd like that."

"That's an understatement," Oryn said, sighing.

I walked to the stables to visit Aramis and distract myself from thoughts of Sadye's health. I devoted myself to currying Aramis until she glistened.

~ † ~

Spring came quickly to Red Castle. One day we were shoveling three feet of snow, the next, crocuses, daffodils, and other flowers burst into riotous bloom. Indecision seemed to grip Oryn; he delayed planting the vegetable garden and made only feeble efforts in his herb garden.

Our food situation was desperate, so Oryn's lack of enthusiasm for gardening puzzled me. This, coupled with an increase in what I called eavesdropping dreams, was unsettling.

After the painful results of Tal's dream, I never spoke of them again, but they had not stopped occurring. Two or three times a month, I woke up with someone else's dream running through my head. Usually they belonged to Tal, sometimes Nanni, and once I relived Morty's dream. Tal had heroic nighttime adventures, Nanni dreamed about burning dinner or staining the linen, and Morty's nightmare was morbid. Sadye evidently didn't dream.

Then for the third time in as many weeks, I experienced Oryn's dream. Each time it was nearly the same; he kissed a maiden with red hair. It was irritating to watch them kissing over and over. The first two times I thought there was something familiar about the woman, but when I woke on the third morning, I *knew* who she was. Oryn was kissing my mother!

As I rose and dressed, I told myself it was immaterial what Oryn did in his dreams. His reticence had convinced me that they had been acquainted when he was young; no doubt my presence had brought back buried boyhood sentiments. Yet as the day wore on, I became increasingly upset. Not only was she too old for him, she was my *mother!*

By afternoon, I was in a black mood. After spilling my second attempt at a tricky solution, I retreated to the storeroom for more ingredients. I found Tal polishing a carving with an oilcloth.

"What are you looking for?" he asked, after I had been through every shelf twice.

"A beauty potion," I said, irritably.

Tal considered for a moment. I was about to relent and apologize when he said, "You should take mararoot."

"Mararoot? Mararoot isn't a beauty potion. It's not good for much of anything."

He shrugged. "'Twould work for you."

I glared at him, confounded by his stupidity. Snatching the packet of herbs—which had been right in front of my nose—I stomped back to the library.

Oryn sat at his desk, bent over a piece of parchment. After my solution bubbled all over the floor yet again, he laid down his pen and eyed me.

I ignored him as I cleaned up the mess.

"All right. What's bothering you?"

"Nothing!"

"Your nothing has cost me quite a few ingredients," he said, returning to the parchment.

I stewed in silence for a few minutes and then burst out, "You kissed my mother!"

Any other time, I would have found Oryn's mingled expression of shock and astonishment comical.

"Kissed who? What are you talking about?"

"In your dreams. You were *kissing* my *mother!*"

A strange expression stole across his face, and he flushed.

Aha! Guilty as charged.

He shuffled his papers, mumbled something, and then said reproachfully, "'Tis rude to eavesdrop on other people's dreams."

"I didn't do it on purpose! But really, Oryn, kissing my mother..."

"'Twasn't your mother."

I crossed my arms and glared at him. "You just *happened* to kiss a red-haired maid who *happened* to look like her? And earlier you called her Elly!"

"It has been years since I saw her—"

"Ha! So you *did* know her!" I said accusingly.

"I'm not even sure Elly *was* your mother. Her given name was something other than Mirella." He looked angry and something else, which I could not identify. "Come now, Arabella. Why should I dream about her? Besides, there are other red-haired women in the world, and...I can't believe you eavesdropped on my DREAMS!" He finished with a roar.

"Other red-haired women?"

"Arabella, I assure you, I didn't dream about your mother...or Elly." He spoke with such sincerity I knew he was telling the truth.

Oryn must have seen embarrassment on my face, for he added, "I would be upset, too, if I dreamt you were kissing *my* mother."

This made me crack a smile.

"Please," he begged. "No more spying on my dreams."

"I'm sorry. I didn't mean to..."

"I know."

"How do I stop?"

He rubbed his hand over his eyes. "What you were thinking about before you fell asleep?"

I pondered a bit. "Before Tal's dream I thought about him, and before yours..." I faltered as I remembered. Last night I had reflected on how much I loved Red Castle: the library, the gardens, watching Oryn's strong hands as he tended his plants.

"You were thinking of me?"

"I...yes...I guess so," I said, blushing.

"Well, that's your answer." He leaned back in his chair and laced his fingers behind his head. "Why were you contemplating me?"

More heat flooded my cheeks, and a grin tugged the corners of his mouth. "I am...intrigued...but please, dwell upon something *else* before falling asleep."

"Yes, sir." I choked out the words.

~ † ~

My thoughts settled on Aramis before I fell asleep, and I dreamed of unicorns deep in a dark forest. Perhaps I needed to focus on inanimate objects before sleeping.

A series of deep, hacking coughs greeted me when I entered the kitchen. Sadye leaned against the table for support as coughs wracked her huge body. Perspiration beaded on her nose and upper lip.

"Sadye!" I gasped. "You ought to be in bed!" Grabbing her arm, I eased her into a chair. She was burning with fever.

Another round of coughing left her doubled over with her mouth pressed to her eggshell blue apron. When she collapsed against the back of the chair, blood specks mingled with the apron's noisy print.

"Stay here!" I commanded. "Don't move. I'm getting Oryn."

I rushed toward the library, but I paused just outside the door when I heard Balissa. Her voice sounded hollow, the way it did when she spoke through the portal stone. They had communicated several times since my dream—Oryn had warned her about the council.

My fist hovered over the door, ready to knock, but I was loath to interrupt.

"You should explain how you feel," Balissa said.

Oryn gave a short barking laugh. "Of course. I love spilling my guts."

I strained to hear, but their voices dropped and I only caught snatches of their conversation.

"—her true reflection," Oryn said.

True reflection? What did that mean?

There was more inaudible murmuring, then Oryn burst out, "Arabella spied on my dreams!"

I blushed.

Balissa's voice rose. "Ah, the one place true feeling and emotion bubbles to the surface. And what were you doing in these dreams?"

Oryn mumbled a reply, and I heard her chiming laugh.

"What did the council say about the location of Pine Lookout?" he said, changing the subject.

"Nothing positive. They claim it is a fruitless endeavor and refuse to send anyone searching."

"Heaven forbid they should accept the word of a miscreant like me!"

There was the sound of shuffling parchment, then Oryn said, "One moment." I heard his measured tread approaching, and I shrank back against the corridor wall.

He yanked the door open. "Eavesdropping, are we?" he asked dryly.

"I'm sorry, I didn't mean to." I stammered. Balissa's face was visible through the portal perched above the desk, and she gave me a wave. "Sadye is coughing up blood," I said in a rush.

Oryn's expression turned serious. "That does it," he said, returning to his desk and grabbing the ring. "Balissa, I'm sending her home. If she continues to worsen and I can't contact you..."

Balissa nodded soberly.

Oryn followed me to the kitchen where Sadye sat slumped over the table.

He laid his hand on her shoulder. "'Tis time for you to go home."

She jerked upright, her feverish eyes darting to the portal. "No!" she rasped.

"I need you to go back to Sperara...now, before it's too late."

Sadye shook her head doggedly. "Who will keep. The boys in line? Who. Will cook. For the cat?" she managed to say between ragged, gasping breaths.

I blinked. It was the longest phrase I had ever heard her utter.

"Dear, stubborn woman," Oryn murmured. He set the portal ring on the floor. "So help me, Sadye, I will heave you through that portal if I have to."

Sadye nodded—in resignation, perhaps—and slid weakly off the chair. She crouched on the floor.

"Do you want my help?" Oryn asked, but she slapped his hands away. Taking a deep breath, she dragged herself to the portal. Balissa helped from the other side. Once through, Sadye erupted in a frenzy of coughs.

Balissa's face appeared at the portal. "She'll be burning the bacon the next time you see her."

"She'd better," Oryn growled. His cheeks were wet.

~ † ~

The castle seemed empty without Sadye's familiar presence. To distract myself after a somber lunch, I galloped Aramis across the green. As she flew over the turf, I loosed my hair and bent low over her neck. After an exhilarating ride, I stabled her and headed toward the keep.

I was pinning up my hair as I entered the great hall. Halfway across the huge room, Morty stepped from a shadowy corner wielding a quarterstaff. He twirled it a few times and grinned at me.

"Where are you going in such a hurry?" His eyes scanned my riding habit.

I had avoided him—mostly successfully—ever since I learned he had read my dream diary. "To the kitchen." He seemed vaguely menacing, and Balissa's warning sprang unbidden to my mind.

"Why don't you join me? I'm thinking of decorating the room for a celebration." He gestured grandly, and the walls of the old keep blossomed with gaudy decorations and garlands of fake flowers. Candles burst to life in a shower of sparks, but their unwavering flames gave no light or warmth. Tables loaded with pastries and other delicacies sprouted from the rush strewn floor. I eyed the fabricated food with distaste.

"What kind of celebration?" I asked in a flat voice.

"Perhaps...our engagement." He studied my face as if to gauge my reaction.

My eyes widened.

"Just think," he said. "I will be Mortimor the Great Enchanter, and you will be..." He paused, but then continued as if inspired, "You will be my *beautiful* bride." He knelt on one knee and held out his hand. "Come kiss me, my lady."

I was in no mood to be trifled with. "I should warn you," I said in a steely voice, "the last lumbering oaf who tried to kiss me got a broken tooth and a bloodied nose for his pains."

His expression hardened. "Don't be so quick to spurn my proposal, Arabella. I offer you all the spoils of Latretta."

I stared at him, unease churning through my gut. "Tell me something. On our journey to the Great Lake, I caught you washing your knife by the river. What *really* happened to those two soldiers?"

He smirked, showing all his perfect teeth. "I stuck my blade between their ribs and left them to rot where they dropped."

I recoiled at his obvious pride, though his confession was unsurprising. Somewhere in the depths of my heart, I had suspected the soldiers had met with such a fate.

"Morty, nothing in this world could induce me to marry you."

His mocking grin vanished, and a savage, wild light burned in his black eyes. He gestured, and his stunning spell caught me and held me immobile. A smug, self-satisfied expression spread across his face. He cocked his head. "Oh, is the poor little maid frozen? Can't she move?" Helpless, I screamed and thrashed inwardly as he reached out to touch my cheek.

Somewhere in the depths of the castle an enraged bellow erupted, and Morty sprang away from me, startled. "Does he see *everything*?" he cried, fear and loathing alternating across his face.

Fear and loathing—that was how he felt about Oryn.

Morty glanced from door to door to door, as if weighing his chances of flight, then bolted toward the eastern hall. The door closed with a bang and locked with a click. The northern and southern doors closed as well. Morty wheeled toward the western door. Looking like a caged animal, he crouched and raised his quarterstaff.

It was Tal—not Oryn—who charged through the door like a raging bull. He lowered his head and plowed into Morty with all of his considerable bulk. The two of them catapulted over each other on the floor, scattering chairs, breaking tables, and tossing food and cake everywhere. They came to rest against an overturned table with Tal sitting on Morty's legs.

Oryn strode into the room. He watched Tal pound Morty's stomach and face with his fists before scuttling them through a portal. I glimpsed a courtyard before he closed it and turned to me. Concern and another indefinable emotion played across his features. He cleared his throat. "Can you free yourself?"

I fumbled mentally, unable to focus. Then my muscles relaxed, and I sagged to the floor. The garish decorations, broken tables, strewn chairs, and scattered food evaporated.

"Well done," Oryn said, sounding pleased.

I shook my head. "It wasn't me."

"Ah," he said, glancing around the empty hall. "That means Mortimor is unconscious. Perhaps I ought to intervene." Yet he remained, worry etching his face. "Are you all right?"

I nodded and leaned my head against the wall.

Oryn still looked uncertain. He knelt and placed a tendril of stray hair behind my ear. "Are you sure?"

I nodded harder. "Go. Tal will kill him if you don't."

He hesitated a moment longer before striding toward the courtyard.

I watched him go, then closed my eyes, physically and mentally exhausted.

32

e's gone!" Tal rushed into the kitchen, ashen-faced. When Morty had not come to dinner, Oryn had sent Tal to fetch him. Oryn rose to his feet, dinner forgotten. "Are you sure?"

"I can't find him anywhere."

A week had passed since Tal beat Morty to a pulp. He had no broken bones, and poultices and salves had soothed his cuts, but his bruises had turned livid shades of green and purple. He was on room arrest, though today Oryn had decided he could return to the dinner table.

Oryn turned from the table, and Tal and I trailed him to the library. Oryn flung his arm wide at the mirrors, and their surfaces sprang to life with different views of the castle.

"This is how you keep track of us!" I said.

"Not well enough, apparently," Oryn muttered. Rooms and corridors flickered in the mirrors, but there was no sign of Morty.

Oryn slammed a fist on his desk. "I should have paid better attention!" Gesturing again, he opened a portal. "Follow me," he said. We found ourselves on the roof of the northeastern tower. Tal went to the edge of the battlements.

"There!" he said, pointing. Far across the rocky wasteland, a tiny dot moved along the top of an outcropping, the only moving thing on the red-stained earth. In another moment, Morty slid over the ridge and out of sight.

"Where is he going? Why is he heading east?" I asked.

"Mortock," Tal said in disgust. "He's going to his grandfather."

"His grandfather! Mortock is the grandfather who stunned him as a little boy?"

"The same," Oryn said. He slumped down against a battlement .

"I'm going after him," Tal said. He rushed for the portal, but Oryn stopped him with a listless wave.

"Don't bother. He must follow the path he has chosen. Besides, he'd be in the marsh long before you reached him." Oryn shook his head, despair etched into his weary face.

Tal turned to the stairs. "I'm heading down." Oryn shrugged, and Tal started the long journey down the tower steps.

"Perhaps I ought to console Tal." I glanced at the stairs, but I was torn. Oryn looked pale and shaky.

"Why would Morty go to Mortock?" I asked.

"Mortock's power is alluring. I knew Morty had fatal flaws in his character, but I hoped..." Oryn drifted into silence. "I promised his poor mother I would try to help, but I could not."

I had never seen him so despondent.

"I am a fool, Arabella. A fool!"

I knelt and took his hand in mine. "Oryn, you are a great enchanter."

"If only." His hand lifted toward my face, then fell into his lap.

I tightened my grip on his hand. "What is it?"

He banged his head against the battlement and closed his eyes. "Just go."

I stood up in confusion. I had never seen him like this and had no idea what to say. I whispered, "You *are* a great enchanter."

"And yet still I am a fool." He gestured angrily toward the stairs. "Go on. Follow Tal."

I went.

~ † ~

Oryn's despondency was short-lived. He shuttered himself away for three days in the library, but on the fourth morning he emerged, armed with scrolls and manuscripts.

"We're leaving Red Castle," he announced, dumping his armload on the kitchen table where Tal and I were eating a skimpy breakfast.

"Leaving!" Tal echoed.

"Where are we going?" I asked.

"Sperara. This is the stuff of irony," he said with a faint smile. "More than ever, the king needs to know what has happened, yet the portal stone no longer works. Since no one will open a portal for us, we must hoof it over the most forbidding territory in all of Atruria and Latretta." He unrolled a map and pointed out our path. "North, across the barren desert wasteland, to the ancient trade road through the Enchanted Forest. Then we must climb the foothills of the Pindars and find a way over huge mountains that cannot be scaled." He grinned. "Sounds fun, doesn't it?"

I smiled. Oryn was in rare form. "How did you get here to begin with?" I asked.

"The council was only too happy to open a portal and kick me through."

"And Sadye?"

"The council sent her a week later. Apparently she threatened to put leeches in their soup and slugs in their salads if they didn't send her." He swiped at his eyes, chuckling. "She probably would have, too."

"What about you and Morty?" I asked Tal.

"We used Balissa's portal stone. No one treks across the wilderness. Why can't we just stay in Red Castle?"

"Morty knows too many of the castle's secrets. He could lead Mortock right to us. We leave tomorrow at dawn," Oryn said. "Pack only what you can carry."

"What about the stock...and Prissy? And Aramis?" I asked in dismay.

"I sent Prissy to Sadye last week."

I had not realized the cat was gone.

"The stock we can release on the green. They'll survive. Aramis will come with us. I hope she does not object to carrying bedrolls."

"No, sir," I said, relieved.

After Oryn left, Tal said in a soft voice, "I made something for you." He led me to his workshop and handed me a decorated longbow. I admired his beautiful craftsmanship, and he blushed. "'Tis for your birthday, but I want you to have it now."

"Thank you, Tal." My birthday was still several weeks away. I was touched he had remembered.

"This is for you as well," he said, handing me a quiver. Soft rabbit skin lined the interior, and intricate stitching and leather tooling decorated the outside.

Tears sprang to my eyes. "Oh, Tal!"

"Oryn enchanted it. He claims you'll never run out of arrows. Handy thing to have."

I wrapped my arms around his massive torso in a sudden burst of gratitude. His neck turned red.

"Geesh. 'Tisn't anything special," he rumbled from somewhere deep within his barrel chest.

~ † ~

Despite the promised rigors of our trip, the prospect of the journey excited me. I would finally see Sperara, the capital of Latretta and the childhood home of my mother.

Packing was easy. I threw everything important into my trunk, carried it to the hall, and watched it transform into a satchel.

Aramis proved more difficult—she did not want to be a beast of burden. I had to give her a stern lecture about her role in the journey and threaten to leave her behind if she did not behave.

I scoured the cellars and scrounged up every bit of food I could find. It barely filled two packs. There was not enough for the trip, but Tal assured me we would be able to snare game along the way.

I spent one last night in my princess-perfect room, and then joined Tal and Oryn on the green just as the sun peeked over the eastern horizon.

"Everyone ready?" Oryn asked as I secured bedrolls and blankets on Aramis's back.

I carried my longbow and quiver, and Oryn and Tal wore long swords sheathed in studded scabbards slung over their shoulders. I had never seen them carry such weapons before.

Oryn led us through the northern gate into the sandstone desert beyond. As we passed under the ancient arch, I felt the familiar tingle of the protective spell. I looked back, and Red Castle had transformed into a massive sandstone outcropping glinting red in the dawn.

Our journey to Latretta had begun.

33

ed loamy soil punctuated by sandstone ridges gradually gave way to a weathered, limestone boulder field, pockmarked with caves eaten into the soft rock by eons of dripping water. Tufts of coarse grass took root in cracks and crevices, and small bushes dotted the barren, rocky landscape.

Aramis was surefooted and adept at picking her way across the boulders, sometimes leaping from one rock to another like a silky-maned goat of the mountains.

Oryn shook his head. "I've never seen a horse act like that. If I'd known the terrain was this rough, I would have suggested we leave her behind, but she is faring quite well."

"Better than I am," Tal said, stopping to rub an ankle he had shinned in a crevice.

We traveled straight through midday. There was not much to eat anyway, and Oryn wanted to get as far from Red Castle as possible before dark.

"See if you can find shelter," Oryn said to Tal as the sun dipped low in the west.

Tal threaded his way through the boulders while Oryn and I rested with Aramis. Fifteen minutes passed before he hailed us from farther up the slope.

"I found a cave. Nice and dry. This way," he called.

We reached the protection of an overhanging crag as the last sliver of sun disappeared below the horizon. Tal already had a fire crackling in the shallow cave, and we roasted a few turnips and one withered parsnip. Oryn doled out pieces of flatbread I had baked with the last of the flour.

"Perhaps we could improve this fare," Oryn said, eyeing his dinner.

"What do you suggest, sir?" I said, giving a sweeping curtsy.

A smile flitted across Oryn's face. "How about some roast duck, madam, complemented by a seasoned vegetable medley and warm bread." He flexed his fingers, and the food transformed before our eyes. "We'll top it off with a dram of perfectly aged wine." Three fist-sized rocks became cut crystal goblets. He poured wine from a jug.

I grinned. Though we were eating parsnips, turnips, and flatbread, it was fun to pretend we were enjoying a grand feast in our humble cave. The duck tasted perfect, and the roll was delicious—a little salty perhaps, but the medley...I could not palate turnips no matter what form they took. Tal finished my vegetables, and we nursed our wine and watched sparks from the fire sail into the sky.

"Does enchanted wine make you drunk?" I felt tipsy and light-headed.

"Only in your head," Oryn said. I caught him winking over his goblet at Tal.

"Nevertheless, perhaps I ought to stop imbibing and retire for the night, lest I stumble over myself ignominiously."

Oryn raised his eyebrows. "She cannot hold her enchanted wine, Tal. How would she fare on the real stuff?"

I ignored him and swept toward the back of the cave, until a rock came out of nowhere and tripped me. I fell in a tangle of skirts and limbs while Tal and Oryn laughed uproariously.

"Should we tell her it was real wine?" Oryn asked Tal in a mock whisper.

I made a face at them, then laid out my blankets and found a comfortable place to curl up for the night. Tal and Oryn were still passing the jug back and forth when I drifted off to sleep.

~ † ~

I had the packs stowed on Aramis by the time Tal rolled out of his blankets, but Oryn was still snoring.

"Wake up, lazybones!" I nudged Oryn in the ribs. "Time to rise and shine!" He grunted and rolled over. I transformed a pebble into a feather and tickled his ear. After rolling back and forth several times, he ended up on his back. I brought the feather down and touched the tip of his nose. His hand shot up and locked around my wrist.

"You like tormenting me, don't you?" He opened one eye.

"It makes your blue eyes flash."

"What about letting sleeping dogs and babies lie?" he grumbled.

"The saying doesn't mention anything about grumpy enchanters." I tried to pull away.

He groaned and gripped my arm tighter.

"Are you going to let me go, or do I have to tickle your nose again?"

"Maybe," he grinned. He sat up slowly and released his iron grip on my wrist. "Perhaps I shouldn't have drunk the whole jug of wine," he said, rubbing the stubble on his jaw with the back of his hand.

"Headache?"

He grunted. "'Twill go away." He rolled up his blankets, and I tied them on Aramis. Oryn slung his sword over his shoulder as we exited the protective shelter of the cave.

"Let's head west for a league," Oryn said, squinting against the brightness of the sun, which was well above the horizon.

"Why west?" Tal asked. "Don't we need to go due north to reach Sperara?"

Oryn nodded. "But if we miss the old trade road, we'll have to travel west to find it."

"The trade road?" I asked.

"It runs east from the Great Lake along the southern edge of the Enchanted Forest. Then it cuts north. We don't want to wander the heart of the forest without the benefit of the road."

We were paralleling the slope of the rise when, from the corner of my eye, I glimpsed a shimmering oval a hundred yards down the slope.

"Is that a portal?" I asked, pointing. Aramis stopped instantly. Her flanks trembled even before the writhing mass of gray bodies began pouring through.

"BACK TO THE CAVE!" Oryn shouted. He drew his sword and ran toward the shelter.

Aramis would not move, though I heaved on her rope with all my strength.

"Leave her," Tal begged, tugging on my sleeve. As if on cue, Aramis bolted up the slope, yanking the rope from my hands. I considered chasing her, but the wolves had covered half the distance already. Tal sprinted back to the cave and I followed, skirts flapping in the wind.

As we entered, I felt the familiar tingle of the protective shield Oryn had placed over the entrance. I strung my bow and nocked an arrow, waiting for the wolves to come close. As the first gray bodies leapt into range, I loosed an arrow, felling a wolf. They sought refuge from my hail of arrows, slinking behind stone piles or groveling in crevices. A massive gray wolf bounded on to a limestone boulder to the right of the cave. He sat on his haunches and gazed at the cave, his eyes blazing red.

"That's the pack leader," Oryn said in a hoarse voice. I shot a dozen arrows toward him, but they fell harmlessly on either side.

The huge wolf's eyes bored into the cave. Oryn clenched his fists, and sweat trickled down his forehead.

"Are you all right?" I said.

He sank to his knees, ashen-faced and glassy-eyed.

Tal gripped his sword with white knuckles. "That wolf," he said, nodding toward the leader. "He's breaking down Oryn's spell, isn't he?"

"I think so," I said, feeling helpless.

"Take care of Oryn and be safe," he said, his voice thick. Grabbing my hand, he pulled me close and planted a kiss on my forehead. Then, with a mighty bellow, he charged out of the cave.

I froze, paralyzed by shock and horror. Tal's initial onslaught carried him halfway to the wolf, whose concentration was broken. He crouched down on the rock, snarling and barking at the pack. They responded instantly, jumping on Tal and biting at him ferociously. He flailed with his sword and arms, knocking wolves away. With a furious yell, he leapt on the huge wolf, hacking with his sword. As the wolf's jaws closed over his forearm, crunching bone and sinew and rendering his sword useless, Tal wrapped his legs around the wolf's body, gripping it in a stranglehold. The rest of the wolves piled on them, until they disappeared under a struggling mass of writhing bodies.

Watching the pack engulf Tal galvanized me into action. "Noooo!" I shrieked, loosing a furious volley of arrows and scattering wolves in all directions. They slunk away, snapping and snarling. Oryn—somewhat recovered now that the leader was dispatched—unsheathed his sword and bounded down the slope after the remnants of the pack, yelling hoarsely. He reached Tal before I did. Blood spread from Tal's broken body, pooling on the limestone and staining it black. He was sprawled atop the huge wolf, its body pierced by his sword and its neck broken by his bare hands.

"No!" I sobbed wretchedly, stumbling toward him. "No, no, nooo!" Oryn tried to restrain me, but I slapped his hands away and crumpled at Tal's side, cradling his head in my arms. I moaned and wailed, my shoulders shuddering, and my chest heaving. My tears wet his face and cheeks, mingling with his blood. I pushed his unruly hair back from his sweat-dampened forehead, laid my head on his chest, and wept.

Oryn eventually pulled me off Tal's body and buried him in the cave. I lay pale and listless, silent at last, but unable and unwilling to move. Murmuring about the cave not being safe, Oryn hoisted the bedrolls and packs on his shoulders and placed me on Aramis's back—who had returned after the wolves dispersed.

~ † ~

The next week passed in a blur. I rode in a fog, slumped forward with my head bowed, barely conscious of anything. I never fell off, but I do not know whether that was due more to my innate horsemanship or Aramis.

Each night, Oryn found a place to camp and eased me off her back. He made a fire, tended Aramis, and forced food and drink down my unwilling throat. Then he laid out two bedrolls, one on each side of the fire, and tucked me into mine.

Then came the nightmares. *Real* nightmares. Every time I closed my eyes, I watched Tal die over and over. When I woke in a cold sweat, shrieking and tearing at the blankets, Oryn was always ready with a warm cup of tea. After drinking, I rested my head on his lap, and he stroked my hair and whispered endearing words until I fell into a dreamless—if not restful—sleep.

A week after Tal's death, I awoke from the nightmare without the usual scream on my lips. Instead, tears streamed down my face. Oryn offered me tea, but I shook my head. He pulled me into his comforting arms, and I listened to the steady beating of his heart until my sobs subsided.

"He knew he would die, didn't he," I croaked, my voice rusty.

"Yes."

"Why did he do it?" Fresh tears spilled down my cheeks.

"So we might live."

So we might live. Oryn's words echoed in my head. Tal had sacrificed his life for us. I rubbed my cheek against the rough homespun of Oryn's tunic. "He was in love with me, wasn't he?"

"Very much so." Oryn's voice caught as he spoke.

I thought of the small chores Tal had done for me, the care he taken on my bow and quiver, the blushes whenever I came near. A fist seemed to squeeze my lungs, and I vowed his sacrifice would not be in vain.

"I dreamt of his death when I was young," I whispered after a pause.

Oryn's breath sucked in. "Why didn't you tell me?" His tone carried no accusation, only grief.

I struggled to sit up, desperate to explain. "It was many years ago. I was so little."

Oryn wrapped his arms around me, pulling my head against his chest again. "Hush. 'Twasn't your fault. No one should be burdened with such dreams."

I relaxed against his chest. For the first time since Tal's death, I slept peacefully.

~ † ~

I brewed a strong pot of tea on the embers of the fire, and when Oryn finally awoke, I handed him a steaming cup. He looked startled for a moment, then a smile crept across his face. "Welcome back to the world of the living."

I gave a wry smile. "It's good to be back, but for how long I don't know. I'm little more than a bag of bones rattling in the wind." I stood and tightened my sash around my waist. My hipbones jutted out, and Oryn's face looked gaunt.

"Our most pressing need is food," Oryn agreed, savoring his tea. "There is precious little left in those packs. Even Aramis hasn't had a decent meal since we left Red Castle."

I glanced over at her. All her ribs showed. Every blade of grass or green plant within reach of her tether was nibbled down to the crevice from which it grew.

"What about water?" Surely, there was not much of that around either.

"I found a spring three days ago. Aramis drank enough for three horses, and I filled every flask, but we're running low again."

"How long until we reach the forest?"

Oryn unfurled a map and studied it intently. With a sigh, he rolled it up. "I have no idea."

We ate sparingly of the remaining flatbread, which was lasting longer than expected without Tal to feed. The thought brought a lump to my throat.

We made good progress throughout the morning. The day grew warmer, and I shed my cloak when we rested at noon. My dress was travel-stained and torn where it had caught on sharp rocks.

"How did the wolves...?" I hesitated, unsure how to articulate my question.

"How did they find us?"

I nodded.

"I'm not the only member of my family with my particular gift. Given enough time, Mortock can find almost anyone. And I'm sure Morty pointed him in the right direction."

"He must have been to that rocky hillside if he was able to open a portal there."

"Not necessarily."

I frowned. "But I thought—"

"I know...we can only open portals to places we have been. But Mortock may have fashioned a seeing stone. With the right enchantment, he could locate us and open a portal." Oryn cocked his head. "'Tis possible *you* could open a portal to a place you've only seen in your dreams."

"Does Mortock have dreams like mine?"

"No. Yours is a rare gift. It only surfaces once every century or so... usually in the hour of Latretta's most desperate need."

I shook my head. "It hasn't proved very useful so far."

"It will."

I wished *I* could be so sure.

By evening, the boulder-strewn hills gave way to a gently sloping plain covered with fist-sized rocks and smaller pebbles, interspersed with increasing vegetation. Our progress slowed because Aramis stopped at every tuft of grass, and it was difficult to persuade her to continue. By nightfall, a dark smudge was just visible on the horizon.

"That has to be the Enchanted Forest," Oryn said, sounding relieved. "There will be water and food, if we can find the trade road."

We camped under the stars. As the fire burned low, I sat up. "Oryn, are you sleeping?"

"Yes," he answered in his deep voice.

I chuckled softly for a moment. "I want you to stun me."

"What?" He sat up in his bedroll. "Why?"

"When Morty stunned me, I felt helpless, vulnerable, and humiliated. I want to learn to free myself, and the only way I can do that is by practicing."

Oryn sighed. "All right. Stand up, and I'll stun you. Let's hope I don't go to sleep or you might be frozen till morning."

He stunned me, but I could not free myself inside twenty minutes.

When he released me, he said, "Some people can't break the enchantment unless they are desperate." He rolled over and promptly fell asleep.

I stewed in my blankets. How could I be more desperate than when Morty froze me in the great hall?

We got underway as the first pink of dawn blushed the sky. Aramis had eaten to her heart's content throughout the night and behaved better. I wished grass might satisfy us. By midmorning, a lush carpet peppered with brilliantly blooming flowers covered the ground underfoot. I found several roots, which appeased our hunger when Oryn boiled them for lunch.

On the horizon, the huge forest spread in both directions as far as the eye could see, but there was no sign of a road. "Is it possible it has disappeared with time and disuse?"

Worry lines marred Oryn's forehead as he studied the ground underfoot. "I don't think so. Portions of it may be gone, but the trade road was broad and paved with huge stones. It cannot have disappeared entirely."

By afternoon, I could make out individual trees in the forest.

Oryn kept looking at his map, then at the sun. "I'm *sure* we've come far enough west," he said several times.

The line of trees marking the edge of the forest was only two hundred yards distant when Aramis's hooves struck on a stone. She pawed at the ground, ate the head of a flower, and yanked the rest out by the roots, pulling a large section of moss with it.

"Oryn! Look!" The stripped moss revealed a paving stone.

Oryn came back to look. A closer inspection revealed paving stones buried under a thin layer of dirt and moss. A smattering of flowers and grass grew from the dirt, making it appear, from a distance, like any other section of the plain.

"The moss gives it away," Oryn said, pointing to the east. Now that we were standing on the road, it was visible, snaking along disguised by moss and flowers with broken paving stones sticking up at odd angles.

"You found it," I said, patting Aramis's neck.

"She deserves a whole bucket of apples for this."

We proceeded eastward down the road. It was almost dusk when the road curved to the north.

"This is where we enter the forest," Oryn said. "I think we'd better camp here tonight. I don't want to spend more nights in the forest than necessary."

While Oryn hunted for likely spots to set snares, I searched for plants. What I found was nutritious, but not filling, and we went to bed with hunger gnawing at our insides.

34

aybe you didn't set them properly," I said as we stared at three sprung snares.

"I know how to set a snare."

With my hopes of a hare for breakfast dashed, I searched for more plants. I gathered dandelion leaves and roots, purslane, sorrel leaves, spearmint, bergamot blossoms, chervil, small chicory plants, wild onion greens, wild parsley root, and lemon balm.

The plants helped quiet our stomachs, but we needed meat to maintain our strength.

We headed into the forest after breakfast. With a name like the Enchanted Forest, I had expected it to be dark and forbidding, but the sun peeked cheerfully through the trees, and flowers and plants flourished in glades. The road had disappeared under centuries of leaf mold, but the wide path free of trees revealed its location. Water was plentiful. The original architects had built small reservoirs at intervals, and water from hidden springs seeped into the leaf-choked aquifers.

"How long will it take to cross the forest?" I asked while we rested at noon. I nibbled on a birch twig I had stripped from a tree.

"I hope to only spend three nights in here. By the fourth day we should be close to the northern edge."

Dinner once again was sparse and green, but Oryn set snares, which we both hoped would be full in the morning. We had spotted deer, quail, partridges, and hares in the forest.

We laid our bedrolls on the road and tried to sleep despite our hunger. After midnight, I woke suddenly and sat upright. The light breeze had stilled, and I was certain I heard hoof beats. Then the leaves rustled again, and my certainty wavered. I glanced at Aramis's silvery form tethered to a tree and laid back down. I watched stars twinkle through the treetops before I rolled over and went back to sleep.

The twittering of birds woke me at dawn. I rose and stretched. Oryn's bedroll was empty, and Aramis was gone. I blew on the embers of the fire and made tea from some spearmint leaves I had saved.

Oryn looked glum when he returned. "I don't understand. The snares were sprung again."

"Where's Aramis?" I asked.

"Tethered over there..." He trailed off, frowning.

I jumped to my feet. "I thought you took her with you to get water," I said in a shaky voice. I hurried to the tree where I had tied her. Her lead was still knotted around a sturdy branch, but the buckles on her halter were neatly undone.

"How could she have gotten free?" I ran a short way into the forest, calling, "Aramis! *Aramis!*"

Oryn studied the halter, a doubtful expression on his face. "She couldn't undo her own halter."

"Well, who then?" I asked, running to the other side of the road to call her again.

"She's gone."

"She *can't* be gone!" Tears slid down my cheeks. I could not bear to lose *another* member of our party.

"Somebody—or something—unbuckled her halter," Oryn said.

"I should have watched her better." I sank to the ground and cried in earnest.

"This is an enchanted forest, Arabella. Strange, inexplicable things happen here." Oryn shook his head. "I'm sorry she's gone. I'm going to miss that little horse."

I dabbed my eyes with my tattered hem and clambered to my feet. Crying would not bring Aramis back. Oryn divided the load, and I hoisted my scanty share. He insisted on carrying the water.

We made steady progress through the forest. The road ran straight through its heart until the canopied path disappeared into the misty distance. There were times when I was sure inquisitive eyes were watching us, but I never saw a whisper of movement beyond the flashing of a white tail or a startled bird.

Oryn set snares when we made camp, and we ate the few plants I had found along the path. I gazed at the stars as I prepared to sleep, but they did not twinkle as merrily as they had the previous night.

~ † ~

I woke to the aroma of roasting hare. "All three snares were full!" Oryn announced, offering me a piece as I sat up. My mouth watered at the enticing smell, and we gorged our shrunken stomachs on most of two animals. "Three fat hares," Oryn said contentedly, patting his stomach. He had suffered even more than I had from the lack of meat.

I leaned against a tree. For the first time in a long while, my hunger was appeased, and it felt lovely. "Now I'm sleepy again."

"No time for that. We have a lot of traveling to do before nightfall. Maybe tonight we'll get a fat partridge."

A slow smile spread across my face. Though still sad about Aramis, I was pleased we had finally gotten a decent meal. That night I slept like a baby.

Oryn was overjoyed when he found two plump partridges and another fat hare in his snares the next morning. The third morning he caught two hares and a partridge. Since we had eaten plenty for two days, we agreed to save some meat. Oryn thought we might reach the end of the forest before nightfall, and game would be scarce in the Pindar foothills.

The road climbed steadily throughout the day, and in late afternoon, the trees thinned dramatically. The road disappeared; a thicket of brambles and scrub closed in. We pushed through and emerged on a steep grassy meadow.

A shout of joy rose to my lips. Dropping my pack, I ran into the meadow. "Aramis! Aramis! You found us!" I threw my arms around her neck and hugged her. She gazed at me with her brown eyes, as if to ask what had taken us so long. "You silly horse. How did you end up here?"

Oryn strode over, shaking his head. "This is unbelievable. A huge forest, limitless mountains, yet somehow she is waiting for us when we reach the foothills. Unbelievable!"

I entwined my fingers in her silvery mane. "I missed you so much. Don't ever run away again." She tossed her head and pawed the ground.

"She looks so healthy!" I said. She had no marks, cuts, or bruises. Her coat shone as if someone had curried her for hours. She had put on weight, and her flowing mane and tail looked freshly brushed and tangle free. I lifted her hooves to inspect her feet. My breath caught. Two of Tal's horseshoes were gone. I traced my fingertips over her front hooves where his nails had clinched them in place. Tears misted my eyes. "Where have you been, and who took your shoes?" I murmured.

Dusk approached, so we selected a flat area fifty yards from the edge of the forest to set up camp. Oryn set snares while I prepared stew from a hare and some tubers I had gathered. We still had a partridge and one hare, which I cut into strips and dried on a clever rack Oryn devised for me. It felt good to be in the open again, and we all slept well.

~ † ~

"Three fat hares," Oryn said, glancing toward Aramis. "You'd almost think she had something to do with it."

"That's silly. How could Aramis have anything to do with the snares being full?"

Oryn shrugged. "I didn't expect to catch anything. There weren't any good places to set traps." He dangled them by their ears and grinned. "'Tis a good thing I like hare so much."

The foothills of the Pindar range were larger than the actual mountains of the Aurals. And though I was certain we were climbing the Pindars themselves, Oryn assured me we had a full day's journey before reaching their sheer faces.

"How are we going to cross them?"

"We'll find a way."

I sighed. Sometimes Oryn's secretiveness was frustrating.

I kept my hand on Aramis's side as we climbed. Massive granite monoliths dotted the steep foothills.

"Look! A wolf!" I cried.

"Where?" Oryn swung around.

I frowned. "Over on that huge flat rock, but it's gone now," I said, pointing.

"Was it an Ayr wolf?"

"No. It was different."

He strode toward the boulder. I grabbed Aramis's rope and followed.

Oryn was staring at the rock when we reached him. He mumbled several inaudible phrases and then commanded, "Show yourself!"

Long moments passed. At last he mumbled as if the words had been wrenched from him, "Please."

A shape on the rock shimmered, and a sitting wolf took form and substance. He had clear gray eyes, a large ruff, and a regal bearing. He gazed at us like a king looking over his subjects.

He turned to Oryn and spoke in a deep rumbling voice, "A little humility and courtesy go a long way, enchanter."

Oryn flushed. The wolf turned his penetrating gaze on me. "Long has it been since I have seen one with such strong vision."

When I recovered from my surprise, I shook my head. "I think you are mistaken."

"As old as the hills I am, and only twice before has anyone seen me when I did not wish it." He turned to Aramis. "And who is this?"

"This is my horse, Aramis," I said, patting her neck.

The wolf raised an eyebrow and cocked his ear, which gave him a quizzical expression. He made a series of yips and barks. Aramis tossed her mane, pawed the ground, and snorted, fearless. I wondered at this, considering her terror when the Ayr wolves appeared.

The wolf nodded. "Your horse it is, then."

I looked from Aramis to the wolf and back. Could they possibly talk to each other?

"I assume you seek a path through the mountains," he said, turning his gaze on Oryn.

"Yes," Oryn said, bowing his head.

"Then follow me." The wolf leapt from his perch and set off at an easy lope. We followed as quickly as we could. When he was almost out of sight, he sat and waited for us to catch up.

"What kind of wolf is he?" I panted. We were jogging, but he easily outdistanced us.

"He's a Syr wolf," Oryn said over his shoulder. "They are the guardians of the mountains."

When we caught up to the wolf, he grinned at me. He looked almost comical with his lolling tongue. "We are also the keepers of the gates."

"The gates?"

"Great portals through the mountains," Oryn said.

The wolf blinked. "Perhaps you could use some provisions for the rest of your journey."

We nodded. He turned and gave a short shrill bark. Answering yips reverberated from a ledge above our heads, and four frisky furballs tumbled down a steep path worn into the rock face. They bounded into the wolf and knocked him over as they worried his ears and tugged on his tail. The wolf and pups romped until a stately wolf with a plumed tail stepped sedately down the path. She turned her large intelligent eyes in our direction and bobbed her head. Unsure of how to respond, I curtsied in return.

She barked sharply, and the four pups scampered off their father and scrabbled back up the path. In a moment, they reappeared, hanging over the ledge, watching us with curious eyes. I smiled at their antics and waved to them, which set their little tails wagging. The male wolf still lay on the ground, and the female nosed him and bit him gently under the chin. "The female one has some manners, at least," she said to her mate in a low voice, flopping by his side.

Oryn flushed and bowed deeply. She acknowledged him with a nod. The male yipped, and she rose and leapt up the path to the ledge. She returned in a moment, dragging a large pack.

"We caught some soldiers lurking west of here about a week ago," the wolf said. "We relieved them of their burdens. Perhaps you can find something useful in there."

I was already tearing into the pack. "There's jerky and flatbread, all in good condition, and even some tea!" I pulled out a small packet of rolled tealeaves and sniffed them, delighting in their pungent aroma. "They're fresh, too."

The female sat up straighter and sniffed the package when I mentioned the jerky.

"Would you like some?" I asked.

She backed away, but her mate gave a short yip. "Perhaps one piece," she said. Her tail thumped as I opened the wrapping, and she took the piece I offered right out of my palm. She closed her eyes as she chewed it. "I do like a good piece of jerky," she said when she finished.

"Would you like some more?"

"No dear," she said, nosing my hand away. "You need it much more than I do. But thank you."

She reminded me of a queen, so I dropped my best curtsy to her. She did not speak, but I could tell she was pleased, and as she returned to her pups, her elegant tail waved regally.

The male watched her. "She's feisty. Perhaps you'd like a feisty mate, too," he said to Oryn. A deep blush spread up Oryn's neck, and he coughed violently. The wolf grinned as if he were laughing and said, "Enough fun. We must be off. It will soon be dark."

I squinted up at the sun high in the sky, puzzled.

He led us up a faint path toward the cliff above. He padded along, surefooted, stopping often to allow us to catch up. When we reached the sheer cliff face and could go no further, he said, "Yonder lies the gate."

I looked for an opening, but granite cliffs stretched endlessly in either direction, broken only by jagged fissures and tumbled boulders. The cliff soared a thousand feet above us, obstructing the view of the snowy mountain summits.

"Where is it?" I asked.

"Look closely," the wolf said. "Tell me what you see."

I walked along the cliff face for several yards, but I saw nothing and felt no telltale tingle. I turned back, trailing my fingers along the surface. Suddenly I stopped and flattened my palm against the stone. "Here, it feels different, as if it were—"

"Good." A rumble echoed from deep in the wolf's chest and reverberated off the cliff. The stone beneath my fingers shimmered. I took a quick step back and watched wide-eyed as the gate materialized. It was not a portal as I had expected. Two massive stone doors met in a soaring arch thirty feet over our heads. Strange symbols marked the lintels and carved stone rosettes lined the doors.

"Where does it go?" I asked.

"To the other side of the mountain," the wolf said with amusement. "I must warn you, enchanter," he said, turning to Oryn. "Be cautious but make haste. Evil has seeped into the Pindars." Then he turned and padded down the path.

"Wait," I said, but Oryn shook his head to silence me.

"It's time for us to go, Arabella. Hold on to Aramis and stay close." He pushed against the doors, straining with all his might. Slowly they grated open with a protesting rumble.

I gripped Aramis's halter rope and followed Oryn down a short stone passageway. A breeze played lightly on my face, then the doors closed behind us with a shudder. I watched them shimmer and disappear into a solid cliff face.

"Are we through?"

Oryn nodded. We stood on a ledge overlooking a lush plain far below. He pointed toward a city where lights were shining in the twilight. "That is Sperara. And this is Latretta," he said, making a sweeping gesture over the plain.

"What happened to the sun? It was barely past noon when we entered those doors. Now the sun is setting."

"The gate warps space...and time, only we don't feel it. Hours passed that seemed like moments to us."

"That is…amazing! Who built the gate? And the Syr wolves…"

Oryn laughed. "Later, Arabella. We might as well spend the night here. 'Tis the only flat place for half a day's journey."

"But I'm not tired. We woke six hours ago."

"The extra rest will do us good."

Oryn was right. After dining on roasted partridge, flatbread, and tubers topped with a steaming cup of tea, I felt comfortably drowsy. Ensconced in my bedroll, I watched lights twinkle in the far off city. We were almost home.

Home. I liked the sound of the word. It had been so long since I had called Heyden my home. Two birthdays had come and gone unmarked since then.

"I'm seventeen now," I said to the night sky.

"Congratulations."

"How old are you, Oryn?"

He rolled over and propped his head on his arm. "How old do you think I am?"

"I don't know. Twenty-nine."

He chuckled. "Not bad. I'm twenty-six. How old do you think Balissa is?"

"Sixty."

"She's eighty-two."

"Eighty-two," I echoed. "I never would have guessed."

"And she'll probably live to be one hundred and twenty. Latrettans age more slowly than our southern counterparts. The average life span for women is one hundred ten years. And men can live just as long."

I pondered this for a while. "She is very beautiful," I said at last.

"Does beauty matter so much to you, Arabella?"

"No, but I appreciate it when I see it," I said.

Oryn fell silent, and I thought the conversation had ended. Then he said, "You are beautiful, too."

Heat rushed to my face. Thank goodness he could not see me in the darkness. I managed a choked, "Thank you," before burrowing into my blanket in mortification.

35

e were at a high altitude, and I shivered in the morning chill. Hoarfrost coated the rocks and sparse vegetation.

All morning we zigzagged down the mountainside. The sun was well overhead before we paused on a ledge to drink from our leather flasks and eat a cold lunch of jerky and flatbread. I explored along the ledge for twenty yards. A hardy vine had found a place to send down roots, and its runners crept up the face of the rock, clinging to the pitted surface. I reached an area free of vines and felt a familiar tingle. I whirled around and hurried back to Oryn.

"Are you ready?" he asked, buckling his sword belt.

"I think there's a masking spell further up the ledge," I said, breathless.

His expression was instantly wary. "Show me."

I led him along the ledge until I felt tingling again. "Here."

Oryn peered at the rock face, then held out his hands and murmured a few words. The rock shimmered and dissolved, revealing an opening. "'Tis a cave...and within sight of Sperara." Oryn glanced over his shoulder at the city. "Stay close behind me." Unsheathing his sword, he took a few cautious steps into the interior.

As my eyes adjusted to the dim light, I saw a spacious area, well-appointed with articles of furniture and a cot. I moved toward an area obscured by a curtain and yanked it aside.

"Oryn!" I cried, jumping back. "A portal!"

As I spoke, an impossibly tall figure clothed in black ducked through the portal, followed by...Morty. The bruises on his face had yellowed, but there was no mistaking the familiar sneer.

Oryn lowered his sword at the man in black. "Mortock."

"The little wench does have extraordinary abilities, doesn't she, Oryn?" Mortock said in a sibilant whisper. "She found our comfortable little lair." Threads of stark white hair clung to his scalp in sickly wisps, while pasty skin stretched taut across sharp facial bones, and cloudy, sunken eyes burned in hollow sockets.

I shrank behind Oryn.

"You will regret this intrusion, nephew. Now I do not even have to hunt you down to kill you." He yanked a short sword from a scabbard at his waist. Strange etchings marked the twisted black blade.

"You can try," Oryn said between clenched teeth. The challenge hung in the air between them. Then Oryn lunged.

Mortock parried with a slash of his blade and sidestepped, countering with a thrust that nearly caught Oryn under the chin. Oryn spun and sliced downward, striking Mortock's blade with a resounding clang.

I backpedaled from the two men intent on killing each other, until my spine pressed against the back wall of the cave.

Mortock crossed his arms across his body and shoved Oryn, sending him stumbling backwards. During the momentary pause, his hands swirled.

"No!" I gasped as he hurled a ball of blue fire at Oryn's head.

Oryn ducked, and the fireball imploded against the wall, showering the cave floor with rock shards.

With a hoarse shout, Oryn threw a starburst. Mortock deflected it with his blade, and a chair to his right exploded into a thousand splinters.

I lifted my hands, watching for an opening to throw a spell as they wove around the cave in their dance of death, but I had no experience, and I feared I might just as easily hit Oryn as Mortock. Besides, my mind was blank—every spell I knew had fled.

"Is that the best you can do, nephew?" Mortock taunted as another starburst missed his head and zinged harmlessly out the cave entrance.

"You're not dead yet," Oryn answered between gritted teeth.

As they parried and slashed, Morty snaked his way around the perimeter of the cave to my side. "When my grandfather kills Oryn, I'm going to take you back to Ravensdell."

I glowered at him. "Over my dead body."

"Now that wouldn't be any fun, would it? By the way, how's Tal?"

With a cry of fury, I threw a spell at him, which he blocked easily.

"Ah, the battle of the apprentices. Who's going to win this one, I wonder," he sneered.

"At least I'm not apprenticed to a mad sorcerer," I flung back at him. I longed to cast another spell, but I was well aware his skills surpassed mine. I edged away from him, seething with helpless fury.

Oryn and Mortock still circled each other, but Oryn had slowed. Sweat stained his tunic, and he grunted with effort as he parried Mortock's blows. Oryn lifted his sword high and hacked at Mortock, who countered with an upward slash. Their blades clashed again, then Mortock whirled around and slammed the hilt of his sword into Oryn's ribs with a sickening crunch.

"Oryn!" I cried.

With a desperate yell, he lunged at Mortock and knocked the ugly weapon from his hand. It flew across the cave floor, landing a dozen feet away.

Morty threw out his hand and uttered a harsh, unrecognizable word. Oryn's muscles spasmed, and his body went rigid. His sword clattered to the floor as he sank to his knees, mouth working soundlessly.

I screamed and rushed toward him.

A stunning spell flung me against the wall.

"Well done, Mortimor." The red slit that passed for Mortock's mouth gaped in a horrible grin. He kicked Oryn viciously in the ribs.

I screamed and struggled inside my head, but Morty's spell held. Mortock landed another kick as Oryn tried to crawl across the floor.

Morty turned his attention to me. "Ooh, look at you," he said with a twisted smile. "So pretty, even through all that dirt." He covered his mouth with his hand. "Oh, I forgot! No one's allowed to say that." He leaned so close I could see the stubble sprouting on his unshaven chin. He ran his hand over my hair and across my cheek. My skin crawled. "You'll be wickedly beautiful, once you have a bath," he breathed in my ear. "A little scented lavender water..."

He gave me his most charming grin, but I would have spit in his face and kicked in his teeth even if he hadn't planted a kiss on my lips.

If I wasn't frozen like a wretched statue.

Over Morty's shoulder, I saw Mortock pick up Oryn's long sword and hold the tip to Oryn's throat. "I've dreamt of spitting you like a dog," he said, gloating. He jabbed, but Oryn jerked away. The tip grazed his right cheek, and the gash welled with blood, spilling on his torn tunic.

I watched the scene play out in an agony of helplessness. Tal died for nothing, I thought bitterly. A single tear trailed down my cheek, and with a jolt, I realized Morty's spell had melted away.

Morty turned his back to me as he watched the battle play out. I scrabbled for a stone on the cave floor and struck him on the head . He collapsed to the floor, unconscious.

Oryn's body crumpled as the enchantment broke.

Mortock straddled Oryn's prone figure and lifted the sword high over his head, cackling in insane exultation.

I darted across the cave, snatched up the black sword, and drove the blade into Mortock's back. The tip of the blade emerged from his right shoulder. Oryn's sword fell from Mortock's limp hand and tumbled to the floor. Mortock's breath whistled as he exhaled, and blood spurted from his wound. Staggering heavily, he reeled toward the portal. He fell through, and the portal closed after him.

Sobbing, I knelt by Oryn's side and dabbed at the bloody gash on his face. His hand caught my wrist, and he said thickly, "Did that wretch touch you?"

"It doesn't matter," I wept, cradling his head in my arms. I ripped a strip from the ragged hem of my petticoat and pressed it on his wound to staunch the blood.

Morty moaned and stirred. I stretched out my hand, and long tendrils of vine crept from the cave entrance. They wrapped around Morty, pinning his arms to his sides. He thrashed as he came to, but the vines held. With Morty secure, I turned my attention back to Oryn, who was drifting in and out of consciousness. A cursory inspection revealed cracked ribs, countless bruises, and several abrasions. I mopped his brow and cried.

Morty began cursing.

My fury resurged, and I rose to my feet and opened a portal. I cut the vines with Oryn's sword and pointed the tip at Morty.

"I saved your life," he whined when he saw the grisly scene through the portal.

"Yes, twice. And because of that, I'm not taking yours. Can you swim?"

"Please, don't send me there," he begged.

I poked him with the sword, forcing him to stand. He edged away from the portal, so I whacked him on the backside with the flat of the blade. He stumbled through, howling. Water closed over his head. I waited until he surfaced and started swimming before closing the portal.

Oryn groaned and I rushed back to his side. He was trying to sit up.

"Don't you dare! You have cracked ribs and who knows what other injuries."

"Where did you send him?" His words were thick and jumbled.

I tore cloth off my petticoat until I stripped it to my knees. "When we crossed the Great Lake, a dead Sardonian soldier was caught among the roots of a huge snag."

He tried to laugh, but he clutched his ribs and grimaced in pain. "Stop it!"

"So I *did* see a skeleton," he wheezed.

"Yes. The flesh was picked clean off the bones." Sending Morty there gave me a measure of satisfaction, though he was too good of an enchanter to be stuck for long.

Unless the luminescent creature ate him.

I transformed a stone into a knife.

"What are you doing?" Oryn asked.

"Now is not the time to be prudish! I have to take off this filthy tunic and bind up your ribs." I brushed aside his feeble protests and slit his shirt. When I peeled away the last remnant of his tunic, tears welled in my eyes. His torso was turning black and blue from the vicious kicks Mortock had planted on his ribs.

"Look what he did to you," I wept, brushing my fingertips lightly over his bruises.

He was fading again.

"Don't you die on me."

He moaned, seemingly unconscious.

I leaned over him. "I love you, Oryn," I whispered.

His eyelids fluttered. "'Tis...about time." The words were faint.

I sat back, flustered. "I...I need stores from Aramis's pack." Oryn's head slumped to the side. *Now* he was unconscious.

Panicked, I rushed out of the cave. Aramis was waiting outside, her lead trailing on the ground. She nudged me, as if to tell me she was all right. I patted her nose and took the pack. Then I started a fire and made a poultice. Using my petticoat, I bathed Oryn's wounds. He groaned as I tended him. The gash on his face would leave a scar—one I was all too familiar with.

After I did all I could for his wounds and bruises, I turned my attention to his fractured ribs. He stirred and moaned as I eased him to a sitting position. I propped him up with blankets and bound his ribs tightly. He turned ashen but made no sound except for his labored breathing. I laid him down when I finished, and he promptly slipped into an exhausted sleep.

He slept through the afternoon and night, waking only briefly to eat some watery soup. Toward midnight, he grew restless and broke out in a cold sweat, and I spent the night mopping his brow with a compress.

In the morning, he was more alert. The gash on his cheek had stopped oozing, although his bruises looked much worse.

"Did you sleep?" he asked, his voice still hoarse.

I helped him drink. "Do you think Mortock will survive?"

"Depends what he poisoned his blade with. If he had nicked me with that sword..."

"What spell did Morty put on you?" I said, taking his hand in mine. It had been awful to watch helplessly as he struggled under that enchantment.

"I don't know," he said in a flat voice. "Perhaps Mortock's invention, or something Mortimor came up with himself. 'Twas not a spell you will find in any book."

He squeezed my hand. "Now, will you do something for me, my sweet Arabella?"

I blushed. "Of course."

"Heal my ribs."

I tried to pull away from him, but he would not release me. "No. Don't ask me to do that."

"I saw you grow the vine. I know you can heal my ribs."

"I won't do it!"

"Even with the bindings, I cannot move. If you don't heal them, we can't proceed to Sperara."

Tears quivered on my lashes. I shook my head.

He massaged my icy hand. "Why not?"

"I—I can't put you through that agony."

"You must, darling. If you could stand it, I can, too. 'Tis the only way."

I vividly remembered the excruciating pain when he healed my arm. How could I make him suffer like that?

Tears spilled down my cheeks. He reached up and swiped them away with his thumb. I could tell the movement pained him horribly. "Please," he whispered.

He was right. There was no other way. "All right."

His hand fell to his side. "Thank you. Once you start, don't stop for anything."

At Oryn's direction, I moved two large, smooth stones against his legs, pinning them together. He placed one hand on each stone. Then I knelt by his side, wishing I had whiskey to numb the pain.

Oryn gritted his teeth and his breath whistled in and out, but in the end he could not hold in his screams of agony. By the time he finally succumbed to unconsciousness, tears were running down my cheeks in rivulets. I could hardly see to knit his last few ribs. I curled up next to his still form, covered us with a blanket, and cried myself to sleep.

36

t was dark when I awoke, and a fire was blazing. Oryn sat tossing small rocks into it, which exploded when they hit the fire. "Oryn! What are you doing up?"

He gave a wan smile. "You were right. 'Twas excruciating...but worth it. Look." He peeled back the blanket wrapped around his torso, revealing amazing improvement to the horrible bruises.

"How did they get better so quickly?"

"When you healed my ribs, I think you fixed most of the bruises and cuts as well."

"How do you feel?"

"Sore, but like a new man. I can move...slowly. You've taken weeks off my recovery." He grinned like a schoolboy. "Well done."

"Thank you." I blushed at his praise.

"I think we'll be able to start out in the morning."

"Are you sure you're well enough?"

"Probably not," he said, sobering. "But I don't want to spend one more minute in Mortock's lair than necessary."

I could not agree with him more about staying in the cave, but one slip because of his weakened condition might prove disastrous. I would not let him take any foolish chances.

We traveled slowly and stopped often. Oryn protested initially, but soon he welcomed the breaks, sinking down on a rock whenever I announced a rest.

"How long until we reach Sperara?" The city lay far across the plain.

"A mounted troop can reach the mountains in half a day's hard ride. At our pace, 'twill take three days." He sounded depressed to be so close to his home—yet so far.

Dusk came early in the shadow of the mountains. Stars twinkled above the mountaintops as I set up camp in the twilight, even while the spires of Sperara to the north reflected the rosy glow of the last fingers of sunshine.

As I unrolled my blankets, I asked, "Is now a good time to ask about the gates through the mountains?"

Oryn smiled. "They are one of the great mysteries of Latrettan history. There is no mention of their origin in any of our history books." He dropped his flask and winced when it banged against his side. "They are used so infrequently, some do not even believe they exist. 'Tis said you can find them only in your hour of greatest need. Or—if you're lucky—you happen to have someone with you who can see things usually unseen," he said, winking at me.

I blushed and fumbled with a pack until I regained my composure. "How many gates are there?"

Oryn shrugged. "Only the Syr wolves know, and they don't tell. The wolves *are* invisible, after all. But there are other ways through the mountains," he said under his breath.

"I thought you said no one could cross them."

"There are ways *through* them." I gave a silent expression of surprise, and he said, "Mazes of tunnels riddle the range, dug by dwarves searching for treasure...and *other* things." He shuddered. "Trying one of those holes would be a desperate measure of last resort. Few go in— fewer come out." He did not elaborate.

~ † ~

The sun was just peeking over the horizon when I opened my eyes. I enjoyed the luxurious warmth of my bedroll for a few precious moments before sitting up to stretch. My hair cascaded over my shoulders in waves. I reached up, surprised. It tended to tangle, so I wore it pinned up for bed. Each morning I brushed it before pinning it anew for the day. My pins were gone! I searched around my bedroll in vain.

I hugged my knees. Someone had taken them, and since Aramis did not have fingers...I crept closer to Oryn's sleeping form. Sure enough, the tip of a hairpin was sticking out of his closed fist.

"You scoundrel." How was I to get my hostage pins back?

First, I tried opening his hand. No luck. His fist wrapped around them like iron. I tried calling them to me. I managed to retrieve two before his fist tightened.

Aha. He was only pretending to sleep! Next, I transformed a blade of grass into a feather and tickled his cheek. He lay unperturbed, like a stone giant. I leaned over and whispered fiercely in his ear, "You are a rogue, Oryn. Only a rogue would steal a girl's hairpins." He did not stir a muscle, and I sat back, flummoxed.

"It's as bad as stealing a petticoat," I said in a normal voice. I wondered what ransom he would require for my pins. I ran my feather lightly up the inside of his arm. His skin quivered, but he did not loosen his grip. Then I bent and kissed his wrist. The result was instantaneous. His fist relaxed, I called my pins, and they flew into my hand. *Now* his eyes were open, and he gazed at me with a bemused expression. I rose, dropped him a mock curtsy, and flounced away to pin up my hair.

Our pace increased on the flatter ground, and I made Oryn ride Aramis part of the time. He objected, and so did Aramis, but I was implacable. He was not going to arrive in his home city injured *and* exhausted.

We camped beside a stream that evening, and Oryn banished me from the fire. He wanted to prepare our meal himself. I spent the time exploring and found a small pool suitable for bathing. The icy water took my breath away, but I was determined my face and hands would be clean when we arrived in Sperara.

"Don't you look all clean and sparkly," Oryn said when I returned. I twirled for him, and he clapped.

Oryn had spared no effort on our supper. He'd made a savory stew from jerky, roasted tubers, and our herb supplies. We dipped our flatbread into the gravy. For drink, there was refreshing cold tea, brewed strong and chilled in the icy stream. I was not sure how he made everything so delicious—he claimed no magic was involved—but the meal tasted wonderful.

After supper, we talked as lights appeared in the city. After a while, we lapsed into companionable silence.

"Will you marry me, Arabella?" he said, his voice barely above a whisper.

I watched an early firefly glow above the rustling grasses. My heart thumped in my chest. "Do you love me?" I asked.

"Exceedingly."

Only Oryn would tell a girl he loved her 'exceedingly.' "Of course," I answered breathlessly.

After remaining quiet for a long time, he rose and walked some distance away. Raising his arms to the sky, he gave a long whoop of exultation, followed by a wolf-like howl to the heavens. Then he shot fireworks into the sky. They soared into the air and burst over my head in a shower of green, blue, purple, and orange sparks. I lay on my back, exclaiming as pinwheels and stars burst overhead.

I fell asleep long before Oryn returned to his bedroll.

We ate our cold breakfast in silence, punctuated by grins from him and shy smiles and blushes from me. I was packing our bedrolls on Aramis when we heard the thunderous sound of horses approaching at a hard gallop. In a moment, twelve riders with white plumes on their helmets swept over the crest of a small hill. The leader signaled his troop to pause and walked his horse down the rise toward us.

"Oryn?" he called as he approached. "Is that you?"

Oryn strode forward several steps and waited until the rider dismounted. "Of course it is," he said, sounding irritated. "Who else would traipse across the wasteland to save your backside from the wolves?"

The rider removed his helmet, and a slow smile spread across his face. Then they embraced, slapping each other on the back as they greeted one another.

Oryn put his arm around the man's shoulder and led him back to me. "Regys, meet Arabella, my apprentice. Arabella, meet Regys, my baby brother."

I was astonished, but I recovered enough to drop a curtsy.

"So pleased to make your acquaintance," he purred, catching my hand in his and raising it to his lips.

Oryn slapped him. "Hands off! This flower stays in the field." Turning to me, he said, "He's an inveterate womanizer. Ignore everything he says and don't ever get caught alone with him."

"I'm wounded," Regys said as they turned away. "I've reformed. I'm a changed man."

"I'm sure," Oryn said. They talked and chuckled as they walked toward the rest of the troop. I followed, leading Aramis. "How did you find us?" Oryn asked as I arrived at the crest of the hill.

"The queen saw fireworks last night and informed me this morning that you had announced your arrival. She told me to take a troop of soldiers and escort you back to the city." Regys lowered his voice and leaned closer. "To tell the truth, I thought she was crazy, but being a dutiful soldier, I brought my men. And here you are!"

"Count on the queen to send a welcoming party," Oryn muttered. "Come, Arabella. We'll walk with them."

"No, sir," Regys said. He ordered two of his soldiers to dismount. "The queen will tan my hide if I allow you to walk back. You must ride with us."

"What about them?" I asked, nodding toward the two dismounted soldiers.

"They can walk, or run, as it pleases them," Regys said with a shrug. "They'll take your pack horse with them."

"Aramis stays with me," I said, gripping her lead tightly.

"As you please, miss." Regys cast a questioning look toward Oryn.

Oryn was mounting a huge sorrel stallion. Regys offered to put me on my horse, a lovely bay mare.

"I can mount myself, if you will hold this a moment," I said, handing him Aramis's lead. I swung expertly into the saddle and retrieved her rope. "Thank you."

Regys mounted his own horse and pulled it next to Oryn's. "The little vixen can ride, can't she?" he said. Oryn shot him a sour look.

We rode hard toward the city for two hours. I was impressed at how well Aramis matched the pace. She frisked and tossed her head as if she found the run invigorating. The gleaming walls of the city drew nearer; we swept on to a wide paved thoroughfare, and Regys signaled us to slow. People and carts choked the road, but they moved aside as we approached.

As we neared the gates, Oryn pulled his horse next to mine. "Are you ready for this?"

I was not sure how to reply, so I smiled bravely.

"A true diplomat's answer," he said with a grin. Then he added, "No one is ever ready for Sperara. Not even me."

The soldiers fell in line on each side, hemming us in with their mounts as we entered the huge city gates. "Make way!" Regys shouted. "Make way!"

We swept up a broad, tree-lined avenue toward a gleaming white palace set on a rise in the middle of the city. A tall, square tower stood in the center, flanked on each side by sprawling four story wings. Built of cream-colored marble, it gleamed in the late morning sun. We entered a palatial courtyard and dismounted. Grooms scurried from every corner to lead the horses away. At a nod from Oryn, I reluctantly relinquished Aramis to a small boy.

"Take care of her," I said. The boy nodded, wide-eyed, and hurried toward the stables.

Regys removed his helmet and led us toward the imposing entrance. With a grand sweeping gesture, he announced, "Welcome to Ivory Tower."

37

f I could have imagined a meeting with the king and queen of Latretta, I would never have dreamed I would be wearing a torn, dirty dress and half a petticoat, with mussed, wind-blown hair and grimy face and hands last washed in an icy stream. I tried to console myself that Oryn was just as filthy, but even with dirty clothes and dried blood caked around his scar, Oryn still looked dignified and potent. Feeling small and insignificant, I lagged behind as Regys led us toward the dais at the head of the room.

"My liege," he said, bowing low. "I offer you Mortoryn, the enchanter, and Arabella, his apprentice."

Oryn knelt on one knee, bowed his head, and laid his sheathed sword at his feet. I followed his example, laying my bow and quiver on the floor.

The beautiful, silver-haired queen rose from her chair and glided down the steps. She raised Oryn to his feet and gazed at him. Tears glistened in her eyes, and she cupped her hand over his cheek. "My dear boy. What happened to your face?"

"Hello, grandmother," Oryn said. The queen opened her arms, and they embraced.

I rose to my feet, stunned beyond words. The king descended the steps with the aid of a golden-headed walking stick.

"Hello, grandfather," Oryn said, bowing.

"Welcome home," the aged king replied. They embraced as well. The room was full of people and courtiers, and a wave of murmurs swept through the onlookers.

The king turned to me. "Welcome, Arabella. I am Beris."

Still in shock, I blurted the first thought that popped into my head—"You must not be an eldest son."

The courtiers covered their mouths and tittered.

A genuine smile creased his tired old face. "Quite right. I am not an eldest son."

The queen took both my hands in hers. "Welcome, my dear. We hope you will be comfortable." She turned and glanced over her shoulder. "I think there may be someone here you know."

Even before she finished, Balissa separated herself from the crowd, and I flew into her welcoming arms.

"You're safe!" I cried.

"Yes." She held me at arm's length. "Look at you. You have become a woman in the months we've been apart."

I blushed at her compliment, thinking of Oryn's proposal. Though I longed to tell her, I held my tongue. He would announce our engagement when he was ready.

"How is Sadye?" I asked.

"Still recovering," Balissa answered. "Yesterday I caught her in my kitchen trying to starch her kerchiefs." She shook her head. "I threatened to stun her if she wouldn't go back to bed."

I grinned. "That sounds just like Sadye."

"Come," the queen said, taking my arm. "You must be tired after such a long and difficult journey. Asper!" she called. The shortest woman I had ever seen popped out of a doorway.

"Yes, mum," she said, dropping a curtsy.

"Take our guest to her room. Make sure she has everything she needs."

"Yes, mum," the tiny lady replied.

Balissa squeezed my arm and whispered, "We'll talk later, dear." Then she vanished into the growing crowd. People seeped out of every doorway, talking excitely in low undertones. As the tiny woman led me toward an exit, I saw beautiful ladies eyeing me and whispering to each other behind their hands.

Asper led me through several grand rooms, and then through a series of halls and corridors. "I'm taking you up the back way," she said in a shrill voice. Though scarcely three feet tall, she was plump with a long blond braid that would have dragged on the floor if she hadn't looped it up several times. "The front staircase is fer grand entrances and such. You'll be more comfortable going this way."

We turned a corner and started up a long staircase. There were landings, but by the time we climbed five flights I was puffing. The staircase continued upward, but Asper led me down a hall. "'Ere we are," she said, pushing the door open.

The room was lovely. A huge bank of windows filled one wall, allowing sunshine to highlight tasteful decorations and comfortable furnishings. A burgundy velvet canopy hid matching bolsters and pillows on the walnut four-poster. If my bedroom in Red Castle had been the room of a princess, this was the room of a queen.

"Are you sure this is for me?"

The tiny woman shook with laughter. "Of course it is. Did you think they was going to put you in the stable?"

I shrugged, feeling out of place in such a room. Perhaps the stable was more fitting.

"I'll prepare yer bath in the ant'room. Is there anything else you will be needing?" Asper asked.

"No, I don't think so. Wait. The satchel on my horse..."

"I'll 'ave it sent up immediately." She turned to go, but looked back at the door. "I'm a blonde dwarf, in case you was wondering."

"I was."

"There be red dwarfs and black dwarfs, also, but we be the only ones 'oo can get along with big people."

"Have you always lived here?"

"Fer three gen'rations." She beamed. "Me grandmammy was born somewhere in the 'eart of the Pindars. But we like the sun a bit more'n our darker cousins. They be too busy mining their stones an' forging their steel. The mountains can keep 'em."

"I'm glad to meet you, Asper."

"You sweet on Oryn?"

"Why do you ask?"

"'Cause an awful lot of ladies is going to be sorely dis'ppointed," she said with a smirk. "You keep yer secrets to yerself. Let 'em stew fer a while." She dropped a quick curtsy and backed out the door, leaving me to sort out my thoughts.

A boy brought my satchel, and I dug into my trunk once it transformed. After a hot, luxurious bath, I dressed in my cinnamon velvet and sat down at a table to read. I had no idea whether I was permitted to explore the castle, and I did not want to overstep my bounds.

A gentle knock sounded on my door. "Arabella?" called Balissa.

I threw the door open and hugged her again. "I was worried about you, and I missed you so much."

"Oryn is downstairs regaling everyone with stories of your exploits." Her breath caught and her hands flew to her heart. "I had no idea you would encounter such danger. When I heard about Tal..." Tears sprang to her eyes.

We clung to each other and mourned together.

"What Mortimor did," she said, shaking her head. "After everything Oryn tried to do for him. And how you killed Mortock—"

"Maybe," I said slowly. "Would I be wrong in assuming he was the king's elder brother?"

"He was," she said in a flat voice. "When he was young there was some question about his temperament and self-control. There was an illegitimate daughter." Balissa sighed. "He was always a favorite with the high council. When the people voted to make Beris king instead of Mortock, well, the council was furious and blamed his subsequent volatility on the citizenry. All the signs were there, but the council refused to face the truth. Making Beris king was the wisest thing the people have done for an entire generation."

I tried to sort things out in my head. "So that makes Morty—?"

"The son of his daughter. The queen took the poor girl under her wing, and Morty was raised in this household. After Oryn went to Red Castle, she begged him to take her son on as an apprentice. Though he had reservations about Mortimor's character, he never imagined things would turn out so badly."

"And what about you? Did you get your necklace back?"

"Not yet, but when the council hears your story, they won't have a choice. Those thickheaded mud brains can no longer hide from the truth. Mortock attacked the heir of the king."

I grinned at her description of the high council, though I was still digesting the revelation about Oryn's royal lineage. Why hadn't he told me he was the grandson of the king?

"Come," she said. "Enough about politics. Let's explore!"

We spent the rest of the day inspecting the grounds, visiting Aramis, and strolling through the palace. Ivory Tower was truly impressive. Larger than Red Castle, the palace was a bustling, busy place. Not only was it home to the king and queen, but parliament filled most of one wing, and the council met in the other. The tower was the only part that belonged exclusively to the royal family; the kitchens, dining hall and throne room on the first floor of the wings were accessible to both council and parliament.

In the afternoon, I returned to my room to rest for an hour before dinner. I had just closed my eyes when I heard the queen's excited trill in the hall.

"Arabella! Ara*bella*!"

I threw open the door and ushered the breathless woman into my room.

"What is wrong, my lady?" I asked, dropping a curtsy as she sank into a chair.

"Goodness, we don't stand on ceremony around here," she said. Her cheeks were flushed pink, and her eyes shone. "I have the most wonderful news!"

"What is it?"

She gripped my hands in hers. "The men have just found out, and I couldn't wait to tell you. My dear..." She could hardly speak as emotion overwhelmed her. "There has been a coup."

"A coup?"

"The Sardonian monarchy has been overthrown!"

"Overthrown? How?"

She shook her head. "We have few details as of yet. But we do know university students started a massive riot in Pithark. Sarduk abandoned the capital and fled."

"From some rioting students?" I found it hard to believe Sarduk the despot, Sarduk the oppressor, would flee from a bunch of students.

"We don't have the whole story yet, dear," the queen assured me.

"I saw some students in the gallery during the trial," I said, trying to wrap my head around what she was telling me. "Still, most of the spectators seemed to want my head."

"Bah!" she snorted. "'Twas all staged—part of Sarduk's propaganda machine."

"The pillory, too? The crowds seemed to relish pelting me with muck!"

The queen's brow furrowed. "Sarduk probably employed the usual tactics. People will do almost anything if soldiers threaten to burn down their village."

That was true enough.

"Do you know what this means, Arabella?" Her voice turned breathless. "You might be able to go home. Depending on who becomes the next king, of course!" She squeezed my hand. "But only if you wish," she added. "Nothing would make us happier than to keep you here."

She clasped her hands. "I must fly, dear. The king has called a special session of parliament and council. They will be discussing and debating this turn of events for weeks." She patted her perfectly coiffed hair and smoothed her dress. "I have to make sure the kitchens are prepared."

After she left, I leaned back on my bed and digested the queen's report. What had happened? Why had Sarduk, the tyrant of Atruria, fled Pithark? I longed for accurate news.

As the evening shadows lengthened, I was sure everyone had forgotten me. When Asper brought my supper, I plied her with questions, but she had heard nothing but wild rumors: giants from the west had invaded Atruria, the mer king had destroyed Sarduk's fleet, a pox had felled his army and half the population. She was no help at all.

A jaunt through the palace gleaned me no better information. The corridors were rife with speculation, conjecture, gossip, and hearsay, so I returned to my room to pace impatiently. Did no one have any answers?

Finally, worn out with nervous pacing and the fanciful scenarios of my imagination, I crawled into bed. I had just fallen into a fitful slumber when a knock sounded. My nightgown billowed in the breeze through the window as I opened the door.

"Balissa!" I cried. "Please tell me you have news!"

She set down her candle. "I do," she said.

"What have you learned?" I asked.

"Patience," she laughed as she lit the lamp. She sat on the bed and drew me down next to her. "'Tis official. Sarduk is deposed, gone, disenthroned...possibly even disemboweled, according to the reports." She laid her hand over mine. "And 'tis all because of you."

My eyebrows shot up. "Me? How is that possible? I haven't been in Atruria for over a year."

Balissa smiled. "An axe had been hanging over Sarduk's reign for years. Nobility, soldiers, peasants—they all had numerous reasons to be dissatisfied with him."

I frowned. "Of course they were dissatisfied. Everyone hates a tyrant."

She nodded. "In the past, Sarduk crushed any opposition without mercy. But in recent years, his iron fist had loosened, causing his dissenters to grow bolder. Your trial brought the fomenting unrest to a head."

My brow furrowed. "But how?"

"Many people were unhappy with your sentence. They felt Sarduk had overstepped his authority. After your mysterious disappearance, rumors circulated that Sarduk had you murdered. Months of unrest ensued, culminating in riots by university students."

I raised an eyebrow. "Yes, the queen told me. But why didn't Sarduk just dispatch soldiers to quell the riots?"

"He did. But they were the same soldiers Sarduk accused of 'aiding and abetting your escape,' and who lost a number of their compatriots on an ill-advised search for you." Her voice sobered, and she squeezed my hand. "Instead of subduing the protestors, they joined them and laid siege to the palace. Sarduk called more men to his aid, but when they arrived, those troops also joined the ranks of the besiegers. With half his army turned against him, Sarduk had no choice but to flee."

I shook my head. "Sarduk deposed. It hardly seems possible."

"There is one other thing you may find of interest. Apparently, Sarduk's nephew led the insurrection. He was a much-loved general in the Sardonian army until Sarduk demoted him." She cocked her head. "I think you might have known him. His name is Taren."

My jaw dropped. "Taren was the king's nephew...and a general?"

She nodded. "And if succession is followed, he is next in line to the throne of Atruria."

"Taren?"

Balissa squeezed my shoulder. "'Tis late, dear. I shall leave you to rest. Good night." She planted a kiss on my temple and swept out the door, closing it behind her.

I laid back on my bed and contemplated Balissa's news.

What did all this mean for the future of Atruria? Who would be the new king? Taren? Some Atrurian noble? More importantly, should I go back to Atruria, and...did Oryn want me to go back?

Overwhelmed, I buried my head in a pillow.

~ † ~

News circulated quickly through the palace. In every corridor and around every corner, clusters of people huddled—councilmen, members of parliament, aides, servants, kitchen staff—all discussing the downfall of Sarduk. Words like "provisional government," "constitutional monarchy," and "republic" were bandied around like foot soldiers on a Kings board.

In the days that followed, Oryn was frenetically busy arguing with the council, speaking to parliament, and meeting with the king and his advisors behind closed doors.

Oryn seemed to have no time for me, so I spent my days with Balissa.

"What do you think will happen in Atruria?" I asked her as we rode back to Ivory Tower after a visit to Sadye.

"These are tenuous times," she answered.

"Meaning?"

"There is often a struggle for power when a leader dies or is deposed. With proper leadership, Atruria could emerge from this turmoil stronger than ever."

"Or they could trade one tyrant for another," I finished for her.

She nodded, her face pensive.

"Do you think I should go back?" I asked.

"Tired of Latretta already?" she asked with a sidelong glance.

"Of course not." I halted my horse and fussed with the buckles on the reins. "Why didn't Oryn tell me he was heir to the throne?"

"All his life he has been the eldest grandson of the king. Everyone knew who he was and measured his achievements by that yardstick. People treated him differently because of his lineage, and he hated it. Then you came along, and you had no idea who he was." Balissa smiled. "To you, it didn't matter that he was a talented enchanter or the grandson of the king. At Red Castle, he was just a man, and he wasn't willing to give that up. After Red Castle..." She raised her eyebrows and said, "Maybe he thought you would refuse to marry him if you knew the truth."

"You know about our engagement?"

"I guessed as much," she said and laughed. "I've never seen Oryn walk with such a bounce in his step. Besides, he has eyes only for you."

"So he didn't actually tell you," I said, disappointed.

"He will in his own good time. He'll make a grand event out of it if I know him."

I was not sure I liked the idea of a 'grand event,' and living in Ivory Tower under the watchful eyes of the courtiers was not what I had imagined.

Balissa patted my hand. "Don't worry, dear. I've never seen him so happy."

I smiled in return.

"I think you've answered your question." She clucked to her horse.

Of course, I wanted nothing more than to stay in Latretta. Yet weeks passed with no announcement of our engagement, and I began to doubt the magical proposal had ever happened.

After all, there were beautiful women everywhere I looked—and not a single one had frizzy orange hair. They had white hair, gray hair, golden hair, sable hair, brunette hair, and every shade of red hair imaginable—but not one woman in all of Sperara had carrot-colored frizz. Except me. Every day I gazed at my reflection in the mirror as Asper helped me dress and wondered why Oryn had chosen me over the flocks of beautiful women in Latretta.

I occasionally saw Oryn at meals, yet I never had a chance to speak to him. He sat with the king and his counselors, while for some unfathomable reason the queen had seated me at the other end of the table across from Balissa—and next to Regys.

I soon discovered Regys warranted Oryn's depiction as a womanizer. Ignoring him proved futile; he always had a gallant new line for me, and he would not take my continued silence as a hint. Oryn was usually so engrossed in discussion with the king that he rarely noticed when I ducked out of the dining room. The one time he *did* head in my direction, I escaped to my room. Perhaps it was childish, but I was piqued at him. Surely, he could have finagled a better seating arrangement with his grandmother.

Moreover, each glimpse of Oryn's scar reminded me of why I didn't dare open my dream diary anymore. The account of the gallant prince with the scarred cheek marrying the lovely maiden was like a canker sore gnawing away at my happiness.

38

re you sure I have to attend this gala?" I asked Balissa for the umpteenth time. Oryn and I had been in Sperara two months. The news everyone had been waiting for had finally been confirmed—Taren had been crowned as the new king of Atruria. The political tension had eased, and in celebration, Oryn's grandmother had announced a huge banquet the next day.

"Of course you do," Balissa said and laughed. "'Tis in your honor."

"It's in *Oryn's* honor," I said, correcting her. "Surely they won't miss me." I had no desire to watch the fashionable ladies of Sperara gawk and titter over me. I was still hoping to find a crevice big enough to hide in.

"I would miss you, and so would Oryn. I know you don't like all the pomp, but 'twould be a grave snub to the king and queen if their guest of honor did not attend."

Guest of honor or not, I was dreading the whole affair. And I still had to decide what to wear. With a sigh, I dropped my dresses in a heap on the bed.

"These are lovely gowns," Balissa said, straightening and arranging the dresses as she inspected them.

"Explain the sequence of events again," I said, flopping over a bolster and idly stirring through the jewelry in my box.

"First comes a luncheon with the king and queen and other distinguished guests, such as the high council and select members of parliament. 'Twill be boring and stuffy," Balissa said with a humorous twinkle in her eye. "I recommend the white damask."

I sighed and ran my fingers over the beautiful fabric. It was too lovely for a frog like me to wear.

"In the afternoon there will be wine and delicacies. Either the lavender or the brown velvet will be fine. And then...the gala event. You and Oryn will make a grand entrance down the main staircase into the ballroom, and there will be dancing and a light repast. For that, you should wear the evening gown."

I groaned and buried my face in a pillow.

"Let's see what you have to wear with your dresses," Balissa said.

I rolled over and watched through half-closed lids as she searched my jewelry box.

She removed my pearl, amethyst, and garnet jewelry. "These are exquisite," she said, laying them on the dressing table. Suddenly, she gasped and a hand flew to her mouth. Reaching into the box again, she removed another piece of jewelry. Her eyes glistening, she whispered, "Where did you get this?" My mother's tiger's-eye brooch nestled in her palm.

"That was my mother's. She gave it to my nurse, and then Nanni passed it to me when I was in prison."

Tears streamed down her face, and she sank into a chair. "'Tis the third stone."

"The third stone?"

"Oryn—"

"At least *one* of us is talking to Oryn." I flopped down on the bed.

"This stone..." She held the brooch to her cheek and closed her eyes. "Three portal stones set in jewelry have been handed down through my family for generations. When I inherited the stones, I kept the necklace and gave the ring to my husband. When Oryn went to Red Castle, I lent the ring to him. The third stone belonged to my daughter...Elissa."

I sat up. "Elissa—the woman I was accused of consorting with— was your daughter?"

"Yes," Balissa whispered.

"But this is all so confusing. How did her brooch and books end up in my mother's trunk in Atruria?"

Balissa sighed. "My husband was from a proud and ancient family. He was a member of the council, and when I failed to give him a son, he decided the family seat would be carried through his grandson."

She pressed her lips together tightly. "Elissa's father wanted her to marry a man from another prestigious Latrettan family to carry on the family seat in the council. 'Twas a way to consolidate power since this family already had a seat, and a family with two seats is powerful indeed. However, Elissa refused. She was an idealist and uninterested in her father's ambition. I tried to sway him, but he remained unmoved by her tears and petitions." Balissa closed her eyes, and tears welled out under her lids. "She crept into my bedroom one night, weeping, and told me she could not stay. She left home twenty years ago and never returned, and I assumed the stone she took with her was lost." Balissa looked up at last. "The third stone..."

"Was set in a brooch," I finished in a faint voice.

She nodded and wept softly before she continued. "We never heard from her again. For years, I thought she was dead, but at your trial, I realized she had somehow crossed the Pindars into Atruria. She made quite a name for herself for speaking out against Sardonian tyranny, didn't she?" Balissa swiped at tears with the back of her hand. "Elly always was an ardent believer in liberty and freedom."

"*Elly?*"

Balissa nodded. "That was our pet name for her."

"Oryn called my mother Elly."

A tear coursed down Balissa's cheek. "I think Sarduk's soldiers were closing in on her, so she fled to the last place they would look. A little town, north of the Aurals."

"Heyden," I whispered.

She nodded. "Elissa must have changed her name before she married your father."

"She became Mirella, my mother," I murmured.

Balissa's voice choked with emotion. "You are my granddaughter, Arabella."

My breath caught, and when she opened her arms, I buried my head against her shoulder as we embraced. I had a grandmother!

I rubbed my wet eyes with my sleeve. "What about my grandfather? Is he still alive?"

Balissa patted my hand. "He was furious after your mother left. He hired the best searchers in the kingdom, and they scoured the country for her, certain she was hiding somewhere nearby. When it became apparent she was gone, he fell into despondency and died two years later."

"I'm sorry." I leaned forward. "But why did Oryn send you to rescue me? Did he suspect I was Elissa's daughter even then?"

Balissa's brow furrowed. "Perhaps he guessed, though he is a scoundrel for not telling me of his suspicions."

I wrinkled my nose. "Oryn likes his secrets."

"Too true. Regardless, two years ago, Oryn contacted me through the portal stone and told me an Atrurian lass was in trouble for learning Lattrian." She laid her hand on my arm. "We weren't about to stand by and let you fall victim to Sardonian injustice. He lent me his apprentices, and we traveled south to Pithark. During your trial I wondered if you might be of Latrettan descent." A faraway look came over Balissa's face, and she tucked a stray hair behind my ear. "You resemble your mother."

I shrugged uncomfortably, and her hand dropped to her lap.

"Where did these dresses come from?" she said suddenly.

"My trunk," I said, nodding towards the corner.

"There was another heirloom in the family..."

I raised an eyebrow. "An enchanted trunk?"

"My husband gave it to me as a wedding present. 'Twas in his family for generations, passed from mother to daughter, but he had no sisters." She shook her head. "I should have guessed when I saw your raggedy old satchel."

"What about the brooch? Does the portal stone still work?"

"Elly no doubt enchanted it, but that should be easily undone." Balissa waved her hand over the brooch, then handed it to me and undid the clasp on her necklace, which the high council had returned to her at Oryn's insistence. "Watch this," she said.

I sat on my bed and curled my feet under me, holding the brooch gingerly in my hand. From across the room, Balissa gestured over the stone. A portal yawned over her necklace, and a similar one opened over my brooch. I almost dropped it. "Hi," I said shyly, waving to Balissa through the portal. She was close enough to touch.

"This is the first time your stone has been used in over twenty years." There was a peculiar echo because I heard her both through the portal and in the room at the same time.

"This is strange," I laughed.

She chuckled in reply and reached her hand through the portal. I leaned back as her hand appeared above my portal stone.

"Okay, that is really odd," I said.

She nodded and pulled her hand back through. "But they are useful when you are separated by a hundred leagues. Our family has used them to maintain contact for centuries." She gestured, and the portals closed, first hers, then mine.

"Where did the stones come from?"

"My grandmother claimed red dwarves mined them out of the Pindars, but no one knows where, when, or how." She replaced her necklace and joined me. "I'm overjoyed to have you for a granddaughter," she whispered, putting her arm around me. I leaned my head on her shoulder.

"I haven't met anyone I would rather have as a grandmother."

39

he luncheon *was* boring and stuffy. It began with long introductions of each one of the fifty or so guests. By the time lunch was served, I was famished. The only redeeming point was that Oryn put some kind of spell on Regys, which affected him every time he opened his mouth to speak to me. He conversed quite eloquently with his other neighbor, but I smiled into my soup when he turned to me and could produce nothing but grunts. Adela cast a questioning look in Regys' direction, and he turned bright red. He glowered at Oryn, who sat across from us, next to a stunning auburn-haired woman.

Oryn ignored her during the meal, and she seemed quite put out. The wide table made it difficult to have a conversation with those across from us without yelling, so I did little but eat and nod at Oryn whenever I glanced up. He seemed to be watching me, which I found unnerving, so I spent much of the meal with my eyes downcast. At last lunch was over, and I escaped to the peaceful serenity of my room, where Asper helped me take off the white damask and pearls.

I had decided on the lavender for refreshments, and Asper fixed violets in my upswept hair and fastened my amethyst jewelry.

"You sure are beautiful," she said in her shrill voice. "All the ladies will be jealous. You've got a fresh face and a lovely gown. They'll be running 'ome to their dressmakers and ordering a gown like yers, 'specially when they spy you in that evening gown."

I tossed my head . "I'm sure their gowns will be just as stunning."

"'Ardly. Those ladies would die fer a trunk that gave 'em fancy gowns. I hain't never 'eard of such a fancy bit of magic b'fore."

I shrugged, unconvinced, and surveyed my reflection with dissatisfaction.

The gathering was well underway when I arrived, and I hovered in a corner, vainly hoping to escape notice. Several eager young women swooped down on me, showering me with questions about our escape from Red Castle, our encounter with Mortock, and about Oryn. Soon a ring of women surrounded me.

"What is Oryn like?" one woman asked.

"Such a shame he has been gone so long. He's the most eligible bachelor in all of Latretta," said another.

"Doesn't that scar make him look distinguished?" a third said, gushing.

When I could take no more, I put my hands over my ears and pushed my way out of their circle, fleeing toward an alcove. My heart was pounding, and I felt faint and dizzy. Looking concerned, Oryn moved in my direction, but an elderly member of the high council detained him.

"I'm sorry, sir. You must excuse me," I heard Oryn say in his deep voice as he pushed through the press of people.

I could not face him, so I fled. I paused a moment to gather my bearings, then headed for the staircase—back to the sanctuary of my room. Oryn entered the stairwell behind me as I topped the first flight.

"Arabella," he called. "Where are you going?"

I was nearly in tears already, and I did not trust myself to speak. Ignoring him, I hiked up my skirts and took the stairs two at a time.

"Arabella!" he called. "Wait!" His feet pounded behind me, and I rushed headlong up the stairs, willing my feet to be fleeter than his.

"ARABELLA!"

As I reached my floor, I paused. For whatever reason he had stopped chasing me, and I peeked over the railing. He sank down on the top step of the third flight and put his head in his hands. I studied him for a moment until he looked up and saw me.

"Arabella!"

I scooted away from the railing and ran toward my room.

He shouted after me as if his heart were breaking, "ARABELLA!"

I dashed into my room, flung myself on the bed, and yanked a pillow over my head. I lay sobbing until I cried myself to sleep.

~ † ~

A gentle touch on my shoulder woke me. It was Balissa. I uncovered my head and turned toward her. I'm sure signs of my recent tears were still evident upon my face.

"What's wrong, dear?"

I lay quiet for a moment, wondering how I should answer. "Will you open a portal for me?" I asked. "Now that Taren is king of Atruria, I think it is safe for me to go back."

Balissa smoothed my hair with her hand. "Of course I can, my dear. But why do you wish to do that? Oryn is here."

"I don't think I'm going to marry Oryn," I mumbled around the lump in my throat.

"Why on earth not?"

The lump threatened to choke me. "He doesn't wish to marry me anymore. I think he asked me in haste and has had time to regret it in leisure." I turned away to hide my misery.

"What makes you think that?"

"Oryn hasn't told *anyone* of our engagement!" Tears welled in my eyes, but I blinked them away angrily.

"A decision I'm sure he regrets bitterly right about now."

"He hasn't spoken ten words to me since we've arrived. I know he is busy, but surely he could find the time if he wanted to. And I have to sit next to that idiot brother of his at every meal."

Balissa laid her hand on my arm. "Oryn is worried about you. He sent me up here."

"Why does he send you instead of coming himself? Don't tell me he is so busy he cannot find the time to traipse up the stairs himself." I broke off because Balissa was laughing softly.

"There is nothing he would like better than to waltz up the stairs and woo you, but he isn't permitted."

"What are you talking about?"

"This is the women's floor. The queen is quite strict about the rules of propriety, and—"

"He could come up here if he really wanted to," I said.

"No, dear. He cannot get past the men's quarters on the third floor. Not even the king can leave the stairwell on the women's floor as he travels upward to his chambers. The rules are strict."

"A boy came up here the first day I arrived. He brought my belongings. Other livery boys have been up here since then as well."

"They were boys, not men."

"Oryn can do anything he sets his mind to," I said in a huff. "A simple spell couldn't keep him away."

Balissa laughed. "Oryn also likes to believe he can do anything, but complicated magic thwarts him."

I sighed as I remembered that he had stopped at the third floor when he chased me.

Yet I had saved my most convincing argument for last. "I don't think Oryn is supposed to marry me."

"Why ever not?"

I flopped back against a pillow and covered my face with my hands. "When I was a little girl, I dreamed about a lovely wedding. A man with a scar on his face was marrying a beautiful girl with red-gold hair." I uncovered my eyes. "The man was obviously Oryn, but the girl cannot possibly be me. Not in a thousand years."

"I see," Balissa mused. "Have you ever seen the girl you dreamed about?"

I hesitated. "Once."

A perplexed expression furrowed Balissa's brow. "Where?"

Twisting my hands, I said, "I saw a girl like her in one of Oryn's mirrors. But Morty must have done something to it."

Balissa's forehead smoothed, and she rose from the bed. "So you saw this lovely girl in the mirror." She took me by the hand and drew me to her side so we could view our images in the full-length mirror on the front of the wardrobe. I buried my face in her shoulder, refusing to look at my reflection.

"Were you taking mararoot at the time?" she whispered in my ear.

"Yes," I answered tonelessly.

She hugged me. "You know mararoot suppresses magical abilities?"

"Of course, which is why I shouldn't have seen such a thing in the mirror!"

Balissa squeezed me harder. "You don't like mirrors, do you?"

"No. They aren't trustworthy."

"Have you ever considered that perhaps they don't show you an accurate reflection?"

Though momentarily stupefied, I recovered quickly. "That's the most ridiculous thing I ever heard."

"Is it? How many times has someone told you how lovely you look, or how pretty you are? How many times have you disregarded them?"

I opened my mouth to protest, but she continued, "You said yourself mirrors aren't trustworthy." She shook her head. "The reflection you see is the image you have trained your mind to see. 'Tis not what other people see at all."

I stared at my reflection, dumbstruck. Could she possibly be right? All these years, had I been deceiving myself?

"But when I was a child..."

"You were clumsy, ungainly, and had flyaway hair and freckles smattered everywhere, right?"

I nodded.

"But you've blossomed into a lovely woman. Most girls can watch themselves mature in the mirror, but for you..."

My mind whirled. Nanni said my freckles were gone—Oryn commented about my "green" eyes—Tal told me to take mararoot for a beauty potion.

I gasped. How could my eyes have betrayed me so?

As if reading my mind, Balissa said, "You have the gift of sight, but the gift is notoriously unreliable when it is turned upon the bearer. I have never heard of such a thing happening before, but you lost your mother at a tender age, and no one else understood your abilities." She hugged me. "'Tis time to unveil your true reflection. Are you ready?"

I wasn't, but I nodded blankly.

"Close your eyes and remember how you appeared when you took the mararoot. Picture that woman in your mind's eye."

I did as Balissa instructed.

"Now open your eyes."

When I opened my eyes, the image of the carroty-haired girl staring back at me faded away. Slowly she transformed, one feature at a time, into a lovely girl with red-gold hair—the maiden of my dreams. I stared hard, expecting her to waver and evaporate, but she remained, staring back at me in skepticism. My gaze traveled over the reflection. My hands seemed different than I remembered. More delicate, with long tapering fingers.

"*I'm* the girl in my dream," I murmured.

"Yes, dear," Balissa whispered.

My eyes widened. "Oryn was kissing *me* in his dreams."

Balissa's lovely laugh chimed. "That he was, my dear. He was mortified when he discovered you had been eavesdropping and mystified that you thought it was your mother." She squeezed my shoulders. "Are you ready to go to dinner? Oryn is waiting for you, and you will break his heart if you don't attend."

I took a deep breath. "I'm ready, I think."

Balissa smiled her approval and helped me don my green evening gown and garnet jewelry.

"You look truly lovely, like a princess."

I gazed at my reflection, and for once, I had to agree with her. She held out her hand, which I took tremulously, and she led me along hallways and down a flight of stairs until we reached a balcony leading to the grand staircase. The staircase split—one long flight swept down to a landing two floors below, and a second flight descended from an opposite balcony. Then one grand flight traveled down at a right angle into the ballroom, two floors below the landing. I heard noise from the ballroom below and peeked over the railing. Hundreds of people dressed in gorgeous clothes filled the room. Music was playing, and two trumpeters lounged against the railing at the top of the banister. Oryn waited on the opposite balcony. His face brightened when I appeared on Balissa's arm. The trumpeters leapt to attention and blew three long blasts in harmony. A crier had been nodding on the landing, but he jumped to his feet and stood at attention.

"Announcing the lady Arabella, and Mortoryn, grandson and heir of our most noble king Beris and his lovely wife Adela, our most excellent queen, in celebration of the return of their grandson from the savage and untamed wasteland," the crier bellowed. He obviously enjoyed his job, drawing out each word and accenting every syllable.

Balissa nudged me gently, and I composed my face into my best blank smile and began the slow descent down the staircase. I did not think I could maintain my composure if I looked at Oryn, so I fixed my gaze on the opposite banister until my feet reached the landing. Oryn was waiting for me. I graciously took the hand he offered, and he drew me close, his eyes anxious and somber.

"Why didn't you tell me you were the heir of the king?" I asked.

"I was planning to tell you in the morning, but then my brother arrived and—"

"Speaking of your brother, if I have to listen to one more glib saying of his, I shall run screaming from the room and throw myself off the parapet."

"And if I have to watch him ogle you one more time, I shall crawl across the table and claw his eyes out!"

I allowed myself a tiny smile. "I've hardly seen you."

A low growl erupted from his throat. "You've been avoiding me. Every time I tried to speak to you, you vanished out a door and retreated to your room."

"I didn't know you couldn't follow." It was my turn to be apologetic.

"I've been going wild trying to get news of you," he said, his voice an urgent rumble. "I've had to rely on Balissa and Asper for every tidbit, and when you went running out this afternoon..." He swallowed hard, and his hands trembled.

"Ladies swarmed around me. Beautiful ladies. They were asking questions and swooning over you. It all became too...overwhelming."

A look of understanding flashed over his face, and a smile tugged at his lips. "You were jealous."

I nodded and looked away. Suddenly Oryn went down on one knee, and the crowd below drew in an expectant breath.

"Arabella, will you marry me?" he said, loud enough for everyone to hear.

I felt my face flame. "What are you doing?" I whispered.

"Proposing," he whispered back. "And if you say 'no' you are going to embarrass me in front of the whole of Latretta." He shot me an incorrigible grin, and I smiled despite my embarrassment.

"Yes," I said softly.

The crier had retreated several steps down the main staircase when we arrived on the landing, but he surreptitiously returned a step or two when we stopped to talk. He heard my answer and turned to the crowd.

"The lady says, 'Yes!'" he shouted. The crowd erupted into thunderous applause, and Oryn rose to his feet, grinning.

"Shall we go down?" He proffered his arm and led me down the staircase. Balissa had somehow appeared at the bottom, and she was beaming. The king and queen stood beside her, both smiling in warm approval. When we reached the floor, the crowd overwhelmed us with offers of congratulations, but Oryn propelled us expertly to the king and queen.

"Sir. Madam. May I introduce Arabella, my bride-to-be."

The queen took both my hands in hers and kissed me on the cheek. "Congratulations, my dear. I am so happy for you." The king likewise offered his congratulations and blessings, and then the music started.

"Shall we dance?" Oryn asked, taking my hand in his. The floor cleared miraculously, and we sailed around the room in a lively waltz. When the music slowed, Oryn took me in his arms.

"Why didn't you tell me I was beautiful?"

Oryn raised an eyebrow. "I did tell you. But you didn't believe me." He squeezed my waist.

I smiled shyly and ducked my head. We turned slowly around the room, and more couples joined the dance until the floor was nearly full.

"You were jealous of Tal, weren't you?"

"I was," he said slowly. "I knew how much he loved you, but I didn't know if you returned his feelings."

"I liked him very much, but only as a good friend." Tears welled in my eyes as I thought of his sacrifice, and I laid my head on Oryn's chest, listening to his steady heartbeat. "I only loved you," I whispered.

"What was that?"

I looked up, and by the twinkle in his eye, I knew he had heard, but I smiled and repeated again, "I only ever loved you."

And then he kissed me.

Epilogue

n the days that followed, I was blissfully sheltered from the winds of politics churning through Sperara. Oryn was furiously busy during the day, but in the evenings, we supped together in the garden or stable, then rode through the city side by side or climbed one of the towers to watch the sun set in all its splendor and glory over the city.

"Come," Oryn said one evening. "Follow me."

He led me up an outside staircase to the top of Ivory Tower. A garden flourished on the flat roof, complete with fragrant herbs, luscious vegetables, and brilliant flowers.

"You've been busy."

He grinned and led me to a bench near the western parapet where we could watch the sunset. I leaned my head against his shoulder and snuggled closer to him.

"Oh!" I said suddenly. "I forgot to tell you. Aramis is going to foal."

"Foal?" He sounded incredulous.

"Ahh," I said, teasing him. "Is Oryn the Enchanter surprised?"

"Surprised? I would hardly be more surprised if you told me *you* were going to foal!"

I felt my face blush, and I turned to watch the sunset again.

"When in the world—?"

"It must have happened during the three days she disappeared in the Enchanted Forest."

"But there weren't any horses around, certainly not any amorous stallions."

"I heard hooves the night she disappeared. More than one set."

"You heard hooves?" He looked thoughtful. "Hmmm. I wonder."

"You wonder what?" When he did not answer, I nuzzled him, but he sat like a statue contemplating the view.

When he did not continue, I sighed and said, "You aren't going to tell me, are you?"

"Cheer up." He laughed and pulled me close, planting a kiss on my forehead. "'Twill wait."

I took a deep breath, taking in the heady scents of the burgeoning rooftop garden. I turned my attention back to the glorious sun as it set over the city. It lit up the spires and towers, turning them shades of gold, silver, and every imaginable hue of red, mauve, and purple. I exhaled slowly in appreciation as the blood red sun sank below the horizon. Crickets and other night creatures sounded all around us. A million lights twinkled as night descended over my city.

My city. I squeezed Oryn's arm contentedly. At last, I was home.

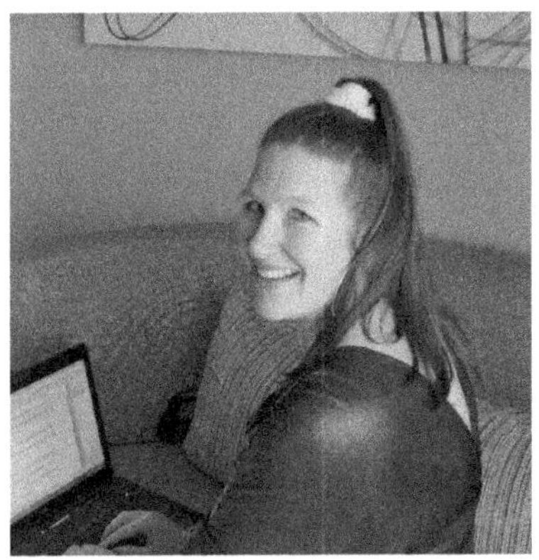

T. M. BECKER

T. M. Becker, called Steph by her friends and family, is always a fan of second breakfasts, hobbits, and Grimm's fairytales. She spent her childhood afternoons buried in a book or acting out scenes from her imagination in the woods beside her house. In high school, she discovered a passion for theatre and even began a recording of The Hobbit for her younger siblings, complete with different voices for each character.

She lives in Pennsylvania with her husband and nine children in a log house full of books, soccer gear, and perpetually mismatched socks.

One of her favorite things about writing is how a single image or idea can blossom into an entire series. In her spare time (what is that?!), she enjoys teaching, cooking, trail running, and watching her sons and daughters play soccer.

Visit her at www.tmbecker.com

www.ingramcontent.com/pod-product-compliance
Lightning Source LLC
Chambersburg PA
CBHW071749190726
48292CB00003B/918